KATIE MUNNIK is a Canadian writer living in Cardiff. She is a graduate of the Humber School for Writers in Toronto, Canada, and her first novel, *The Heart Beats in Secret* was a *USA Today* bestseller. *The Aerialists* is her second novel.

Praise for *The Aerialists*

'A heady and stylish read that had me swept away from the first page. Munnik has captured a fascinating world of daring with both beauty and heart' **Mahsuda Snaith**

'Vivid and meticulous, Katie Munnik's *The Aerialists* captures the tangled desires of people living on the thin air of their own daring – a glorious vision of a time, a place, a welter of human manipulations and hopes, and ultimately, their tragic effects. A really fine read' **Joan Barfoot**

'Based on a true story, this rich novel will capture your imagination' ***Best* Magazine**

'Munnik movingly conveys the fragility of the real Louisa's life and afterlife' ***Historical Novel Society***

'Exquisite' ***Woman's Own***

Also by Katie Munnik

The Pieces We Keep
The Heart Beats in Secret

THE AERIALISTS

★★★

KATIE MUNNIK

THE BOROUGH PRESS

The Borough Press
An imprint of HarperCollins*Publishers* Ltd
1 London Bridge Street
London SE1 9GF
www.harpercollins.co.uk

HarperCollins*Publishers*
Macken House, 39/40 Mayor Street Upper,
Dublin 1, D01 C9W8, Ireland

This paperback edition 2023
1

A catalogue record for this book is available from the British Library

ISBN: 978-0-00-847323-5

Poster for The Cardiff Fine Art, Industrial & Maritime Exhibition of 1896
'Man on trapeze' from The Modern Gymnast by Charles Spencer, first published in 1866
'Main Entrance to Exhibition from Park Place' from the South Wales Echo, 4th May 1896
(with thanks to The National Library of Wales)
'Mdlle. Albertina Fully Equipped' from the Evening Express, 24th July 1896
(with thanks to The National Library of Wales)
Vintage Hand-crank Sewing Machine © Sergey Pykhonin / Alamy Stock Vector
Excerpt from True Stories by Margaret Atwood (Simon & Schuster, 1981). Permission granted.

Set in Adobe Garamond by Palimpsest Book Production Limited, Falkirk, Stirlingshire
Printed and bound in the UK using 100% Renewable Electricity at CPI Group (UK) Ltd

This book is produced from independently certified FSC™ paper
to ensure responsible forest management.

For more information visit: www.harpercollins.co.uk/green

For Isla

The true story lies
among the other stories . . .

Margaret Atwood

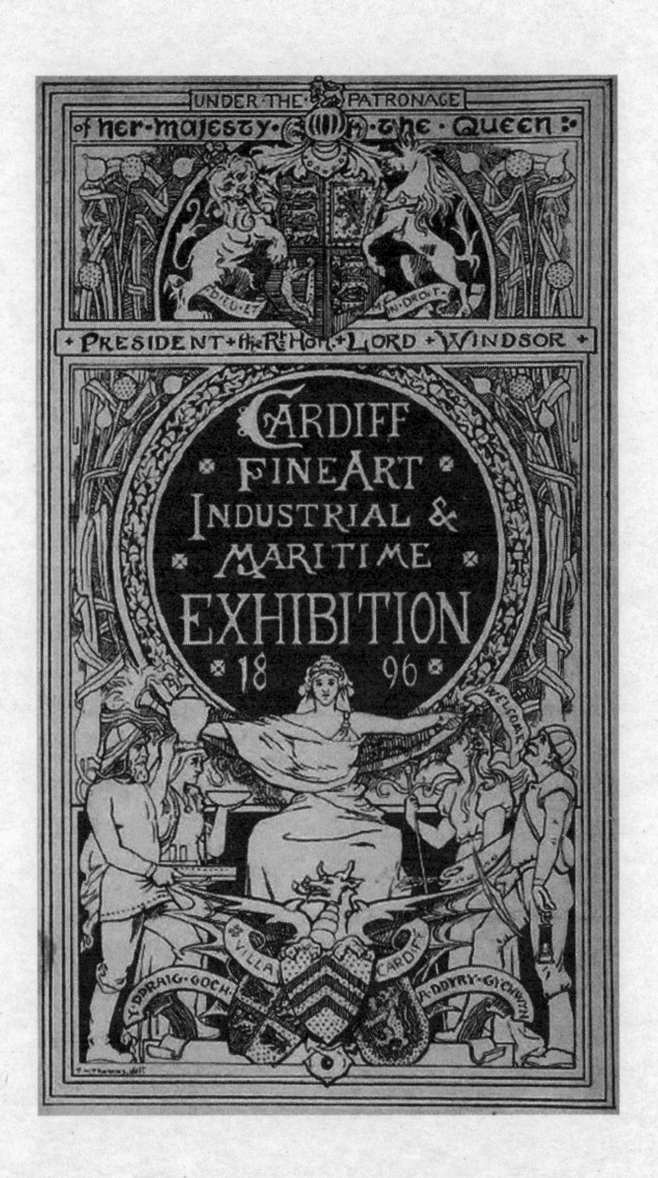
UNDER THE PATRONAGE
of her majesty the Queen
DIEU ET MON DROIT
PRESIDENT the Rt Hon. LORD WINDSOR
CARDIFF
FINE ART
INDUSTRIAL &
MARITIME
EXHIBITION
1896
WELCOME
VILLA CARDIFF
Y DDRAIG GOCH A DDYRY CYCHWYN

PROLOGUE

And up.

The earth fell away, and she looked down into the opening space beneath her, then quickly up again for courage. Overhead, the ropes spread like tree branches and the belly of the balloon blocked the sky. Her hands gripped the ropes tightly, and she looked down again to the vanishing grass, the surge of people left behind, all their voices, then the castle tower on its hill with its bright ring of water. All the trees looked soft from above.

Not yet afraid. Good, she thought. So, it was a good day for flight.

The light above the city was still bright, but the air felt cool and the evening close, and she kept rising. She concentrated. Balance, patience, persistence, strength. The parachute's lines were fast and ready, the clips in place, the webbing secure. Not yet time to think of the valve and the right moment to release. For now, that strong west wind was carrying her out into the open, away from the city, and all would be well. It was simply a matter of well-timed science.

She started counting churches. They were easy to see from above and easy to navigate by. Did the builders think of that, how their towers might be useful from up above? Of course they did. Isn't that the point of church towers? Getting God's attention when He looked down from on high? Maybe.

She'd climbed a church tower once. Where was that? Bristol? No, somewhere in Cornwall, away from the hills. Built of granite, grey and heavy, and every surface carved and decorated like sailors' arms with flowers, animals, and patterns every which way. There were a lot of stairs and she thought she'd be dizzy when she reached the top because it looked so high from the churchyard. When she got there, it wasn't like that at all. She was just above the roofs, their slates close beneath her like paved streets, and the sky above unfinished, unthreatening. Looking out to the horizon, she saw gentle fields beyond the town lifting to a ridge of trees silhouetted in the distance and if she stepped out, if she could, up and over the tower's stone wall, she could walk there quickly, she thought, long strides right over everything until she reached the edge of the sky.

The wind teased her hair loose around her face and it tickled, but she couldn't brush it away. This wasn't a moment to let go her grasp. She tried to focus and looked down on the city. So many people there; she could see them crowded in the streets, moving about, looking up, watching her. What a show. But she shouldn't be distracted by them, either. She needed to focus. Remember the map, the pencilled arrows and that cross out on the moor. She wished she had that bit of paper now, just to check and to be sure, only no point in wishing. What good would it do? There was no going back and very little steering. She held the ropes tighter.

Now, too many churches below and she'd lost track. The wind was strengthening, the city slipping away below, and her shoulders ached, but she told herself it was all right. She was safe; it was a sturdy system, well made, with every modern innovation, and her harness was secure. Still, the wind slipped inside her clothes like fingers, and she shivered. Fear started. The prickle, the clench. There it was, and maybe she'd been waiting for it all along, expecting it like church towers expect God. Now, she needed to rise above it and let the fear stay below. It could be the field she left behind, the city she was flying over. It could sink away, and she could rise up higher. Show them all.

Who knows if anyone down below could see her clearly? For all the brightness of her careful costume, she and the balloon may just have been a distant smudge against the evening sky, and soon enough the crowds would look for some closer distraction or simply walk away, off down the streets, back towards their houses, their own filled lives. They'd forget this latest spectacle and that hardly mattered now. With the quick wind behind her and her eyes fixed on the horizon, she let go of the rope with one hand. The skin on her palm was unexpectedly cool and light, and she smiled, threw up her arm and waved to whoever might still be watching.

SPRING

Paris: 1891

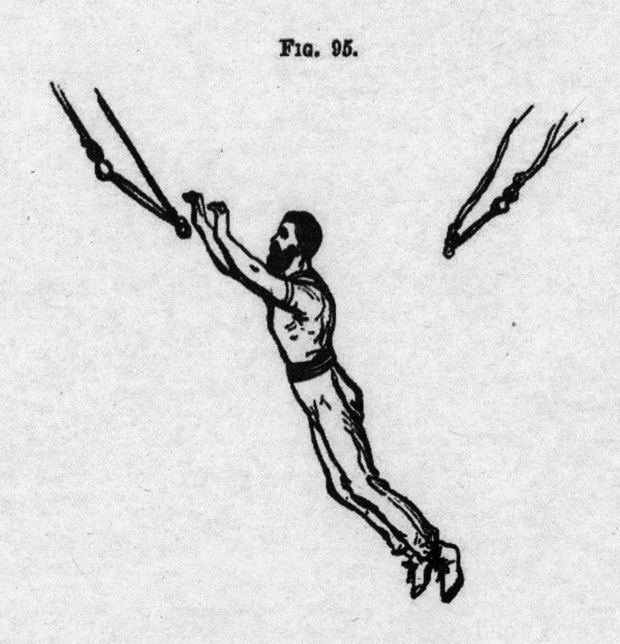

Fig. 95.

1/

Hooked. That's how she did it, easy as that. Like a hook that snagged me, that look she gave me, bright flash in dark water, and I swallowed. Yes, there was a moment of strain, struggle as she drew me close and I pulled back, muscled and thought I'd got away, but she reeled me in, drew me out into her brightness, out into the air.

She was wearing blue that day and I was alone, sitting on a stone step when she caught my eye. Kingfisher blue, peacock blue, the blue of March skies, sashaying down the street towards me just when I was thinking it couldn't be winter forever. The cold afternoon light was fading and if I'd been with someone, we could have huddled together like birds on a branch, puffed up against the cold, but there was only me, and I wasn't trying or wishing anything at all. I swear I didn't do anything at all. Just sat alone, thinking.

That morning, there'd been a discussion about me being alone. Madame Jacq said two children might make more money, especially if one was smaller and preferably crying. The older one – me – could offer comfort, maybe spark sympathy that way. It might even be more respectable, sending kids out in pairs. They'd keep each other safe, she said, but Jacq didn't like the fuss of it, the complication.

'Kids alone cover more corners. And don't cover that yellow hair. Keep it out where it shows.'

He'd been wondering if he should be working me nights now instead of days, and Madame Jacq argued there wasn't money for those kinds of clothes, proper clothes and paint.

'She's old enough, but not pretty. She'll need lots of paint,' she said.

'Lemme take a look,' Jacq said, lurching to his feet, and the kids scattered. I got behind Madame Jacq before he could get anywhere close. We were used to this. He stood almost perfectly upright in the dingy room like a beast at the circus, and I wished Madame Jacq had a whip.

'Bah, you're a' bastards anyways,' he growled. 'Get to work, and don't come home without money, y'hear?'

I'd headed out to the streets near the Opera where there were shops for the wealthy and people came and went. Wealthy? They seemed wealthy then. All gentlemen, I thought, in their dark city coats and the ladies, too, beautiful in stylish dresses, sweeping over the pavement like swans on a pond, safe and always moving. I anchored myself in a doorway, my feet already cold, my dress thin, and my hands sore and chapped. I rubbed them together hard so they looked worse and stretched them out to the moving ladies who could be spooked into reaching for a purse or a pocket and find a warm coin for me. They never took time to pay attention, just dropped the coin into my cold hand and hurried off.

But not her in royal blue, cobalt blue. She stopped in front of me, and this was new. This was different. This lady looked to see me, and her expression was confused, almost excited, not with pity but recognition, as if my face meant something to her. Her gentleman noticed her look and his face turned, too, more curious than hers, as if he expected to see something wonderful.

They were both young and clean, his moustache trim, his eyes dark and flickering back and forth, confident and watching. She matched his height, and her shoulders were swung round with a blue cape, embroidered and fancy as anything and a matching hat. I lowered my eyes and didn't lift my hands her way. I didn't want to be a curiosity, to be looked at like that. I concentrated hard and thought of other things, because it was hard enough asking for money without that sort of look.

'Are you well?' Her English voice made me look up so quick, I caught the moment the blue lady gripped her gentleman's arm and, though her next words were soft, I caught them, too. 'See? I was right. She isn't French. I can spot an English rose anywhere.'

'Peut-être. Or she is attentively alert because you addressed her.'

I said nothing. In a moment, they would go. Only they didn't. She turned back to me with another question.

'But *are* you well?' she asked again. 'It is such a cold afternoon, even for March. Do you have somewhere warm to sleep tonight?'

'Marina, really,' he said.

'Well, would *you* like to have to sleep in that cold doorway, my dear? I'm sure we could help in some way. She is very young.'

I wanted to fight because twelve wasn't young at all and I was practically grown up, but why fight with strangers when they're only talking?

'Marina, we really must go. Your appointment.'

'But this girl. I can't leave her. I must do something.'

'Non, Madame,' I said, trying to sound very French. 'Tout va bien.' They stood right in front of me and I couldn't get past without shoving them out of my way, which would alert Jacq and bring trouble. I waited, willing them to go. Any moment now, they would go away. They just needed to go away.

The blue lady stepped towards me, bunched her skirt up and sat down. I'd never seen a lady do that before. I didn't think they could. Not on a step like that, practically on the ground. Of course, ladies could sit at café tables and on the graceful iron chairs in the park, but not down like this. The colour of her skirts was shocking down here, so real it would leave puddles on the ground beside me.

'It is rather cold, isn't it? You must be perishing. And you're far from home. Well, me, too. How did you get to Paris?'

'My . . . my father. He was French.'

'Ah, like my husband, then. Frenchmen can be very handsome. And your mother? English, I assume. From your looks and accent. Though your French is very good, I must say.'

'She was American.'

'Then you *are* very far from home. And on your own?'

Too much. She smiled and her long earrings swung back and forth and she was beautiful and English and looking at me. Far too much.

I cracked right open and ran.

Pushed past the people walking, pushed and turned, kept my head down, kept running now not even looking, and my heart thumping thunder all around and the deafened crowd stepped back so I'd get away down the street, I'd get away, I was going to, could – then he grabbed my arm hard enough to stop anyone.

Jacq.

'Tout va bien?' Words spat out and his eyes all trouble.

'Oui, Monsieur.' Only he could see it was an act or why would I be running? He asked if I had made any money yet and I said no, but he grabbed me all over to check, then snarled and slapped me back into a doorway.

'Don't even think of trying that again, would you? You so close to being grown up, too. You stay there and hold out your little hands until you have my coins, you understand? The money they give you, that's mine, isn't it? And if you even think about running or trying to get away, I will teach you to swim, you hear?' He stood up straight now and smoothed his coat, then slowly, gently walked away as if he were a gentleman with all the money in the world.

When I looked up again, the crowds had thinned. The blue lady was nowhere to be seen. I shouldn't have expected anything else. She looked like the sort who'd only scoop you up to drop you off at the nearest church, and Madame Jacq warned about that sort. Useless optimists, because what did the church want with a tangle of ratty gutter kids? It wouldn't even feed them despite whatever bread the priest promised the do-gooders. Best case was he'd open the back door and push you out again, but Madame Jacq said some priests might keep you and Lord help you then. You might as well say your prayers. Madame Jacq was good at those kinds of vagaries, and between all that and Jacq's threats of swimming lessons, there wasn't much time to be anything but terrified.

I'd spent all winter terrified or sad, or maybe those were the same thing when you're alone. I might have said I wasn't old enough to be alone, but how old do you need to be for loneliness to be good? Ma said sometimes even she was lonely, and she was old and it sounded bad when she said it. And she had me, so her loneliness was different. The loneliness of not being where you want to be, not doing what you feel you should. I get that now, though I didn't when she said it. Being without her meant I had time to remember things she used to say and turn them over and over to find the truth underneath.

The first two nights without her in Paris, I really was alone. I'd left the room where she lay and ran away. I didn't know what else to do. Her open eyes. I walked beside the river and when the street lights went out, I walked faster. I tried to look like I knew where I was going, like I had a purpose and a mission and people waiting for me. My shawl was still in the room, stretched out on the bed, useless. I was so cold that night, and for a while, I hid under a bridge, curled in a shadow away from the wind. But the ground was hard and it hurt to lie on. As soon as it was morning, I was walking again, trying to get warm. I found an apple in a puddle and ate it. I didn't beg. I was thirsty and dipped my hands in a fountain. The water was colder than cold. The next night, I didn't sleep, but kept walking.

Madame Jacq found me that day and I didn't know any better, so I went with her. She gave me a bun from a bakery, and it felt warm to hold.

'Put that inside,' she said. 'It's best put away. You'll feel better fed, won't you now? That's right, eat it up and things will be better.'

I wasn't scared of her for the first few days. She kept me close and fed me plenty. Yelled at the others, but it was easy to see they were gutter kids and wild. She told me I was different and safe now and her special one, and she fed me more buns and something strong to drink from the bottle she kept inside her clothes. She said it would make me well.

Now, she didn't do that any more. Just got me to work with the rest of them, got me to do what I was told.

I didn't mind the streets by the Opera, not a bad place to beg, really. In the late afternoon when the lights came on in the shops, everything looked beautiful. You could see all the colours of the bright things to buy, and the colours in the street changed, too. Everything looked gold when the lights came on. Not gold like a cold morning, but proper gold set against the shadows of the street, shining like something precious dug out of the ground, something expensive and worth all the weary work. I could love the Paris streets then and even see them as my mother saw them, brighter and better than all the stars in the Colorado sky.

Then that English voice again, sweet and loud. 'She's there. I can see her on the corner!'

I turned to see the blue lady and her gentleman coming right towards me again. He was carrying parcels now, and his wife quickened her pace and came towards me.

'He said I'd never find you, but I did. I was certain you wouldn't have gone too far. Well, certainly hoped. I should introduce myself. I am Madame Gaudron. Marina. Ena. And this is Auguste, my husband. My Frenchman.'

'What's your name, American girl?' he asked.

'Laura.' The answer came out too quickly, but before I could regret speaking, the lady took her gloves off to reach out her hands for mine and I let her. She didn't want to shake, only held both my hands between hers and I looked down again because I didn't know what she wanted me to say. I looked at her hands and saw they were rough with short nails and calluses on her fingertips. Working hands.

'Well, Miss Laura, we were feeling a bit peckish and this wonderful husband of mine said that if I could find you on this street, I could feed you, too, so if you like, if you will, you're coming, too.'

And the blue lady – Madame Gaudron – tucked her arm through mine and manoeuvred her husband to shift his parcels to one arm and take my other arm and together we walked down the street. I felt caught up in a wind, a change in the weather.

It was only a block before Jacq caught up.

'Marie-Laure! My daughter, my dear lost daughter! And these kind people have found you to return you to me.' He spoke with a wide, trusting face and something in his eye looked almost warm.

'Oh, yes?' Monsieur Gaudron spoke politely, then cleared his throat and turned to look at my face.

I met his gaze but risked no reaction.

'I am not certain,' he said. 'Perhaps you have made a mistake. There is very little family resemblance.'

'Ah, she takes after her mother's side, I'm afraid,' Monsieur Jacq replied. 'Her poor lost mother. A beautiful girl from Nice. We fell in love walking southern sands, but oh, such a sad story. Drowned in the Seine, she did. Tragic. And left me all alone with no one but Marie-Laure. I'd be devastated if I lost her, if she shared her mother's fate.'

'Marie-Laure?' The lady spoke the name as a question, but neither her husband nor I could answer.

Monsieur Gaudron looked at Jacq and shook his head. 'No, my friend, I believe you are mistaken. This young lady is my dear wife's cousin and not French at all. We have travelled all the way from her home and have been hunting Paris to find her. Now, we are overjoyed that we will be able to return her to her family and we will not let her out of our sights again. I am so sorry to disappoint, but perhaps in grief, we do not always see so clearly. Here,' and he let go of my arm which made my heart stop, but he was only reaching into his pocket and now he held out a coin to Jacq. 'Use this to continue your search. I am sure you will find your lost daughter if only you look a little longer.'

Jacq took the coin and looked hard at Monsieur Gaudron before beginning to nod.

'Perhaps, perhaps you are right. But what if I am making a mistake now, distracted as I am by this small coin. A weighty mistake to make and so very much for me to lose.'

'Oh, here, let me help.' The lady spoke and surprised us all.

Her French was forceful. 'You have my husband's coin and here are mine as well. Three more's enough?' This wasn't a question, though she looked at him as if she dared Jacq to reply, and as soon as she put the money in his palm, he closed his hand and stepped back, agreeing, promising to keep looking, apologizing for his embarrassing mistake, and then he was gone.

'Now, Ena, was that necessary? I do feel that my own action would have been sufficient if we'd given the man a moment.'

'Or he would have thought up some other way to terrify our new friend. Are you all right, Laura? We'll get you right away from this street, and dinner, too, because we promised dinner, didn't we? Oh Auguste, don't be a bear. Put away that look. You might have married me for my money but that's not to say I can't still spend it when I want to. And this was the noblest of causes.'

She spoke English, but he was a Frenchman, though nothing like Jacq. Maybe he was like my father. For all her talk, Ma had told me little about him that was concrete and real, so I collected all the differences between her and me and gave them to him as virtues. He didn't mind about rules and loved stories. He loved music, staying up late and two pillows in bed. And sugar sticks and the burnt-on sticky bits of bread pudding left in the skillet and he was brave and never burnt his fingers or at least not badly. And he loved me. He'd do anything for me, only he couldn't because I got lost. Me and Ma together, moving towns like we did, every year a new town, a new job for Ma, a new bed and our old blankets.

My papa would always love us if he could find us. He'd look at us with those dark eyes of his – not blue and tired like hers, but maybe something like Monsieur Gaudron, brown and strong – and I'd know him right away because he'd be smiling and he'd make everything all right again, wouldn't he?

They took me to an apartment in a grand building, with ornate ironwork and a concierge at the desk who greeted them graciously by name. Monsieur Gaudron was polished and perfect in responding, meeting the old woman's eye and distracting her with a now-embroidered version of his cousin story while Madame Gaudron kept her arm around me, shielding me from scrutiny. With the key in hand, Monsieur Gaudron led us towards a decorated grille set into the wall and we stood watching a lit dial slowly move. Then something moved behind the grille – a cage, lit and decorated artfully, but definitely a cage that slid down from above – and Monsieur Gaudron took hold of a handle I hadn't seen, pulled the grille open and gestured for me to step inside.

'No,' I said. 'I won't.'

'But it is easier this way. There are so many stairs.'

Madame Gaudron turned and looked at me with a smile starting, then she stepped in first.

'See? It's perfectly safe. It's only a lift.'

'A lift?'

'Yes. In you come and we'll go up together.'

2/

THEY'D BEEN OUT SHOPPING THAT DAY, HE TOLD ME, setting parcels down on a chair. Madame Gaudron pulled its opposite away from the table, nodded to me and asked if I'd like a cushion.

'No. Thank you.'

'You must be cold. Here, take this shawl and wrap up better. These Parisian rooms get so chilly. Auguste, let's call for more fuel, shall we? Warm this room up a little more?'

He shrugged and said he might try. 'Only it would take some time, I should think, as we haven't arranged it. We hadn't expected to be in this evening.'

'Yes, I know, but of course it is best to be here with Laura. We couldn't leave her. Not after—' and her husband interrupted, assuring her with warm tones that she'd done the right thing. She had been kind.

I pulled the shawl close and looked out the window. I'd never looked down on Paris like this. I'd never been so high. The street-lights stood in a line below me, bright moons like buttons down a sleeve, pearl buttons on dark cloth. I looked down on the people walking past, saw their hats, their shadows and heard the clock of horses' feet and church bells in the distance, telling the time.

Across the street, I saw lights in other windows, some curtained, some open, and people, too, standing, looking out or crossing a room. A hand reaching up to take a book from a shelf. A couple standing close against each other. There was so much to see, and I thought someone might even see me, sitting at the table in this impossible room, only this close to the window, I'd be silhouetted, and they'd never recognize me. I'd only be a shape, shoulders, head, a shadow in a rectangle of light.

On the other side of the room, the couple chatted together, probably trying to make me feel at ease. They talked quietly about things they'd seen in the shops, things they'd considered and the ones they bought. The cotton flowers would look good in her hair and the wires would be easy enough to conceal. The green silk was excellent but too dear, even for trim, but the gold might be effective, catch the light splendidly, work out fine. I didn't turn to look at them, only looked out on the city and saw my own listening face reflected in the glass like someone else, and maybe it was. A new Laura, a listening Laura, glad to hear English again. I heard the lady say she'd liked the earrings, but Monsieur was unsure if they were remarkable enough, and everything they were saying was about appearance. Everything for effect. Madame Jacq all over again.

'Would you like to open the box now, my dear?' he asked. 'Take another look at your purchase?'

'No, no, dear. Not now.'

'Why not? It seemed to be an excellent piece of craftsmanship. I should like to look at it again.'

'But perhaps . . .' her words trailed off as she glanced towards me.

'Hardly something to be shy about. It isn't a private instrument. You'll need to get used to gripping it in public.'

'But the girl . . .'

'. . . will be curious about these mad rescuers of hers, aren't you Laura? You know our names and something of our nationalities, but who are we? What sort of business do we do? I'm sure you'd like to find out about that, wouldn't you?'

'You're actors, aren't you?'

Monsieur Gaudron smiled, his dark eyes twinkling.

'Ah, she has us sussed, my love. She can see through our glamorous illusions.'

'You were shopping near the Opera. You were shopping for costumes.'

'You are very observant,' he said.

'And you're being smug, my love.' Madame Gaudron threw a glove at her husband and he caught it deftly, throwing it back at her in a single fluid motion which made her laugh. 'Oh you. You do know how to put on a show. But Laura, you shouldn't believe him. We're not really actors. Performers when required, but only then. Actually, we fly.'

She folded her hands and gracefully raised them above her head like a dancer, the arc of her arms a perfect balloon.

'Aerialists and Aeronauts with Charles Green Spencer and Sons of Highbury,' she said.

'And people like to watch whenever we do fly,' her husband continued. 'So, she's not far off the mark to call us actors. We put on a show, they give us pennies and then we have money.'

'To spend on aeronautics. And experiments and innovations and inventions. We're scientists, really, and that's the line you should use with Lachambre, my dear. He needs to hear how we're trying to do something different. We're not run-of-the-mill circus performers.'

'Now, Ena, we agreed that I would tackle Henri. He knows me – taught me the trade – so he understands me well enough to know what I can do. Aspirations, if you will.'

'Ambition. Plans,' she said firmly.

'Yes, of course, but asking for money is a tricky thing. He knows me as an apprentice, you realize. I need to convince him I am more, but I need to do it gently or he will not hear. This isn't like England. You can't just weave a story about scientific advancement and glory for Queen and country and expect investment will flow. You need to make it sound practical. And I think he will appreciate the emphasis on aerial news distribution. It could well be the way of the future. When I meet him in the morning, I will make a strong case that it is no gimmick but a progressive and innovative idea. Scientific, even.'

'And our purchase today?' She picked up the wrapped box and held it on the flat of her palm. 'If word gets out we bought this?'

'A mere plaything, isn't it? Proves we have money to spend on frivolous items.'

He took the parcel from her and held it with both hands.

'Well, you have my permission to open it,' she said.

'Yes? It is your box.'

'And my money. And your decision.' She sounded stern but when she met his eye, they both smiled.

He took a pen knife from his pocket and carefully sliced the paper, revealing a black leather box with a small brass button to release the catch. Inside, the lid was lined with red satin, with an elegant, printed address. *M. Alexandre.*

And then I saw the hook. Shining steel and no thicker than a finger, the circle of it two inches across. It was attached to a black metal ring like on a harness and, above that, something grotesque. Pink, solid, shaped like an ear, but all around the edge, it was marked with the impressions of teeth.

'An aerial mouthpiece, Laura,' Monsieur Gaudron said, catching my eye before looking back to the hook. 'Finest of its kind, the very same sort used by Madame Leona Dare. More commonly, these pieces are a simple hook fastened to a bit of leather, but this is Grade A ceramic and made from a personalized mould. And look, it swivels most graciously. M. Alexandre does excellent work.'

'But,' I said, with my voice too soft, too curious, 'what is it for?'

'It holds me up. You will see. Auguste, will you?'

'Certainly, my dear. Let's see, how shall we manage this? The mantelpiece? Will that give us the height?'

He picked up his walking stick, set its tip on the high shelf above the fire, and climbed onto the seat of his chair holding the stick parallel to the floor. On tiptoes, his wife hooked the steel around the stick and twisted it, testing the swivel.

'No,' she said. 'I've a better idea. Slide that chair over here, will you? And you can put that stick down. I won't be needing it.'

She stepped up onto the seat of the chair and hooked the device from the chandelier. When she gave it a tug, the glass tinkled, but she seemed pleased because she smiled, then opened her mouth, bit down on the mouthpiece and kicked the chair away.

Slowly, she started to spin. She bent her knees gracefully and arched her back, curling up like a leaf, like a hook herself, holding her arms out like a bird. She was right; she could fly.

Monsieur Gaudron laughed and I clapped my hands.

'She says she's not an actress but look at this. Look at that form! A dancer! A delight!'

She straightened and let herself drop down to the carpet where she gave a deep curtsy, then rubbed her jaw, opening and closing her mouth, eyes bright and locked on Monsieur Gaudron.

'And it works? It feels right?' he asked.

'Just as it's supposed to,' she said, still smiling.

They kept me that night. Fed me soup heated in a copper casserole on a kitchen grate and ordered more fuel for the sitting-room fire. When the warm room made me yawn, they made me a bed on the couch with cushions and blankets and, with Madame Gaudron's shawl still around me, I'd never been so warm and comfortable. She showed me the bathroom with a modern odourless toilet and basin and told me that there'd be hot water in the morning when a hotel maid would fill the tank.

'Don't worry. I'll leave you to your own devices now. It is an intimidating arrangement here, I know, and I must say far more up to date than what I'm used to as well, but it's convenient and lovely not to have to share with strangers. Other guests, I mean. Oh dear, I do hope you and I can be friends. But no rushing things or coming to decisions before morning. That wouldn't do. I hope you sleep well. It's always difficult in a new place.'

But it wasn't. Not at all. I lay down and a brief worry crossed my mind my clothes might smudge the pale blankets, but quick as rain, I fell asleep. Maybe wishing did it or will power because I shouldn't have slept well. I should have been terrified. First, of these strangers who'd just bought me, and also Jacq who'd sold me. He and Madame Jacq had only looked after me – if you can call it that – a handful of months and now, here they were selling me on. Unless this wasn't permanent and wasn't that a thought? I might have to go back. Back to that cold room with the other looked-after kids, that silent, sleepless space where we tried to lie under thin blankets after cold days in the streets. Madame Jacq liked things to be silent at night. Said she didn't want the neighbours getting curious, and besides, when Jacq came in, he needed to see she had everything under control. So, it was my job to listen and keep those kids comforted if anyone tried to fuss and Madame Jacq showed me how to be good at that. How to hold your thumb against a neck right, just enough, how to twist an ear if things got worse. She liked that I was good at my job and gave me extra bread when no one was looking. I hid it to eat at night when I was sure everyone was sleeping. A hard crust tucked inside my cheek to soften. The sound of others breathing, the weight of that darkness and not thinking about Ma. That was the hardest thing: not thinking about Ma. Lying cold in that room, listening, I might as well be tucked away in her grave, lost in the dark and forgotten. Not forgotten, and that was when I started to think about wishing and will power, muscles like any others. They must be. You could exercise them, make them stronger and then you could use them to do things. Control what you thought about and remembered. Maybe even more, if I could remember how. Wishing changed things, even made you think new things, though now it was hard enough not to think the wrong things about Ma. I needed to be stronger. Things weren't so hard when you're strong. Like when you're sweeping and you can't see any dust on the floor but you're sweeping anyway and you do it over and over and then in no time, you find you have a great pile of dust. Or you're watching a tree out the window and you're thinking and thinking about how perfect it would be to get away, far away, and you keep thinking that until suddenly there's a bird and you've made it with your mind because it wasn't there before and now it flies away with wide wings spread out across the sky and it's getting away all because you wanted it to. Thinking like that could change everything.

3/

IN THE MORNING, LIGHT, AND I LAY WITH MY EYES closed, my head on the pillow, deciding to leave. I'd take the shawl with me, close the door quietly and get out to the streets again. I'd need to be careful, but if I could get across the river, things might be different. Jacq wouldn't bother looking for me too long. There'd always be someone else. And if I started walking, I could keep going, couldn't I? Not everything was Paris, and maybe there'd be a small town out in the country where someone might be kind, a place where I could learn proper work. All these thoughts, a farm with chickens to feed, the smell of things growing after the rain. Only there was coffee in this room, I could smell it now and, opening my eyes, I saw a cup on the table, steaming. I stood, saw Monsieur Gaudron's walking stick wasn't by the fireside nor by the door and the bedroom door was slightly open. Outside, I could hear someone whistling and horses and birds.

'If you are awake now, Laura, you should bring your coffee and come through here.' Madame Gaudron's voice from the bedroom. 'Did you sleep well?'

She sat on the floor in front of the window, pointing her toes. Her legs were stretched out in front of her, and I could see her drawers, pale blue and fastened at the knee with small white buttons. Her shoulders were bare, and her hair hung loose over her chemise. She looked at me over her shoulder and smiled.

'Do you like the coffee? I stirred some sugar in.'

'Yes. It's good, Madame Gaudron.'

'Please, it's Ena. And coffee helps when we're waking up, doesn't it? Well, it helps me. I thought you might like it sweet. I do.'

'Thank you. It's very good. Ena.'

'You slept a long time. I was beginning to think about waking you. Auguste has already gone out for a walk before his important meeting, but I made him be as quiet as he could on the way out. I didn't want to startle you first thing in the morning. Girls your age need to sleep, I think. How old are you? Eleven?'

'Fourteen,' I said quickly, straight-faced. 'I'm just skinny.'

'Slender. And of course you are. I'm sorry. I don't really know girls. You can sit down beside me, if you like, or over there on the bed. When you're done with the coffee and I've finished stretching, we'll both get dressed in going-out clothes.'

But I didn't have any other clothes, and she must have seen the look on my face.

'Of course, I'm going to lend you something, silly. I don't expect you have a whole wardrobe tucked away in a hidden pocket. But you're about as tall as me and we'll make something work. I'm good at adjustments. You wait and see.'

'Like costumes for the theatre?'

'Yes. I thought you were listening to all that. Yesterday was all about that side of things for us. Only it really is merely a side project to make some money. Let's see, what would suit you?'

Now, she got up from the floor, opened her cupboard and spent a few minutes considering options before handing me a dress. She said it would make me more comfortable when I was sitting in a café and café-sitting was most certainly on her agenda for today.

'Shopping isn't really my favourite pastime, to be honest. I'd much rather sit somewhere bustling and watch the world go by. Isn't Paris perfect for that?'

Ma would have laughed out loud at that one. Not back home, though. Back there she would have nodded and looked dreamy, but once we got here and got hungry, settled down and saw Paris for what it was, then she'd have laughed. I could hear her doing it. Like she laughed at the travellers who came into the store looking for newspapers from the East. *If they wanted to keep reading all that New York news, they should have stayed in New York*, she said, and laughed like they'd asked for turtle eggs and caviar. Ma wasn't good at seeing someone else's sense. She knew what was what, and everyone else wasn't up to snuff. My determined Ma.

So, what was Paris perfect for? Ma had thought Paris would be the perfection of everything, so maybe she and Ena Gaudron would have got on fine. For me, Paris was just a good place to get cold. But the dress in my hands was made from heavy navy-blue cotton with twisted cord embroidery on the shoulders and at the waist. The lady handed me a corset, too, and laughed at my look.

'Not to draw you in, silly. It's only for healthful support, what the magazines call a good line. It will keep you warmer, too. Slip down what you've got on and I'll lace you in.'

It did feel warm and rather rigid, encasing me and changing how I stood. She helped me step into a flannel petticoat and then the dress, too, and I felt protected.

'Perfect. I'm not sure it needs much of a change at all. How's that hem? Walk across the room for me and we'll see how you do.'

I took slow steps and the dress made a moving, sweeping sound.

'With proper boots, you should be fine. And a hat. And we'll see about your hair. Do you wear it up sometimes? Is that something you've started?'

'No. I . . .'

'No matter. I'll show you how. Probably best if you do, because it will be as good as a disguise and make things smoother, too. I'm not quite old enough to pass as your mother, but a sister? No, we said cousin, didn't we? That could be convincing.'

She stood behind me at the mirror and gathered my hair in her hands. I was a different Laura. Older, taller, strange.

'Do you like it?'

'I'm an actor. Someone new.'

'So, ready for Paris then.'

Monsieur Gaudron at the door, calling out cheerfully, and when he came into the room, he carried a large trunk.

'My love,' Ena said. 'You look like a pirate.'

'I'm afraid it isn't treasure. Lachambre wasn't that forthcoming. We did have an excellent conversation, though, and he has agreed to meet with me again.'

'But no investment.'

'Not yet. Still, no reason to be disheartened. Time will tell. And in the meantime, I led him to believe I was meeting with other investors today and he, in turn, gave me a box of supplies. For experimentation. A good gesture, I thought. Materials are always welcome.'

He opened the lid to show us a pile of folded fabric. There was a smell, and Ena wrinkled her nose.

'Materials? Spent parachutes, more like it. How exactly are we going to innovate with these?' She lifted a piece of pale silk to the light. 'Yes, definitely worn.'

'Salvageable?'

'Maybe. Looks like a lot of work for the girls at the factory.'

'So, not now, then. Let's go outside. Get some fresh air. The park is lovely this morning. And you two are probably hungry, yes?'

In the dress, the streets felt different, and the day clear and warm as if it really was spring. Ena looped her arm through mine and talked about ladies' hats. As soon as we left the rooms, they'd switched to speaking French which felt right and safer in the street. Monsieur Gaudron walked behind us, and I liked that, too. Another bulwark. A wall.

I asked Ena if they'd lived in Paris for long, and Ena explained they didn't live there at all.

'We're only visiting. We live in London with the rest of the family.'

'The ballooning company.'

'Yes, that's right. We're only here for a short stay.'

'But all your beautiful things,' I said.

'Rented. When you rent a suite of rooms in this city, you rent everything in them, too. Isn't that strange? Carpets, coffee cups, bed linens and the bed, chairs and the clock, too. Everything can be paid for here. Even time,' she said, laughing.

'Even me?'

She stopped and looked at me, quizzically.

'You? Oh Laura, that's not what happened. We may have paid that horrible man, but we didn't buy you. We paid for you to get away. Like . . . like a key to a prison maybe. Like a train ticket. You looked like you needed to be free.'

Free.

Free on board that ship with Ma and the wide ocean all around. She breathed so deep I thought she'd swallow the sky. *We can begin again now,* she'd said. *Everything gets to start from here.* She squeezed me close and I breathed in her excitement. Free. And there was a band playing somewhere in the ship, a brass band and they'd already played through 'Hail Columbia' and 'My Country, 'Tis of Thee' and now something new and Ma's mood turned sour, singing out the words with an edge in her voice.

'The land of the free. Home of the brave. That's all a joke, isn't it? You've got to be brave or die, only women don't get to be free, least not without money or a man and how's that free? But that's going to change for you and me, my girl. Liberté, égalité, fraternité. That would have been a good name for you. Could have called you Liberté, only the school marms would have you as Berty then and that's not you, is it?'

The wind blew hard in our faces and it stung my eyes, but she told me not to cry and I said it was only the cold even though it felt like the sky had wedged itself in my head, pushing. It was like that all the way. All that ocean sky, impossible to take in. How could it be bigger than the prairie sky at home? But it was. In every way bigger.

When we got to Paris, I missed the sky. It wasn't really there any more, and I missed the feel of it. At home, the sky gave everything shape. It gave towns their edges, strict perimeters to each farm and, whatever the weather, it made you look up. It could be every colour, every slice of the rainbow and the clouds were mountains and castles and cities, always changing like the rest of us, just passing through. In Paris, the same clouds covered the sky for weeks, slate grey and heavy over the rooftops. Ma would have liked a room right up under the roof, a garret room like she dreamed of, but these were occupied by the servants of grand apartments and she was lucky the shopkeeper who gave her work also offered us a bed in the entresol above the door. It was just a storage space between the shop's ceiling and the apartment above, a cold crouching sort of space, but she called him kind and sympathetic because he might have given her no space to sleep at all. Only, he docked rent from our wages because of that room, and our savings didn't last long. At night, Ma sat peering out the small window, craning her neck to see the sky between the buildings and I'd ask if there were stars and she'd say it was too early. They'd be coming out later.

Madame Gaudron's skirt danced down the street and my own sighed as I swung out my legs trying to keep up. I might be almost as tall as her, but she walked easy and I was nervous. I'd never walked like this before, walked like it was a joy and everything was allowed.

Then the Place de la Concorde opened around us and there we were, right in the middle of everything, watching the fountains and all the water and sunlight falling. She reached out and gripped my arm tight, as if she could feel what I felt. All that space and this was France, at last. Ma would have loved this. The elegant couples walking together, small children in hats and white clothes. This was what she dreamed of.

Monsieur Gaudron leaned towards me and asked if I knew this place. I shook my head, and he smiled, telling me it hadn't always been so beautiful. A hundred years before, it had been a horrible place, hell on earth, he said. La Place de la Revolution, he called it, where the guillotine sat and all those heads and all those eyes that watched. If you closed your eyes, could you hear them? Could you imagine the sound a crowd like that would make, and Madame Gaudron scolded him for that thought, telling him he was frightful and should be ashamed of himself, trying to scare me like that and I looked down at the heavy fabric I was wearing, the polished leather boots that weren't mine.

I'd describe him as young, if a man could be young. Sailors and cowboys and Frenchmen. But when did that shift happen?

When were they no longer children? Wagon boys and what? The boys in the schools I went to were always boys, the teachers always old or women. Monsieur Auguste Gaudron was young with an energy about him that made you watch. A kind of confidence, the inevitability of a wound spring. He was a man born in a village that knew his family, a village where they'd always been. I knew that the way you know a dog's a good one or a bad one from how he stands in the street. And here he was, a small man striding, smiling, at ease in this wide, open space, almost a sailor, so steady on his feet and sprung with tight energy. When he was older, he'd walk with a heavier step, and when I knew him better, I'd know his quickness linked with a quick mind, a facility with figures, a head for memory work, and a quick imagination, too.

'But, of course,' he said, 'the fountains weren't yet here then, nor the obelisk.' Walking stick a pointer as he spoke, he led my eyes around the circle of space and up the stone column. A spire with no church, a tower with no clock, the surface engraved with gold and black pictures: monkeys, men, geese and lions, and all manner of shapes and lines. An ancient language, he told me, from Egypt. This obelisk was one of two given to France by the Khedive of Egypt, the other too heavy to travel.

'And there was trouble erecting this one here, too. It almost failed. The stone was hauled here and those in charge had made their calculations and arrangements – weight, height and pulleys – but in the moment, disaster. Half-way up, more than that and the ropes proved too short. Such a panic. But luck, too, because there was a sailor in the crowd who watched and saw and called for water. He knew rope shrinks when dry and swells when wet. Imagine if he hadn't been there. The grand Luxor obelisk brought all the way to Paris only to lie in the dust for want of practical knowledge.'

'Don't believe him, Laura,' Ena said, with a laugh. 'That's all a grand story. My husband likes those, but his science needs adjusting. Wet rope expands in width not length, unless it's badly made. I imagine King Louis Philippe would only have had the best rope for a spectacle of this nature.'

Auguste shrugged and raised his eyebrows at his wife, who laughed again.

'But, my love,' she said, 'you do tell pretty stories. And I didn't know this obelisk came from Luxor. I wonder if my brother saw its pair when he was there. Wasn't Percy at Luxor?'

'Might have pricked his balloon on it, perhaps. But yes, I believe he was. After India.'

'And he said we're mad coming over here for investment.'

'We all have our own adventures,' he said, and Ena arched her eyebrows. 'Well, we do. You married me, didn't you?'

'A whole different kettle of adventures, that one,' Ena said, laughing. 'Though I'm sure my brothers all agreed with my choice. They do like you, you know. Even Percy. And even if you are French.'

'And trying to get ahead in the family business?'

Monsieur Gaudron told me how Ena was fourth in the family after three brothers, and Percy was the eldest and maddest of the bunch. All balloonists, her brothers and her sister, Julia, too, though the company name left off the daughters. Ena had hoped that might change when Percy took over from his father, but Percy thought legacy better than innovation and kept it the same.

'Not very modern,' she said. 'We could be doing so very much better about that sort of thing.'

'So, you see how this fits together,' Monsieur Gaudron said, still explaining things to me. 'This big family of aerialists and aeronauts, balloonists all, and the power and money doesn't quite trickle down to the younger ones, even if they are the ones who bring glamour to the whole arrangement.'

'Do you really think Percy has no glamour? What do you think got him to India? And out again in one piece?'

'Luck. Nothing more. All an aeronaut can ever rely on.'

'You don't believe that for a moment. It's a whole lot of skill and courage that does it. And luck and glamour, too.'

They told the story together, interrupting each other, deferring and interrupting again, and I heard how Percy had been invited to India by an entrepreneur who wanted to establish ballooning in Bombay. Government House was eager to host the event, delighted that the first-ever Indian parachute jump from a balloon should be witnessed there, even providing the highest quality coal gas to help inflate the balloon.

'And everything went perfectly,' Monsieur Gaudron said. 'Percy charmed them all.'

'So, naturally,' Ena said, picking up the story, 'there was pressure for a second jump, which took them off to Calcutta. Sadly, the racecourse that hosted them there was a long way from the gas works and the coal gas was of poor quality, to boot, so it wasn't any good. Percy decided to try with hydrogen, which takes an awfully long time to inflate and meanwhile the crowd grew and grew. And the viceroy was there and umpteen maharajahs, so Percy got impatient for his chance to show off.

'He took a risk and improvised. There was supposed to be a basket and ballast, and a gas release valve and ropes, not to mention a parachute, but he left all that behind in an effort to amaze the crowds. Just swung himself up on a sling of rope under the balloon itself and took to the air. We read about it in the papers. Made quite an effect, only the sun sets so quickly in those parts and soon the crowd couldn't see him at all, and he couldn't see anything. The crowd waited and waited and then trekked over to his hotel to wait for him there but all with no luck. He didn't come back. And someone calculated that, based on the wind and his speed, if he'd come down that night, it would have been right amongst the Sunderbunds mangroves where the tigers live.'

'And did he . . . come down?' I asked.

'Oh, yes. Right as rain. Walked back into Calcutta three days later to read the newspaper reports of his tragic death. It turned out he'd managed to land – not in the mangroves – but near a small village. He spotted their lights in the dark and walked towards them. Of course, they were terrified he was a ghost, appearing suddenly like that in the night and out of thin air, too. He had to take out his notebook and draw sketches of his balloon, which might have been what convinced them, but more likely it was the money he gave them. Either way, everything worked out happily in the end and he even managed to salvage his balloon. When he got back to Calcutta, there was such a glorious fuss with all the rajahs and officials treating him like a hero. He told

Harry he was even invited into the zenana to celebrate – that's a harem – but may just have been bluster. Who knows with Percy?'

Monsieur Gaudron explained Harry was another of Ena's mad brothers. 'And my soon-to-be business partner, all being well.'

'I can just see him there, surrounded by smiles and silks. Percy, I mean, with his glasses and walrus moustache, and that grin on his face,'

'Sounds quite comfortable, I should think.'

'You are a devil.'

She sparkled at him and he laughed only at her now, so I slowed and let go of her arm which made her turn to look at me, asking if I was well. I half-smiled, sort of nodding, looking about, and let the two of them walk on together.

I looked up at the obelisk. It was very old against the spring sky, but once upon a time it was new and must have looked it. Something completely modern and unthought-of before. Someone made it and stood there at its base – not here, but somewhere far away in Egypt where the ground was sandy – looking up like this, thinking *If only they could see this? They'd never have dreamed of this.* Did ancient civilizations have ancient civilizations? Who did they look back to? And did they look ahead and think of us following after, standing here gazing at their carved language, all made up of pictures? That was something new to me for sure. Old and new. I remembered Ma pointing to the letters in her old school reader, teaching me the sounds, and above each word, a picture. An apple, a cup. She taught me everything twice, once in English, pointing to the printed words, and once in French, a secret, second language only we spoke. And how did she learn the French? Maybe my father taught her. I liked to imagine it that way, that the language was something he gave her, something that mattered, and she gave it to me, showing me how each picture had two names. When I started school, I was surprised the teacher only used one way of speaking. That meant I had to choose. It wasn't fair. Every second word I knew was wrong and I needed to remember the right sounds, if I wanted to be understood. But with a picture language, it wouldn't be like that. There'd be no division. The meaning could be simply there, and no one would be wrong.

High overhead, the clouds stretched out against the blue, thin lines like hair, like prairie grass.

Then voices, carrying.

'Ena, you must be sensible. She isn't to be your pet. She's practically an adult.'

'She's a child.'

They'd circled back and didn't see me there, standing behind the obelisk. I kept still and Monsieur Gaudron's voice kept going.

'We simply do not have the security to extend the household on a whim.'

'The household,' Ena laughed. 'As if we were that established. You know we're making this up as we go along. She could be useful. Helpful. And we could help her.'

Two small boys ran close by with toy boats for the fountain. Their noise covered any words that followed, and I turned away.

Later, they took me to a café and Ena ordered far more food than we needed. Her husband raised an eyebrow but said nothing. I sat very straight in my borrowed corset and watched everything

Ena did, every careful fork, every bite. On the table, the cutlery was shining clean and overhead there were lit chandeliers despite the sunshine. Everywhere, on every wall, mirrors hung reflecting the light.

Auguste called the waiter back to order a fresh bottle of wine and when it came, he poured me a glass.

'My father used to water mine when I was young,' he said. 'Claimed it would improve my palate to take learning in stages. I wonder. A French fancy, peut-être. Taste this and tell me what you think, Laura.'

I took a slim sip and carefully set the glass on the table again. The wine was light and white, almost sweet. Nothing like the rough red Madame Jacq sometimes passed my way in the dark, when the children were all silent and I was awake. In the morning, her lips would be stained, her teeth black, and her temper rough to match.

'It's beautiful,' I said. 'A little strong.'

Ena smiled and turned to raise her own glass to her lips, and I thought her profile was lovely. If it wasn't for her, I wouldn't be here, not sitting inside with food set in front of me. But what brought her here? That hook. A thought. Another one.

'You look perfect, you know,' she said softly, leaning towards me and sliding my wine glass across the white tablecloth. 'You must feel awfully relocated right now, but you don't show it at all. A real actor. Practically a lady.'

That night, I woke in the dark. Light came through the shutters, etching itself against the painted wall, the mantelpiece shelves, and I remembered Ena hooked, dangling from the chandelier, turning in flight. A different night, different room and Madame Jacq standing solid at the end of my bed, her breathing like an empty street before the storm. And the night my mother died. Three in the morning. Church bells and I conjured my father pacing in the street below. I could hear his step.

I undreamed myself and remembered the day that was. The wisps of clouds, the taste of wine, words and light and all that had passed, all that really was.

4/

ICE FOG IN NEW YORK BEFORE WE LEFT AMERICA. THE river frozen, ferries on the East River locked in and impossible. In the morning, the light came feeble and we couldn't see anything but white, heading down through the gridded streets, the horses' breath same as the sky.

'It gets like this,' a woman told us, on a corner that might have been nowhere. 'Cold comes on and gets in the air. Keep a scarf up or your lips will crack. Try to keep the girl warm. Kids freeze fast.'

She walked away down an invisible street, not even a ghost in the white. Ma stepped out bold and fast, saying she wanted to see the shore and that we'd walk between Manhattan and Brooklyn like over a field, the ice was that thick. But when the white streets were all behind us and we got to where the water must be, she changed her mind.

'Can't see anything anyway. No different from anywhere else.'

A white wall. A white island and feet frozen through to cold white bones.

We might have stayed in New York. There was work there that winter and Ma made some money. We had a good room and there was no trouble, only she kept telling me we'd left the west because she was certain now and that meant something. She was ready. She had money saved so we only had to wait for the spring to come. Then we'd get our steamer tickets and head across the sea. She said it was the right thing to do, and that in ten days – only ten days! – after we left, we'd be in France. Ten days of waves and wind and salt and sailors' whistles, it turned out, but standing on that deck, Ma put her arm around me tight, and the wind blew our prairie hair out like flags, and we turned our backs on America as dismissively as we knew how.

All the sailors whistled like cowboys, but I really mean wagon boys because they were the ones I met. The horse boys. The travellers. The ones heading west. They came into the store, each with their Pa, sunburned, dusty, hands in their pockets and standing just the other side of the counter, close. I only saw real cowboys at a distance. They stood around in the street, spitting, silent, or I heard them at night making a fuss, fighting and singing songs Ma would have preferred I never heard. Once she caught me whistling one in the store when I was sweeping and the store wasn't empty. A family of travellers was there buying supplies and the wagon boy caught my eye, a hot prickle of needles ran up my arms, through my hair and there was a look in his eye while the sound of my whistle kept going, like a sound I was listening to, a song that came from elsewhere. Ma pinched my arm, took my broom, and marched me to the back.

'What do you think you're doing?'

I didn't know and she said she never wanted to hear that again and she better never catch me flirting like that, by gawd, never.

That night, she made me sit long at my sewing, even though it was just dolls' clothes, and I had to stitch an extra line of buttonholes for practice. She sat in silence, not even watching my stitches, just watching the fire. When I'd finished, she didn't look at it and I put my work away, then she told me I needed to understand wagon boys were only ever passing through and their hands were filthy from collecting buffalo chips to burn in their stinking campfires and what did I want with all that when something so much better was coming our way?

Funny she should warn me about just passing through because that's all we were doing, too. Most folk were heading west, but not us, if she could sort things. She saved all the money she could and kept me respectable in hand-me-down clothes, just waiting for her chance. It struck me the only thing she bought in those days was writing paper and stamps. Because how was he ever going to find us if she didn't let him know where we were?

My father was in the French Navy. Or maybe it was the Army. She wasn't sure any more, so she wrote to both, and anytime she read in the store newspapers about a military exploit or a naval battle that concerned France, well, she'd sit down and write another letter addressed to Monsieur Michel Grenier and whatever kind of address she could piece together from the news. I'd grown up believing she'd find him, that her letters reached him, and things would turn out the way they were supposed to, but by the time I was ten, I wasn't sure any more. He might have left the navy years ago. Or the army. Honourably, of course, or he might have run away and settled in New York City or New Orleans. Or not been French at all, but Belgian or Swiss or Canadian. How were Ma's letters going to do anything when she knew next to nothing? How could she be certain who he was? But I said nothing about any of that, and she kept on writing and telling me stories about how wonderful he was.

The store we worked in then belonged to Mrs Yeo, a barn of a woman who sat in the backroom while Ma helped the customers. She wasn't bad-hearted, just sad. Said the travellers made her that way, all those poor, dumb boys running away from their families and homes, trying to find what? A new life. A shining California. And streets paved with sluts and gold to be sure. It was worse when families came in. Hairy husbands with their scrawny wives and kids, still running, always running.

Mrs Yeo said it would have been far better if everyone just stayed put where they started and left this hard land to the Indians. They seemed to like it and knew how to live there. Sensible folk, the Indians, who never did try to farm wild grasslands or build railways or make whisky until we came along and ruined things. Then she'd give me a stick of sugar candy for listening to her talk and tell me to scat before Ma found me another job to do.

I liked to take my sugar candy out to the prairie and sit on a rock and suck. On a good day, I could watch the wagons pass and the dust wasn't bad. I could count the dogs and red bandanas, the wagon boys who walked behind and the mothers with their teeny tiny babies who sat up front behind the horses. The wagons were all different – and all the same. Hooped and tented, cracked paint and weathered rope. None of them were new by the time I saw them. We were too far west for new.

I wished for something new. Wished so hard my fingers cramped and the skin beside my nails got thin and dry and bled when I chewed it, still wishing.

And then? A photograph. Blown into town by magic. I was sweeping the store, always sweeping, and that one day, she'd helped me move the sugar barrels from along the wall. White sugar, brown sugar and molasses, and all winter they'd been heavy as sin and we couldn't shift them, but now there were travellers coming through and goods were moving, the barrels got light and needed sweeping behind. Then I found it, that bit of newspaper.

It was dusty from being on the floor for so long and I swept it up with all the rest of the fallings back there – old leaves, mouse turds, fluffy dusty stuff. The paper was too big for the dustpan, though, so I put it on the counter while I looked after the rest. It was all just bound for the stove, just floor sweepings, only Ma saw the paper while I was crouched down on the floor and she smoothed it flat with her hand. A look on her face. Like stars at night, like dreaming.

'It's Paris,' she said, and I came over to look. She pointed out the letters on the page. 'See? That's French. *Le Petit Journal*: *Supplément Illustré*. And look! Photographs.'

I thought they were nothing special, really. No animals, nothing happening. Just streets and buildings, some boats on a river. Trees in a park and a fountain. People.

She pointed.

'Him.'

'Who?'

'Him. It's him.' And when she said it like that, I knew she was talking about my papa. Which couldn't be real because how could it be? My father was a giant, not a face in the newspaper, a black-and-white smudge with a café behind him. Ma said she would have known him anywhere.

'And see? It says . . . *FABRIQUE CHOCOLAT* and something else there . . . *et fils*. Yes, that's him, and a business now. My word.' She stopped and said nothing more. Took the paper from the counter, folded it carefully and gently asked me to finish the sweeping so we could move the barrels back.

She told me the date on the top of the paper was from two years before, which meant he'd be waiting for her. And all these moves we'd had. Had word got through? How could she know? Except she could – she would – write to the newspaper and ask them to send word. She could tell them exactly which day, which edition and which page her lover's face had appeared on and surely they'd be able to go round to his store and pass on a message for her. She struggled to know whether or not she should send the paper itself. It might make it easier for whoever took the message, but what about her? When now, finally, after all this time she had an actual image of *him*. How could she put that in an envelope and send it away? She stayed up late with these questions, talking to me, to herself, counting and recounting her money on her folded blanket. Enough. It would be enough.

And it was, apparently. Enough to get us east and then on a ship. She'd make it work, she said, and this was a better plan than sending word, because how would she know if it ever got through? She'd go herself. And me, she wasn't going to be leaving me behind. We'd go to Paris and find him and be together again. Everything would be all right.

The Gaudrons' odourless toilet was cold to sit on, but clean, so clean and the room was bright. On the shelf behind the toilet, I found a stack of cut newspaper, ready for wiping. Seemed the French, even in swanky apartments, had the same system as the privy behind every store. Except here, the newspapers were French. Made me think of Ma before we came over here, all those French words to read, only then she'd have found it impossible to use up these words for wiping. Precious things when France was far away. Now, just plain bog paper, words and words and words. I took the top sheet – a printed advertisement for ladies' stockings with a row of cut-off legs sausaged round in black, and tied with lace and bows – and I scrunched up the paper because it worked better that way to make yourself clean. Hot water from the tap felt good and soap, too. I could steal the soap, hide it away in my clothes because I'd need to be leaving soon and how do you leave all this behind and how could I tell them when they'd been so good? I'd have to sneak away.

They sat at the table, clean and dressed, with coffee and bread, talking. What I could hear through the toilet door was a close kind of talk, a sweetness between them unpinned from their words.

It felt like their mouths might be talking about one thing – exercise apparently – and their minds and hearts and who knows what else were saying something different. I was glad they didn't sound like that when we were together. I wouldn't know where to look.

'Deep knee bends,' he said. 'And running on the spot for twenty minutes every morning. That's the way to start.'

'Auguste, is this really necessary? Couldn't we manage some other way?'

'That isn't the point. We need to be disciplined. We have one week.'

'And nothing to wear and no money to buy anything. We'll be laughed off the stage.'

'Well, that's an intriguing thought, isn't it? Nothing, you say. But it isn't that kind of theatre. Might need to come up with a better plan. We have time.'

'I didn't imagine we'd actually be performing here. Wasn't it supposed to be our secondary plan after Lachambre?'

'But, my dear, that would mean one stream of revenue from this Parisienne trip, not two. Why turn our backs on easy money?'

'Easy for you to say. You aren't the one holding on by your teeth.'

I pulled the chain and the water flushed, and I hoped the noise alerted them to slide their hidden selves away because I'd be through in a minute. Then Monsieur Gaudron said something else but I couldn't hear what and his wife laughed as I washed and dried my hands, leaving the soap where it was.

'What about some new manoeuvres?' he asked, as I came through the door. 'Something to go with your new equipment.'

Ena laughed again. She was standing by the fireplace now, stretching her arms, and he still sat at the table, turning the pages of a small red book, and then he looked up at me and smiled.

'Bonjour, Laura. It is a fine morning, is it not? Are you well?'

That might have been the moment to say thank you ever so kindly and I'd be leaving soon, but I couldn't because Ena sprang towards me, grabbing both my hands and asking me to join in her morning exercises.

'Best to tackle callisthenics before corsets. Let's go through to the bedroom. Auguste has some reading to do. Reading for inspiration, he tells me. Best to be avoided.'

'Wait a moment, ladies, and listen to this nugget. Let's see, where does it start? He's writing about the benefits of practical gymnastics. Ah yes, here:

'I knew an instance of a person falling from the great height of seventy feet, but, from being a practical gymnast, he came down in such a manner as to receive comparatively slight injury; whereas to anyone unacquainted with gymnastics, fatal injuries would most likely have been the result.

'See? Your father gave us performers some wise words.'

'Performers. Is that what he means by "practical"? I hardly think he'd be thrilled to have his daughter practically naked and performing for a paying audience. Now, don't look at me like that. I'm serious. This whole thing has me flustered. And it isn't easy, you know, having you casually talking about him like this. I've only just put away my jet.'

She lifted my hands above my head and I felt the stretch in my back muscles then like ropes in the back of my legs. She was going to stretch me taller, I thought, pull me right in two.

'Perhaps Laura would like some coffee before callisthenics?'

He lifted the pot and smiled. Ena let go of my hands and I let them drop, heavy at my side.

'Not much coffee left in there, I think,' she said. 'You'll need to make a fresh pot.'

'Excellent, my love. A good practical exercise in its own way. Here, Laura, you can look through this till I come back.'

He held the book out towards me, then a look on his face and a smile and he told me there were many illustrations amidst the text, in case I needed them.

He meant if I couldn't read and he watched me to see what I'd do. Ena was watching, too, so I took the book and looked down at the cover.

'English?' I asked.

'Bien sûr. My wife is English, after all, as was her father, who wrote this book. The famous Charles Green Spencer.'

I turned pages and found a sketch of a gymnast, a young man with thick, dark hair and a solid beard. 'Is this him?'

'Well, maybe at one time. A rather simplified sketch. More representative than anything. The beard, though, is accurate and very characteristic. Percival told me that fame of his father's beard precedes him on his travels because of all those little sketches in the book. That's why he wears his own beard similarly styled. It is expected, that handsome grooming.'

'I hope you're not considering a change, love,' Ena said. 'A moustache is one thing. Looks fairly dashing and athletic. But a beard is too . . .'

'Too what, my dear?'

She bent in half at the waist, pressing her palms flat on the floor.

'Too much,' she said, straightening.

'Ah well, then I will continue to refrain. But yes, Laura, to return to your question, the book in your hands is written in English, the language of capitalism. Percival manages to sell hundreds of copies wherever the wind takes him.'

'The Sunderbunds mangroves,' I said.

'Exactly. Many a tiger is said to have purchased a copy.'

'Their English must be excellent.'

He laughed and took the empty coffee pot through to the kitchen. Ena followed him and I sat down on the soft chesterfield, turned pages, looked at all the weird gymnastics, promised myself never to take to a trapeze.

When Monsieur Gaudron came back through to the living room, he carried the coffee pot, and Ena followed with a plate.

'Oranges. Don't these just look like heaven? I thought you'd like them for breakfast.'

Half-moons as orange as copper, as cats. I couldn't believe how orange they were inside, how impossibly orange and wet. We had oranges in the store at Christmas, but never one for us. I'd only seen their skins before, not what was hidden inside.

In the afternoon, he suggested they go visit the theatre to look at the space there, but Ena refused. She didn't want to be seen there; she didn't want any suspicions raised.

'Really, my dear. You are worrying about nothing. What does it matter to Paris if you are here to perform?'

'I am still a Spencer.'

'And Spencers are not known for their performances? For their gymnastics?'

'Things are different now, Auguste. We are trying to be different.'

He left the apartment alone and said that after the theatre, he'd go over to the gentleman's gymnasium and spend time working with the rings and the trapeze. Ena said we'd stay in the apartment and be ladylike, but as soon as he left, she grew restless, and we went out for a walk.

'Exercise. Best medicine there is,' she said, skipping down the stairs. She asked if I was all right, by which she meant was I frightened? I told her I trusted the dress. No one would recognize me dressed like that.

We followed the street down to the river and walked along the banks, and as we walked, she told stories. She was a good storyteller. I heard more about her brothers, Percy's foreign escapades, and Arthur's, too, and about Stanley's public lectures and demonstrations. She said he had a voice that seemed stitched to a megaphone and he was proud of it, always looking for ways to gather a crowd. She told me about Julia and her friend Alma, a lady balloonist the brothers hired for fetes requiring a little female glamour, and about all the gymnastic equipment they kept at the balloon factory for anyone who wanted to practise – pilots, gymnasts, family friends, anyone. It had always been understood that she'd also want her fair share of time on the family gymnastic equipment.

'But come to Paris and things are difficult. Not a place anywhere for a lady to really exercise. Briskly walking is all well and good, but it doesn't exactly tone the arms, does it? Well, we're just going to need to improvise.'

She put out her hand and touched a lamp post as we walked, then the next one, too, and swung herself around like a thing caught. Heads turned and around she went again and again before letting go and spinning back to me.

'If only there was a bit of grass, I could practise somersaults,' she said, with a grin, then tripped and skipped and I saw it was more of the act, a tumbling kind of funny walk like dancing to music I couldn't hear. 'And if we were in London, I wouldn't need to worry about costumes, either. We have everything we need there and lots of hands to help. Not me, I'm afraid. I'm hopeless at that sort of thing. Hems and darning, sure, but not proper dressmaking. That's for Julia and Alma. You should see the two of them working, pins in their mouths *and* whistling away, making their own suits. They can sew anything you can dream up, lickety-split.'

'I can sew,' I said.

'You can?' Now it was her head that turned, and she looked at me with interest.

'Yes. My mother taught me. Showed me how to work from pictures and make up my own pattern pieces. I could help you.'

The words slipped out and how was I going to get them back? You can't unsay anything, even if you want to. And an offer like that? Ena would be foolish not to jump at it.

By the time we'd returned to the apartment, she'd come up

with the idea of cutting up Lachambre's parachutes, and I offered to make something wearable in exchange for meals and a bed for a couple more nights.

Ena stopped with her hand on the street door, her yes surprised. 'But I never thought you might be leaving elsewise. Where would you go?'

Upstairs, we pushed the furniture against the wall and rolled up the fine carpet to make space for the parachute. Unfolded and spread out on the floor, the material looked worn, the seams stretched with use. It was obviously a cast-off, but probably usable for some kind of garment. I smoothed it with my hand, the silk cool to the touch. Ena watched and nodded at me.

'You know what you're doing,' she said. 'I can't imagine what you are seeing and learning looking at that scrap.'

Imagining's more like it, but I didn't say that. I told her my mother was good with fabric. I didn't say I was born among needles and pins, all the small sharps scattered on the table while Ma pushed me out on the bed and the midwife held the scissors to cut me free.

Instead, I said, 'She had a sewing machine. Back home, only we didn't buy it. One of the wagon families left it with us. They were trying to cut down on weight in their wagon and said it was too heavy for the horses. When they got where they were going, they were going to send for it, but they never did. Then we moved on, too, and had to leave it behind when we came over here. Couldn't bring it with us because it was too heavy and besides, we needed the money.'

'We could get you another one. If it would help.'

'I'll be fine with a needle and thread. And scissors. And paper.'

She gave me letter-writing paper and went downstairs to ask the concierge for the rest. I picked up a pen from the table and started sketching. A woman's dress with a square-cut neckline, the hem ruched and gathered into draped valances and the waist tight-tied and trim.

When she returned, she stood behind me, close.

'It's just a first idea,' I said. 'I can do it another way if you don't like it. If you have other ideas.' I wrote *Idea Number One* under the sketch and put down the pen. 'What do you think?'

She leaned over and put her hand on the table next to the paper. She didn't touch me, but I felt she was warm from climbing the stairs. Her fingers made a mark on the polished table like breath on a window. She looked at my work.

'Remarkable. I didn't know.'

And I didn't know what she meant. I'd told her I could do this, hadn't I? Did she think I'd been lying?

She spoke with a smile, shifting to look at my face. 'I thought you wanted to make a pattern. A cut-out thing with the scissors.'

Now, I got it, and flushed. That trick with the book earlier, pretending I couldn't read. I shouldn't have done that. What was I playing at?

She was still smiling, only in a way I didn't understand. She was waiting to hear what I'd say next, how I'd explain this lie.

I could leave. Right then, stand up, wearing her clothes, but still I could go. I didn't need to stay and explain anything. I didn't owe her that and if she and her fancy husband wanted to think

I was trying to con them, well, let them. No one honestly understands anyone else, so what did it matter?

But I wanted to stay. The chair was comfortable. I was warm. I did nothing.

'You lied,' she said, and here we go, a blade to start the argument, only she kept smiling. 'We were trying to help you and you outright lied to us.'

'I didn't. You – he jumped to conclusions. He never asked if I could read.'

Her smile widened, and I still didn't know why, but pushed on anyway.

'He assumed someone like me wouldn't be able to. I was only being careful.'

When Ma got angry, her mouth got very thin, and I knew what to do next. First, I'd give her space on her own. She'd leave the house, walk out to the edge of town, wherever that was, stomp about and rage and scream at the sky. I used to follow her when I was little, pretending to be a cat, slinking after her, watching and all careful, hidden in a shadow. When the night came on and she was back in our room, I'd sit close like I needed her, like I didn't know what to say, but couldn't stand being anywhere else. That doesn't sound true, but it was because I couldn't stand it. And it didn't matter if she was angry with me or someone else. Away from her – and her anger – I got scared. I worried she'd up and leave without me. She was usually angry when we were leaving. Angry about something some man had said or tried or wouldn't do. That was the kind of anger that lasted. When she was angry with me, it was gone by morning and I just had to sort out how I behaved.

Afterwards, she got tired, and she'd hug me then, and I'd act tired, too, just to be held close.

Madame Gaudron didn't leave the room, only pulled out a chair and sat down across from me. She still didn't look properly angry at all. She was watching me. I looked out the window. There were pigeons settling on a roof and a band of cloud across the bottom of the sky. I picked up the pen again and tried drawing a different kind of costume, one with draping scarves and a thin, split dress. It looked like a lily flower, so I added grass. Prairie grass nodding in the wind. A bird in the distance low on the horizon. A few clouds in the sky. I didn't look up at her, just kept the pen moving.

'You're taking a risk,' she said. 'Coming along with us like this. I don't think I really thought that through. I feel I should apologize.'

'I didn't try to lie,' I said. 'He just didn't actually ask.'

She laughed at that and put her head on the table. 'You are something, Miss American Girl. I think we're going to get on just fine. Both of us actors after all.'

5 /

IN THE EVENING, SHE BROUGHT OUT HER CLIPPINGS BOOK to show me, and we sat together on the couch, looking at all the pages she'd filled with notes, sketches, and things she'd collected. There were newspaper stories about aviation and Arctic exploration, advertisements for gymnastic equipment, foreign postcards Percy brought back from his travels, Chinese lettering on rough paper and etchings of balloons. She told me she used it to keep track of things that happened and ideas she wanted to remember, everything neatly clipped and pasted in, kept safe and orderly between clean leather covers.

We sat together on that soft couch, looking at the clean white pages and things that happened far away, and I felt safe enough to know I was tired, simple as that. I yawned and she asked if I'd like a cup of warm milk. When it was ready, she stirred in a spoonful of sugar and suggested I get some sleep. I took it, sipped, smiled, and did what I was told. She and Monsieur Gaudron went through to their bedroom and closed the door, so I thought they wanted time for loving and what was that like, but I wasn't going to listen, only I could hear them talking softly and then opening the shutters on their window, closing them, then opening again.

Long past midnight, I woke in the darkness with a voice close by my ear.

'Pull on your things and your shawl,' she was saying. 'Then through to the bedroom. We'll talk there.'

Ena's voice was almost too quiet to hear, and I was still dreaming, mixing her up with Madame Jacq.

'No, Laura, don't close your eyes again. We need you. Please.'

I was dizzy, getting up like that and maybe it was the darkness, but my head spun. I sat down to put my feet in my shoes, my eyes gritty.

In the bedroom, the lamp on the table was shaded with a cloth and Ena was wearing odd clothes. Her dress lay on a chair, and she stood against the wall with her legs showing, their length wrapped in tight dark cloth, and her body and arms were wrapped, too, like stockings all over. She looked like a spider. I wondered if she always looked like this underneath her dress. But Monsieur Gaudron was the same, thin, wrapped and dark. Good clothes to wear if you wanted to vanish in the night. My own clothes felt pale and cold and small, as if I'd outgrown them in the past few days.

'We need a lookout,' Ena said. She explained: she wanted me

to stand in the street, hidden if I could manage it, and watch to see if anyone came. 'It won't be difficult and won't take long. An hour maybe. You can trust me. Both of us. I promise. Here, take this handkerchief.'

'But the concierge downstairs,' I said. 'We won't get out. The door will be locked.'

'We're not going through the door.'

Monsieur Gaudron smiled and held up a tangle of rope, a thin, complicated thing like a fishing net but black like their wrappings, and said it was stronger than it looked. He'd lower it from the balcony, fix the top to the railing as firmly as he could, and then he'd climb down. I would follow.

Ena suggested I take my shoes off; it was easier to grip when you could really feel the rope.

'And you can tie the laces together and string them around your neck to carry them down. You wouldn't want to stand out in the street shoeless.'

Monsieur Gaudron moved like a shadow out to the balcony. There was no thought, nothing tentative, just movement. It didn't take him long to tie the rope ladder and the knots were reassuring, fat as fists. I didn't want to watch him descend. I looked up instead, my feet heavy and I was part of the balcony, as fixed as iron railings, and no moon at all, only needle-prick stars. Then Ena's gentle hand on the small of my back, not pushing, but there to let me know she was beside me.

'When you are ready. The railing is the hardest part. You swallow and climb over, okay? The rest isn't tricky. You hold on tight and you climb down. You can do this.' Her breath was warm in my ear and I wanted her to keep talking, so I could keep listening. She asked if I was ready. I nodded. Now.

She helped me, held me as I shifted up and over the edge, and she held on tight. Then, one foot and another, each one in its place. My hands looked pale on the dark ropes but there was no way to hide them now. Next time, I thought, and that was strange. Next time. Goodness.

When I reached the street and stepped down, my shoes swung against my collar bone, and I let go of the rope and steadied them. Monsieur Gaudron was beside me, his hand on my arm, but he didn't say a word, turned his head, looked both ways down the street, a good long look. The night was dark, and the street lights had gone out. There would be gendarmes walking these streets and I was to raise Ena's handkerchief above my head if I saw one.

'I have very good eyes, you see,' she said. 'Just be sure to keep it hidden unless you need to signal.'

I nodded, crossed the street and slipped into a shadowed doorway. Empty, a small relief. The street was silent and behind me, the door felt solid, the stone wall cold. I looked one way, then the other. Nothing moved. Monsieur Gaudron was gone, now, nowhere to be seen, and I couldn't see the ladder any more. I hadn't asked him what I was to do if things went badly. I'd run. Only thing to do. The mildness was gone from the weather now, the night cold as winter.

Then I looked up. Until that moment, I thought the night was dark, but there, high above me, I could see them silhouetted against the sky. They stood in the middle of the street, high up in the air, swaying, and then I saw the rope. Somehow, they'd strung it from their bedroom balcony railing to one across the street like some sort of laundry line, except they stood on it, balancing like pegs, like thin, black crows.

I glanced back to the street, one way, then the other. Nothing, but I was frightened now. Nothing, but if anyone came round a corner and happened to glance up . . . I looked up again and this time I saw the trapeze suspended from the rope's centre, and now the couple both gripping its ropes, dangling. He leaned back as if against a tree. She leaned towards him, then into him and they looked like one shape, one shadow. She pulled back and he leaned into her, and I saw what they were doing. This back and forth, this swinging, was pumping the trapeze and building momentum. Then he fell.

My breath sharp, the city awake all around. My heart loud loud crashing loud and I left the shadows to find his body on the cold, hard ground.

But nothing. Only darkness. Cold cobbles. An empty street.

Overhead, Ena did not cry out, and none of the windows opened. The trapeze kept swinging back and forth and now I looked and saw he was up there, still there, not fallen, but not standing. He hung by his feet from the sling of rope, upside down, his arms outstretched in flight. The show continued.

I ran back to the doorway and only watched the street. This was impossible. These people. This night. I would not watch a moment more.

I couldn't not. Maybe the old Laura could have turned away like that, could have ignored what was really happening, but not now. These people. I willed him to be safe. And her, that hook surely in her teeth, her mad, determined, beautiful smile.

When I looked up again, Auguste was standing on the trapeze with his feet wide apart and Ena hung below, yes, gripping her mouthpiece, her arms dancing. She pointed her feet and raised them up, dancing, and when she spun around, the white of her face flashed clear now gone now clear again, still dancing and the starlight like music.

Every night that week, they practised like this, and every night I was delighted and afraid. It was all too good to last, and I was certain things would turn, and I'd be left standing in the shadows again, hiding and cold. But every night, when we were safely back in the room, we sat down on the carpet and they were both so happy, reaching out and touching each other as they whispered back and forth about what happened and how it went and they thanked me – me – for keeping them safe. I whispered they were wonderful, and our faces were so close together. This was mad and beautiful, dangerous. Not something I could understand, really. Nothing had prepared me for this.

Every morning that week was bright and every afternoon warmer than the last. Ena sat with me as I worked on the parachute, cutting through the tiny stitches with a small pair of scissors she bought for me, and pulling out the scraps of old thread. When she opened the window, a spring breeze filled the room, fluttering the silk so it moved like something alive. Ena drew sketches for me: figures dangling, dancing and costumes, too. She showed them to me and asked if I could make something like these, something stunning and beautiful? Because she wanted something decent, but decadent, too. Something fantastical. Some performing women wore next to nothing, just corsets and some sort of drawers, but that wasn't the look she wanted. It wasn't going to be that kind of performance.

'Leona Dare's all well and good with her American stripes and high-cut pants, but I'm not trying to build an audience here. This isn't about making a name for us.'

She told me about her husband's on-going admiration for the American acrobat – *la belle Madame Dare, he calls her, and she is extraordinary, a legend!* As a boy, he had seen her perform in Paris – *such grace, such strength, such remarkable courage as she worked with the elegant hook* – and then he read her tragic life story in a newspaper. Her father, a Confederate Colonel, her mother, a beautiful, mad Mexican and the two of them so in love, but they got caught up in the turmoil of the Civil War. One betrayed, one killed, and leaving behind them three orphaned children. Leona, the eldest, tried to look after her brothers and together they refugeed their way to Indiana but tragedy, tragedy and they were lost, lost. Leona travelled to New Orleans and the circus. Nerves of steel. Skimpy costumes. A wonder. Graced the stages of the Americas and Europe with her flying presence.

'Which has created an audience for that kind of madness,' she said, with an edge to her voice. 'Flesh and hagiography. Not the game we're playing at all. I've made him promise one performance, maybe two at most, and then back to London with whatever money we've managed to make. The last thing I want to do is build a legend.'

She wanted clean lines, modest necklines. She wanted flexibility, innocence, modern clarity. Something lovely and fresh and new. I told her the white silk would be perfect, that they both would be perfect.

When I brushed out my hair in the evening, I found tiny curls of snipped thread, clean and white like snow.

'How long have you been over here?' she asked. We were sitting drinking coffee one morning. Monsieur Gaudron had gone out again to the gentlemen's gymnasium and Ena had washed her hair. Now she sat by the open window with it tumbled down over her shoulders, drying and curling in the sun. The coffee was strong, and I felt jittery, maybe the coffee, maybe the question.

How long? I might have said anything, and she might have believed me. I could take the scrap she knew, snip the stitches and make something new. A rich uncle. A shipwreck. A fortune lost. A year or two. A promise broken. It might have worked, and it wouldn't have mattered, so why did I tell her the truth? Because she wore blue that first day and she bothered to look at me.

So, I told her the truth about the photograph and the savings, the ship and the entresol room and Ma's cough. How quickly she died and watching it happen. It only took a day. I watched in the morning, the sunlight a line across the floor. The room was cold and I was cold and Ma cold, but what could I do? Every blanket was on her and my shawl and hers. Our breath visible like ice fog. That line of light moving and, in the afternoon, it was gone, the room darker and her breath grew loud. I touched her lips to see if she'd take a glass, but she didn't respond. I dipped my finger in the water and touched her lips again. Don't know if that helped. Her breathing roughened anyway. Later, I watched the light fading in the room, but outside, the sky was still there, a washed blue. I went to the window, craned my neck like she did, saw trees silhouetted, so there was still light there, just. Her breath was hard, awful.

Ena sat, listening, with her hands cradling her coffee cup, but I didn't look at her face, just kept talking, telling her everything. I told her I stood by that window watching the cold evening coming on and listening to that breath, that horrible rasp. I told her I kept looking at the sky.

Ena wrapped her arms around me and said she understood. Her father had died, too, and she'd been there with him. She knew what it was like, waiting, and scared, and she sounded nice about the whole thing and understanding, but I don't think she really did because how could I tell her it was my fault? That I'd wanted that breath to stop. That I'd looked out the window instead of at my mother, looked at the tree and wanted the birds to all fly away. It wasn't scary because it happened; it was scary because I'd wished it and then it happened. The room went quiet, the light changed, her breath gone.

'Not easy,' Ena told me. 'Watching like that. Not when it's someone you love.'

Then she asked me about my father, and I said we never found him.

'I could help,' she said. 'We could look, Auguste and I. We could find the right people to ask and I know we'd find him for you.'

Except there was no point because she couldn't. I showed her the newspaper, the folded scrap I'd taken from Ma's cold clothes, the smudged face that told nothing.

'See?' I said. 'She really didn't know at all. You can't tell anything from a photo like that. He might be anyone.'

I lost my father twice.

When I was growing up, he was so far away, and never visited, never wrote, so he was as good as lost then, whatever stories Ma told. I tried to imagine him, to find him in some forgotten memory, but he wasn't there.

Then, when Ma died, I lost him again. When she couldn't tell me about him any more, when she couldn't cry about him or dream about him, when she was cold and still and dead, then he was dead, too. I lost them both when I lost her.

I wasn't sure Ena understood that, either.

* * *

The theatre was like nothing I'd seen. All paint and glamour and every surface blazed. We stood in the wings, watching a line of black girls dance in fringed costumes, their dark hair billowed like clouds, their lips painted gold.

'That girl in the middle also works the trapeze,' Ena said. 'She's very good, very disciplined and strong. There's an artist who comes to draw her. Every performance, they say. He never misses one. She's that good.'

Ena looked out across the audience, then pointed.

'There. Do you see him? That sad one with the sparse beard.'

There were so many people in the audience, so many men looking, and ladies in fine dresses and paint and feathers. I spotted the artist and was glad he wasn't looking at me. He didn't look like he could hear the music at all, he was that sad, but Ena beside me tapped her feet, letting it flow right through her.

'It's a good crowd tonight and not long now. How do I look? Are you all right? You look pale.'

'It's terrifying,' I said, and her laugh rang out, but honestly, how could she do it? Go out there in front of all those faces and manage to hold on? And not just hold on, but dance – high up in the air, in that secret middle-of-the-night balancing dance she'd perfected with her husband. I had to look down, dizzy, my own feet flat on the wooden floorboards.

'Well, it's all a glitz and tizzy, but it brings in the beans,' Ena said, and handed me a white parasol. 'Now, just like we said. You stand right there with this in your hands as if it's something you need to pass to me during the show. Prop girl, that's you. You just stand still and you'll be fine. The stage manager will give you no trouble if he thinks you've got a part to play.'

I'd met him that afternoon, or seen him at least, when the Gaudrons reported to the theatre office to make their final pre-performance arrangements. They'd waltzed in like they owned the place and he'd been grim, looked ready to say no to everything, but Ena persisted.

'Well, she'll need to stand completely still,' he'd growled. 'And touch nothing. The ropes are all precisely set and any slight change of tension, then nothing is safe any more.'

'She'll be as good as gold,' Ena said, charming him with a smile. 'She always is.'

But the light in the theatre was silver, not gold, and I wasn't good at all. Good didn't act like this, start over pretending things could be new. Good didn't try to forget the past. Good didn't need to.

I stood holding the parasol as Monsieur and Madame Gaudron climbed up into the height of the theatre, wearing the white silk costumes I'd stitched for them, and I saw how good they were. If I could be like that . . .

I would. I could, I thought, and all through their performance as the music played and the two of them danced, I focused. Because if I could make those costumes, those bright white sails fashioned from old scrap cloth, if I could sweep and conjure paper when I put my mind to it, I could do anything. I could hold Ena and her Auguste in my focus and they would never fall. Like I did in the dark street when I was so scared. This new Laura did that, and I'd do it again. Watching from the wings, I'd hold them up, keep them safe as houses.

And the old Laura? Still outside in the dark, still hiding in the shadows. She'd still be there, only harder to see. Things in the shadows generally are.

6/

WE LEFT FRANCE LOOKING BACKWARDS, AT LEAST I did. Standing at the railing as the steamer pulled away, I watched the flat land, grey-green under low clouds, and let myself get sentimental. I imagined the church spire in the distance was Ma's gravestone. Might as well have been. She wouldn't have a real one. And, with me leaving, who'd remember her here? Maybe the landlord who found her, or maybe not. She wasn't the first corpse for him, just one more hard-luck story that turned out sad. I kept my eyes locked on that spire and thought of her hard, kept thinking until the ache came on and after that, too.

'There you are,' Ena said, her pace quick across the deck to stand beside me. 'I lost track of you in the crowd. Quite something, isn't it? You'd think it was a holiday with all these people. A bit smaller than your last boat, of course.' Her face was flushed and her hair tendrilled by the wind, her expression lively and kind.

'So, my dear, I have something I want to give you. This feels like the right moment. Let's come away from the railing and stand out of the wind. Would be a shame to drop it right into the sea.' She drew me back against the cabin's wall, then made a show of reaching into her pocket and pulling out a small parcel wrapped in a piece of parachute silk.

'More scissors?' I asked, and she laughed.

'You'll need to open it to see.' She adjusted her shawl, drawing it closer against the cool Channel wind. In my hands, the parcel felt heavy, and I pulled the silk away to find a square leather box that looked expensive.

'You shouldn't spend money on me.'

'Oh, I didn't,' she said. 'Don't worry about that – and don't let the box mislead you. It isn't a fancy aerialist's mouthpiece, either. I hope you'll think it's better than that. It was mine, but I want you to have it now. I thought it might help. Open it up and see.'

Inside the box, there was a dark brooch, oval and carved with petals like a flower, each curve empty so you could see through to the hollowness behind.

'It isn't jet,' Ena said. 'It's bog oak, which I think is nicer. It's ancient wood that's been preserved and hardened till it's almost stone. I like the idea of things getting stronger with time. My mother gave us all mourning brooches after my father died. Something to mark the occasion.'

The brooch felt light in my hand and I touched its surface with my finger.

'The petals look like teardrops,' I said.

'Or maybe balloons, I thought. I found it comforting to wear when I was missing him. I hope you like it.'

'I do. It's wonderful. Thank you.'

She adjusted her shawl again and smiled. 'Goodbyes are hard. They never get easy.'

London, but not what I expected. I'd pictured it like Paris only filled with English voices. But from the train, it looked short, spread flat and everything was prisons, factories with painted English words for plain things – hats, pianos, window glass – and square-towered churches that looked unfinished, their pointed spires left off and their stone walls grimed with soot. Near the railway station, a cluster of men in pale clothes stood out against the dark background, and Ena said they must be in from the countryside which was a paler place. America was paler, too, I thought, at least my part of it. White cotton and calico, bonnets, aprons and wide, washed skies. This London was dark and not clean at all. Ten minutes in and my nose felt smutted.

The railway station arched high above us and, all around, people knew where they were going, everyone in a rush, everyone moving.

'Ah, yes,' Monsieur Gaudron said, quietly. 'The natural Englishman, scuttling about as the sun descends. Pity there are no good cafés where we might retreat for a civilized rest before continuing.'

My stomach grumbled just then, and Ena laughed and clutched my arm. 'Me, too, my dear. We have been too long on the road and goodness, I can't even remember when we lunched. You must be starving. We'll need to put on a good meal as soon as we get home.'

They'd said I could spend the night at their house, and in the morning more suitable arrangements could be made.

'Otherwise, there'd be talk of impropriety,' she said. 'And my brothers are rather particular about talk. But of course, you'll take your meals with us. If you like. It's all a bit more humble than Paris, I'm afraid. Not half as romantic.'

'Nonsense, my dear,' said Auguste. 'Think of the excellent English names. Highbury and Holloway. What's not romantic about that?'

'It wasn't romance that moved us up here. Land's cheap in North London,' Ena said, looking at her husband sideways, but he kept with his own train of thinking.

'You have good place names in America, too. I always liked Soda Springs. Salt Lake City. Names you can taste.'

'That's not fair. You're making us both ravenous! You should go and find us a cab before we faint.'

That first night in England, I slept with the brooch in my hand and it felt good to have something to hold. It was colder than Paris, like spring was only just starting here, a slow northern spring, a new kind of weather, and the brooch in my hand was warm like wood and hard as stone. I was amazed someone had been able to carve it. But then, they carved stone, didn't they? Like that stone pillar in Paris with all those secret symbols. And the brooch was a symbol, too – of mourning, of grief. Holding it hidden in my hand, it felt like grief itself, like something that grew, then hardened, something that you might, if you looked at it right, carve away, pattern and make beautiful.

7 /

IN THE MORNING, THEY TOOK ME TO THE FACTORY ON Ringcroft Street. It was busy and Ena said it was always like that in the spring and summer, people coming and going, lots of workmen hired in. Jackets hung on pegs along the wall and the men worked in shirtsleeves. There was a balloon, just back from service, spread out on the floor, and a rotary fan blew air through its neck, causing it to inflate. It looked like a whale, fished out of the sea and caught in this boat of a building. A group of men walked its length, laying hands on the swelling cloth and examining the seams. Another painted canvas with a wide brush and a clear paint that smelled strong. Hanging from a line along one wall, a wide net was being knotted by hand, men standing on stools reaching up, working the rope. More men sat right on the floor with more ropes around them, knotting and splicing like sailors on a ship. I said that to Ena and she nodded and said I was right. A lot of them were retired sailors, men who'd seen the wide world and come home wanting land work.

'And now they make sky ships.'

Auguste cleared his throat.

'The family will be upstairs,' he said. 'Percy has something he wants to discuss. Everyone should be there already.'

We climbed a twisting staircase and the room up there was as large as the one downstairs, though not quite so high, and cut through with rafters. Above them, the slanted roof was windowed with skylights, and everywhere there was more equipment. Ballooning baskets stacked like teacups, coiled ropes, heaps of silks and canvas, more balloons tied up to the rafters, and a peg board hung with tools. Things everywhere, but no one was working and the sewing machines on the long table under the skylights all had their covers closed.

There was a smaller table set up in the centre of the room where three men stood, looking down at papers. and two young ladies leaned against a balloon basket, talking together. No one seemed to notice us until Ena put her bag down on the floor with a bang and they all looked up.

'Ah, you have returned. Percy said you'd be joining us, but no one had seen you yet.' One of the ladies came towards us, almost running, and she must have been Ena's sister, they were so alike. 'When did you get back?'

Ena met her hug and I hung back, trying to keep behind her.

'Just yesterday evening,' Ena said. 'And *what* a long journey, though nothing went wrong on the train, so that felt like a victory. It's good to be back.'

'Did you buy up Paris? Did you bring me anything?'

'Julia, really. And did you send me with any money? Paris is expensive, you know. But I did bring bits and bobs for sewing. French thread and buttons and things. Just essentials.'

One of the men at the table stuck out his hand towards Auguste.

'It's good to see you both home again,' he said. He was a thin man with teasing eyes, and he wore a thin modern moustache, trimmed and waxed at the ends. 'All these honeymoons you're taking with my sister. What a scandal.'

'It wasn't a honeymoon, Stanley. A bit of investment research.'

'They're all honeymoons until the babies arrive.'

Another brother at the table, this one older and with a beard and small glasses that perched on his nose. He looked over them as he spoke, and he also seemed to twinkle. On the ferry, Ena had told me all about her family. This would be Percy, I thought. Mr Percival. The eldest adventurer. He who'd seen Egypt and India and told them all what to do.

'And did you manage to talk money out of the great Henri Lachambre?' he asked. 'I hear his factory is doing very well for a French business. Perhaps not as ambitious as ours, but still with some rather enviable connections. I hear he's selling to the American Signal Corps. What did he think about your small suggestion?'

Auguste pursed his lips before shrugging his shoulders.

'Well, it may yet work out,' he said. 'For the moment, no commitment, but he was interested in all I had to say, and he was generous with his time. Two meetings and coffee *and* a cigar, which I enjoyed very much. For now, he has donated a trunk full of materials to our cause. I haven't sorted everything yet, but there seem to be some useful parachutes and pulleys and things.'

'And no money. That is a pity.' He looked down at his bare arms and unrolled his shirt sleeves, nodding slightly to himself. 'But I see you've brought a friend instead.'

'A new employee,' Ena said. Julia looked surprised and the lady by the basket gave an edged smile, looking me up and down.

'Well, isn't that just what we need?' she said.

'It is, isn't it?' Ena replied, smiling. 'She's very good with the sewing and very reliable. And American, like you, Alma. Laura, let me introduce Miss Alma Beaumont, our international glamour. And my sister Julia and brothers Percy and Stanley, and the quiet one is Harry. Don't worry; he's friendly. And he likes Americans, too.'

'The more Yanks the better,' Harry said. 'Isn't that what they say about business?'

Julia frowned. 'If she's under thirteen, she'll need to be in school two hours a day. They've passed laws now. Child labour. We need to be sure of provision.'

'She's fourteen,' Ena said, and Percy looked at me, as if calculating.

'Fourteen last November,' I said.

'Well, then,' he said. 'No worries about that.' He gathered the papers from the table into a neat pile and said it was time to sit down to talk business. Alma and Julia joined Ena at the table with the brothers, and Percy told Ena I could stay, too, but suggested I'd be more interested in looking at the sewing machines than discussing the accounts and maybe she could set me up at the worktable.

They could talk for an hour: that was all Percy could afford that morning because time was tight, but he'd really like to hear what the family had to say about the purchase of new expedition baskets – solid, sophisticated things with modern developments – and there was need to continue the discussion about developing a second branch to the company. Perhaps an entirely separate company made more financial sense. The new branch could focus on training pilots for scientific expeditions, both within Britain and abroad. But to fund this, there would need to be a strong season of performances, perhaps longer.

Ena stopped him there. She wanted to know what kind of performances.

'Popular ones. You know, fairs and fetes and festivals. Exhibitions. Events that draw big, ticketed crowds.'

'With girls?'

'Perhaps. There are advantages.'

'The advantages,' Ena said, 'are that they're costumed and badly paid.'

'Not badly,' he said, and now the other ladies piped up.

'Yes, badly paid and never right away.'

'And never full time, though we're always here, aren't we?'

'We do what we can, ladies,' Stanley said. 'It's a business. And we pay well per shift.'

Then, more papers spread out on the table and talk about accounts, risk and investment. The young ladies held their tongues, though they watched like hawks and listened carefully, and all the men ignored them.

I looked at the sewing machine in front of me. It was bigger than Ma's, and the wooden cover was clean and polished. The key sat in the lock like it was waiting. No treadle under the table so it must be a hand-crank. I wondered what the decals were like.

Talk around the table continued on, voices quiet back and forth.

I turned the key and lifted the lid. Golden flowers in gold rings so they looked like church windows in Paris against the black lacquer. And it had a fiddle base and good strong hinges with the paint unchipped. A lovely machine and well maintained, and this was just one of them. How many were there? Four, five others on this table, maybe more somewhere else around the room. I pictured what it would be like with all these machines working, the whir of those turning wheels, the thrum of needles up and down. So many machines meant so many workers, and I tried to picture them, too. Young ladies like Julia and Alma, or girls like me, sitting with shoulders hunched, eyes set, hands in motion. Or would they be older women? Old as Ma? Older?

So, what was I doing here? Me in a place like this. Didn't make sense, did it?

Ena laughed over at the table, and Auguste coughed as if to cover whatever he'd said.

I ran my fingers over the machine, the cast iron black and cold and the gold paint delicate. A flat pin cushion was strapped to the top, tied on with red ribbon, and beside that, a spool of white thread stood up on its spindle. I opened the machine's small panels and looked at all its workings. The smell of oil and a cache of small tools. Needle threaders, presser feet, fine dust brushes, a small screwdriver.

Ma's machine was a Singer, too, I learned to use it by watching, the way a child learns any important thing. How to tie back your hair, how to welcome a woman into the store, a man. I watched as she set the bobbin in the shuttle and tucked it into the little cave under the machine. She turned the crank, the needle started, and the hidden shuttle made a rackety sound as she sewed. Sometimes, when the thread was spent and the bobbin needed winding again, she let me slide the door open with my thumb and take the shuttle out, and then it was a shiny boat in my palm, heavy and pointed at one end like a knife blade or a bird's beak. I had to be careful. And it had a small screw in just the right place, too, just like an eye, and I thought about it looking around in the dark when my mother closed the door, looking and looking and seeing darkness.

I put the lid back on the machine and turned the key again in the lock. At the other side of the room, the men talked on, the women listening. Now it was advertising, clients, commissions, and debt. All stuff I didn't understand, but then they didn't know about bobbins and shuttles, thimbles and thread, did they? When I was sewing the costumes in Paris, Monsieur Gaudron had watched with such interest as I made my paper patterns with their notches and matched points. I'd wondered then but didn't ask who stitched his balloons together and where did he get his clothes?

How could anyone be so surrounded by so much they didn't understand?

When the conversation finished, Mr Percival walked over to where I sat and told me I'd do.

'Do what?' I asked and he laughed.

'You'll do fine. I trust Ena's choice. You can work here, if you like. We can always use another pair of capable hands.'

'Thank you. I . . . I'll do my best.' I hadn't realized Mr Percival had the final say.

The men left the room, but the ladies stayed.

'Time for some exercise, you think?' Julia asked, and Alma was on her feet fast as fast. She moved the chairs and Julia helped with the table, clearing space. Ena gathered an armful of rope from behind a stack of baskets and laid it out on the floor, then with a quick pull, she found a weighted end and hoisted it up and over the central rafter above our heads. Quick work; they'd done this before. In no time, a swing hung suspended in the centre of the room.

Alma stepped up and stood on the seat, holding the ropes in her hands. She leaned and pulled, arching her way up into the air, her dress flattening against her as she swung. In that long room and with that much rope, the swing simply flew, high and higher and all that swinging made a wind in the room. Down at the far end, a parachute hung from another rafter and its pale silk fluttered. I watched it rise and fall, and listened to the young women's laughter, their easy, swinging jokes.

There was a swing in one town where Ma and I lived. Just a board attached to long ropes tied to a tree branch, and in wet weather, a puddle collected underneath. At lunchtime, there was always a line of girls waiting their turn. I can't remember what the boys did at that school. Marbles, maybe. Some game with sticks or balls. Something pushing. But the girls all lined up, waiting their turn. At first, I thought they were all polite, but it wasn't that. You needed to watch to see there was something else going on. Sometimes the girls changed order, and sometimes there was a look or something said. A game they were playing, but they didn't explain it to me. I waited. Other girls swapped places. I tried to as well, only then they called it *budding*, and they whined and scolded so I shuffled back. I didn't like that word. *Budding*. Made me think about tree buds, how hard and green and sticky they could be. And false, too, because they were supposed to have leaves inside and looked like little packages, but when you sliced them open with your thumbnail, you never found the leaves at all. Just hard and green like vegetables.

Once the teacher asked me to stay late after school to clean the blackboards, and when I'd finished, she asked if I'd like a go on the swing before I went home. All on my own. No line-up. My hands felt chalky clutching the rope, and I pushed off and pulled myself into swinging, back and forth until I went so high I could see over the school, down the road and the road kept going. I could see forever from way up there. The teacher stood small at the school door, her hands folded, her eyes on me. When I came down again, she was smiling, and she locked up the school and walked me to the store where Ma was waiting.

Late that night after swinging, after coming home, I woke for no reason, and lay in bed listening. Ma in her bed was still and sleeping, her breath steady and soft, and out in the night, I could imagine the swing hanging empty, moving a little in the night wind.

'Hey Laura! You want to?' Julia's voice startled me. 'You know about swings, right?'

'Everyone knows about swings,' Alma said, laughing. 'They've even made it to America. Expensive imports, but only the best, eh Laura? Isn't that right?' She sat on the floor now, her legs stretched out in front of her, and leaned back, bracing herself with her hands flat on the floor, as Julia took a turn on the swing. 'Where are you from anyway?'

'All over the place, sort of. Colorado. Then Wyoming. Montana.'

'I'm from Nebraska. Omaha, Nebraska. A good place to leave.'

'That's a well-rehearsed line,' Ena said. 'You are such a performer, Alma.'

'That's why they hired me. I bring the spice to this business.'

'We were spicy enough before you came along,' Julia answered.

'Sure, you were,' Alma smirked.

'It's not about spice,' said Ena. 'We're not that kind of entertainers.'

'Tell that to Percy. Did you see the last lot of costumes he had made?'

'I'm going to change that. We're going to. That's why Laura is here. As I said, she's a seamstress. We hired her in Paris and she's wonderful. She can make anything out of anything.'

'And how does she manage with altitudinous work?' Alma asked, holding out the swing. 'Because it would be a waste of her youth for her to be chained to a sewing machine when she could make a name for herself and a bit of cash, too. We could train her up, Julia and me.'

'Training's all well and good,' Julia said, 'But all a girl really needs in this business is good looks and a good grip.' She took the swing from Alma and held it steady for me. 'You don't have to stand if you're not ready. Sitting's fine. I'll start you off with a nice big push, okay? Hang on tight.'

'Laura, don't let them bully you,' Ena said. 'You don't need to if you don't want to. Really.'

'Don't listen to Ena. She thinks she's all respectable now that she's caught a husband, but she's a trapeze queen like the rest of us.'

They all laughed, but I remembered Paris. The chandelier. The height between the rope and the cobbled street. And that night at the theatre. All the light in the world. Ena caught my eye as I sat down on the swing, and whether she was pleading silence or revelation, I couldn't tell.

I sat down and started pumping slowly, slow as this strange English spring. That's how most things start, I think. Little by little, slow and steady as you lift your feet off the ground and start to feel the wind.

* * *

It turned out, in England, spring came slowly every year, but the years between sprinted. By the next spring, London was home. I'd grown used to the smell of the local streets, the Highbury brewery sweet and strong, and the industry furnaces with their heavy coal smoke all day until the very last moment of night when it finally lifted and then I could smell wood smoke starting from the bakeries, a faraway country smell, a new day beginning. I had a small room of my own in the Ringcroft Street factory and my own sewing machine, too. It was a gift from Auguste and Ena at Christmas. He called it a recompense for supporting the new branch of the business – Harry and Auguste's branch – and for spending all those hours making new equipment. Ena said, yes, it was partly that and partly to set me up for business myself. She said I wasn't bound to them and could always go if I wanted to. Just give notice and make my own plans. But I decided to stay.

That summer, they taught me how to fly. We left the performing to Alma and Julia, and together we talked about science. All through the autumn and into the winter, I learned so much, but another spring came and now Ena was pregnant. She worried about money, about the baby, Auguste and us girls, too. She asked me if he was putting on the pressure and maybe he was. I worked hard that summer, hoping she'd stay home and rest, but still she came to the factory to watch me when I trained, climbing up to the rafters to jump down and practise parachute landings on cloth stuffed sacks.

'There must be a safer way,' she said.

'Softer than some of the places we have to land,' Alma said.

'And fewer cows,' said Julia, laughing.

'And no lakes.'

Ena stood with her back against the wall, her hands pressed

against her hips. She closed her eyes and slowed her breathing, concentrating. Auguste watched her, his face uncertain.

'Tout va bien?' he asked.

'Yes, of course, dear. Only I'm turning into a balloon and this little pilot has a mind of his own. Come on, Alma. Let's see what you can do. Laura needs a good example.' The factory windows were open, and a scrap of breeze crept in, catching her hair.

I pulled myself up and settled beside Julia on the rafter. Looking down from that height, it looked like landing was all guesswork and gravity. I swung my boots back and forth and Alma scolded me.

'I'm trying to focus,' she said.

Julia laughed again. 'As if any balloon trapeze ever was still and stable. You kick out for all you're worth, Laura. We need to cope with whatever comes.'

Below us, Ena's upturned face was a chalky white thumbprint.

The child was born in the summer. Not a little boy at all, which turned us all inside out with surprise because Ena had said she was so certain, but there you go. You can't tell how things will work out. They named her Marina like her mother and brought her to the factory in a wicker basket, sleeping sweetly, wrapped up in clean cotton and starched lace. By Christmas, she was sitting up under the sewing tables, and playing with a rag doll I stitched from new cloth.

'She'll be flying in no time,' Auguste said. 'No time at all.'

8/

THINGS I LOVE ABOUT BALLOONS:

The fabric first, all strength and readiness. I take the cut gores from the worktable and lay them together, pin each in place and check the edges, making them ready for the machine. With one hand, I touch and guide the fabric and with one, I turn the wheel. This is my first work, each stitch mine. Small, secret, holding everything together.

The miles of thread I use, thin as hair, heavy to hold.

Then the varnish, its sharp, hard smell, the boar-bristle brush, and the broad strokes the painter uses like he's casting out a fishing line, like he's waving to a ship that might now come to shore.

The room in the factory upstairs, hung round with waiting balloons, and mainly women there. The towers of baskets and the shadows they make. The heaviness and lightness of ropes and cotton and silk suspended, all waiting until we need them.

So many things.

I love the plans we make and the maps. Decisions. Even arguments. Schemes.

I love the experiments, the equations, the new ways of making things.

I love looking ahead.

I do not love the costumes the girls wear, but love my own when I can choose it. A man's suit, a well-cut waistcoat, buttoned close, the warmth of layered wool. I wear these when we try new balloons, when it's just us and no audience, no paying passengers. Just me and Ena and Auguste in the basket, working together, talking things through.

Sometimes, though, they do make me perform. A crowded fairground and wearing the girls' suits. Low-cut, high-cut, stripes, edged in gilt. I hate all that. They paint my face, my lips red, each eyebrow a rising arch. I frown until it is time to perform, and then I smile.

I love the groundwork before each flight. We take the balloon from its cart, lay it on the grass, then the hard work of inflation over fire, or if we have it, over gas. We hold on together, resisting, straining as the balloon starts to swell and tug. Above us, the quiet sky.

The ropes and calls, the hope of height and lift and ease. The rising. The holding. The wait.

Sometimes, we attach a basket and sometimes just use a webbed loop. At first, this terrified me, sitting on a swing and flying up so high, but when you know the ropes, all the work of hooks and valves, the drift and thought and way of the thing, it can be beautiful. You can trust it.

It's never what you'd think. It's silent. You move with the wind, carried, not buffeted. You feel safe. It's the shrinking world that falls away. You stay where you are.

All around, the bright edge of the summer sky touches you and birds rise, companions in the air. You look out and can see forever. You are held and moving. You watch the sea.

But now, it isn't worth it. I won't go up any more. Those days won't come back.

SUMMER

London: 1896

MAIN ENTRANCE TO EXHIBITION FROM PARK-PLACE.

1/

If it was a newspaper, I might ignore it. Not my business. Just something the wind snatched up and tossed high. I looked out the open window at that scrap of white caught against the factory chimney, trying to decide what to do. It might be nothing, but probably it was drawers.

I'd been drying laundry that morning, all the small bits I could wash in a tub, and I laid them out on the flat roof under my window, weighing everything down with pebbles like always, only maybe the wind was stronger than I thought. It seemed a perfect day to get things dry. The sky was clear, a morning that asked for more with no clouds at all, and my room felt fresh and breezy.

I reached out to feel the closest chemise and it was dry already, so I gathered up the pebbles to use again, folded each chemise, then counted the pairs of drawers. One was definitely missing. Oh dear.

So, that was it. I'd have to climb out the window. I couldn't just leave them there because every time I looked outside, I'd see them, looking at me. I had to get them. My window wasn't far from the ridgeline and looking out, I could see a manageable valley sloping up from my flat bit of roof. If I took off my shoes and socks, I could get a good grip on the shingles. And once at the ridge, the chimney wasn't far along, really – only six or seven steps. Twelve or fourteen, if I counted there and back.

The pebbles in my pocket tinked against each other as I sat on the sill and swung my legs out into the sunshine. The shingles were warm, almost hot to the touch, and, climbing hand and foot, I was up to the ridge quick enough, trying not to think about what I was doing. I'd learned to be fine with heights and it wouldn't do to waste perfectly good clothing. Next time I did laundry, I'd be more careful.

At the top, I was glad to see the smooth tiles along the ridge. Fine for sitting and they'd be easy enough to walk on when I got to my feet. I hoped no one was looking up. That was the trouble with cities; there were always people watching. Sure, you might be anonymous, but you were likely to be witnessed, too. But no helping that now. I couldn't think about that up here or I'd worry and throw myself off balance. I stood up slowly, held my arms out for balance, and then, one foot in front of another, stepped out carefully. One, two, three – pause – four slower, five, six don't look at the birds now, seven and my hand now flat on the red brick chimney. There. I could breathe again.

In the courtyard below, a cab arrived. I saw Ena step out, lift little Marina down and set her on uncertain feet. From up here, they both looked tiny, and I wished I was brick-coloured. If only I'd thought to change into flight clothes, I might be mistaken for a man up here doing some work rather than a conspicuous girl out on a limb. But Ena didn't glance up.

I shifted my feet closer to the chimney and looked around, feeling stupid. What a mad idea this was. Not exactly clever problem-solving and where were those drawers, anyway? How high had they been? From the window, it had been hard to tell and now, up close, I wasn't even sure which way to look. Far below, I could hear Ena laughing, but when I glanced, she was only looking at Marina, clapping her hands about something.

And then relief, because from the corner of my eye, I caught a glimpse of white, and looking up, there they were, those fly-away drawers close above my head after all, caught on a ridged bit of brickwork. With one hand steady on the chimney, I reached up, then stretched taller and hoped and there! I managed to hook one finger in the waistband and pulled to get a better hold, only just then a crow flew close, black and cawing, and maybe it distracted me or the wind gusted right then, but off they went. My white drawers flapping away.

I suspected they were the new ones Ena had given me. Wide-legged and flared, and she called them fashionable. A kind gift, really, and they were a comfortable pair. I liked the lacework above the hems. And now, gone.

The factory was quiet, with most of the balloons out away from London, making money. Auguste was in the West Country at fetes and festivals in Taunton, Exeter, Redruth, all the industrial towns down there, and Alma travelled with him to draw the crowds. Ena had said she wasn't interested in funfairs, and, besides, she liked London in the summer, the heat and the different pace. She brought Marina to the factory most days, and she and I kept up our experiments, making miniature balloons and parachutes in new designs, making use of the slow days and the empty factory.

I tried to imagine what it would be like packing up and travelling on, country fair after country fair, all those posters and printed banners. Glitz and glamour or a bit of a trudge? Hard to say from this distance. In London, Redruth felt flat, a thing of paper, printed words in a newspaper cut up for the clippings book or to make jointed puppets to amuse Marina, papercut shapes glued to rolled paper straws with fancy paper clothes watercolour-pale. *He flies through the air with the greatest of ease*, I sang, making the puppet dance, and the little girl sang with me. *The daring young man on the flying trapeze.* She liked the song, but I wasn't being fair because before they left, there'd been an almighty argument. Ena was furious that Auguste took the trapeze along. The same old argument about science and performance and business and, as always, Auguste won because of the money. That didn't make it better. Alma stood to the side, smiling, which was maddening, particularly because she, too, argued money with Auguste. After they left, Ena spent three days fuming and then we settled down to quieter times. Cornwall was miles away, and London was hot.

We read the newspapers each morning, hoping for news from the West Country fairs but finding little. Only that the crowds were very large, the factories' owners concerned at the lateness of the fair's operating hours, a tiger escaped from the menagerie, was missing all night, but was found in St Ives in the morning in a fish shed. Nothing about our aeronauts.

'We should consider that lucky,' Ena said. 'The papers report happenings which ten to one mean bad news. I'd rather not hear about Auguste and Alma in the papers, thank you very much.'

Auguste sent postcards home, polychrome seasides with very few words. I wanted to imagine he was the kind of husband who sent his wife fat love letters, overflowing with poetry. He had the perfect handwriting for that kind of thing, and I'd seen it frequently enough on balloon sketches, but the postcards were brief and lacked even technical detail. *Flight went well. Good crowds. Fair wind. Coastal weather.* All flat as the sea and no mention at all of trapezes.

Ena said she'd paste the postcards in her clippings book, and she rather hoped he'd enjoy Redruth and work to make connections whilst he was there. It was a town known for development. Plenty of mining and the investment associated with that, but also inventors, she said. William Murdock had lived in Redruth, the one who developed coal gas lighting, and she showed me she had a clipping in her book about that, too. *One hundred years of clean gas lighting: Murdock remembered.* The clipping next to it was a death announcement for Mrs Garnett of Vernon, near Crewe who died aged 105. *She had been a member of the Wesleyan Methodist body for 90 years. On her farm, there is now living a labourer who had been working on the farm for over 80 years. Mrs Garnett retained all her faculties to the last.* In blue ink, Ena had added *1789: Wilberforce, Mutiny on the Bounty, Herschel discovers Saturn's moons.*

When I got my shoes back on and myself down to the factory floor, I found Harry sitting with his left leg propped up on a stool. He'd twisted his ankle earlier in the summer from a wonky balloon landing and was still convalescing. In front of him, there was a stack of company record books, and Ena was standing posed at the door, waving something white with a look of triumph on her face. For a brief moment, I froze, electrified, but then I saw it was an envelope.

Harry didn't turn to see me at all, just kept laughing at his sister as she put on a show.

'Are you going to show me at all or simply use it as a flag?' he asked.

'It is a grand moment in the history of this grand company. You will see. Something entirely new! Or at least, on a grander sort of scale altogether.'

She took the letter from its envelope and unfolded it carefully, looking at her brother with twinkling eyes, as I sat down and surreptitiously tied my shoelaces.

'Listen to this. *The Cardiff Fine Art, Industrial and Maritime Exhibition under the patronage of Her Majesty Queen Victoria.* Now, that's a mouthful, isn't it? And they want an aerialist. Isn't that grand and advantageous! Of course, Vicky won't be there herself, but I read in the papers there was a royal visit to the Exhibition earlier this month. The Prince of Wales himself and his lovely wife Princess Alexandra. And the Marquess of Bute is in Cardiff, too, of course. A crowd to be associated with, don't you think?'

'Bound to be a good purse in it. I'm surprised they didn't contact Percy,' Harry said.

'But they wouldn't. It's Cardiff. They won't want the Spencer name in Cardiff. Not after Stanley and the Horticultural Society. Disaster.'

'Hardly a disaster. A captive ascent, wasn't it, and the winch jammed whilst pulling them back to earth.'

'And a strong wind crashed the balloon into a nearby tree. The whole show committee had to jump ship and climb down the tree to safety.'

'Well, I'd still say disaster is a strong word. We've had worse. Mishap, perhaps.' He leaned back in his chair and adjusted his foot on the stool. 'But I can understand why they've asked Auguste this time around. Brothers-in-law are useful. Maybe we should find some more.'

'Julia would never agree.'

'No, I don't suppose she would. She's still in a snit Auguste didn't take her to Cornwall. As if Redruth was Paris herself.' He fanned himself with one of the record books, pulling a face like a grand lady.

'Julia just wants adventure.'

'And Auguste doesn't want to pay for two girls. I can't blame him. These numbers, I tell you. But you should send that invitation on to him. He'll want this opportunity.'

'Of course he will. I want this opportunity. Much better publicity for investors than country funfairs.' She looked over the letter again.

'A Royal Exhibition. It'd be a chance to meet people, too. The right people. Of course we're going. And what about you, Harry?'

'Only if you put me in a wheelbarrow.'

She laughed and swatted him with the letter. 'Well, I'll want Laura there, at least,' she said, smiling at me. 'With your sewing machine, of course, and your fine eye on hand, and to help with Marina, too. She dotes on you.'

Ena sat down, and when she'd finished writing a note to Auguste, she asked if I'd like to come to the post office and then for a walk with her and Marina.

'Need a bit of fresh air, don't we? And a chance to run on the grass. We'll go up to Highgate and have a walk on the Heath before the day heats up too much. Sound good?'

An omnibus up Holloway Road, up Highgate Hill to St Michael's Church and Ena said she wanted to go in. There wasn't a service or anything and she said I could wait outside with Marina. I thought of the posts on main streets in Wyoming, the way men tied up horses when they stopped in at a saloon. No posts here, and no gravestones either, but then they were behind the church, hidden away in the great cemetery there. Marina wanted to pick daisies and I didn't let her. I held her hand tightly, told her we needed to keep our feet on the path, our dresses clean. Waiting felt dusty, dried out and flat.

Two jackdaws circled the spire, calling, and I thought their black wings must be hot in this weather, though maybe it was cooler higher up. I watched them perch on the cross-topped spire, take flight, then land again and in another moment, Ena came back out through the red doors, looking calmer. Marina ran towards her, and she bent to catch the girl, gathered her up and spun her around in a circle which made Marina laugh and the jackdaws fly away.

'Now then,' Ena said. 'A walk in the cemetery, I think, and a run on the Heath. The vicar says he'll let us in through the gate here, so we don't have to circle back to Swain's Lane.' She set Marina down on her feet and held her hand and both their faces were happy.

'We could just go to the Heath, couldn't we?' I asked. 'We don't need to go near the graves.'

Ena smiled like I hadn't understood.

'My father's here,' she said. 'It isn't far.'

The cemetery was overhung with trees, the neat grass divided up by tidy paths. I followed Ena and wished Marina wanted to hold my hand. I tried not to look at anything. Ahead of us there were stairs and below, a sunken corridor curved round in a ring. Closed tombs with heavy doors like a street of silent houses, and everywhere stone, iron, ivy and carvings. In the centre, one tree stood tall, an ancient cedar like in the Bible, with flat, reaching branches dark against the hot sky, an impossible tree.

'He isn't in this section,' Ena said. 'These are rather grand and expensive, aren't they? I'm not sure he'd have liked it if we'd planted him here.'

I followed her down the path and out to where the graves looked humbler. Crosses, veiled urns, angels with lowered eyes.

'All this stone,' I said. 'It makes me feel heavy just to see it.'

'Auguste wants to be buried here. He told me that after my father's funeral.'

'I've never been to a funeral.'

'No. Ladies don't, do we? I'm glad of that. Waiting in the chapel was difficult enough. So many visitors wanting to say something. Ghastly. All the comfort and cards and condolences.' She unpinned her hat and took it off. 'Isn't it strange weather today? Too hot for a hat, but you need the shade.'

Everything all around us was bright and sunshot.

'I should have brought the guidebook,' Ena said. 'Maybe you'd be interested. It shows you who's buried where. Politicians and scientists – Faraday the Sandemanian, for one – and writers and artists. All sorts. Lizzie Siddal's just over there, actually.' She pointed away off the path towards a lush rosebush.

'I don't know who that is,' I said, and Ena was quick not to look surprised. She forgot sometimes that I was a different sort of person from her with a different sort of memories. A faraway person, though I tried to fit in.

'One of the glamour girls. A muse. She posed for artists and married one, too. Rossetti, and when she lay dying, he sat by her bed, writing poetry, and he buried the manuscript with her. Terribly romantic, and people said at the time it was a fitting sacrifice of mourning for such a loss. Then, imagine that, he changed his mind. Well, not right away. Seven years after she died, he decided he wanted the poem back, that it would be worth the trouble.'

She told me how he had her dug up. Got permission from the Home Secretary and paid his friends to exhume her one night. He himself stayed home, which might be understandable, though so would his curiosity as he was an artist. It must have been such a scene. Autumn – he didn't want to risk another season of frost and thaw – and they lit a great bonfire beside the grave for warmth and earthly comfort, too.

I shivered, imagining the shadows and the falling leaves.

We turned onto a smaller path, the gravel crunching under our shoes. Marina stooped to pick some up and Ena waited a moment, then kept walking and the girl followed after.

'And the poems? Did they find them?'

'Yes. Tangled in her hair. She had such beautiful hair. That's what drew the artists to her in the first place. Masses and masses of flame-coloured hair.'

'Will you be buried here?' I asked.

'Oh, I don't know,' she said. 'Probably. Seems likely it'll become the family thing to do.'

'I think it's a nice idea, being together like that.'

'Is it? I wonder. It probably means nothing at all to the deceased once they're gone. Might bring comfort while you're dying, knowing that detail is sorted and no one will need to worry it through for you after you're gone, but that's not really what comes next at all, is it?'

'It could be nice for those that come after. For family, I mean.'

'To be confident they'll find us all here in one place. A tidy unit? Perhaps.' She didn't sound convinced. 'I'd rather be out in the open. Somewhere like the Heath, except they'd never permit that. But you could just lay me down out there. Wrap me up in a spent parachute and lay me on the grass where the winds blow. I'd like that far better than all those richy tombs and extravagance.'

'These ones here are better,' I said. 'Less showy.'

Another few paces then she stopped by a grave and held out her hand again for Marina.

'This is the one,' she said, softly. 'Your grandpapa's grave. See the balloon? Your uncles thought it would be nice to have a balloon carved there because he liked balloons, didn't he?'

'I like balloons. And trapeze,' Marina said.

'Me, too.' Ena kissed her daughter's cheek, tucked her hair behind her ears and told her she could sit down on the grass now if she liked. The girl smiled and trotted off to find the best place to sit. 'Keep an eye on her, will you please, Laura? I don't want her to go too far from us.'

I stepped away to give Ena her space. For what? Whatever she needed to perform out there. Bow her head, say a prayer, touch her toes. I thought about her father's book, all those small illustrations bending this way and that, all those trim beards. What would her father want now? What can we do for the dead? Say we are here. That they are remembered. That we don't understand.

I looked up at the sky. There weren't so many trees in this part of the graveyard and that helped. I could breathe better. I saw the jackdaws were still settled on the church spire, the same jackdaws or different ones. I thought about the church spire in France, the one I'd decided on. And I thought about Ma and what remembering her felt like and the mourning brooch Ena gave me, that matte black heaviness I could pin at my throat when I wanted to remember her. A useful thing to wear.

Ena took off her hat again and plucked out one of the feathers. It was blue as the sky and, for a moment, she held it between her fingers and looked at it, then she set it down on the marble gravestone. There was a sort of ledge under her father's name and space below where more names might be added. *In Affectionate Remembrance*, it said, and I saw he died in June. It wasn't cold in June. You could have warm nights then. Fireflies.

When Ena had finished by the grave and Marina found her feet again, we walked the length of Swain's Lane and out to the Heath where everything opened up. I wanted to say something to Ena about the open space and maybe about Wyoming and how open space really felt around you. I wanted her to know, but couldn't find the words, so I kept silent. In the distance, hazy London stretched out at our feet and a bit of breeze ruffled our hair and I was glad we'd left the cemetery behind.

'Right,' Ena said. 'Next stop Cardiff, is it? I wonder what the Welsh will make of our balloons.'

* * *

Auguste would stay in Cornwall until the end of his current contract. The invitation had said nothing about Alma, only inquired after the fee for one balloonist and three flights. In his reply to Ena, Auguste wrote he would travel straight from Torquay and meet us in Cardiff with the equipment. Ena arranged for a storage place near the Exhibition grounds, a rented house for the week and a housekeeper called Mrs Warsow, who would send her husband out to meet us at the station and help us with our things when we arrived.

Brown flat cap, brown trousers, brown dust on his shoes and he spoke slowly, saying hello and asking carefully if we found the travel pleasant. When Ena answered him quick as a wink, he grinned, all surprised, and said he'd been sure she was a foreigner with a name like that.

'Ah, Gaudron, you mean,' she said. 'Yes, it trips people up sometimes. And all the different ways people say it. Goodness, such imagination! But I imagine yours causes trouble, too. Is it German? Or Bohemian?' Ena was full of friendly chat and Mr Warsow seemed completely charmed.

'My husband, you see, is French,' she said. 'We met in Paris. But his English is excellent. He understands everything. And we are both so glad to have this opportunity to come to Cardiff and the Exhibition we have heard so much about.'

'Of course, you have, lovely. All of London must be talking about us and our Exhibition. It is the wonder of the age, I do believe.'

He didn't sound German, so maybe his family left a long time ago. Voices can change. I liked his singing way of speaking, the lift and lilt that was different from how they spoke in London. Different but not disconnected. So many ways of speaking the same language. I wondered what he would think of my American when I opened my mouth, but decided not to surprise him again so soon.

The rented house was 19 Edward Street in the centre of town, not far from the Exhibition. The front hall smelled of soap and floor wax which I took to be a good sign. The housekeeper was diligent. Hopefully, the food would be good, too.

'My husband will be arriving later this evening,' Ena said,

explaining that he was travelling separately. 'But he may not be coming straight to the house. There was some confusion about the shipment of our equipment, and he may want to go directly to the Exhibition Grounds to inquire there about its delivery and storage. I've arranged for use of a shed there. He hasn't sent word here yet, has he?' Mrs Warsow shook her head and said nothing had arrived, nothing at all.

'Well, no matter. He'll arrive when he arrives, and I am sure he can sort out all arrangements then. In the meantime, we'll set up here and maybe a cup of tea? Would now be a good time for that?'

I would sleep in a room with Marina, so I could look after her. Ena and Auguste would be across the hall in a larger room that looked out on the street through fashionable bay windows. The curtains in both rooms were heavy and lined – a sign of comfort, Ena said, approvingly.

Later, when the light was fading in the evening, I heard church bells striking the hour and a train down at the station. It was so much quieter than London, and I felt I could hear everything happening everywhere in the city. Every echo coming and going, everything ahead of us, every little thing. Only I didn't hear her, small footsteps on the darkening pavement. She'd have been arriving then, her train pulling in with that whistle blowing. She'd climb down to the platform just like everyone else and look up at the clock, its face like the moon maybe. Or a cup. Or a coin.

* * *

Shakespeare Street is half an hour from the train station if you know where you are going. She didn't, but didn't mind. She was tired after the day of travel, but glad to be in the city at last, and glad to be walking after all the time on the train. The streets opened up around her and she could go anywhere now, be anyone, ask for anything she wanted because you weren't going to get it if you didn't ask. And she would, wouldn't she? Everything she wanted could start here. She swung her arms and took long strides, trying to look purposeful and confident. The first thing she needed was a place to sleep. The hotels by the station had seemed too grand and she didn't even have a suitcase. Well, she'd aim a little lower. A rooming house would do fine. And she'd tell them her things had been sent on separately. That sounded good. They'd be delivered on arrival. 'They' even sounded plural. Imagine suitcases.

The evening was warm and comfortable, lovely, with ladies and gentlemen walking arm-in-arm and tall city buildings all around. There was a gracious air about this city, an elegance and freedom, and along all the streets, the trees were leafy and green. She wondered which way it was to the Castle. It was supposed to be right in the centre of the city, only the buildings were getting in the way. So many shops with bright windows, so many things on display. She walked slowly, taking everything in, and kept her eyes open for theatres.

A man smiled at her as he passed, so she smiled, too, and the evening was coming on and the light beginning to fade. The streets narrowed and there were train tracks and houses, then a church on the corner with fancy brickwork and a great square tower which made the houses around look smaller and dirty, and children played outside. There were no adults here, and no one telling them to be quiet. She passed them by, ignoring their laughing which might have been Welsh or maybe Italian, all those dark-haired children singing. Past the church, a small square of grass unfolded between buildings, centred with a tall, white statue of a mother and child. The grass looked soft enough to sleep on. Might be as good a place as any and it looked safe enough, only those children were still noisy in the street and they'd see if she stopped, maybe wonder if she was going to pray, maybe bother her if she wasn't. And here was one of them right behind her now, still teasing, not teasing, she couldn't tell, but he grabbed her hand, pulled hard and pointed towards a house with a paper in the front window. ROOMS. Well, there was the answer then.

She knocked on the door and a tired-faced woman answered, wiping her hands on her apron. When she asked about the rooms, the woman smiled sadly and shook her head.

'These ain't rooms for you,' she said. 'Just working men. They stay by the night, never more than a week. I always move them on.'

Standing there, she was suddenly tired, only wanting to lie down, and she might have told the woman one night would be fine, but the woman was shaking her head again, so she'd have to go back to the grass and hope the kids were gone inside.

'Here, I know what we'll do,' the woman said. 'There's a better house – a boarding house for young ladies – not far from here. I can take you there myself and get you sorted. You shouldn't be walking about at night like this all on your own. I'll get my shawl and then we'll go together.'

The house on Pearson Street looked larger and cleaner and there was no sign in the window. A young woman answered the door and said she'd find the landlady, a Mrs Pugh. The woman from Shakespeare Street turned and smiled encouragingly, but when Mrs Pugh appeared, it seemed she suited her name. The sturdy type who shrank you with an up-down look. Only she didn't. She said there was a room available, not smiling, not moving her head as she spoke. Upstairs to the left. They'd talk money and arrangements in the morning.

2/

I woke in the rented house Monday morning hearing seagulls. I'd forgotten we were near the sea and thought at first they were squally babies, a whole street full of babies. Marina was still sleeping, curled up in a white night-dressed ball in bed beside me. I didn't mind sharing a room with her; she was a nice little thing and kept to herself, happy enough with her bag of wooden animals and a quiet place to play. I'd made her that bag from a scrap of canvas she'd found under the worktable in the balloon factory, stitched it with thick red thread which looked cheerful against the white, and gave it a drawstring close at the top that she could manage on her own. The wooden animals were made by one of her uncles. Harry, I think, who didn't have children of his own yet and liked to practise.

I rolled over and looked out the window. The houses were close together, but there were trees, too, filling in the spaces in between. I'd slept with the curtains open for the heat, sheers closed for modesty, so looking out now into the morning the whole world had a gauzy look, a vague dreaminess about it. It was like looking out through a cocoon, this thinness all around, or an egg, the shell translucent, almost ready to break.

The sound of more seagulls shook me out of these dreamy notions, all squawking and scratching at the roof shingles overhead. A right riotous racket, Ma would say. Would have said. Time to get up.

There'd be a lot to do at the Exhibition Grounds that day before Auguste's flight in the evening. The crates we brought from London needed to be opened and gone through to be sure nothing had been damaged en route, and all the equipment Auguste used in Cornwall needed to be aired and examined. Sometimes flight damage was obvious. A jagged hole, a snapped rope system. More often, though, equipment weakened slowly through wear. Seams stretched, fabric thinned, and one small tear could imperil a whole panel if it wasn't caught in time. Then there'd be hours of work to do, removing and remaking the balloon's gores and reinforcing every connected seam. We'd made sure to bring plenty of extra material from London just in case it was needed, and I brought my sewing machine, hoping to find a decent work surface wherever it was that the balloons were kept.

The shed Ena had arranged was just beside the Exhibition Grounds in the Castle Gardens. When she let the concessionaires know how much space we needed, they had put her in touch with the head gardener, a Mr Andrew Pettigrew, and he was happy to offer use of one of the garden's winter storage sheds which would be locked and made secure when they weren't using it, the only keys kept by Mr Pettigrew himself.

'Perfect,' Auguste said, smiling at his wife. He was delighted not to need to hire anyone to guard the equipment this time. At the country fairs, that was always a concern and expense to consider.

'Well, this isn't a country fair,' Ena said. 'Quite another layer of sophistication.'

Walking through town towards the Exhibition Grounds, Auguste swung his cane and Ena smiled.

'They are right by the Castle, yes? The Grounds?' asked Auguste. 'So then, we will see the famous Animal Wall.'

'We're not here to be tourists today,' Ena said, but she looked glad to be with him again. She matched his stride as they walked down the street and I followed behind with Marina in the pram. I didn't mind pushing. It was a bit of a struggle with the wheels jamming on kerb stones and there were tramlines everywhere, embedded in the cobblestones. If you didn't keep an eye open, they'd easily trip you up and send you sprawling. And the passing trams were noisy, rushing east and west, and every trip a penny as it said on the side. Ena said someone was making money in this crowded Exhibition town.

The sun was bright, the sky alive, and Ena had tied a white bonnet on the child's head which made her look like a mushroom.

'You see then, tourism has its benefits,' Auguste said. 'But if that is not to be our morning, well, we'll need to make a point of exploring later, my dear. Each and every display and exhibition building. I'd like that.' He caught her arm up in his and described all the wonders on offer, the tents and entertainments, stalls and stands and shows. He said there was an old Welsh Fair – all historically accurate, of course – and an Indian bazaar, a reproduction of Shakespeare's birthplace and a great concert hall, too, filled every evening. And space for afternoon athletics, with a tended field, sand pit, bicycle track where they'd launch the balloon, bicycle railway, and an aerial railway, with dangling cable cars that passed overhead like a machine man's dream. They'd engineered a new lake and a canal that twisted through the park, past the bandstand, the gardens and the Avenue of lofty elms, which was illuminated every evening with thousands of electric lightbulbs. I tried to imagine that, all that electricity, all the brightness.

'It's all noted in the handbook,' he said, taking it from his pocket. 'I had the concessionaires send it on to me in Cornwall. A nice bit of reading for the train.'

'Oh, let me see that, my love.' She disentangled her arm from his and grabbed at the book, and winning it, she walked along beside him, flicking through the pages. 'All sorts of useful things in here. Just a pity that you aren't in the listings, though.'

'I'm sure it was printed months ago. You can't expect a late addition sideshow to be added in.'

'A sideshow with a good scientific angle. You have told them you plan to give a brief lecture before each flight, yes? Atmospheric conditions and the principles of lighter-than-air flight. You did remember?'

'Yes, yes, I mentioned it. We shall see how things configure, my dear.'

She threw him a quick look, but didn't push the question, turning pages instead.

'There's a note in here about our Mr Pettigrew. Seems he's growing grapes – the only vineyard in Britain – and he's making wine.'

'Wine? Here? In this cold, grey land?'

'It isn't cold today, is it, my dear? I'm sure they do very well. The Marquess will have good taste. He can afford that. And it says it's Gamay Noir. Beaujolais. Lovely. But the vineyards aren't here at the Castle; they're on the outskirts of town where Lord Bute has another castle. Goodness me. I do hope we have the opportunity to meet this man. I wonder if he likes balloons.'

We found the shed and Mr Pettigrew, a sturdy bearded man with a soft Scottish accent. He unlocked the door and showed Auguste the worktables, the hooks on the walls that might be useful for drying ropes, and the rafters where there was space for both balloons to hang safely and air. Auguste was pleased. He was pleased with everything that day. After Mr Pettigrew shook his hand and left again for the gardens, Auguste stood in the middle of the shed with his arms open wide.

'How could we imagine things more perfect? Everything is in its place.'

He praised the size of the space, and the quality of light inside. The neat way the crates had been stacked, the faithfulness of the men who had delivered them, the quickness of his wife to arrange the details and even the grand Exhibition clock now chiming the hour. Each time it chimed that morning, he remarked on its perfection and the quality of the time it kept, as if time relied on the clock that kept it and not the clock on time.

He organized us to sweep the floor before he'd let us unroll the balloons and parachutes for inspection. Ena and I hitched up our skirts and, shoes off, worked together, inch by inch. First, the newer model – a hemisphere parachute with clear calculations. Six gores, with the radius at each point proportional to the width of each gore, and the end of the parachute flat-pointed. Ena and I had worked this design through ourselves, she on the maths and me sewing. We made small versions first, trying different shapes, and climbed the factory rafters to test them. With the full-sized model, we developed a system for checking wear, working towards each other along each seam to meet in the middle then swap, so every bit was double-checked. Six gores meant six seams up and down is twelve and we called out each half as we went. *Start! Half! End! Switch!*

We worked all morning while Marina played with her toys or napped in her pram. Anywhere you put her, she seemed happy enough. She didn't look around or didn't check if anyone was watching. She was solitary and content, and I wondered how the Gaudrons had managed to make such a self-contained little girl. Ena had told me her own father was always performing, and that made sense. She always knew what to pull to get attention when she wanted it. She described her mother as the stubborn one, hauling the family through to the other side of bankruptcy when her brothers-in-law fumbled the family business. Sheer bloody-mindedness, and wasn't that just another ingredient in the Ena pot?

Auguste never talked about his parents, so I didn't know anything about them at all.

And mine? Ma, of course, but what was my father? A story not quite told. A star in her evening sky, pulling us east. A magnet. A blur.

Music from the Exhibition came in through the open shed doors, the sound of a band striking up a polka. Ena put her coil of rope down and started tapping her feet, turning her face to Auguste who only shrugged. She shrugged, too, and spun herself round, one arm around her own waist and the other hand held out for an invisible partner as she danced herself across the room in wider and wider circles.

'And you say you do not want to perform,' said Auguste, laughing and clapping his hands.

'I'm not performing, you donkey. I'm enjoying.'

'Ah yes, all the difference in the world. But perhaps not for the audience.'

'Oh, I'm tired of audiences. I'm glad it's you up in the balloon and not me any more.'

'You talk as if you're never going up again. I cannot believe that. Not you.'

'Well, we shall see, won't we? I'm making no promises.' She whirled past again and came to rest next to me and the sewing machine where I was fussing with thread, her breath coming fast. 'And how's all the fabric looking?'

It was musty but seemed strong. There was one stretch that might need a run through the machine, but that was easy enough to manage and soon done. She smiled encouragingly, then the music swelled again, as if carried in by the breeze, and Ena held out her hands to me, but I shook my head and turned back to the work.

When I finished with the seam, Auguste found a ladder and set it against a rafter so we could haul up the two balloons. They filled the shed, heavy lungs, waiting for air.

At midday, we ate the picnic Mrs Warsow had packed, thick-cut ham sandwiches, boiled eggs, and slices of cake. Auguste said he was happy with the morning's work – said we'd all been much more efficient than he'd expected, but then he was used to working with Miss Alma Beaumont, and Ena laughed at that and so did Auguste. The shed grew warm, and we finished the picnic, folded the sandwich papers, and Auguste lit a cigarette.

'I think I'd like to seek out the concessionaires this afternoon,' he said. 'Have a talk with them before preparing myself for the evening's flight. I would like to hear their perspective on the spectacle.'

Ena said she would take Marina home for a nap.

'So, Laura, it seems the afternoon is yours,' he said, turning to me. 'You won't need to worry about an entrance ticket; your name is on the exhibitors list. Wander where you like. See the sights.'

Ena gave me the book and made sure I could find the page with the map. 'You'll be fine,' she said. 'Just keep an eye on the clock and you'll always know where you are.'

'And when,' I said.

She smiled. 'Yes, of course. Auguste, when will the cart come to collect the balloon?'

Four o'clock. So just before then, he said, we should all be together back at the shed, ready to go.

'Well, that's enough time for a decent exploration,' Ena said. 'You can do what you please.'

I went into the Museum Hall where it would be shady and cool, and all manner of antiquities and ancient coins were on display. Flint knives, axes, arrowheads and early pottery, thumbprint ridged. Each case was closed behind glass so you couldn't touch these things, though I could see they were made to be touched. Looking was only half knowing. Like a glance at a sewing machine in a shop window. You might think you see – just turn the handle and the needle stitches, how clever – but you can't know a tool at arm's length. You fool yourself you understand and move on quickly.

I stayed. Looked down into the glass case where a collection of ancient bone needles lay in rows like wingless dragonflies pinned to felt. *Needles and pins*, I thought, *needles and pins. When a man marries, his trouble begins.* A skipping rhyme from a playground at home, another circle of girls not letting me in. They all knew the words, wore blue dresses, their hair in neat braids. *Buttons and lace, buttons and lace, who'll marry you with that look on your face?* They lived in big houses, had brothers and horses and their skipping ropes were white. *Thimbles and thread, thimbles and thread, the skinny old spinster is better off dead. Tallow and wax, tallow and wax, the wandering gander is good for the axe.* They laughed hard at their songs and went home to their mothers, their fathers homing later when the field work was done. Their mothers sat sewing by the fire, pink flowers on blue cloth, and the needles were all bought at the store where Ma worked. *Needles and pins. Needles and pins.*

Ma would smile to see how I liked making things now. I could see the work before I began – the shape of a bag, a seam, a jacket – and see the making, too. How I'd need to turn my fingers, make the crease hold, pin and stitch and tie. I liked watching my hands working, making things happen. Trustworthy work that would last well. Steady though all the world may change. I liked work I could hold on to. An old way of working and knowing and truth.

Museum-case gazing, my own face reflected and I wished Ma could be here, too, looking with me. She'd have liked the neatness of this display and the thought of all these bone needles. She'd have asked me what animals I thought they were from and we would wonder together about that. Deer, maybe. Wolf. Buffalo. Not a bird because bird bones were hollow and brittle, and you could break them too easily. That was something she taught me, and I thought about it whenever I was flying, about how the birds around me were different inside and out and how where I have strength, they have emptiness, but that's what helps them fly. Maybe Ma would like the balloons, too. Not the performing, though sometimes that was necessary, but the work together and the feeling of flight. I might be getting more like her the older I get, older and more capable, and more adventurous, too. These days, I often thought about her and what she'd think about what I was seeing and doing. I wondered if she'd done that with her own Ma and why she never talked to me about her, but then maybe you get to the stage when you don't need to say these things out loud. You just keep them inside, their emptiness and strength.

* * *

When I got back to the shed, the cart was already there for the equipment and the first of the hired men. They stood bunched up, watching Auguste as he leisurely coiled a length, all their arms folded, their shirts pale. When he finished, he introduced me, saying I'd be the one they'd need to watch on the field. I'd be in charge of orchestrating the launch and they'd need to ensure they'd be able to see me. One of them said something about me being a little short for the job and the others laughed.

'Don't worry at all. She will be standing tall on a strong box and everyone will be able to see her as clearly befits.'

I didn't like the way he said that, the implication in his voice, but what could I say without raising more laughter? He continued, explaining that the rest of the hired men would be waiting at the bicycle track and he'd already been out there to see them and check the gas supply and the weather.

'It looks promising, I think. Still hot, but not unpleasant at all, and a warm evening will encourage the crowds. And what is more, it shouldn't affect the balloon too much. The best thing is there isn't much wind.'

Wind was dangerous and blew balloons off course. Then you might land anywhere. And rain cancelled the whole show.

Ena caught my eye and beckoned to me. She and Marina were sitting on a crate, eating biscuits, and the two of them looked rested and happy, their faces flushed, their clothes changed since lunchtime.

'Did you have a nice afternoon, Laura?' she asked.

'Yes,' I said. 'All sorts of interesting things to look at.'

'I'll look forward to it tomorrow. Auguste and I can go together and see the machines in action. Might find some ideas for our new liberator.'

All spring, the new liberator had been their pet project, the two of them working together to develop a new method of detaching the parachute from the balloon in flight. It needed a system that supported a light cord attached tightly enough to both balloon and parachute to hold up in a wind, but loosely enough to pull away easily when it was time to descend. The current method worked, but was inelegant, according to Auguste. He'd prefer something that worked with a single gesture rather than the swivel and tug required now.

'There's plenty to see. I'm sure you'll find inspiration.'

Marina finished her biscuit and Ena wiped the crumbs away. 'Plenty to see everywhere here, I think. As Mrs Warsow's good man told us, the whole world's come to Cardiff. Are you going to be all right overseeing things? It will be a big crowd and that might be distracting.'

I told her I'd be fine. The size of the crowd wouldn't make me twitch. I'd ignore the noise and focus on Auguste and the balloon, and everything would be fine.

'You know I'll be right there if you need me. I can always hand you Marina and take over if you're uncertain at the last minute.'

We walked behind the cart to the bicycle track, the crowd curious and stopping to watch us pass. When we arrived, I saw that the area in the middle of the track had been roped off and a banner flew between two tall poles. *Monsieur Auguste Gaudron and his Fabulous Balloon.*

'Pity the company name isn't on display,' Ena said. She lifted Marina to her hip and stood gazing across the open space. 'I hope there is an illustrator for the papers. Or a photographer. Imagine that.'

Auguste turned to the men and started getting them organized to unpack the cart and then spread the balloon out on the grass to inflate. He introduced me again, this time to everyone and told them he trusted they were all dependable men.

'You will all keep your eyes on this lady when the balloon is inflated. As I explained before, I will not be giving instructions then as I will be busy preparing myself for the flight and she will be in control of the launch. If you find this complicated, you will step away from this job now. Anyone she deems unreliable in the instant will receive no payment.'

'And just when you going to pay us? 'Fore or after you crash land and can't count straight?'

'You will be paid tomorrow morning and I assure you I will

be well and able to pay you all. But, if I am wrong and unexpected disaster strikes, my lady wife will see to all the arrangements and will pay you what is owed. You will be able to contact her through the Exhibition officials, should the need arise. But it will not. My flights are always successful, just as my hired men are always dependable.'

I climbed up onto the empty balloon crate, and no one tried a whistle, which seemed a good start. Ena stood back with Marina in her arms and smiled at me so I smiled, too, then focused on the balloon. It was important there was someone watching because it was hard to see what was happening when you got up close and the balloon started to inflate. I liked that work – the rope-work, the adjusting of cloth and the togetherness of it all, but I liked the watching, too. Standing higher and seeing what they couldn't. Watching and keeping things safe.

The inflation always took time, but the gas supply that evening was good, and I could see Auguste was happy with how smoothly it went. The balloon swelled and began to lift, and the men watched me and did as I signalled. Then, the gas-filled balloon pulled up and the restraining ropes held tight while Auguste took his place on the webbing seat. I watched as he gripped the balloon's wooden hoop and clipped the parachute's trapeze to the safety lanyard. But no harness for him, I noticed, and Ena wouldn't like that. She wanted him clipped to the parachute and nagged him when he skipped that step, though he was quick to assure her that a man could take his own weight and didn't need safety clips. I glanced over to her, but Marina had her attention, clapping her hands and squealing at a magpie that had landed on grass.

I liked the clips myself and couldn't imagine wanting to fly without them. Sitting on a loop of webbing, dangling under the flying balloon and then leaping off, trusting the parachute would open and catch your weight, and all that supported by nothing more than your own tight grip? No thank you. How could anyone hold on tight enough for that to be a good idea? Bravado, Ena called it. Madness.

The hired men were all watching me now. When I saw Auguste was ready, I gave the sign and they loosened the ropes, then released them and the balloon began to lift. Up, and so slowly at first some spectators ducked their heads as he drifted over, but up he rose and still up and then he was away. The crowd watched, swaying, cheering, pulled by the balloon as they always are, every crowd, every time. Now the balloon rose swiftly, and Auguste looked small, a dark shape swinging beneath the lifting balloon.

The parachute hung from the side of the balloon, like a flag waiting for the wind. Even from here, you could see the ropes it held, and the light cord that would pull away neatly from the balloon when he jumped. Swivel and tug. He'd need to find the right place to do it, but he was good at that. We'd looked at city maps together and decided the East Moors would be best, out away from the city's roofs and spires. A hundred-foot free-fall, then the parachute would open, and he'd drift down.

The crowd thinned, and I climbed down from the crate. Ena stood close by, still hoisting Marina on her hip, who looked tired and ready for bed. I wanted to ask Ena about clearing the ropes away and what she wanted to happen next, but she was speaking with a man who carried his own small child on his shoulders, gripping her legs tightly. That child was older than Marina, a girl of maybe four or five, who clutched her father's flat cap and tried to get his attention.

'Dada!' she cried out. 'Is that man going straight home to heaven?'

Ena laughed and said she truly hoped it would prove otherwise.

The child had this amazed look on her face, and kept her eyes fixed on the vanishing balloon. She let go of her father's hat and threw her arms up, waving, and it looked as though if he loosened his grip at all, with all that flapping, she'd take to the skies herself.

3/

THE NEXT MORNING, AUGUSTE WAS DELIGHTED TO FIND an article in the newspaper with the headline *THE PARACHUTIST'S DESCENT.* Ena had been less pleased that it began by placing Auguste alongside other acts such as Monsieur Diamond, the champion knife-thrower of the world, Senor Don Pablo, the leaping marvel, and Professor Garford's troupe of acrobatic dogs.

'It's honest,' Auguste said. 'These are all new sideshow acts for the week. But listen, it continues on to say so much more:

'Of course, the aerial ventures of Mons. A. E. Gaudron are the chief and most exciting of all, and on Monday evening these drew thousands of spectators.

'Excellent, isn't this? Precisely the sort of publicity we would aim for, my dear one. And more again:

'Ascending in a balloon from the ground inside the bicycle track, he was loudly cheered by the crowd, and borne slowly south-eastwards towards the sea. After sailing on for a mile or so, at an altitude of 9,000 feet, he found he was getting near the sea, and, as he had not donned his lifebelt, he released the parachute and attempted to land on one of two fields in Splott Ward.

'Perhaps, the reporter needn't have added that, but I did give him the details when he asked me.'

'Perhaps you should be more circumspect,' Ena said.

Auguste kept his finger on the page and read on.

'*He somewhat missed the mark* . . . Well, yes, I did . . . *and dropped on an outhouse at the rear of Janet Street* . . . unpleasant detail, but true . . . *Happily, he was not injured* . . . hooray! . . . *and was able to return to the Exhibition Grounds to give an assurance of his safety. The balloon fell soon afterwards in a street adjoining, but, unfortunately, it alighted on a glass-topped wall and was slightly damaged. M. Gaudron will repeat the performance on the evenings of Wednesday and Saturday next.*

'Well, is that not fair? Perhaps a too-detailed description of the event, but fair. My hat off to the Welsh reporter.'

The newspaper man was right that the balloon was damaged, though he wouldn't have said 'slightly' if he'd seen it. Auguste and Ena came to the shed later that morning to help me assess the damage, and together we sorted out which seams could be strengthened, which gores needed replacing. It looked like a whole day's worth of work on the sewing machine, and that meant me working alone. Auguste said he would arrange for someone to lock the shed after I'd finished and I could meet them at the house in time for tea.

'And you'll be all right with lunch?' Ena asked. She offered to have something sent over, but I told her how Mrs Warsow had packed my pockets with sandwiches.

'Funny,' she said. 'She didn't do that for us. Must have thought you looked more in need of feeding. Well, isn't it nice we have a motherly landlady like that? We'll find plenty of options at the Exhibition, I shouldn't wonder,' she said, turning to Auguste, and he smiled at her, but looked distracted. Maybe he hadn't slept well. A new bed can throw you off.

They wheeled Marina's pram out through the shed's open door, suddenly silhouettes against the day and I remembered their Paris nights, only there was no rope this time, no fear, just two dark shapes moving together against the light, and then he stepped back to let her go first through the doorway, so there was only one.

I didn't mind working on my own. You know where you're going with a seam to sew. There's a clear beginning, the stretch of work before you, and then you know when you come to an end. You could let your mind drift, the work in your hands ballast enough to keep you steady. Time falls away. Slivers, wedges, and it was a night in Paris, a cold afternoon, a morning under the western sun and Ma hanging out the washing, pegging each shirt on the line. The sun was bright in the sky, and I had a green neckerchief I held up against it, the penny of the sun shining through and I thought it would be just like that to lie down under the grass, buried with the grass growing over you, every muscle relaxed to sleep but my eyes open still looking up through the green at the sun.

The Exhibition clock struck the hour, and I was stitching past the grommets now, every metal circle an eye, the blind sun, a clock. Why do we keep time in circles? Watch faces, standing stones, medicine wheels on the open prairie. Seasons and years and wedding rings. I turned the machine's crank around and the seam continued.

At the end of the seams, there was still time to fill because I couldn't leave the shed with the door unlocked. I ate my sandwiches and drank a jar of water, then walked back and forth the length of the shed, rolling my shoulders to stretch out the stiffness of a morning of table work. I decided to open the crate where the parachute harnesses were kept. Auguste didn't like the bulk of them. The rigidity. The way they stuck out awkwardly when worn with a lifebelt. And if you wore them underneath, they were awkward to unclip if you landed in water, but you needed to or you'd be dragged under when the parachute saturated through. I wondered if there was a different way to make the clips accessible. Maybe if the hooks were stitched to a jacket's shoulders with slits to pass the webbing through. That would be more discreet, which Auguste would like, and it might feel lighter and easier, too.

At half past two, Auguste came back to the shed himself, so I got the chance to explain my idea to him right away. He seemed to like it and nodded to himself as he made a quick sketch in his notebook.

'You might have something here,' he said, smiling. 'Thank you.'

Then he pulled out his pocket watch just as the Exhibition clock chimed and checked the time.

'It looks like you have had a good day's work.' But he didn't even glance at the balloon where it lay spread out on the ground, the repair on top, clearly sound, only thanked me again warmly and patted my arm, so I asked where Ena was, and he said she'd most likely gone back to the house with Marina.

'The little one seems to need a quiet time in the afternoon.'

'That sounds sensible,' I said, which made him laugh and he told me I sounded like Ena.

At the house, Marina was not quiet. She sat in the hallway, banging on the floor with a wooden spoon. Ena was sitting on the stairs when we came through the door and looked irritated.

'There you are,' she said. 'I thought you would have been back earlier. There's no time to go back to the Exhibition this afternoon now.'

'We can go in the evening,' Auguste said, smiling. 'See? I have tickets for the concert hall. Music. Won't that be wonderful?'

She stood up and looked at him without comment, then turned and walked through to the kitchen.

'I imagine she's checking about our tea. It is coming up on that time. Un petit goûter, n'est ce pas? Perhaps a nice Welsh cake or two?'

Marina liked the mention of a snack. She stood up, holding out her hand to her papa, and pulling him towards the kitchen, too.

'No, little one. We will sit in the parlour. Your mother will see to it that Mrs Warsow will bring things through when they are ready. I'm sure of that.'

Over tea, Mrs Warsow warned us the next day would be full of excursionists come for the Great Temperance Fete. Societies throughout Wales had been handing out special cut-rate tickets to the Exhibition for the day's festivities, hoping to bring in the young.

'Young people love a day out. And there will be races. Competitions and all that and the preaching will be good for them. Some wonderful preachers are friends of the Temperance Society. Plenty of clergy in the streets tomorrow, of that I am certain.' Auguste raised an eyebrow and Mrs Warsow might have caught it, too, because she quickly went on to say she was certain the crowds would still be gathered by the evening when it came time for his next balloon flight. 'Young people stay in town when they can, when there's something interesting happening.'

'Like Laura, staying away all afternoon,' Ena said. 'As soon as she can, she's away to find something more interesting to do than spend time around here helping. Despite the fact she'd been hired to. And I need to cope with Marina on my own.'

What could I say? Nothing, and Mrs Warsow clucked her tongue. Ena's face was fierce, but she wouldn't look at me and I didn't know what she was talking about. All day working in that shed and my neck stiff with it and now this attack like I'd been skiving.

No point in doing anything but shut up right then, but Auguste stepped in and started talking over the awkward pause.

He said he'd want to visit the Exhibition buildings again the next day by himself. If the streets were going to be crowded with processions and young people, wasn't it likely there'd be few people actually at the Exhibition in the morning looking at the machines? At least not early in the day. It might be a good chance to speak to the men.

'But you,' Auguste said to Ena, 'you and Laura should take Marina out. No point in making her sit through scientific conversation when there's excitement to be had. The three of you might have a jolly day.'

Ena didn't answer. Mrs Warsow poured out the strong, dark tea and served us slices of bara brith, the raisins soft as melting butter. Ena broke hers into small pieces and fed them all to the child. Later, when Auguste went out to buy tobacco for his pipe, Mrs Warsow told Ena how concerned she was about the baby and the crowds tomorrow and offered to keep her home.

'She'll be fine with me in the kitchen. I'll be baking and she seems to like having a spoon of her own to play with. Far too young for the Fete, and the excitement won't be good for her. She won't see anything anyway, not in a pram, and it wouldn't be safe to hold her.'

Ena agreed, thanking Mrs Warsow for her kindness. 'It is so good to have local advice about this sort of thing,' she said, with a wide, intentional smile. 'Coming in like this for a quick engagement, we don't really know the lay of the land.'

'It's always like that with flying visits,' Mrs Warsow said, then laughed at her own accidental joke. 'You being balloon people, I mean. Flying, you see.' And she coughed and went back through to the kitchen.

It was hard to sleep that night. The moon wore a storm ring and the air felt hot and damp. Swampy, but Mrs Warsow said humid when she brought me a glass of cold water, and that was a good word because it sounded unpleasant. Like a hot bowl turned over on top of us all, heavy and keeping us down. I wished it would rain. That would change things. The air would be clearer afterwards. Open.

4I

In the morning, Auguste didn't eat with us, so he must have had his breakfast somewhere else. Maybe at one of the Exhibition tearooms. Ena said in Paris they regularly found coffee and something to eat while on their morning walk. It was something he liked to do.

'He won't go hungry,' she said, looking into her coffee cup at the table. 'And we'll find him later in the morning. He said he'd keep an eye open for us. Can you remember if I spooned sugar in here already? I'm not sure.'

'Be hard to find anyone in the crowds today, I expect,' Mrs Warsow said, bringing through a refilled toast rack. 'There, that's just what you need. A lush bit of breakfast to set you up for the day.'

'Well, he'll do his best to find us. Of course he will.' She dipped a finger in her coffee and slipped it in her mouth, then reached for the sugar tongs and dropped a cube in her cup. 'And it doesn't matter because we'll always know when to meet him at the shed if we don't meet him before. In the meantime, we'll have a bit of an exploration ourselves, won't we? A treat, just the two of us,' she said and smiled at me. She was still trying, I could see that, but she seemed softer than the day before. Maybe the weather was wearing on her. The room felt stuffy, and Marina in her highchair looked overdressed, her face flushed. I'd dressed her as Ena instructed in pale blue pantalettes and a petticoat that morning, and it had been a struggle to get her dress on top, her hot soft arms refusing to go through the armholes, and none of the ties reaching right as she twisted about. If it hadn't been for Ena's instructions, I wouldn't have bothered, which would have been better in this heat, but Ena said she didn't want to leave the child half-dressed. Marina sat up at the table now, eating bread and jam, and looking very happy with herself. Mrs Warsow touched her fingers to the girl's rosy neck as she passed behind her chair and called her pet names.

'She likes her plain food, doesn't she now?' she said, and Ena agreed, the two of them talking on about what Marina should eat while we were away and when she should nap and what she might like to do. 'There's plenty to keep her busy in the kitchen with me, spoons and the like, but don't you worry, I'll have her away from there for the heat of the day. Perhaps a walk if it gets too warm, just up and down the road and nowhere near town. It will be quiet enough here, I wager.'

We put on our hats, said our goodbyes and stepped outside, and we weren't halfway down the street when Ena put her hand on my arm and apologized.

'What for?'

'For yesterday. I was in a mood. Auguste had . . . been difficult after we left you with the balloon. You might have guessed we argued, and he stomped off. So, I was left pushing the pram through the crowds, fairly miserable. I should be used to his Gallic tempers by now, only that one caught me. I shouldn't have taken it out on you.' Her hand was hot on the sleeve of my dress, and she held it there as we walked, so I reached out and put mine on hers and we walked like that together.

'He's been away all summer,' she said. 'We need to get used to being together again, that's all.'

A turnabout to be sure, but I was glad she talked to me like this. I was quiet, but glad, and the sun was overhead, clouds at the end of the street, the air like canvas, and people all walking in the same direction. Halfway to the Exhibition grounds, we were stopped trying to cross a street, a stout woman in a broad hat and a bright sash looked Ena in the eye and told her the Procession was due to come past now in a minute and we'd have to wait and watch from there.

The woman turned, her dress sweeping behind her, and the letters on her Society sash bold and carefully spaced, *Temperance* across her breasts. A gong word ringing out, so close to temper. I knew about temper. Mac Goulding and his temper and Ma's black eye and us leaving that town, just another good-for-nuthin' town. That's what she called it when she said he had no right, and she said it like a cuss word, not a Sunday school word like Temperance. Charity. Forgiveness.

And here came the girls in white, marching, six in a line right across the road, carrying a banner. *The Innocent Suffer with the Guilty.* Drums and flags and girls marching and behind them children carrying another banner. Then carts and wagons stacked with more children, all clean, all waving, wearing white and carrying flowers and Sunday school teachers and clergymen marched alongside carrying placards: *Dry is Best. Drink and Poverty Go Hand in Hand.* More girls marched with arms linked under a large flag that read *The Lips That Touch Liquor Shall Never Touch Mine* and a roar rose from the crowded street.

I turned to ask Ena what she thought of the spectacle and she laughed, saying it did offer balance and maybe it was right to give the next generation good role models. A cheerful man beside us said the children had worked hard decorating the wagons and there'd be prizes offered for the best emblematic design illustrating temperance truth.

'Well, that's a mouthful,' Ena said, and the man looked at her and wagged his finger, his eyes shining, and told her not today, which made her laugh.

Band music deafened us as the Procession marched past, and I felt the whole street swaying, as if we'd all topple over if someone started to push. I wanted to sit down but there was no room, no solid place, nowhere to be steady. I remembered a rock on the high prairies where I sat, watching the wagons pass when everyone else was moving, and it was only me staying still, left behind, dizzy with watching alone.

'I don't know why Auguste doesn't like this sort of thing,' Ena said, leaning in to speak in my ear. 'With all his interest in performance, you'd think he'd breathe in a procession like this. I mean, the music is a bit blustery, but it's powerful. Alma would love it, wouldn't she? That drum beat and those drummers. She'd get the whole crowd's attention.'

The man beside Ena tapped on her arm. 'You have a fine day to see the city,' he said, as if we'd travelled in from the valleys together for a day's bit of fun. She nodded and smiled, then winked at me as another band came down the street like a river, the music pushing in at me.

After the bands and the carts and all the cheering children passed, the crowds joined the Procession and followed down the street and into the Grounds, buying tickets and showing passes at the gates. The children were sorted by the marshals – Sunday school teachers all, Ena said – and there were refreshments for them, provided by the concessionaires and an afternoon full of races and amateur athletics. Ena bought a bottle of lemonade and we found a bench on the Avenue.

'They've certainly made this town something special for today,' she said. 'And endless soft drinks for everyone. Here, you take the glasses and I'll sort out how to open this thing.' She held the bottle in both hands and looked at the marble at the top, held in place by a rubber seal. 'I'm sure Auguste could manage it. Can't think I've opened one of these before.'

'You need to push the marble down hard. Just give it a push with your thumb. It keeps the bubbles in. And the lemonade, too.'

She put the bottle on the bench beside her, set her thumb against the marble and gave it a good push. 'Ah, isn't that clever? Did you have these in America, then?'

I told her we sold them at the shop. I tried to keep *shop* singular as if there'd only ever been one because the real story felt complicated and made Ma sound unsettled. Or that's what I told myself. Best to keep the story streamlined.

I held out the glasses and Ena filled them with lemonade. 'Now, doesn't that look lovely? Perfect thing for a hot day.'

The band started playing again from somewhere over near the lake and Ena leaned back, tilting her face to catch the sunshine.

'I think Auguste simply doesn't like following a band,' she said. 'Someone else setting the beat. And then for him to feel pulled in and compelled to be part of it? I think that's the trouble for him and bands. How's your lemonade?'

'Perfect,' I said. A cold sip, my lips on the glass and I held it there for a moment to keep feeling that cold.

'So, you had this at home? In America, I mean. I suppose you would with all those California lemons. Must be beautiful out there. As sunny as this only all year round.'

'Not where I was from. We got thunderstorms. But we got lemonade, too.'

I missed thunderstorms. The wind before they come. The colour of the sky and the space it takes up. Then, the crack. The world split in two. Sky-torn. Scar-marked. Crack. That sound. It gets inside you. The whole raining world does, and the rolling waves of thunder and it isn't anger and it isn't grief. Only power. Raw and better than horses. Louder and better than anything. And after? That calm. That smell. Wet earth and grass and the left-out sheets on the line hanging heavy and straight, white windows to a world you can't yet see.

Ena sat up straight again with her glass in her hand.

'I remember lemonade – at dances when I was young,' she said, slowly. 'I remember the fizz. The surprise of that. As delightful as dancing. And then Percy said wait until you get to India where lemons grow wild and you could buy lemonade on every corner. He told me they put salt in it, too, and something spicy, which I didn't think sounded nice, but he said made it more refreshing in tropical temperatures. Only I never got to India, at least not yet. He took me to Russia, though. I liked Russia.'

She told me how Percy had met the Tsarevich in Madras, and he'd been so impressed with Percy's balloon that he invited him to the Alexander Palace.

'Of course, our papa insisted on an entourage. It was one thing for Percy to trek off to India on his own, but Russia would offer opportunities to young ladies, or so he said. I expect he would have been quite happy if we'd all married Russians. Maybe we would, too. No, I shouldn't have said that. Only Russia was so very romantic and grand. A complete delight. Nikolai Alexandrovich was a dear, too. He's the Tsar now, though he wasn't yet when we were there. He's the same age as Stanley, I believe and a very handsome man. This was before I was married, and goodness, splendour like you've never seen, never dreamed of. But he didn't want a circus act; that wasn't what interested him. It was the science of balloons. A man after my heart. Science and the applications, too, Percy said, which he thought might mean military contracts, geographical exploration, meteorological inquiry, economic development, who knew? The vision afforded by balloon might unfold all manner of possibility. You can see why I found him so interesting. Why did I start talking about this?'

I took a sip. 'Lemonade.'

'Yes! Of course. Only I don't remember lemonade in Russia. We drank something red there made with berries. A little tart, like lemonade, I remember. Does Russia have any colonies with lemons? I can't remember.'

Ena wiped out our empty glasses with a handkerchief and returned them to the lemonade stall. It was too hot to eat anything, too hot to be inside, so we stayed in the field to watch the races in the bicycling ring.

They were silly races, not real athletics at all, and it felt like a Sunday school picnic, especially with all the marshals standing around and making sure the children sat in straight lines. Ena got right into the spirit of the day, whooping and hollering to beat the band. At one point, they asked for volunteers to join in a twenty-yard stone-picking race and she took off her hat and waved it madly, hoping to be selected, but the marshal chose all young men and she sat down again, disappointed.

'I only hope they don't ruin the ground with all their efforts compliqués.'

'Auguste, there you are! We thought you must have been eaten by a printing machine or turned into a modern biscuit or the like.'

He laughed indulgently. 'You worry too much, my dear. I am perfectly well and have had a charming day of restful conversation with men of technology.'

'You shouldn't have given us the slip this morning. I would have liked to join in those conversations, too.'

'Yes, well, perhaps . . .' but he didn't complete his thought and instead, suggested that we might like to join him in the Indian Bazaar for cucumber sandwiches and tea.

'A light and elegant repas before your next victorious flight? Yes, I think we can accept that invitation.'

'It would be very pleasant to drink crisp white wine, too, but I am afraid we will find nothing of the kind today. Have you seen the water fountains they have installed throughout the grounds? Very clever, these teetotallers. And they seem to have attracted so many people today. Who would have believed such an endeavour would be so popular with the Welsh?'

'It looks like a promising crowd,' Ena said. 'I do hope they all stay for the evening. And that the newspaper men write it up nicely for tomorrow's paper. That would be a great one for the clippings book.'

'I'm sure they will be here in number,' Auguste said, with confidence. 'The newspaper men like a spectacle and what could be better than a balloon?'

'A balloon and a dashing Frenchman, to be sure. And a safe landing, too.'

Auguste laughed, and there we were, sitting down to lunch, together again.

51

Over the promised sandwiches, Ena started worrying. 'We haven't even been to look at the balloon today. And a flight tonight. Of course, I trust Laura's work, but how can we catch each other's mistakes if we don't even check? We really should have tested it this morning rather than coming down here for a jolly.'

'We need time to enjoy ourselves. Did you enjoy yourself this morning, Laura?'

'Yes, I did.'

'Ah, good. Isn't that good, Ena? I enjoyed myself as well. So important. But you shouldn't worry about the balloon, my love. We will test it tomorrow together. Tonight, I am planning to use the replacement one, the older one I like best, and it is already inspected and ready to fly. There was no problem at all. All will be well.'

Ena looked at him and he held her gaze until she finally smiled.

'Yes?' she asked. 'What is it?'

He reached for the last sandwich on the plate and when he had finished it, asked if either of us would like ice cream. 'It seems an ice cream sort of day, doesn't it? Shall we walk and see if we can find some?'

It was a hot afternoon. Not a cloud in the sky, and the light was blistering. We walked towards the Avenue where Auguste said we'd find another refreshments stall and could enjoy the shade. A hot wind blew dusty and dry which made me think of home, but Auguste sighed and wiped his neck with his handkerchief.

'Not a pleasant wind,' he said. 'This morning a journalist tried to worry me about it. He suggested it would most likely direct my balloon to the Channel this evening. I asked if perhaps he thought that would make a good story, but no, he merely wished to warn me. I told him I wouldn't fear a dunking.'

'You didn't mention to me that you'd spoken with the journalists today. You did speak about the science, didn't you? Our emphasis on innovation?'

'Of course, I did. You need to relax, my dear.'

'Of course. Of course, you would.' She adjusted her hat, then turned back to her husband with another question. 'Did he seek you out or was it a lucky coincidence? He must have found you with the inventors in the Exhibition Hall. We couldn't have planned that better.'

'Well, to be honest, it was more of a coincidence, actually. And I hadn't quite made it to the inventors yet.'

Something in his voice prompted her to ask where he'd been.

'Do not worry so, my dear. I was with one of the professors. Professor Garford. His work is with animals.'

'Garford. The dog trainer.'

'Yes, most fascinating work it is. Such intelligence. He only uses kindness, he says. Never a whip. Kindness and liver.'

Ena slowed her pace, her eyes now fixed on the ground, as Auguste continued, telling her about a French Poodle named Peter who could stand upright on his hind legs upon a trapeze and swing to and fro to see-saw music.

'Exceptionally clever,' he said. 'You would have been delighted to see it.'

'So, it wasn't just talk? You had a demonstration, too? And you think I will be pleased to hear this?' She stopped walking and her voice had yesterday's edge. She looked straight at her husband and let her questions hang in the air. He seemed to have nothing more to say.

'Dogs?' she pressed. 'And trapezes! Professor Garford my eye! And Professor Gaudron. Well then, you two had something in common. High-flying fools. And more fool me, too, trusting you to be the public face of our enterprise, the scientific authority; I never should have left Harry at home.'

Auguste swung his cane like a long metronome, then caught the end and examined the dusty ferrule.

'It was a very good demonstration,' he said, quietly.

'Bah!'

I didn't know where to look with all this going on. I wasn't part of it, but they didn't seem to want any privacy. Or maybe they didn't think of it. Ena started walking again towards that promised ice cream as if that still mattered, and what could I do but follow? I resolved not to answer if Auguste spoke to me. That was probably wise. I didn't want to get between them. So, what would I do? Pretend I didn't hear? Or start coughing or something, anything to distract. Maybe I could faint. It was a hot day and that could be a useful excuse. I wondered if I could make it look convincing. I'd have to fall completely and not stumble or try to catch myself. Be tricky to pull it off, actually. I hoped I didn't have to.

Ena swung her head towards me and held out her arm, so I fell into step beside her.

'I have made a decision,' she said, loud enough for Auguste, who followed, to hear. 'If you and I, Laura, are to be real women of science – real innovators, real New Women – we must take a pledge. Not this Temperance nonsense, that's not what I mean. Everyone needs a good glass of wine from time to time. No, our pledge is for a different kind of purity. We will refuse to perform. We will never fly as entertainers again. No flaunting, no flirting, no aerialisting. We will only be scientists. What do you say?'

Of course, I said yes. I couldn't say no. And I didn't want to.

Auguste said nothing but strode off to the refreshments stall and bought, not the promised ice cream after all, but extravagant cups of punch for each of us. Bright green with cucumber, sweet, pink, iced strawberry, and lemon sharp as a blade.

That evening's flight was to be prefaced with a lecture about the possible application of high-altitude aeronautics to the pioneering field of meteorology. Ena organized everything. The launch was scheduled for 7:30 p.m., a full hour and a half after the field races were to end, so we had plenty of time for Auguste to answer questions after his lecture and for Ena to oversee the launch proceedings. My job was backup, circling the balloon during inflation and keeping an eye on the groundcrew and equipment.

'This will be a straightforward flight, I should think,' Auguste said, in a reassuring voice. 'Now that I know the lay of the land.'

'The wind is still constant,' Ena replied.

'Nothing to worry about at all. The newspapers call it *fair generally*. I will be fine.'

'And you will wear your life jacket tonight?'

'Perhaps. But it would be very warm, I think. The temperature, like the wind, isn't dropping. I might prefer to trust my strong swimming arm if it comes to that.'

'You are impossible. You know that.'

'It is part of my charm, no?'

Auguste promised fish and chips for dinner as a treat after the flight and I looked forward to that all afternoon. Ena had us working together in the shed again, with me sorting and reviewing extra equipment while she went over the speech with Auguste. She had him rehearse his gestures as well as the material and made him repeat everything until she deemed it suitable. When I finished with the last crate and could find no other work, I cleaned and oiled my sewing machine to keep busy.

We were a little later to the field than Ena had hoped, and she was flustered about that.

'I'm trying to run a tight ship, you know.'

Auguste moved slowly, perhaps trying to keep a calm head before his speech, but Ena hurried things along, organizing the groundcrew to clear the field. There were markers and ribbons left over from the day's races, and water cups and newspapers. She emptied the rope crate to use as a rubbish bin and we soon cleared the field to get the balloon ready.

Ena wished things were going more smoothly. She worried about the children lingering on the field and how Auguste was pacing rather than helping.

'He's nervous,' she told me. 'It's his English. When he gets nervous, he forgets words. And the thought of that makes him nervous. I wish I could convince him he'll be fine.'

She sent one of the groundcrew for a bottle of water and a glass, but he didn't want a drink. He kept marching back and forth across the grass.

I wasn't surprised when he cancelled his speech. Ena, on the other hand, was furious.

'He says his voice isn't strong enough out in the open like this. That the wind is carrying it away. I can't believe this. After everything.'

It was hardly the time to try an argument. She told him it wasn't a waste; there would be another opportunity to give the speech. Perhaps even tomorrow. They could arrange something with the Exhibition. A special additional education event.

'The crowd will love that. And it will boost numbers for your final flight.'

I went to check how the inflation was progressing. The ground-crew said they should really speak with M. Gaudron about it, so I told them I could be trusted to carry a message. It wasn't going as quickly as they'd like. It seemed as though it was taking too long.

'I'll tell the Gaudrons.'

'Tell him it feels like it's pulling away sideways. And it's more than the wind.'

Ena was on her own with the parachute harness when I returned, and, though she listened, I wasn't sure she'd understood what I was saying. I asked where Auguste was, and she shrugged.

'I hope he's almost ready. It's coming on quarter past. I'd really rather he was here with the balloon.'

'I'll tell him when I find him.'

He was standing with the Exhibition concessionaires behind the stage at the edge of the field. When he saw me approaching, he smiled widely.

'Laura! Our American angel! I was just telling these gentlemen about the extent of the shining new branch of our business. Laura is one of our lady pilots, you understand.'

They all smiled at me.

'But I think,' Auguste continued, 'that I am needed by the balloon. Isn't that right, Laura? I am just on my way this instant. You shall see me soon, gentlemen. Simply look and aha! There I will be.'

They laughed as we walked away, and I tried to explain about the message from the groundcrew, but Auguste was humming under his breath, interrupting me to agree, and seemed not to listen at all. When we drew near, there was a shout from the gathered crowd and Auguste took off his hat to wave it in the air. The shout grew louder. He turned and doubled back, showing off, tap dancing on the grass.

The balloon was ready now, pulling at its tether ropes, and Ena had the hoop and parachute waiting. I started to walk towards her, but she waved me off and it was obvious she'd rather I circled the balloon again to check all sides. Maybe she did hear me after all, I thought, and I let her and Auguste get on with the work of settling him in the sling for the launch.

But things weren't fine around the back of the balloon. It was obvious now something had gone wrong. The seams were squint, and the ropes strained off balance. Everything looked crooked and caught by the wind so it might have been a badly tied rope or even a leak. A hazard any way you looked at it and I couldn't let the flight happen. So, I ran.

Then the balloon started to lift as the crew started easing the tether ropes and I ran faster. As soon as Ena could see me, I pointed up with both hands, crossing my arms above my head to signal stop. She seemed to hesitate, numbed. I did it again, this time shouting. She couldn't greenlight the groundcrew. I couldn't let her. There was something dangerous happening. She had to stop.

Then finally, she moved. She understood. A hand to her neck and she found her whistle then four long blasts. Flight cancelled.

Auguste threw up his arms, his face furious, and he leapt back to the ground. The crew held firm, but without Auguste's weight, the balloon swung wildly, and two ropes tore loose. Men shouted and grabbed, and the balloon quivered, lingered a moment, then ripped completely free and up and away.

The crowd rushed forward, chasing the balloon and Auguste ran with them, but turned back when it was clear the balloon was going to fly over the walls of the Exhibition grounds. Ena organized one of the groundcrew to drive the cart, climbed in and sat beside him. Then Auguste joined her, shouting for the crowd to move out of the way. Ena waved to get my attention.

'Laura!' she shouted. 'This is all bound to take some time. Can you go check on Marina?'

I told her I would, and she promised to send word as soon as she could.

Marina was already in bed and sleeping when I got back to the house. Mrs and Mr Warsow had eaten their tea and Mrs Warsow was washing a pot in the kitchen when I came in. She told me there wasn't much to eat – the grocery boy would be coming in the morning – but if I liked she could pull something together.

'You'll have had a proper dinner at the Exhibition midday, I imagine, but it's nice to settle with something in the evening. And won't you be glad to have this unexpected evening all to yourself? Not often that happens, I imagine. Lucky girl tonight.'

I smiled and she told me to sit myself down at the table while she busied around me. Then it was brown bread and butter, cold, cooked vegetables, and weak tea.

'There,' she said. 'Nice and light for the end of a warm day. It was a scorcher, wasn't it?'

I ate my tea, trying not to think of fish and chips, and when I had finished, I told Mrs Warsow I was stepping out to the garden. A mess of sparrows flew up from the paving stones as

I came through the door and hid themselves in the heavy leaves of the tree. The light was fading, the evening warm and the wind still blowing. Cardiff had west winds blowing in from the Atlantic, all down the coastline and on towards Bristol and the West. London winds were mainly west-southwest, and that made a difference. Ma taught me to pay attention to the way the wind blows. On the prairie, you can always feel it, one way or another.

All being well, the balloon would have passed right over the house. Auguste had told me he'd looked down and seen it on Monday. He'd seen the tree in the yard, the length of the little street stretching between the canal and the train station. I remembered that and looked up. The sky was empty.

* * *

She was watching from the crowd. Paid the sixpence admission and took her place in the field with all the others. She didn't want to get too close, but wanted to be sure she'd see. That was how she'd get her nerve back. Stand with the audience and see what they see, feel their fire around her.

She'd spent the day going round the other shows: the grand aquatic battle, the Elizabethan theatre, and the concert gazebo. First-class entertainment with real professionals which was only right for a Royal Exhibition, really. It was a real chance to be here with all this splendour going on. Everything she'd ever wanted. And somehow she had to get ready to take her turn.

But a balloon show isn't like the others; it doesn't have a stage. Or you might say, the stage is the wide open sky, which leaves nothing to visit on the ground. For most of the afternoon, the field where the balloon would launch was filled up with races and games and one of the stewards had the audacity to ask if she wanted to participate. She slowly, theatrically, shook her head, then asked the steward if he knew of a good place to purchase a newspaper.

She found the notice on page 4: THIS EVENING at 7:30 p.m. Professor A. E. Gaudron, the World-Famed Aeronaut and Aerialist, will ascend in a balloon to a height of 8,000 feet and descend in a parachute.

So, there'd she'd been, standing in that pressing crowd, watching as Monsieur Auguste Gaudron checked the tether lines, the hoop and the valves. First time she'd seen him since Cornwall. She might have made herself known, but this was better, watching from the audience. She'd seen how the groundcrew worked together, with the tether ropes and the gas line, and how the overseer got them organized. With all the action, it was easy to get distracted, but she tried to focus and keep her eye on M. Gaudron. She'd seen his hesitation, then the moment he took his place and that second hesitation. She'd also seen the angle of the balloon at full inflation or almost and the awkwardness of its attitude. She saw it all, but she was still surprised when she heard the whistle, and he threw up his arm, then his quick leap down and the whole thing was over. What happened? What went wrong?

She knew she'd never have done that. Disappoint a crowd like that. Not in a hundred years. She'd have taken the risk.

6/

SHE WASN'T EVEN PRETTY. AFTERWARDS THEY SAID SHE was, but they said all sorts of lies then. She was interesting and that's what worked for her. When you saw her, you felt interested.

The girl had yellow hair, very fair and thin, and the first day I saw her, she wore it half pulled back around her face. Her chin was pointy, her skin pale and delicate, and her eyes very unusual, very wonderful. Wide-set and grey. When I knew her better, I saw they changed – sometimes blue, sometimes green. I hadn't seen eyes like that before, and she'd look at you and blink slowly and you'd watch, fascinated. Did she know the effect she was having? Did she understand?

The middle of the night and she knocked on the door of the Edward Street house. Only I didn't know it was her. When I heard the noise, I assumed it was about the balloon and maybe trouble. Auguste and Ena had only been home about an hour, coming in late, arguing in hushed tones. They'd woken me up, but I stayed in bed, glad to hear both their voices and know they were together. Marina was sleeping and I didn't want to wake her, so I figured if they needed me, they knew where I was. Whatever the problem, it could be explained to me in the morning. It wasn't like I was going to be sewing in the middle of the night.

After a while, their voices hushed, and then much later that knock on the front door, waking me up again. I heard voices downstairs, then walking back and forth. Doors opening, closing, chairs and more doors. Ena's voice asking questions. Maybe the balloon had been lost and now was found. That happened sometimes. Half asleep, I thought about all the times I'd been out with a cart late at night, looking for some lost balloon and the moon overhead and the stars shining on and I must have half-heard her then, too, a different, higher voice because I thought Alma was down there or I might have been dreaming when that thought came, dreaming about carts and balloons and Alma in the dark, Auguste flying overhead trailing a blazing paper banner and the faraway Cornish sea and London still so hot and dry.

In the morning, Mrs Warsow knocked softly on my door and brought warm water in.

'Can't say I expected this household to be raucous,' she said. 'Do the French always keep mad hours or is it just performers? And with a little one in the house, too. Must say I'm surprised.' She put the water on the dresser and straightened the towels.

'Is everything all right?' I asked.

Marina stretched in bed, kicking her feet under the covers.

'Oh, probably, though I'm hardly sure,' Mrs Warsow answered. 'I just didn't expect to be woken to hammering on the door after midnight. Not a respectable time for house guests, if you ask me. But perhaps it's the foreign influence. They do things differently, don't they? Your mistress and her coffee for breakfast.'

She straightened the rug on the floor and looked over at Marina in her little bed. Marina grinned and waved, and Mrs Warsow smiled, softening.

'I expect coffee is popular in London. Even heard about it from the pulpit recently, a Temperance preacher, you know. It wasn't in my house when I was small, but days change. Now, seeing as you're awake, I'll be getting the things on the table. You get ready for the morning and come down as you like with the little one. I have some berries set aside for her. And cream, if her mother agrees.'

The breakfast table was set but there was no sign of the Gaudrons. I put Marina down and she stood on the carpet, looking around.

'Would you like your bread and milk now?' I asked.

She shook her head and scuttled under the table to play. Well, that was fine. The coffee pot was already on the table, ready for me to help myself, which made me feel grown up and awkward. I sat down, smoothed my dress and looked out the window. The street was empty, and the day clear, promising more heat. A day to find a shady place to sit under a tree, away from everything. Of course, that's not what I'd be doing because if there'd been balloon trouble, that meant I'd be back in the shed, but it was nice to think about anyway. About green spaces and a good fresh breeze.

A rustle under the table and the child's weight on my feet. She leaned against me but didn't make a sound.

'You'll need to come out when your mother comes through,' I said. 'You'll eat your breakfast then.'

I put a slice of bread in her shallow bowl and left the milk in its jug for the moment. Then the door opened, and I heard Ena's voice.

'Just through here, dear. Best get some food in, I think. That will settle you a bit.'

A girl came through the door. Slight, younger than me, with pale hair and a careful set to her shoulders. Ena followed her in, speaking in a voice full of charm.

'Mrs Warsow said she'd put on extra food this morning to feed us all, and judging from the last few days, she's good at heavying a table. Hmm, that coffee smells wonderful.' Ena pulled out a chair and sat down, reaching for the coffee pot. The girl stayed standing beside the door, and I saw Ena glance at Marina's empty chair, so I pointed down, saying nothing. Her eyes brightened and she kept her voice light and deliberate. 'Oh, there's nothing like a nice cup of coffee in the morning, is there? Makes you fresh as a daisy. Do sit down, Grace. Laura, would you like me to pour you a cup? Ah, but you have one already. Clever you, first to the table. Did you sleep well?'

I nodded and smiled, and under the table, Marina shifted off my feet.

'Well, we had some excitement last night, to be sure. This is Grace Parry, a friend of Auguste's from Cornwall. Well, not from Cornwall, but she was there for the summer fairs, I believe. I think that's what he said. Grace, would you like some coffee?'

'Oh, no, thank you. I'm not too fond really.' The girl spoke in a soft voice, and Ena said she was sure Mrs Warsow could make a pot of tea, if that was better.

Another shift under the table and a quiet giggle this time. Then Ena on her feet and acting.

'Oh! My goodness, Laura!' she cried. 'What *is* under the table? Did you let a dog in the house?' Ena pushed back her chair and knelt right down on the carpet, lifting the edge of the tablecloth. The hidden Marina erupted with laughter.

'Me!' She crawled out right into her mother and buried her face in her dress.

'You little monkey! Scared me half to death. I thought you'd run away with the gypsies, so we were going to have a quiet morning without you. You raggle-taggle monster!'

Marina squealed with laughter and looked around the room to find her father's chair was empty and a stranger watching her. She stopped and Ena waited, but Marina didn't flinch or hide herself away, just stayed sitting by her crouching mother, looking at the girl.

'Hello,' she said, eyes wide.

The girl smiled.

'Hello,' she said. 'You're a funny dog.'

'I am a dog.'

'I thought so.' She blinked and Marina laughed. 'I'm Grace.'

Marina stood up and stepped towards her to get a better look. The girl tilted her head one way, then the other and waggled her fingers to make Marina laugh again. Then Ena stood and picked the child up, a crumple of white dress and chubby legs.

'Come on, pet,' she said. 'Let's sit down and eat some breakfast.'

Ena settled Marina on her lap and cut her toast into small pieces. 'Here, you can dip them in the jam, if you like. And Laura, would you pass me that milk jug? And Marina's cup, too? Thanks, that's perfect. Grace, do sit down and eat. There's plenty here.'

Grace took the chair beside me, and I smiled at her, or tried to. I wasn't sure what my face was doing. She smiled back.

'You are Laura,' she said, making my name sound long and warm. 'They told me about you, that you're practically family and you sew.'

'Grace had some difficulty with her landlady and needed a place to stay.' Ena helped Marina with her cup of milk. 'That's it, isn't it? I find details hard to remember when I haven't slept properly. I hope you slept well enough on the couch.' Ena turned on another smile, then looked back to Marina, and Grace looked at me.

'You're in Cardiff for the Exhibition?' I asked.

'Of course. I thought the Redruth Fete was something, but this is colossal. Thank you, this is wonderful,' she said, taking a piece of toast from the rack to set it on the plate in front of her.

'So, it was Cornwall then,' Ena said. 'When you met my husband? You said Redruth?'

'Yes. And with Miss Alma, too, please. I worked with the W.C. and S. Hancock Empire. He and Mrs Sophie were right kind to me.'

'Professional people, the Hancocks,' Monsieur Gaudron said, coming into the room with a newspaper under his arm. 'I did like them. They ran a tight ship and very modern, too, when it comes to funfairs. All manner of mechanized rides and engines.'

'Ah, there you are, Auguste. I hoped you'd join us and not go straight to the balloons.'

'Well, my love, that would never do. I need family first thing in the morning like you need coffee. Perks me up. Makes me – what's the word?' He pulled out the newspaper and set it on the table, running down the text with his finger. 'Ah, yes, here it is. Plucky. That's me, isn't it? Says so in the morning paper. Another bit for your clippings. And there's a joke, too, you'd like in here. Let's see, where was that?'

'Hang the joke, what's this *plucky*? That is not an adjective we agreed on.'

'Not in the advertisement at all, my dear. It's a real article. All about last evening's exploits.'

'Oh dear. Exploits. Is it bad?'

Ena passed Marina into my arms and took the paper from her husband.

'Here,' he said, jabbing at the paper. 'This is what they said about me. *The plucky Frenchman was much distressed and felt the disappointment as keenly as the crowd.* Plucky.'

'Well, it's a good thing you acted as disappointed as you did. They could have been writing a much worse story in the paper today.'

'It wasn't an act. I was disappointed. I am. I wanted to fly and am not satisfied when a flight must be aborted. I am sorry I showed how angry I was. I should have been able to manage things better and fulfil my contract with the concessionaires.'

'But we did the right thing. We cannot fly if the conditions are dangerous, and the balloon is acting unpredictably. Is it a leak, you think? Something we missed?'

He sat down and sighed. 'You are right, of course, ma chérie. But now I will need to think things through better for Saturday's flight. Ah, these difficulties that appear. And Grace, the Hancocks' lovely Grace. I did not know you were coming to Cardiff for the Exhibition. Had I realized, we might have travelled together.'

'I didn't mean to inconvenience.' She looked down, carefully, and spoke softly.

'But you are inconvenienced yourself. What a difficult thing, to be turned loose from your lodgings. Friends arriving to visit? That was the landlady's excuse? I'm sure friends with shinier boots and heavier purses is closer to the truth. Well, I'm glad you thought to find us out. My lovely wife and I are quite good at finding accommodation for those in need, aren't we, Laura?' and he winked at me.

'I will sort something today,' Ena said, looking down at her toast. 'I'll ask around.'

Auguste nodded and reached again for the newspaper. 'Now, about that joke, ah yes, it is here. Ena, listen to this: *A maiden lady of not very attractive appearance was the other day boasting that a man almost committed a crime to please her. A fresh young damsel of seventeen naively asked if the man had tried to steal a kiss. It is a good job that looks cannot kill.*'

'Oh, you. A sense of humour like an old plank. Frenchmen!'

She threw up her hands and looked to me, so I laughed, too.

'But it is in an English paper, is it not?' Auguste pressed. 'So, how can it be my French fault? Perhaps I should sigh *wives* as you sigh *Frenchmen*.' He laughed at his own words, and the girl laughed, too, and he caught her eye, still laughing.

'Now, Mademoiselle Grace, who are you working for now?' he asked. 'Hancock is not here in Cardiff. Who did you sign with?'

'No one,' she said. 'Not yet. I'm still finding my feet. But I have a few friends and . . .'

Mrs Warsow came into the room then, carrying a dish of sausages. As soon as she put it down, Auguste reached over, dug his fork in and pushed three of them onto Grace's plate.

'Well then, eat up. The unemployed need feeding.'

She smiled, looking round at all our faces.

'Thank you. I can't say thank you enough.'

She cut her sausages into ragged pieces and forked them into her mouth as fast as she could. Ena took a sip of coffee and so did I, watching. The girl looked around, quick like a bird, bright eyes seeing everything, and Auguste filled her plate again. She must not have eaten in days, I thought, though she looked clean enough. When I was first with the Gaudrons, I felt filthy, my skin grey and stiff with months of cold dirt. I used to plunge my hands in the wash bowl every morning, letting the warm water sink in through my skin. When I ate, my hands smelled like soap.

Ena started organizing the day, telling us she planned to be out for the morning and that she would be taking Marina with her.

'Errands and arrangements,' she said. 'With any luck, I'll have news to share at lunch. Mrs Warsow said we should be ready for cold chicken today, which sounds nice. There will be plenty, if you'd like to join us, Grace. No, don't make a decision now. You can play it by ear.'

She advised Auguste he'd best spend the morning at the shed with both balloons. I could go, too, to help, as Marina wouldn't need me, and I was wondering where that left this new girl when she piped up that she'd be coming with us to the Exhibition Grounds, if we didn't mind. She really needed to find work and the best way to do that was to ask around, wasn't it?

'You'll find work easily enough,' Auguste said. 'There's always work for smart, young girls.'

'Just be careful,' Ena added. 'You need to trust an employer. If you feel any hesitation about a man, heed it. Don't promise anything until you are certain.'

'And if you aren't certain, come and ask me, of course,' Auguste said. 'There are many people I know here in Cardiff now.'

He leaned back in his chair and launched into more municipal information he'd read, this time about the Cardiff coal barons and steelworks set up by the docks, about the ships from all over the world, every nation coming for South Wales coal, willing to pay the earth.

'And they call it Tiger Bay,' he said. 'For all the internationals heaving black gold. Every colour of stevedore imaginable. One of the concessionaires told me there is an Arab expression from the Yemen – *getting a bit Cardiff* – which means coming home from these Welsh docks flush and flashing cash around.'

'So, it isn't only Bute who is making money here,' Ena said.

'Though, probably, he is making the most. I suppose Marquesses do. Must be pleasant to be the richest man in the world.'

'Here in Cardiff? The richest? Well, perhaps . . .' Auguste let his voice trail away, and Grace gave a low whistle which caught his attention and made him laugh. 'Just your thing, Grace Parry. You are a one for chasing the money. The docks are no place for pretty pale girls like you. You will have better and safer luck at the Exhibition.'

71

Mrs Warsow was worried that we would be over-heated on such a warm day, so she filled two glass bottles with water and packed them in a basket which Grace insisted on carrying. The handle proved awkward, so she clutched the basket to her chest and walked along quickly beside me.

When we got to the shed, the door sat unlocked, and Auguste strode in, calling out for Mr Pettigrew. I followed him, and Grace trotted after, quick as she could. She found the worktable and set down her basket next to my sewing machine, then shook out her hands dramatically.

'You all right?' I asked.

'Oh, yes,' she said. 'Fine and dandy. Just need to do some stretching, I think. My arms feel a bit stiff. Late nights do that to me.'

She reached up, then folded herself in half and put her palms flat on the floor, echoing Ena, though she didn't know it. Then she kicked up one leg high behind her, straight as a board, and Auguste quickstepped out of the way, before he, too, stooped to pick up a length of rope from the floor.

'This should have been properly wound,' he said. 'I do not like it when things are left in a muddle. I thought I'd hired better men. All this thrown down in the dark when I was not here to watch it was done properly. I should have come and done it all myself. But what is this? I only see Monday's balloon here and where is the other one? Last night's balloon is missing. Ridiculous.'

He told us he'd have to go and find it. I reminded him someone had unlocked and opened the shed for us this morning and was probably right now in the process of bringing the other balloon, but he said he would rather chase than stand idle and if anyone came whilst he was away, they could jolly well wait. Grace said she'd like to wait, too, if I didn't mind. It was a good place to exercise in private.

'Because you know I'd rather not put on a show,' she said, folding herself in half again.

I sat down by the table and unlocked my machine to check the thread supply. I'd need thick thread for repair work, and I wanted to be sure I hadn't run the bobbin down. Long seams needed lots of thread.

'Well, if anyone does arrive, keep them here,' said Auguste. 'I want them to tell me where the balloon spent the night and why it wasn't delivered as promised. And do not start examining it without me. I need to see everything. Everything.'

I smiled and nodded, and after he left the shed, Grace turned to me and laughed.

'He really is something, isn't he? You should have seen him in Redruth. Dashing as all get-out and all the ladies chasing him. They all begged for a chance to fly in his balloon and he refused them all, every one. Said it wasn't a sport, though obviously it is. I can't wait to have a go. Another go.'

'You like flying?'

'Don't you?'

I smiled a little, but didn't answer, just pulled a crate over to the table and sat down on it. I took the sewing machine key from around my neck and unlocked the case. Grace straightened and watched everything I did, young and silly, like Alma must have been before I met her. Or Julia maybe. Silly show-off girls, playing mad games and wanting all the attention.

'How old are you, Grace?' I asked.

'Seventeen.'

'You aren't. I'm seventeen.'

'Nearly seventeen, then.'

Why did she bother to lie to me? What was she trying to win? Or prove? Or hide. It might have been any of these. Because she wasn't seventeen at all. Not just because she had no hips to speak of, no breasts at all, but there was something in the way she carried her excitement around like a parcel in her hands, right out in front where anyone could see it. If she was older, she'd have been better at hiding. She hadn't been at this game long.

'Have you always worked for them, sewing and everything?' she asked, with her head tilted towards me.

I told her yes, and that I didn't just sew; I was also a balloon pilot.

'A lady parachutist like Miss Alma Beaumont?'

I paused. 'Not really. Just a pilot.'

For me, flying wasn't like that. It wasn't a game. It was beautiful. I wished it didn't have to be about fetes and exhibitions and not even about science or discovery. If I could decide, it would be something private I could do on my own without everyone watching. Like Ena and Auguste high above that Paris street, up high in the night where no one saw them. Well, no one but me, and I didn't count. I would fly in the dark when everyone was asleep, and the stars were out and the moon like another balloon so I wouldn't be alone. And I'd look down on the sleeping world, the quiet streets, the church spires and cemetery trees, the fields, the lanes, the coastlines beside, and everything would be there, dim and silver, everything silent as I passed above.

'A pilot,' Grace said. 'That sounds exciting.'

'Oh, yes,' I said. 'Quite.'

Grace sat down on the ground with her legs stretched in front, still stretching.

'Anything to do with balloons is exciting,' she said. 'I love balloons.'

I told her there were a lot of things to learn and she shrugged, then nodded as if she agreed.

'Oh yes, balloons are a complicated business. But are you an acrobat then, too?' she asked.

I shook my head.

'I thought Mr Goodrun said . . .' but she didn't complete that thought. She looked at me, as if trying to work something out. 'Well, I am,' she said, a little fiercely. 'That's what I did in Redruth when I worked with the Hancocks. One of the things.'

Maybe it was the way she pronounced his name that made me push or how she was showing off.

'And before that?' I asked. 'Before the Hancocks. What did you do then?'

She met my eye and didn't flinch.

'Nothing glamorous. A cloth factory in Bristol. I tended spools on a great clunking machine. Had to climb around underneath it and keep it clean and all the bits threaded, and it was moving all the time. Once I saw a girl get her hair caught and it pulled a fat chunk of it right off with a bloody bit of skin still attached. Big as your hand it was. I left after that.'

'Did you?' I asked, flatly. She was trying to shock me. Thought I was the kind who'd shock.

'Yeah,' she said. 'No point sticking around a place like that. Bad management.'

'And now you've left the Hancocks.'

'Them, too.'

'Why? Did Mr Hancock try something?'

'No, nothing like that.' She tucked her hair behind her ear, and I thought she might go quiet, but she pushed on. 'Only I didn't want to trail around with them anymore. I wanted something different. Cardiff seems like my kind of place, don't you think? I've been talking to so many people the last few days, making lots of friends. There's bound to be someone here who'll take my skills. Just need to find me the right opportunity. Like you did.'

Stupid girl. She really thought it worked like that. That she could play around and find her way, safe as houses. She was going to get scooped up for sure and end up where? And then how was she going to get back home again?

'Sewing's a good skill to pick up,' I said. 'If you can work a seam, you'll always have an opportunity to make some safe money.'

She stood up and brushed her skirt down, like a child making herself presentable.

'Safe money,' she echoed. 'I need to get me some of that. Fair work comes and goes and it's probably important to have something for a wet day. That's a flashy machine.'

She leaned over and laid her hand on the black japanned arm of my sewing machine.

'A Singer, is it? *Latest and Best*. That's what the sign said in Bristol. I passed it every day on my way to the cloth factory.'

'No, this is better than Singer. Monsieur Gaudron says the Germans are best at engineering.'

'Look at that: *Frister & Rossmann.* Sounds German, doesn't it?' She reached out to touch the detailed enamel. 'It's pretty. I like the oak leaves. Is that real gold? You know, I've never used a sewing machine before.'

This girl was good at fishing. Well, I knew that, late-night knocking and all, and it was a useful skill, if she used it well.

'Why don't you look for a spool of thread for me, and then I'll show you how it works?'

She peered into my work basket, found a full spool and passed it to me. I showed her how to wind the bobbin first, then to settle the spool on its pin on the top of the machine and explained how they worked together, each stitch pulling both up and down, making the seam strong.

'Like with balloons,' she said, and I wasn't sure what she meant.

'You have one person up in the air, and one on the ground,' she continued. 'Working together. Mr Goodrun explained it to me when I watched him and Miss Alma getting organized in Redruth. Is she with you here, too?'

'Alma's gone to London. Going to get married.'

'Really? I didn't know.'

'That's what Monsieur Gaudron told us. Ena and me.'

'She's nice. Least she was nice to me. Glamorous and a bit stand-offish, maybe, probably because she's famous. But she was always nice to me. And she didn't mind talking about balloons. Because that's what I do. Balloons.'

'Yes. You said.'

'Yes.'

'You want to learn how to thread the machine?'

'Sure. If you want.'

'It works like this. You need to watch carefully. Thread from the back, always the back, and then over this way, through this catch and between the tension wheels, then like this and through and then you're at the needle's eye.'

She blinked and wasn't paying attention, too keen to have a go, so I popped the shuttle in place without comment and raised the bobbin thread myself.

'Then, place the presser foot down on the fabric and you're ready to go. Like this. Turn the crank with your right hand, gently around and use your left-hand fingers to guide the fabric through. Now, your turn.'

I stood up and she sat down, reaching right away for the crank, and I told her she'd want to check the fabric was flat first. Always check first before going forward. Ma's advice.

'There, once your left hand is planted, put your right hand on the crank, then slowly start.'

The handle on the crank was made of wood, which made it different from the other machines in the balloon factory. They all had white ceramic handles which felt cold when you started. Mine was warm and smooth right away, and I rubbed it with beeswax to make it shine.

Grace turned the handle slowly, so she had been listening. The fabric was a scrap of blue left over from one of Ena's skirts and showed the white stitches clearly. The nice thing about a good machine is that the stitches are always even, whether you go fast or slow. They might go crooked or wave all over the place, but they're always even as bricks in a wall. A pleasing precision. Grace sat awkwardly, turning and checking the fabric again and again, not yet understanding how much she was in control.

'Oh!' she said, suddenly surprised. 'It goes backwards, too.'

'Of course it does. The handle works both ways, whichever way you crank it. That's how you reinforce a seam. It makes it stronger.'

'I know what reinforce means.'

'I'm sorry. I've been spending my days with Marina.'

Grace giggled and said she wasn't a child.

'Well, how about I find you another piece of cloth and we make something together? Would you like that?'

'What kind of something?'

'I dunno, something small with seams. What about a little pouch? A small heart-shaped thing you could fill with lavender. That's a nice sort of starting project, don't you think?' I found a piece of printed calico which she seemed to like.

'Yellow's my favourite colour,' she told me. 'And you'll be here, showing me how?'

'Of course. A project for the two of us.'

I drew a heart in chalk on the fabric and explained about leaving space between the stitching and the fabric's edge so it wouldn't fray. It was a child's task, but she looked happy at it and focused, which surprised me. I watched her turn the handle slowly, then stop mid-seam and frown at the result.

'This isn't working very well. There's something wrong with the machine. The edges go all lumpy. See?'

'We'll snip them later to help it lie flat,' I said. 'Don't worry, it'll look different once stuffed. It's not meant to be empty, is it? Like a balloon. They always look strange lying about deflated. It's not bad at all for a first go.'

8/

Footsteps and a whistle and I expected Auguste now, only it wasn't. This man was my age and looked right at me, surprised, like his eyes were adjusting to the shed's light. He pulled his cap off his head and his hair was brown and curly.

'Hello,' Grace said, loudly, her hand frozen on the machine's crank.

He blinked and didn't say anything, still looking right at me.

Grace tried again. 'You're wanting Mr Goodrun, aren't you? We're with him, only he isn't here right now. We work with his balloons.'

'Grace,' I said, warning. I wanted to stop her bragging, twist her ear to keep her silent, but kept still.

'Yes. I am. He's – I am,' he said, answering her question awkwardly. 'I'm looking for him. Monsieur Gaudron.' The man's voice was soft and hesitant, and I felt shy for him, standing there in front of us both like that. Grace kept looking at him hard. Anyone would feel awkward, looked at like that. I looked down at the table, picked up a scrap of fabric and smoothed it flat between my fingers. White canvas, heavy gauge, frayed at one end, the angles not square.

'Do you work at the Exhibition?' Grace asked, her voice irritating. 'Or with the gardener?' She was too excited all the time, snippy and rude.

'The gardener. I'm an apprentice for him,' he said. I looked up and he was looking at me again. He didn't sound English, and I wondered if he'd notice I didn't either, only I hadn't said much yet.

'Was he the one who unlocked the shed for us?' I asked. 'Or was it you?'

'Me. He asked me to. Reckoned you were coming this morning and asked that I do it. I am Douglas. Douglas Harris.'

Before I could introduce myself, Grace started flirting.

'You're Scotch,' she said, looking at him squint.

'Aye. And you're not.'

Grace laughed. 'No. Clever of you to spot that. I'm just off the train from Bristol.'

'City of pirates,' he said, and she laughed again.

His shirt was white, dirty, the sleeves rolled up. He wore no jacket, only a waistcoat, a fine head of hair, eyes, and he kept looking at me, as if I was doing something to make him, as if I was wishing something new would happen. Or maybe it was Grace, wishing away, bewitching us both with her excitement.

He asked if we knew when Mr Pettigrew would be returning, as if we might know, but Grace said we hadn't seen him at all, only Monsieur Gaudron who'd gone off to look for the balloon and left us here. Maybe they'd find each other, Grace said. She was showing off again, flirty, and I wanted to slap her quiet.

'That's good,' he said. 'I hope that is good. I hoped . . . but no matter. It will be good.'

His voice was deep, and he was worried, but didn't explain. He glanced back at me and our eyes met, then didn't, quick as that. Grace started on the sewing machine again, turning the crank slowly, singing under her breath. I fiddled with the scrap of cloth, folded it back and forth, and opened it flat again. Set it down on the table and looked right up at him. He let me meet his eye, longer now, and I looked down. Grace stalled on the sewing machine and I asked her quietly if she wanted to keep going.

'No,' she said, with force. 'I can do it later.'

'Probably best.' I turned towards the stack of crates by the wall and spoke in a louder voice. 'We'll need to get the spare canvas out for repairs, Grace. Now, which crate was it in?'

'I can help,' he said. 'If you like. I'll lift it down for you.' And I turned towards him, but Auguste came back just then, striding into the shed, and I could see he wasn't happy.

'Rien de tout!' he bellowed. 'Vraiment, rien de tout, quelle surprise.'

'Monsieur Gaudron,' I said. 'The gardener's boy is here.'

'Is he then? Well, he will answer my questions. But where is the gardener himself? And what has become of all the assurances I received? Who – who . . . how? . . . How can I possibly prepare for a public performance with this kind of abysmal support? Maudit anglais.'

'Good morning, Monsieur Gaudron,' the young man said. 'I am sorry that we have disappointed you. That I have.'

'And to think I was *impressed* to be offered storage facilities within the Castle grounds. Bah! Vraiment, quel gâchis.'

Douglas Harris introduced himself and Auguste muttered on in French.

'Mr Goodrun, he's only here to tell you it's all fine,' Grace said, making her eyes very large.

'Oh, is he? Well then, perhaps he can tell me why the balloon wasn't in the shed last night? Why weren't my requests obeyed?'

'I am afraid that was my fault.'

'Of course, I assumed that. Though you do surprise me with the straightforward answer.'

'It was leatherjackets, I'm afraid. I was concerned about them yesterday in my strawberries. I spotted crane fly over the patch and worried they might choose to lay eggs in the patch, so I was fussing with netting to cover them when I should have been collecting your balloon. That never should have happened. I was remiss in my responsibilities.' He stood very straight as he spoke and looked Auguste in the eye.

'And my balloon?'

'You needn't fear, sir. It is safe – and was safe all through the night, just not here in the shed. I arranged for a friend to collect it and bring it to me. But by the time I had finished with the berry bushes and he found me, it was much too late to retrieve the key from Mr Pettigrew so we stored the balloon in another shed by the bicycle track. Over on the other side of the model railway. It was perfectly safe there. I slept beside it all night.'

'You slept with my balloon.'

'Yes. That is what I said and what I did.'

'And your berry bushes?'

'I checked on them this morning. I believe they are well.'

Auguste coughed, and rolled his shoulders, stretching.

'Well, young man, thank you for your honesty. I trust I will be reunited with my balloon shortly.'

'Yes, sir. My friend was arranging a cart to bring it right around. I am sorry we were not early enough with that task to arrive before you.'

'No matter. The worry has passed, more or less. That is the expression, no? More or less?'

The sound of wheels and we turned to see a cart pulling into the shed.

'Ah yes, and here we are. Not quite right on time,' Auguste said.

'Again, I apologize I did not arrange things better,' Douglas said.

The cart was driven by a wiry boy in a canvas jacket and when she saw him, Grace let out a shout and startled me.

'Johnny! Halloo, Johnny!'

'Mademoiselle Grace, you know this man?'

'Of course! We're firm friends, Johnny and me. We met, what – two days ago now? At the Exhibition. He's with *Santiago*.'

'And who is Santiago?'

'The show, silly. The water pageant at the Exhibition. *The Siege of Santiago*.'

'Oh yes. The battle on the canal. I hear it rages on to great applause. Do the Welsh love naval battles, then?'

The boy laughed as he climbed down, shiny brown hair and

brown eyes, the kind of boy who makes everyone smile, and I saw Auguste crack a smile, too. Grace bounced up to him. 'Hey there, kiddo,' he said. 'I've got your balloon. If I'd realized you'd landed balloon work, well . . .'

'The balloon is mine, thank you,' Auguste said, cutting him off. He stepped forward to help unload it from the cart. 'We will spread it out here to take a proper look.'

An initial inspection seemed to show that the damage was largely trouble with the grommets and ropes, something pulled squint making the inflation incomplete. So not a leak at all, despite Ena's worry. The fabric seemed fine, though dusty from its night in the bicycle shed. Auguste said it was all much better than he feared. He wanted to use this balloon – his old favourite – for his final flight on Saturday and, though the grommet situation might need some innovative problem-solving, he was confident he could manage it all right.

'Madame Gaudron says problem-solving is my essential asset, so we shall see. These young men can help me haul the balloon up to this rafter to hang next to the other one and then I will be able to assess matters better. But the morning is going. Grace, do not let all this business detain you from yours.'

He told me he wouldn't need any sewing done until the afternoon and that I was free to go, if I liked, but as I locked my machine, he remembered an errand. There was a basket shop near the Castle and he'd seen a sort of creel displayed that could be strapped to a back and might be useful for a parachutist.

'For aerial leaflet distribution, perhaps. Would you mind? A little errand before you walk home again? There should be no trouble arranging for the bill to be sent to the house. Here, give the shopkeeper this card, and I am sure he will help.'

I agreed and asked if I would see him back at the Edward Street house for lunch.

'Yes,' he said. 'I'm as curious as you about Ena's promised news.'

The shop sign said *Martinot & Pierrard Burluaux*. Inevitably Auguste. I wondered if I should speak in French.

Inside, the shop was small and full to the ceiling, and the smell took me right back to Wyoming. Part wood varnish, part tarred rope, the boot-marked boards on the floor, jute sacks and barrels. There were tins and packets on shelves, stacked baskets everywhere and tubs bristling with brooms and brushes of all kinds. A small man with round glasses stood behind the counter. His hair was rusty and curled, growing mainly above his ears, and the top of his head was a burnished copper. He smiled warmly when I came into the shop, the little bells on the door chiming, and, when I said I was there on behalf of M. Auguste Gaudron, he appeared to know the name, maybe from the newspapers.

I explained what I was looking for and he pointed encouragingly to a high shelf stacked with strapped creels. So many models to choose among, different sizes, different weights of wicker.

'But do not fear, mademoiselle. I shall not ask you to climb to such a height. I have a way, as you will see.'

He turned and retrieved a long, hook-topped stick from the corner of the room.

'Now, you simply choose, and I will retrieve any basket you fancy.'

I thanked him and asked for the smaller models, then more little bells and Grace was there beside me.

'I think the medium size would work better,' she said. 'Let's try the black one, too.'

'Grace, I didn't expect . . .'

'I followed you. Doesn't feel like the right time to try for work, really. Mr Goodrun's right – most of the morning is gone already. It really would be better first thing, I think.'

The shopkeeper cleared his throat. 'Is the purchase for this young lady, then?' he asked.

'No,' I said.

'I'm helping,' she said. 'I work for Mr Goodrun, too.'

'Ah, two charming employees. Monsieur Gaudron is a lucky man.' He lowered the first basket towards me, and I held out my hands to take it from the hook.

'Here, Grace. Turn round. I want to judge size against your back. If you don't mind standing still for a bit.'

'I do have a wide selection of mirrors, if you would like to see how the baskets appear on your own back.'

The back wall of the shop was hung with mirrors of all sizes, and when she spotted them, they drew Grace like a candle flame. With a gentle hand, she touched their frames, and looked into each one like she was peering through windows, trying to see what was inside.

I bought two baskets, one large and one smaller, and the shopkeeper kindly agreed to take back whichever didn't suit once Monsieur Gaudron had decided.

'A favour from one Frenchman to another, far from home,' he said.

I gave him M. Gaudron's card, said *merci beaucoup*, and he laughed.

'Très bien. Et merci à vous. Enjoy your baskets, mesdemoiselles, and perhaps I will see you again.'

'Men like you, don't they?' Grace asked.

'I don't know what you mean.'

'Yes, you do. They notice you, but not like *ooh-la-la*. They see you and you – I don't know – you look at them or something and then they're nice to you.'

'You mean Auguste.'

'Sure. And the shopkeeper there. And the gardener's boy, too. Douglas Harris. I liked him, but he liked you.'

'I don't know about that,' I said, and was going to tell her I really hadn't noticed, but let it drop. 'Shall we go and see the Animal Wall before lunch?' I asked.

'You think I'm a child, don't you?' She looked at me fiercely, her eyes sharp.

'It's just across the road here. I haven't seen it properly yet. Mrs Warsow thought I might like to see it. Lots of visitors to Cardiff do.'

Grace softened a bit and turned round to check her reflection in the shop window.

'I think Mr Goodrun might have mentioned it in Cornwall when he first talked up Cardiff. He's going to hire me, you know. He's going to give me a job.'

'Is he? He seemed to be encouraging you to look elsewhere.'

'For now. But that's going to change. He knows I'm reliable. I helped out in Cornwall, see? Miss Alma said I was a big help, shifting balloons and collecting parachutes. I went out in the cart for them, and I guarded them when it was needed, and Miss Alma said right then that I had a real flair for balloon work. And I do. A flair.'

A bus passed pulled by chestnut horses, the advertisement on its side hawking Whitbread's Beer in Bottles, chocolate letters on an orange background. When it pulled away, we could see the stone wall topped with stone animals.

On our first afternoon in town, Ena and I had taken Marina to see it. The weather had been hot and muggy, and Marina hadn't been interested in anything we pointed out. Travel and being somewhere new had worn her out and made her fussy. She screwed up her face and refused to look. And who could blame her? What did she know about wolves? Hyenas? Bears? Fairy tale beasts so far up at the top of the wall that your neck hurt to look at them, and so many dusty people pressed in and all manner of carts and carriages wheeling past. Hardly story-time. Her whingeing frustrated Ena who snapped that if the child wouldn't look at anything, we might as well be back indoors in Mrs Warsow's cramped living room, and then she turned and marched off. She had such long legs, I couldn't keep up, not with Marina in my arms, and you think I could make her walk? So, the two of us were left behind. I stopped walking and Marina opened up that fierce mouth of hers and let out a bellow like you've never heard, but Ena didn't stop, no one turned round, no one did anything at all but keep right on walking and, in the end, that's what I did, too.

But that was a different day.

'Johnny told me about the Animal Wall, too,' Grace said. 'He's told me all sorts of things about this place. I like how he talks. And he doesn't mind when I call him Johnny, though to everyone else, he's John Owen. Look at those vines on those Castle walls. Johnny told me about them, too. They look like old stones but they're not. The Marquess had them built and wanted them to look ancient and right, so he asked the gardeners to cultivate those vines and water them, which is funny, isn't it, this being Wales. Is it this rainy in America?'

'Some places,' I said vaguely, looking at the green growth on the walls. How did her John Owen know about gardens? She'd said he worked the boats in the *Santiago* show, not the gardens at all, so maybe he got that story from Douglas. The vines did look wonderful. We crossed the street to get a better look at the animals and you could see they'd once been painted; there were stains of old colour in the details of their fur. Grace liked the bear best. She said his glass eyes looked cheeky. On the walk back to the house, she growled and teased me, but there was no point in thinking about the gardener's boy at all. Next week, I'd be back in London.

9/

At the house, Ena must have been watching for us because she opened the door as soon as we reached it, welcoming us in.

'Auguste has only just arrived back himself,' she said. 'He was sure you'd be here first, but I told him you two girls were probably enjoying yourselves. Window-shopping in the arcades, were you? Something like that, I'm sure.'

We were hot from walking and Ena looked flushed, too. She turned and walked through the hallway as we took off our hats and set them on the dresser. In the front room, Auguste was standing by the window, his jacket hanging on the back of a chair. Ena stood beside him and didn't look at him and didn't look at us, either.

'Really, Auguste, you shouldn't be standing there in the window like that in your shirt sleeves.' Ena's voice was sharp, and I tried to read her expression, but she kept her face turned away.

'And you should not worry so much about what hypothetical neighbours may or may not be thinking. But I interrupt. You were about to make an announcement to these young ladies.'

'Yes. An announcement.' She cleared her throat. 'It's because circumstances have changed that we've needed to make new arrangements, and it's for the best all round. But I'm not being clear. What I mean is you can't stay here with us. It isn't respectable.'

'Ena,' I said. 'You mean Grace.'

'No. I mean both of you. I am sorry.'

'But Ena,' I said. 'This is silly. I'm an employee. Marina needs me. You need me. '

'Yes, of course, and if it was only you, Laura, but with Grace now arriving out of nowhere, and Monsieur Gaudron, well. I will say no more. Only I have to, because Mrs Warsow is worried about what people might whisper. And then there is the business. Gossip is the last thing we need. That's why I made arrangements.'

She told us that Grace and I would move across the street to a boarding house run by Mrs Watkins, who would keep an eye on us both as befitted unmarried girls.

'But you'll still eat all your meals with us,' Ena said. 'And you can leave your sewing machine here with us, Laura. Save you carrying it up all those stairs. You're not likely going to want it in the evenings, anyway, are you?'

'It's at the Exhibition,' I said. 'Locked in the shed with the rest of the equipment.'

'Yes, of course. I wasn't thinking. Look, it's only for a matter of a few days. I'm really not trying to make things difficult for anyone. Only, there's one more thing. Mrs Warsow thought it best – actually, we all agreed we shouldn't use your real name with Mrs Watkins or with anyone else for now. You didn't use your names anywhere this morning, did you? Didn't tell anyone who you were?'

'No. I don't think so. At the basket shop. I just gave the shop-keeper a business card. I made a point of doing that. But why does this matter?'

'I don't want gossip. If Laura was working as Marina's nurse one day, and then suddenly *Laura* is living somewhere else, well, it doesn't look good, does it?'

She met my eye now and I didn't nod, didn't want to react one way or another.

'So, what name did you give Mrs Watkins?' I asked.

'Alma.'

'Alma?'

'Best I could come up with in a split moment like that. What about the boys Auguste mentioned? The boys at the shed? Do they know your name?'

'No. We didn't really talk.'

'And Johnny only knows my name,' Grace said. 'I didn't introduce you, Laura, did I? I don't think I did.' She was a little too enthusiastic, I thought, happily skipping along with this plan. The couch may not have been all that comfortable after all.

'But my dear, this works perfectly,' Auguste said, a strange smile opening on his face. 'Ah ha! This is why this has happened. Do I not say that everything happens for a reason?'

He lifted his fingers to his face, and smoothed his moustache, holding back a laugh. 'Well, here is a reason. This morning, after you girls left the shed, the concessionaires of the Exhibition came by, and they had what seemed then a difficult proposal for me. I thought at first they carried complaints about the incident on Wednesday night and the lack of a balloon flight and thought I very well might be losing the job right there and then without a Saturday flight after all. But no, that wasn't it. They wanted more flights. More! Which means more money, of course, my dear. More investment. And they wanted me to include, if I could manage, a lady balloonist.'

I didn't move, didn't even swallow, but Ena sensed my reaction anyway, her look catching mine and cautious. Auguste kept talking.

'Yes, just as I had in Cornwall with Alma, and in London, too. Julia, Alma, all the girls. The concessionaires had heard about those flights and heard correctly, too, that they have a positive effect on ticket sales.' He slowed his speech, and looked right at Ena, his eyes wide and performing. 'But, hearing that, vraiment, I was worried. What could I say? Only now you have given me the solution. Word will emerge that Mademoiselle Alma is here and well, perhaps she will be. Do you think, Laura, that you might be able to perform under that name?'

He'd turned now to face me directly, and I couldn't look away. 'Perform?' I said. 'You mean fly as Alma?'

'You are the right size. And ability. You are most capable. You have proved time and again. All our flights together and the graceful performances you have at all those fetes.'

'I don't think so. I don't want . . .'

'But you are excellent. Elegant. The strong and ideal candidate.'

Ena crossed her arms and glared at him.

'Perhaps we should speak about this in private. Grace, can you please go through to the kitchen. I'm sure you will find Mrs Warsow there. No, Laura, you can stay.'

Grace bowed her head as she left the room, and I stopped watching, not wanting to see if there was a look before she closed the door.

Ena sat down and looked at her husband. 'Auguste, you aren't being at all fair.'

'I am merely trying to cope with our difficult situation. I thought you'd be happy that I found a way of honouring commitments and keeping our business prominent in a place where there are so many potential investors.' He smoothed his moustache again, but the smile was gone. 'I do not mean to put Laura on the spot. I only asked as I thought she might be interested in the opportunity.'

I looked down, not wanting to respond.

Auguste tried again. 'Or perhaps you, Ena? It could be you,' he suggested. 'You've performed under false names before. Would you fly for me?'

'No,' Ena flat-out refused. 'You heard what we said yesterday. We have pledged. We are not your flirty girls any more.'

'But surely, it's not . . .'

'No. I have said no. And anyway, I am a mother now. I can't be fooling around like that. What would Marina do if I had an accident?'

'It would be so much better if Alma had never run off,' Auguste said with a sigh.

'You said she didn't run off. She retired to get married.'

'Do you truly think she retired? Alma? Can you imagine that?'

'As good a line as any. I think she got fed up with your wages and that young man of hers started talking sense. If he has his head screwed on, he'll be setting up his own show and she'll be a star attraction again in no time.'

'*His* star attraction. And where does that leave us?'

'You do know how to make a moan, husband-of-mine. But it isn't fair to pressure Laura like this. She's a pilot now, not a lady parachutist, any more.'

'But it is a lady parachutist I need, isn't it?'

'So, tell the organizers no. We've only signed for you and for three flights. We'll go home on Sunday.'

Grace joined us for lunch, helping Mrs Warsow lay the table and bring through the food. No one ate much and Marina was fussy, which made Ena terse. To break the tension, Auguste suggested going to the Exhibition for the afternoon. 'You might all go together. Ena and Marina and Laura and Grace, too. A party of beautiful young ladies. Just use my name at the gate and you'll be admitted without trouble.' He had obligations elsewhere, he said, but didn't elaborate.

'Marina needs a nap,' Ena said, quickly. 'I'll stay behind with her. But you should go out, Laura. I'm sure you haven't seen everything yet.'

'I want to see the crocodiles,' Grace said, though she looked like she needed a nap, too. Her skin was pale and there were shadowed smudges under her eyes. 'We'll go the two of us, won't we, Laura? Have you seen them yet? The crocodiles in the Jungle? There were boys handing out playbills for them yesterday.'

'Should we move our things across the street now or wait until later?' I asked, and Ena thought sooner would be best.

'It won't take long, and you won't want Mrs Watkins to be wondering about you.'

Grace said she hoped Mrs Watkins wasn't like the other Cardiff landladies and uncommitted to her guests. Auguste assured her everything would be fine.

Before I climbed the stairs, Ena stopped me in the hallway and said she wanted a word.

'I am so sorry about all this,' she said. 'It will only be for a few days and everything will come right in the end. You just see if it doesn't.'

Then she held out her arms and drew me close, pressed her cheek to mine, her powder soft and scented.

Mrs Warsow's husband carried my trunk across the road. Grace only had the clothes she was wearing and a brown paper packet, a handful of a thing like a folded shawl, tied round with a dirty bit of string. She'd probably fit into something of mine. I could sort that before we went out for the afternoon.

Mrs Watkins' house was shabbier than Mrs Warsow's and before she showed us the room, she confirmed both with us and with Mr Warsow that we weren't expecting to be fed. Upstairs, she apologized for the thinness of the quilt and said it was July, after all, and, with the two of us sharing, there was no way we'd be cold. The chamber pot sat under the bed and we weren't to use it during the day because there was a privy in the garden. She pushed back her hair as she spoke, her eyes flicking back and forth between us. Then she left us, closing the door, and Grace flopped down on the bed, her hair fluttering out behind her head.

'We'll look for Johnny this afternoon,' she said. 'He isn't hard to find. Usually around somewhere, and maybe we'll find that handsome Douglas, too, and see if he can spend some time with us. That would be nice, wouldn't it?'

'Don't tease.'

I opened my trunk and found a white blouse near the bottom to pass to Grace.

'That will work well with your walking skirt,' I said. 'And it's clean.'

She looked like she might say no, then smiled, thanked me and asked me to turn round.

'Why?'

'If you want me to change, I don't want to do it in front of you.'

So, I turned to the wall to be kind and kept my eyes fixed on the stained paper. A small red spider walked across the printed ivy and bone-yellow background until it found a place where the paper was torn, and crept in behind.

'I'll really need to get my things sent on soon,' Grace said. 'No good always appearing in the same clothes. But in the meantime, this is wonderful.'

'Can I turn round now?'

'Of course. How do I look?'

The blouse was large on her, but the cloth draped well, and the fresh white showed off her yellow hair, making her shine.

'You look lovely.'

She grinned at me and fussed with her waistband. I looked at myself in the glass and decided to unpin my hair and set it again. And I'd wear my brooch, too, the one from Ena. Finishing touch.

'Don't you look a picture?' Grace said. 'That Douglas is bound to fall for you. Especially when he hears you're going up with the balloon.'

'Don't you dare, Grace. That's not what was decided.'

'Calm down, Alma. I won't say anything if you don't want me to.'

'Alma. What a game.'

We breezed through the main gate just as Auguste had promised but needed to pay separate admission at the Jungle. The ticket girl there was Irish, her face pretty and blushed with the heat, and the fine hairs at her temples curled. My hair hung flat and limp and my dress collar felt scratchy as I paid my penny and Grace's, too, and the Irish girl said the tigers would be fed at half past four and it was worth seeing. They could be quite vicious and wonderfully loud when the meat was thrown out and it made your blood boil. I thought of Percy with his hazardous Sunderbunds landing and how Ena would shudder if she were here. Grace had pulled my hand and insisted we start with the crocodiles.

Through the gate and the air smelled green with growth and damp, not fresh like trees, but hot and dangerous. There was a glass roof overhead, with ornate iron pillars, each rounded with benches at its base. There were pathways between the cages, and a nanny pushed an elaborate pram with a fat baby sleeping on a fat white pillow. A larger child pulled at her arm and pointed to a cage where a brown bear lay sleeping like an overstuffed chesterfield.

'Why does the bear have bars?' he asked.

The nanny laughed and said it was so the bear could see the people, of course, and the child nodded and ran off again.

We saw the *Crocodiles* sign from a distance and the bright green of its painted cage.

'Do you think it will be big?' she asked.

'Oh, bigger than a bucket, I should think.'

And I was right because the cage had a stream running through it, a real river with muddy banks and tall ferns and there were real lilies floating on the water like white tulips. But no crocodiles. Maybe they were hiding. I looked for shadows, for places where the water looked different. Grace whistled, as if she might summon them. Then she walked the length of the cage and peered into the spaces under the ferns. I kept my eyes on the water. Was there a ripple? Yes. There. A slight movement and darkening and then something started to surface. It looked like a log, barked and ancient. One eye. Blinked.

'Grace,' I said, softly, getting her attention. 'There's your crocodile.'

She turned and looked, and the beast kept surfacing, more and more of it coming into view up out of the water, its strange bent legs visible now and stepping up the bank, its tail still submerged.

'How deep's that water?' Grace asked.

'How long's that tail?' I said, and she turned to flash me a smile, then spun back to the bars and watched some more, impatient. The crocodile was out of the water now, turning parallel with the stream, a forced thing piped in, pooling on a tiled floor. The ferns grew in pots; I could see that now. The mud probably came from some Welsh farmer, a shilling a bucket. This was a temporary space, lasting only as long as the Exhibition and then it would be drained and taken apart, the tiles reused maybe or thrown away. I sat down on the bench, and Grace stood by the bars, gripping them in her hands, her fingers wrapped right round the green, but the stream ran between us and the crocodile, so I supposed it was safe enough. It wasn't exactly going to snap her fingers off from there.

'It looks happy,' she said. 'Practically smiling. That's what they say about crocodiles, isn't it? That they smile but you can't trust them. Or is it the tears you can't trust? I can't remember. It looks like it's made of rocks.'

The crocodile opened its mouth. Still smiling.

'Maybe it is,' I said. 'Made of rocks. Maybe it isn't real at all, just a clockwork-made thing for the Exhibition. Wouldn't that be a trick?'

'I don't think so. The water would ruin it. And they'd never get away with that; there's too many people coming through the Exhibition. It's got to be real. Oh, look at you, Laura! You don't think so either. I can see that clear as mud. Sitting there, smiling. You're fooling! I can see you are. Practically a crocodile yourself.'

She sat down beside me, sitting on her hands and the look on her face made me smile, too. The crocodile turned round, its long tail dragged through the stream, making more ripples. Somewhere close, there were jungle birds with loud cries. I looked up and saw their dangling cages, each one with a jagged branch inside like a severed arm. There were small cages filled with small birds who flitted up and down, crowding the topmost twigs, a confusion of hopping and calling and bright wings and quick, short flight. Larger birds sat alone in larger cages, long-tailed and taloned, their eyes bright as feathers and paint.

'It's too hot in here,' Grace said. 'I'm going to go find Johnny. He said he'd like to see us today if we had time. You want to come, too?'

'No, not yet. I'll stay a while. I haven't seen the tigers yet.'

'They'll be sleeping. Not much fun to watch that.'

She left me alone with the cages and I sat a long time on that bench, all those fat, green leaves blocking the glass sky. A weird silence amid the shrieking birds. No echo. No music. No bird fluttered down to land on my hand.

Outside, I found John Owen standing near the Jungle's entrance, watching a group of young men by the refreshments stand. They were laughing and pushing at each other, grabbing at hats and tossing them up into the air. Then he noticed me and gave me a smile.

'Grace not with you today?' he asked.

'She was, but she went off to look for you.'

'She's a good kid.'

'And you're fond of her.'

'Oh, not like that. As I said, she's a kid. A nice kid. And she's on her own out here, so there's that. Maybe it's different now but when I first saw her a couple of days back, she was an absolute kitten, all big eyes and hungry and that's a dangerous look when you're on your own, isn't it? I was like that, too, first time from home. No good being friendless.'

'You said it's different now.'

'Well, yeah. With you lot and Mr Goodrun and all. She told me she was looking for you and it's a good thing she found you. I thought she'd been making up the connection. Glad to know she'd been telling the truth.'

'Some of the time.'

'Well, same as the rest of us, isn't it? And he's a good man, isn't he, Mr Goodrun? You like him? He's on the level?'

He was older than I first thought, older than me, but not by much. He had one of those faces that would always look young, and he smiled easily like his face was made for it. I could see something raw but forgiving about him. A stitched tear, maybe. I was glad Grace had run into him.

And here she came, sauntering up with a lemonade.

'Hey Johnny, there you are! Where have you been hiding? I've been looking all over for you.'

'All the way to the lemonade stand,' Johnny teased her.

'It is a warm day. And one of your friends over there bought me this which I thought was really kind and gentlemanly.'

'You watch that lot. Might have splashed the whisky in, thinking they were doing you a favour.'

'You stop worrying about me, Mr John Owen. I'd know what whisky tastes like,' she said, with a hitch of her hip. 'Isn't that right, Alma? We had a good nip last night when I found the Goodruns and Alma here, too, over at Edward Street where they are renting a house and I slept there last night, too, which was lovely after all the fuss I've had with Cardiff landladies.'

That *Alma* came natural as can be, that born liar, and a story about whisky, too. Ma wouldn't have stood for that cheek, but Grace looked at me all innocence and I had to laugh.

'So, has he hired you on, then?' John asked, but Grace only shrugged that off and rattled on about our visit to the Jungle this morning.

'Far more animals than the Hancocks had in Redruth. And more space to show them, too. This Royal Exhibition is the real deal. But I did think there'd be more. Crocodiles, I mean. The sign said *crocodiles*.'

'Advertising,' John Owen said.

'Johnny, do you know Alma?' she asked, jutting her thumb in my direction. 'She's working with Mr Goodrun, too. A fine American balloon pilot and performer, too, when need be. Alma dear, you look like you're about to melt. Want some lemonade?'

I shook my head and John Owen stuck out his hand to shake. It felt sweaty in mine.

'Nice to be properly introduced, Alma. And to know that Grace has found some good friends looking out for her now. Pleased to meet you.'

Then he asked how I'd liked the Zulus in the Jungle.

'When I was in there last, they were cooking something that smelled terrific. I don't know what it was. Can't imagine they let them hunt in the Jungle and there's not much space in the cages for that sort of thing. Must be squirrels or rabbits or something in the Castle grounds. Maybe they let them out to hunt.'

'Let them out?' Grace said. 'They're keeping people in cages?'

'Just the Zulus. They're part of the display. Primitive Man.'

'But they're people. They're not putting the Gypsies in cages. Not aeronauts or aerialists either.'

'It's not the same thing. The Zulus are interesting to look at.'

'Thank you for the compliment,' she said with a smirk. 'Anyway, I think it's awful. They must hate it, being locked up under that hot roof.'

Everyone needs the sky. I thought about that in London, passing the Holloway Prison and Pentonville. There were locked-up people in there, I told myself, in the stench and the dark, left sending up whatever hopeless prayers they might to a shut-away sky they couldn't see. And then all the sky I left behind at home. The wide prairie sky with its storms and sun, all its fickle weathers. And space enough for everyone that ever was.

Ma saw an Indian war party once when she was young. A line of horses on a ridge against the sky, feathers, spears, guns, too, held up, she said, and fringes on their clothes. She was riding west with a family, helping with their kids, their old lady, and they'd stopped for the night out away from the other wagons. The sky was darkening, but still light along that ridge, and then there were Indians. The wife put her hand on her man's arm, and the kids went quiet. Ma remembered she didn't sleep that night, thinking about them and the family's fear, thinking about the stars shining down.

I'd seen Indians, too, but not like that. Women and kids wrapped in blankets, hunched up together beside a dirty fire, waiting for something. Some town, somewhere, I can't remember. Ma kept hold of my hand tight, pulled me along. Dust. People looking.

Then Mac Goulding's store and there was an Indian out front you had to pass to go in. Carved out of wood and polished brown and shining, but his arms were pockmarked with ugly round holes because Mac Goulding liked to snub out cigars there. He thought it was lucky, or maybe funny.

Grace kicked her toes into the ground and finished her lemonade.

'The Hancocks had a lion,' she said. 'Old and bald and he moved about slowly even when it was feeding time, but when he roared you could have heard him in Bristol.'

'That's where you're from, isn't it?' John Owen said.

A slow, hot breeze pushed along the ground and the hem of my skirt. At one end of the sky, I could see clouds building up.

'Why don't we go see something?' Grace said. 'Any spectacles today? Or bicycle races?'

'Not till evening. They want a crowd, and I'll be working then,' John Owen said. 'We could go see the afternoon side shows. Or Professor Hemming might have a show.'

Grace made a face. 'You've seen that already how many times? You told me about Professor Hemming's Astonishing Floating Lady. The Latest Sensational Mystery.'

'I'd be willing to go again. It's a pretty remarkable show.'

'Is she beautiful?' Grace asked, slyly.

'Of course,' John Owen answered, smiling. 'Every worthy act needs a beautiful lady. That's half the trick to it. But I'd sure like to work out the other half.'

'Does it have to be a trick?' I asked.

John Owen laughed. 'How else do you get a sleeping woman to float off a table?'

'Maybe she's in a trance,' Grace said. 'You know, something spiritual.'

'Well, Alma, I wouldn't have pegged you as a believer in Spiritual Truth.'

I laughed. 'I don't know that I'm that. Only I do think it's possible that our minds are stronger than we think they are. All sorts of things are possible, aren't they?'

John Owen's smile widened. 'You might be right. I couldn't say you're wrong. But I'm pretty sure Professor Hemming has a trick to his levitation.'

'We'd better head over there then and see,' Grace said, laughing. 'That way, you can work it out for yourself.'

* * *

She was an actor. She knew what she was doing. It only took a little concentration, a little deliberate motion, and there you go; everyone gives you the reaction you want, simple as that, just as her mother taught her. Because her mother was an actor, too, a London girl confident in all the big theatres. The Adelphi, the Gaiety, the Royal Drury Lane. She knew how to wear feathers. Or tights to play a boy. She'd taught her to remember that people were watching. That hardly a moment went by when you weren't watched by someone. You needed to be aware. Focused.

Her mother took her to see Nellie Farren play Shakespeare at the Gaiety and taught her about reading the audience.

'See those young men?' she asked. 'Dashing coves, aren't they? And those colours they wear? You watch the colours. They mean bumper for the actress. La Farren's colours are dark blue and light blue and white and look, all those men wearing just those colours. That means they like her, and they've come to see her smile. The theatre manager pays attention to all that, doesn't he, and then La Farren will be hired for more fancy roles and better money. Bumper. So, when she's up there on stage and looking out and she spies those stormy blue seas in the audience, she knows she's shining.'

Her mother was always teaching like this, always giving performance tips and notes, whatever the occasion. Taught her every trick she knew. How to smile and laugh, when to show hunger, how to hide.

None of this was why she'd run away, and if her mother had asked, she couldn't have explained it. Her mother would have argued that if she had this kind of education – support! – when she was starting out, she could be anywhere by now. Anywhere. That's what her mother would claim.

But she didn't know where she was going yet so what did anywhere *matter? She still needed to prove she could manage. That was part of it, though prove to who? Good question.*

She would go back again. She wasn't staying out here on the margins forever. And all this awkwardness and discomfort was just a flash in the pan like the rough train ride and the fuss about the room. All that would be behind her soon. Everything was falling into place.

10/

JOHN OWEN PAID THE ENTRANCE FOR ALL THREE OF US and, when Grace complained, he said she should be watching her pennies and anyway it wasn't that dear because it was an early show.

'Come on, kid,' he said. 'Let's find somewhere to sit. Which is better, you think? Right at the front or further back?'

The tent was crowded with young men milling about, women with children, girls in clean dresses and older men, coughing, everyone waiting and choosing their seats. John Owen explained how the show had been up since the Exhibition opened in the spring and it was always going to be popular

'Who says?' Grace asked.

'Everyone. But I read it in the newspaper. And shows twice daily and five on Saturdays means something.'

He gave her a grin, then turned to lead us to a riser at the back where an extra row of chairs had been set up. He said it was the best view in the house.

Strings of electric lightbulbs hung like modern bunting and rich, red curtains covered the back of the stage.

'Isn't this all perfectly elegant?' Grace said, her performer's voice carrying, and heads turned, but she ignored them and motioned for John Owen to take the seat on the far end so she could sit in the middle.

A tall man in a dark suit stepped through the curtains to the front of the stage and held out his hands, his face serious and handsome. Then the music started, and the electric lights all flashed on. The crowd held their breath and the music swelled. Now a dark lady came through the curtains, smiling, in a red Spanish dress, with a tight low-cut bodice and layers of ruffles below. Her eyes were painted to look smoky, her lips like roses to match the dress and her dark hair was heavy, each curlette perfectly set and no pins caught the light.

It was like Paris but wasn't because nothing here was French. There were no chandeliers, no orchestra, no jewellery on the audience, no perfume. So, what felt the same? The attention. The glamour. The illusion of opulence on stage. And the energy of being together, watching.

I looked out over the audience, the clean and grubby necks, heads, and hats and then his face across the room. Douglas. Strange how still you can be when a face surprises you, as if you knew it was always going to be there. I'd looked and there he was, looking at me. I dropped my eyes. There were so many people in this tent, so many people sitting and standing, all around. He might have been looking at any of them. No need to flush. I looked up again, back towards him. But which row was it? Back a little. There? No. He wasn't there, after all. I was seeing things. And now the music grew softer and the clapping was over and Professor Hemming already speaking.

'. . . light as a feather. Or should I say lighter? A feather floats down but this lady will rise up and float. But not without wind, a breath of sorts. No, not the wind that blows the clouds, the wind we hope will soon bring rain and end this heat, but the wind of reality, the breath of thought. Belief. The spirit wind.'

And there he was, beside me. I knew before I looked. I felt him slip past the railing and he sat down next to me, didn't say anything. John Owen leaned over to whisper hello and Grace raised her fingers to wave. I barely turned to nod at him, then looked back to the stage. The lady was turning in a slow pirouette, her hands beautifully held above her head.

'This pure creature is susceptible,' the professor said. 'We all are, of course, the spirit is democratic. But as you will see, she is more susceptible than most to the mighty winds of the spirit. You will see her unique pureness set her free from the earth's gravity. But I said we are all susceptible and some of you raised your eyebrows. Another lifting, perhaps? Or was it disbelief? I cannot have disbelief in this tent. I cannot entrust my pure lady to the spirit wind whilst there are doubters in this place. I will need to educate you first, I see that now. Teach you – show you – how to trust.'

John Owen leaned over again and whispered. 'He always says this. It's part of the act. You'll see.'

'I require a volunteer,' Hemming continued. 'A man first, I think. Men are heavy and prone to scepticism. Who will step forward?'

John Owen nudged Grace, nodding.

'Then get your hand in the air, silly,' she whispered at him, grabbing his elbow and thrusting it up. Professor Hemming noticed and pointed right at him.

'Yes. Yes, sir, I think you will do splendidly. You have been sceptical in this tent before, I believe. I have noticed you. You see, friends? It is just as they print in the newspapers. My audience returns again and again to be amazed and astounded at what they see. Even the sceptics flock to my side. And this young man has a most sceptical face, does he not? I might have hoped for a heftier volunteer, but I see you are the right man for the job. Come up here at once.'

John Owen slid past us and walked through the whispering audience. As he climbed the steps to the platform, he took off his hat then set it on the floor behind him as if he knew what was coming next.

'Now, sir, will you kindly lie down? Yes, right here on the stage would be wonderful. Well done. Splendid.'

Grace craned to get a better view, and Douglas leaned closer to me, only an inch between his arm and mine. I could feel his warmth.

'Please do not worry, any of you. At present, this young man is difficult to see but he will not remain hidden long. Levitation makes all things visible. Ah yes, and afterwards, he will stand and tell us about his experience. If he is able.' Then the professor called for more volunteers. 'But not strong men now, I think. That would make the lifting seem an easy trick. No, to raise such a sceptical man, I will need special assistance. Are there any willing girls in the audience?'

A sea of hands and Grace was put out that he didn't choose either of us, but I'd kept my arms firmly down.

'Well, I don't know if I actually wanted to be up there anyway,' Grace said. 'He looks dead, lying stretched out like that.'

And he did, lying on his back, with his hands folded over his chest. The chosen girls turned to face the audience, all nervous as cats.

'Now,' the professor said, softly, speaking to the girls. 'You must each kneel with one knee, and touch him with two fingers. Two is the number of truth. Earth and Heaven. Breath and Flesh. Two fingers only, no more will be needed. Then, together, we will gather the spirit, speaking the ancient words, and release this man from the earth, leaving all the weight of his living behind him and he will float as if his very soul was lifted.'

Grace gripped my hand and I shushed her, but reached out for the railing myself to keep steady whatever came next.

Professor Hemming began to speak in a slow and eerie voice.

'Here is a body,' he said, and the girls echoed him, their voices small and timid:

here is a body here is a body here is a body here is a body.

'Here is a body,' he said, more loudly and with strength, and their echoing voices strengthened, too.

Here is a body. Here is a body. Here is a body. Here is a body.

'Still as a tree,' he said.

Still as a tree. Still as a tree. Still as a tree. Still as a tree.

'Cold as a stone.'

Cold as a Stone. Cold as a Stone. Cold as a Stone. Cold as a Stone.

'Light as a spirit.'

LIGHT as a SPIRIT. LIGHT as a SPIRIT. LIGHT as a SPIRIT. LIGHT as a SPIRIT.

Douglas's hands were beside mine on the railing now. They looked strange, very real, very close. Working hands with strength in them. And heat. The whole tent was hot and I was red with it.

'We lift you in the Spirit!' The professor's voice rang out. 'We release you from the earth! You are free!'

And John Owen rose from the stage floor, effortlessly lifted.

The audience gasped as the girls straightened and, between them, John Owen lay flat on the air, floating. The professor raised his hands and smiled triumphantly.

'Released into the Light,' he sang. 'The spirit wind rises among us. This is a moment of peace and beauty for all.'

Douglas's hand was closer now and the space between us felt slim, only a hair's breadth. I hadn't seen him move, but he was closer so he must have. Unless I did.

I drew my hand back and folded my arms. I wasn't doing this. I wasn't making this happen.

How long did John Owen hover in the air? Impossible to say. I was watching but didn't see. Then the girls bent like grasses in the wind, slowly lowering him again to the stage. Professor Hemming placed his hands on each of the girls' heads as if blessing them in turn before he let them return to their seats, and then he helped John Owen to his feet.

'My sceptical friend, you have felt the power of the spirit. You will not doubt again, I think. What can you tell us about your experience? How did it feel?'

'I felt . . . hard to say, really,' John Owen answered, keeping his voice controlled, but uncertain. 'Not what I expected. I felt . . . unhooked.'

'Excellent. Your capacity for truth and trust has expanded.' The professor pressed his hand on John Owen's chest. 'Yes, I can feel it there, as you inhale. Capacity. Go forth and believe, my boy. You are a changed man. Go.'

John Owen looked about, then stooped to pick up his hat. The audience applauded again as he came back to join us. Grace said he looked pale, and Douglas smiled at him, reaching past me to pat his arm. I kept my arms crossed, smiled and watched the stage.

The lady walked slowly to the centre with her red dress trailing like a flag. She held her hand out and the professor passed her a wooden hoop, the kind a child might chase with a stick, and she made a show of testing its weight, tracing its rim to show us there was no trick about it. Then she held it in front of her and stepped right through, raising it up over her head. The professor gestured grandly, drawing our attention to a low table that now stood in the centre of the stage. It looked like a piece of classical sculpture, its base a wide marble pillar, solid and ornate, and its pale stone contrasting dramatically with all the red draperies on stage. Beside me, Grace sighed, as if with the beauty of it all, and when heads turned her way again, she smiled and sighed louder. Then the music grew and the professor helped the lady lie down on the table, her layered skirts trailing elegantly.

'My friends,' he boomed. 'My lovely friends, we have come to the moment. I trust you will need no instruction to keep still and silent as we attend to the moment at hand. The lady needs no assistance, no lifting girls to speed her way, but she does require your trust, your stillness so she might connect with the spirit and release herself. And myself? You wonder what I am doing here beside her, perhaps? My work is hidden, is secret. She is not my assistant; I am hers. I, too, will focus and help the spirit. I will speak no words aloud. Silence is sufficient. Now, friends, be still, be gentle, and you will see wonders.' Now, the music swelled and filled the space, an eerie sound like a glass harp, an otherworldly organ and the light changed, softened and grew red. The audience shifted in their seats, shifted and settled and waited.

I was falling. No, not that. A sudden weight on my arm. No, not weight but warmth, yes? Not a pull, no compulsion at all. Presence when I didn't expect it. My arms were still crossed securely, my right hand hidden under my left elbow and suddenly, my hand in his. Warm, there. His left hand, his arms crossed, too, and, like water into water, he held my hand. Douglas.

If I could make this last, the moment stretch and the music and the movement and our hands holding, lasting and lasting, I'd never need to tell him my name. Because here he was, holding my hand and he didn't know my name. There would be a moment when we'd need to turn and talk and what would he call me? What would I say then? Play the Gaudrons' game and be Alma or try something else? And what would Grace say or when? Any moment now she might look towards me, lean over and say something and how was I supposed to react? He held my hand. He kept holding my hand.

Everything else in the tent was a trick and this wasn't. His hand. My hand. One finger traced a small, gentle circle. There'd be another trick with the hoop at some stage, back and forth, twisted and looped around the prone lady proving she'd really left the table and lay suspended in the air. The pressure of a touch. The soft flesh at the base of his thumb. Prone was such an ugly word. Floating was better. Flying. Yes.

I'd say I was Laura. Or Laura-Alma. I'd tell him the truth or almost.

I knew the act was over when everyone started clapping. Douglas looked at me and I didn't mind. I was smiling, I felt glad and warm and happy. Something had happened and would happen again. I felt sure of that and then I clapped, too, till my palms burned like fire.

Out in the sunshine afterwards, John Owen was trying to explain things, talking about ropes, about mirrors and how he'd tried to see what actually happened but hadn't managed.

'Laying my hat down like that was part of the ploy, a minute or two extra up there and not looking where he wanted me to look, but not a thing. I'm still completely in the dark.'

'Going to take another penny then, is it?' Grace teased him.

'You and how many others, all paying to solve the puzzle. Or to look at her. That's most, I'd wager.'

'Either way, the penny's in his pocket,' John Owen said. 'Ah, well, I can't blame a performer for that. My money's spectacle money, too, though there aren't many who come to see *The Battle of Santiago* to puzzle through how we do it.'

There were so many more people out now and noise and jostling as we left the tent and a group of boys pushed past, getting between me and the others. I looked back and saw Douglas's face – happy and why had I expected anything else? I grinned at him with all those people in between and more people came up behind me and I had to spin round to keep my footing, but wasn't everything perfect? The light and the crowds and the music and the magic of it all?

Then Grace, laughing, coming up beside me, holding on to John Owen's arm. '. . . if it's really her doing it all,' she said, mid-opinion. 'Then it's a wonder her name's not on the banners, isn't it? Professor Hemming's Astonishing Floating Lady. But who is she?'

Grace reached out for my arm, drawing us all together, laughing, and there was something more in her voice, too, maybe more conversation I'd missed. She looked pointedly at John Owen, but he shrugged and suggested another lemonade. Douglas said this was an excellent idea and the four of us walked off towards the lake, and music all evening, everything ahead.

That night at Mrs Watkins' boarding house, Grace couldn't settle in bed, and squirmed in the dark. Across the road, Marina would have the bed to herself. She slept like a starfish, limbs all flung out, and sometimes tossed and turned in dreams and got a hold on my neck and held on tight. I didn't mind; she smelled sweet and didn't mind if I hugged her right back. I hoped it hadn't taken Ena long to get her settled without me.

I rolled over and put my face on a cool bit of the pillowcase. The room was quiet around us both, and badly furnished. In bed beside me, Grace was light as a child on the mattress and curled in on herself. Seventeen my foot. There was no way she was that old. Not even old enough to bleed, most likely. Light and little and pale and too young to be alone no matter how good she was at performing, so maybe it was good she'd found her way here to us. Better than being on the street or standing in a doorway somewhere, waiting to be caught and collected by the likes of the Jacqs. And even if it was only for a few days, a few nights, at least she'd found this bit of safety. She might be one of the lucky ones who could land on their feet. We might have that in common.

'Laura?'

'Yes?'

'Are you awake?'

'Yes. I thought you were sleeping already.'

'Not yet,' she said. 'I'm trying. It's not a bad bed, is it?'

'No. It's fine. Did you want something?'

'No. Only I want to ask you a question. If you don't mind.'

'Okay. Ask away.'

'Do you have a mother?'

'A mother? No. She's dead,' I said. That sounded harsh. I tried again, softer, and asked if she still did.

'No. Only sort of. I think of her as dead, but she isn't. It would make things a lot easier if she were.'

'Don't say that. A curse is a curse and comes home to roost.'

'Is that something your mother said? Sounds like someone else.'

Was it? Or Mrs Yeo? Not Madame Jacq. Ena? I tried to think back, but I couldn't find the roots of those words.

'Doesn't matter who,' I said. 'It's true. You shouldn't curse people.'

She went quiet, then rolled over and pulled the sheet up awkwardly.

'I'm not trying to be mean,' I said.

'No. Me neither. I shouldn't have said that. It's only I saw her today. At the Exhibition. At least, I think I did. There were so many people there and then she was there in all that crowd and I saw her face. She waved at me. Like she wanted my attention.'

'What did you do?'

'Nothing. She wasn't close enough. Wouldn't have heard me if I had tried to say anything.'

A mouse in the wall, moving on small feet. No other sounds in the dark.

'We should sleep now, Grace.'

'Yes. I think so, too. It's been a long day.'

* * *

I saw Ma in Paris six weeks after she'd died. Three or four times, I saw her in the crowds. And again in London. Ma on Holloway Road speaking with a man selling peacock feathers, laughing.

Then Ma buying apples in the market, her back turned towards me. Ma at a fete last year when too many people gathered round, pushing in, and we struggled with an inflating balloon in the wind. Ma's face looking up at me as the balloon lifted, growing small as the earth pulled away and all those catcalls and the things men shouted. Ma's face among the rest, looking, hearing, and every flight after that, I saw her. I didn't need anyone looking at me like that. And now no one would. Ena and I had pledged not to perform so it wasn't going to happen any more and now I could just remember Ma when I wanted to.

11/

'No hitch or glitch,' Ena said. 'This final flight needs to be perfect.'

The table was cleared after breakfast, and Ena wrote notes on a blank piece of paper. I could see dashes and question marks, the quick gasps of dark ink.

Auguste said we'd best test the balloon at midday on Saturday with a fan in the shed, away from public eyes. Ena floated the suggestion of sending word to Harry and of him sending out another balloon from London, but Auguste insisted that was unnecessary.

'And expensive. Best be better stewards of the time and two balloons we have. I'd like to have them both available if Laura is up for the task, no?'

A day to be certain about the strength of each seam. I thought I might manage that.

Auguste said he had marked the seams he worried about and solved the difficulties with the grommets, so my work was straightforward.

'Just a matter of strengthening the leaky seam, I should think, but look it all over if you like. The more eyes the better,' he said. 'Just like with perfect balloon flights.'

Ena reached over and dusted toast crumbs from his jacket, not contradicting him.

'Did you see the newspaper this morning, mon amour?' he asked. 'No article today unfortunately, but I have changed the wording of the advertisement for tomorrow's flight. I amended it to include my projected elevation. Nine thousand feet sounds grand, doesn't it?'

'Are you going that high?' Ena asked.

'I did eight on Monday. All depends on the winds, of course, but perhaps, perhaps.'

'I think nine is too high. Too much of a risk. You said Cardiff was tricky to fly from.'

'Peut-être un peu. It does seem that way. But once you've passed over the Infirmary, the country opens out and the East Moors seem a good place to land as long as you don't get caught up in the new steelworks.'

'Or the dock or the sea. We've looked at the maps, my love. I should think it's best to be cautious and stay lower.'

'Ah, there's the trick. Nine is merely a number printed in the newspaper and how many of the gathering crowd have any possible way of ascertaining if I am at nine thousand feet or fifteen thousand, for that matter? They can't possibly tell. So, it's simply an impressive number.'

'You rogue. Performer,' she said, smiling at him.

'Yes, well, perhaps. But speaking of performers, there is another notice in the newspaper that might interest you, my dear. A theatrical production next week at the Theatre Royal – rave reviews and all that – entitled *The Telephone Girl*. Just the sort of modern technological thing that might catch your eye. We might procure tickets? Interesting?'

'But we are going home on Sunday. Or is this your clever way of telling me you've signed another contract?'

'No, no, or not yet at least. More pressure, but I continue to shrug my shoulders. I know you wish to get back to London. But this production does look amusing. And the Royal is a bit of a spectacular place, I believe. Eight hundred gas lights.'

'Plenty of lights in London. And plays.'

They teased each other, watched each other, tossed words back and forth, and it was almost like Paris, that balance, those shadows falling beneath every word. But Marina played at their feet now, her wooden animals clattering on the wooden floor, and the day promised to be another hot one, filled with changing pressure.

I told them I'd go straight to the shed now, if that was all right, to get started as soon as I could. I expected Grace would take the opportunity to tag along, but Ena turned to her and said she had a little work for her at the house, if she wanted it.

'As long as it won't take too long,' she answered. 'I do want to go to the Grounds this morning to find proper work.'

Ena smiled and assured her she'd still have most of her morning to use as she liked.

'You will need the key,' Auguste said to me. 'The gardener sent word he could be found in the rose garden this morning. A very obliging man, I find him. Communicative.'

He asked if I wanted company, but Ena shook her head at that and told him he'd be needed at the house. There were things she wanted to discuss.

'Laura can cope fine,' she said. 'She knows how to deal with people.'

Walking up Queen Street, it struck me Ena was being clever, organizing us all subtly, and putting Grace to work. If the Gaudrons were paying for Mrs Watkins' room, it was sensible to get Grace helping out with Marina when I was working at the shed. Only it might be kindness, too, keeping Grace off the streets, if just for a morning. Ena would think like that.

What was that day like, walking through the city on my own towards the gardens? Just beginning, with the trams and people passing, bright shop awnings stretched over the pavements, red geraniums in window boxes, and wind on my face like something starting. But something ending, too, and I was happy for it.

I wouldn't see Douglas that morning – he'd be working somewhere altogether else, far away from the rose garden – and probably I wouldn't see him again at all. I didn't care if I saw him again. On Sunday, I'd be on the train to London. I'd look out the window and think of him. Fondly. Sweetly. Like his strawberries. His hand holding tight, that light tight snap, too, in beside my heart, like a white shirt on the laundry line and the prairie wind blowing through.

A cart stopped in front of a greengrocer's shop and two men were unloading crates of cut flowers. I could see the flowers in the crate on top because it was open and I wondered if they were all like that, all open-topped crates, all the flowers only covered and kept safe by the crate on top. I supposed it made them easier to display, although someone would still need to plump them up a little, dampen the cloths that wrapped their cut ends. I didn't like to think about those cloths. A bit bone-coloured, or maybe it was clay, and either way, they didn't seem as clean as the flowers themselves. They were something that would be used again, but the flowers, only once.

A tram rattled past, hot faces at the open windows, more people in town for the Exhibition, too far from the sea. Maybe they'd rent folding chairs and sit by the lakeside and be happy there. The lemonade stalls were going to do good business that day.

I walked on and set to picturing the roses in Mr Pettigrew's garden. White, I thought, growing tall and their blooms full and heavy, bending – and, of course, Mr Pettigrew would be pruning them, maybe standing on a ladder or maybe cutting and collecting the blossoms in a basket he'd deliver to the Marquess of Bute. Later, these blooms would float in a crystal bowl on a polished table inside the Castle, the part the Marquess lived in with his wife and children. I couldn't remember if there were children, but I could picture them, too, standing on tiptoe, peering into the bowl with its cool water and those floating fists of petals, fingers on the tabletop, eyes closed sweetly as they sniffed the fresh perfume.

At the garden, Mr Pettigrew was easy to find, standing not with clippers, but a notebook in his hands, writing while he looked at the roses. There was no one else around and he must have heard my feet on the path because he turned and smiled at me as I approached.

'The balloon girl,' he said. 'You'll be looking for the key.'

We walked to the shed together and he unlocked the door and asked if M. Gaudron would be joining me. I told him I didn't know.

'Will be a scorcher today,' he said, looking up at the pale, empty sky. 'Is that good balloon weather?'

'Can be. Depends on the wind.'

He looked and me and nodded. 'Same as roses then. Some winds dry the soil and tear the blooms. Others open them beautifully and share the fragrance. Best to know the wind in your garden before you start planting roses. Best way to be careful.'

He stood with his hand on the shed door, and the light pooled in. The balloon was laid out on the floor, pale in the shade.

'Right, then,' he said. 'I'll leave you to it. If you need anything, you can always find someone in the gardens. Plenty of muscle there if you need help.' He smiled, tipped his hat politely and left the door open.

I took off my shoes and left them by the door. I might have felt awkward about this if Mr Pettigrew had stayed, but why would he? He had work to do and so did I. And I didn't want to walk about on the balloon in dirty shoes.

The canvas felt cool under my feet. I paced up the long seam, one foot in front of another like a tightrope walker, until I found the place Auguste had marked with two upturned terracotta flowerpots. He'd have found them on a shelf here in the shed, but they looked strange against the slack balloon, like small red houses in a pale landscape. Between them, I could see the seam was stretched and slant, a case of needing a slight tuck and a new line of stronger stitches. Not a difficult job, but it would take the morning.

I settled down cross-legged in the middle of the balloon with my workbox beside me. Then needle, thread, beeswax, leather thimble, one stitch then another.

'You're afloat.'

I looked up. Douglas was standing in the doorway, grinning.

'Afloat,' he said again, like it made sense. 'You look like you're floating on the sea.'

I looked down at the balloon underneath me, then back to his face.

'I suppose I do. I'm fixing it. This seam. How are your strawberries?'

'Strawberries? Did . . . did you want some?'

'No, I didn't mean that. You were worried about them the other day. The leatherjackets.'

'I told you about that? No, I told Monsieur Gaudron, didn't I? And you were there. Wearing a different dress.'

'Yes, I think I was.'

He kept grinning at me, standing at the edge of the balloon.

'No, don't get up,' he said. 'Stay where you are. I'm merely here to get something.'

'Oh.'

'Wickerware.' He pointed up to hooks on the wall where some oblong baskets hung. 'They're my excuse. Mr Pettigrew said you were working in here, so I needed a reason to come by. The baskets are for courgettes. I need to pick them before they turn into marrows and Mr Pettigrew wants them ready for the train tonight to go north to Lord Bute.'

'I thought he lived in the Castle.'

'At times. Other times, he lives in other castles. Wealthy men move about.'

'Like courgettes.'

His smile widened, and I smiled, too.

'Well, usually, we send the vegetables off in the morning, but these are for tomorrow's luncheon. To be stuffed, I believe. An Italian idea.'

'You're showing off.'

'No. Not really. A bit. Saying too much anyway. I do when I'm nervous.'

'Are you?' I asked. 'That's nice.'

He smiled again when I said that.

'No, I mean it,' I said. 'It is nice.'

He was so far away, over there by the door, almost outside, while I sat over here in the shade and the two of us separated by the sea.

'I can't stay,' he said. 'I should get the baskets and get away to the garden again to Mr Pettigrew.'

'Yes?'

'I want to see you again, though. If you will. If you liked, that is.'

'Yes. I would like that.'

'When?'

Tomorrow was the final flight, and I told him I'd need to help in the afternoon so it would have to be earlier, before noon if he could manage.

'Here?' he asked. 'I'll come earlier. First thing.'

I nodded. I'd tell Ena something, that I needed my sewing machine. I needed to repair something. A tear in my dress.

'Then, here then,' he said. He had a nice voice. I thought it carried well across the space between us, swinging across almost like laughter.

The next day, I skipped breakfast across the street and went right to the shed. I brought a basket of my own to the shed with a petticoat on top, so it looked like I had work to do. The door was closed and locked when I arrived and that stopped me in my tracks. Up to then, I'd been rushing, though I only realized it when I got to that locked door. Stopped.

The ground all around was rough gravel and flat. Tall grass and weeds grew up by the wall, spindly where the dirt packed down. I wished I'd had a better suggestion for where to meet, somewhere less dusty. The lakeshore, maybe. The Avenue. But those were leisurely places, public, paying places for Exhibition visitors, and we weren't that today. So, what were we? Background people. Stitching seams, thinking about wickerwork and other people's strawberries. We could take what we could.

If he came as promised.

I felt impatient, the morning about me still too early and nothing quite started. Exposed might be a better word. Here I was, an eager girl waiting around for a man. Awkward, stupid, on display. I kept holding that basket as if it gave me a reason to be waiting around and started feeling awkward about the petticoat too. I should have folded it more discreetly and put something on top of it. A workbox. A book.

These thoughts, then Douglas. He walked up quickly, pulling down his sleeves as he came towards me.

'I can't stay either,' he said. 'Mr Pettigrew is in a mood and he's given me too much work and I can't say no.'

His words rushed out, almost angry till he met my eye. He stopped buttoning his cuff.

'I'm sorry,' he said, softer now. 'But you're here. You came.'

'Yes. Did you think I wouldn't? When I said.'

'I hoped. But I kept you waiting.'

He stood beside me, his shoulders squint holding tension. He was standing close, and I didn't want to move. I wanted to touch him, brush against him accidentally, reach out, touch his shoulder, his back, but we faced each other, and I didn't know how to move. I looked down. His hands. I was smiling.

'I didn't mind.' And I didn't, now, because he came. That waiting made something new. A thing given. A glass of water poured.

Sounds from somewhere else in the garden: the tonk of a bucket on the ground, and a bird overhead calling. Yesterday, there'd been gulls on the river, young ones all spotty-headed, and their parents worried the herons, scolding them to keep to the banks. The young ones were clumsy on the water, making splashy messes, and there were swans, too, peaceful throughout the fuss, gliding by like moneyed ladies. He smelled clean, this close, soap and cigarette smoke. His boots were clean, too. Rough working boots but wiped clean and polished.

'I wasn't sure you'd come,' he said. 'Convinced myself but . . .'

I looked up and he looked in my eyes, stopped and I let him. Enough. No. It wasn't enough. I wanted to touch his neck, one finger on his skin. What would he do?

'And now I can't stay.'

'I'm glad you came anyway. Even if you can't.' I sounded unbearable, just like any girl.

'Yes, I'm sorry. But I'll come tonight and watch the flight. I could see you then. I'll try.'

'I'm leaving tomorrow.'

'I know. I'll come tonight. I will.'

I told him I'd look for him and maybe we could go for a walk afterwards. Then he reached out his hand, so I reached mine out, and the space was bridged so easily. That surprised me, how easy it was. We stood together, our hands touching again, feeling all familiar and warm and we were closer and kissed, his mouth against mine and not like I thought it would be. Not pushy or difficult, but like something I wanted to do. That softness in his lips, that tenderness, everything easy right then.

'Tonight then?' he asked, quietly, and I nodded. 'So, tonight.'

He left and what to do next? No point my going back to the house as they'd all be done with breakfast by now. It felt too early for anything. I wondered if the Jungle was open yet and I might go look at the tiger. Make friends with the Zulus. They might have some breakfast to share. But here was Auguste, striding up towards the shed, hat and cane and smiling.

'Ah, yes, perfect. Wonderful to see you,' he said, looking at me with strange eyes. 'Did I promise to meet you here?'

'No, I'm just here, that's all. I wanted to use my sewing machine, but the door is locked.'

'Ah, yes, yes, of course. And you'd forgotten about the lock and weren't sure about the key. Well, it is perfect then, because here I am. Just as if you'd conjured me up. Or me, you. I'll have that open for you in just a moment and then, ah, here we are, the key. I just collected it from Pettigrew myself. Wanted a little more time with the balloons, you see. Tonight's flight must be perfect.'

He unlocked the shed and opened the door wide.

'And exercise,' Auguste said now. 'That's the other thing I want to be doing this morning. Limbering up, readying for this evening's flight. If you like, you could stretch with me. And then you can sew, and you'll be flexible and comfortable for that. A good idea, yes?'

I had no good reason why not, so I set my basket on the work-table and let Auguste lead me in a series of knee bends and reaching stretches. He seemed to have a lot of energy, vigorously lifting his arms and legs into the air in wide rotations and encouraging me to work hard, higher, better! He watched me as I tried to follow his manoeuvres and I smiled, but that felt strained. I knew that look, that way of watching, that way men have of watching girls that seems to say watch yourself, but really means watch out for me. I stopped looking at him and wanted it all to be over.

'You are not enjoying this, are you?' he asked, suddenly.

'No. Not particularly.'

'I thought not. You are not an athletic girl. I mean in the acrobatic sense. You are capable and strong, but not a performer. No?'

'No. Not particularly.' I sounded stupid. I put my arms back down at my sides.

'Perhaps that is for the best. You did make that promise. Ah well, that is that.'

He stopped with the stretches then and told me to keep an eye open for Ena who should be arriving shortly. In the meantime, he'd go find something nice to eat.

'Iced buns, perhaps. I will bring them here and we can eat them together mid-morning. Ena does like things like that. It should make her happy.'

After he was gone, the shed felt quieter. I sat down, unlocked my sewing machine and was setting about fixing my petticoat when Grace stormed in, shouting.

'Laura? Is this where you're hiding? Lovely Laura! Oh, I'm sorry, I didn't mean to scare you. You've gone all pale.'

I didn't think I had. She was very loud.

'You shouldn't shout my name like that. Madame Gaudron, remember?'

'No? Not even when we're on our own? That's a bit silly.'

'No, it isn't. She asked us to be careful.'

'Well, I'm not really one for careful.' She came up close and stood beside me like she wanted me to notice something, tilting her head, touching her pinned-up hair. Gold earrings. Goodness me.

'Did John Owen give you those, then? Or your mother? Did you find her?'

'No. And no, they're not from Johnny. He's not my sweetheart, you know.'

'No? Only I wondered.'

'No. He's not. I'm definitely not interested in a boy like him.' She reached up and gently touched her earrings, flicking them back and forth. Small gold hoops and the holes looked new, too. 'Do you like them? I got them from one of the Gypsy ladies. They have the most beautiful tent.'

'You make friends everywhere.'

'I could take you over there. You want your fortune told? She'd be happy to oblige. She even said I could bring a friend if I liked. She's wonderful. Absolutely ancient – at least a hundred – and she says she knows the secrets of the ages.'

As she spoke, she looked around and saw the ladder and before I could think to say anything, she scrambled right up to the rafter.

'You be careful up there,' I said, feeling like Ma, and Ma's look on my face, too.

'Careful, smareful. I'm an acrobat, remember? A balloonist. An aerialist.' I watched as she stood up again, balanced out her two arms and started to walk, one foot in front of the other.

'Have you found work yet?' I asked.

'No, nothing so far. I've asked all over the place, but nobody's interested. A couple said I should keep my eye on the notices in the newspaper. Apparently, a lot of the jobs for ticket girls and that kind of thing are agency-run and the employers aren't anywhere near the stalls so you can't just go up and ask. But I've got hint of a lead I can follow up tomorrow, maybe Monday. Don't you be worrying about me.'

The clock started chiming and Grace reached the end of her rafter. A knot in my belly as she pivoted on one foot and started back.

'You should get down.'

'I will in a minute. I'm not staying here anyway. Just wanted to pop in and see if anyone was about. Are you still fixing that balloon?'

I told her I finished that yesterday but didn't talk about the petticoat.

'And I'll be checking the ropes in a bit if you want to help with that.'

'You do a lot of meaningless jobs for those two.'

'It's not meaningless. Checking things well means we know they'll work properly.'

'It's not flying, though, is it? It's not in front of anyone.'

'I don't perform.'

'That's what you said. I only wondered.' That tone in her voice. If she knew how she sounded, but what difference would that make? In all likelihood, she knew perfectly well and was trying to get a reaction from me. Like the pirouettes she was turning up there on the rafter, spinning on her toes like a French dancer, trying to get me to warn her to stop.

'You're mad, you know,' I said, and she laughed.

'I know. And you? You're tied down.' She pirouetted again and grinned at me. 'I'd like to see you get away from here anytime soon. Not even on a contract and you might as well be nailed to the floor. You're not going anywhere.'

'I'm here, aren't I? Seeing the wonders of Cardiff.'

'Only because they chose that. They're making use of you. Maintenance and sewing and nursemaiding, too. Can't imagine the pay is worth that trade. But still, it's probably better than what I got with the Hancocks. They only fed me. Not even pocket money unless I asked extra nice. They'd have tied me down, too, if I let them, Alma-my-dear. Imagine that. Me, tied down!'

She threw her arms above her head, toes pointed, to turn a tidy cartwheel and landed on her feet on the rafter.

'Alors, la fille!' Auguste crowed, returned already with a bakery box in his hands. His eyes were fixed on Grace on her rafter, and maybe it was coming in from outside or the way the light reflected off the white cardboard box, but he looked delighted. Incandescent.

'Mr Goodrun!' she called out. 'Anything to eat in that box? I'm famished.' She was back at the ladder now and half-flew down it, letting her hands slide down the rails as she held out her feet and skipped most of the rungs.

'You are a mad thing, ma fille,' he said, laughing. 'Yes, I have food. Any sign of Ena, yet? Ah, there you are, ma chérie. Just at the precise moment.'

We all sat together at the worktable to eat the buns, the sugar bright pink and crackling on top.

'Weather's pretty good today,' Ena said, between bites. 'It would be nice if the wind stayed light like this for you this evening.'

'I am finding this west wind so difficult to judge,' Auguste said. 'It blows, it stops, it gusts, it doesn't bring rain. And it stays hot hot. What is this?'

'It's just the weather here, my love. Mrs Warsow says it doesn't feel strange to her. She is glad it is warm for the visitors. I just hope she gives Marina enough water today or she won't sleep well tonight.'

In the afternoon, Grace helped us get the balloon and the parachute ready and she seemed to know what she was doing. Auguste kept nodding, happy, smiling at us both and excited the way he gets before a flight, and Ena stepped back, letting Grace and me do most of the work. She coiled extra ropes and put them away in crates, and when it was time for the cart to collect the balloon, she wondered aloud, almost sleepily, if she should just go back to the house and make sure Marina was all right getting ready for bed.

'Oh no, my love. Nonsense,' Auguste said. 'You should be with us. I want you here for the flight. We should all be together. It will be the best of the Exhibition.'

'Yes?'

'Yes, yes. Everything is perfect. It will be a perfect evening.'

And it was. Everything went beautifully at the bicycle track. The crowd was full, but not pushing, and Ena stood tall on the crate, calling out instructions to the hired men. Grace and I pitched in with the hired men, two more sets of hands, helping take the strain. Auguste was incandescent, and even let Ena persuade him to wear a lifebelt, just in case.

'If it makes you happy,' he'd said, and she'd assured him it did and she'd be even happier if he wore the safety harness, too, but she wasn't going to push things. Then she kissed him on the mouth in front of all that crowd, stepped back and gave the signal to release the ropes and let the balloon rise.

'Enjoy the sunset!' she called out to him as he left the ground. 'Blow the sea a kiss for me, will you, darling?'

He laughed and waved, the crowd cheering as he kicked out his feet, dancing in thin air.

I stayed around the bicycle track long after the crowds dispersed, but no sign of Douglas. It was a chancy thing, anyway. Anyone could see I was waiting and what a stupid idea that was, with a train ticket the next day. So, he didn't come? What did that matter? Must have changed his mind and he had every right to, just like I did. None of this made sense with me leaving. We weren't thinking straight. I needed to leave it behind me like a thing that happened, a nice thing, but just a thing. I should just head back to the house only I kept standing there, waiting, looking up at the sky and watching the changing evening light as if it might tell me something.

It turned out Ena had been right to think about the lifebelt because it proved handy. The wind carried Auguste right out towards the docks and, though he managed to avoid the furnace chimneys, he splashed down in the water and needed to be rescued by boat. A soggy dip in the drink, but no catastrophe.

'The crowds love a spectacle,' he said, back at the house, dripping on the carpet, and Ena laughed and sent Grace and me across the street to Mrs Watkins to get our rest.

'We'll see you two in the morning,' she said. 'But let's not make an early breakfast. Sunday can be a slow day especially with us all done up in Cardiff now.'

12/

When I woke up, Grace wasn't in bed. The towel by the wash basin hung squint. Maybe she was waiting on the stairs, letting me wash and dress alone. I hadn't heard her shift so I must have slept well. It was nice to have the room to myself, the bed all for me. I stretched out and expected to hear her skip up the stairs any minute back from the privy, only I must have fallen asleep again because a long while passed and still no Grace.

I washed and dressed and was pinning up my hair when she came in the door out of breath.

'It's a perfect morning out there. The sky's all pearly perfect. And I saw a bicycle on the street with a girl riding it. A funny thing to see on a Sunday morning, I thought. Maybe she wanted to try it out when there weren't people around to see.'

'Hmm?' Pins between my lips. 'What were you doing out

on the street? I thought you'd gone over for breakfast without me.'

'No, I wasn't going to do that. Not on your last morning here.'

'What are you going to do when we go? Has that been sorted yet?'

She hummed a bit and fussed with her own hair in the glass. Half up, half down this morning again. It was pretty like that and she was smiling, as if at a joke of her own. Well, I wasn't going to pull it out of her. I just hoped she'd have some money in her pocket soon enough and be able to pay her own way.

The street was Sunday morning quiet and so was Mrs Warsow's house. We'd come too early, I thought, caught them before they were ready. But no, there were things on the table. Coffee cups. A bowl of strawberries, deep red in the sunlight. A nest of silver spoons.

Ena sat rigid behind the table, her face blank. Auguste stood off to the side, almost behind the door, looking at her. Neither of them moved. Grace and I stopped at the doorway, but neither of them turned or said good morning. Auguste's hands were empty. A newspaper lay folded on the tablecloth.

'You promised,' Ena said, not even glancing our way, her eyes locked on her husband. 'You said you rejected the offer and we'd be going home. And now this? What is this?' She pointed to the paper.

'I thought you liked newspapers, Ena. Material for your clipping book.'

Daggers.

'And it's yesterday's paper,' she said. 'So, already a widely advertised, known fact. You are a piece of work, Monsieur Auguste Gaudron. What were you thinking? You weren't even going to show me, were you? And when precisely were you going to let me know? Wait for when I was boarding the train then off you pop as it pulls away and you stick around this dinky town to wave at all the friendly faces? Only there's more to it than that, isn't there? You!'

'I was going to talk with you.'

'But you didn't, did you? And I found out in the newspaper after everyone else in Wales. It was on the table this morning, a headline. A headline! You must have made friends with some rather fancy newspaper men to get a headline like that.'

'I didn't need to pay for this notice.'

'No? Really. And not for the illustrations, either. Goodness me.'

Auguste turned towards us and smiled weakly, sadly. He held out his hand, ushering us in. We both looked at Ena who looked up at us.

'Yes, of course, girls. Come in. You have caught us in a moment, I'm afraid, but you will want breakfast. And Laura, this might concern you, too, if I'm reading my liar of a husband correctly.'

'Please.' Auguste breathed the word, but she didn't look at him.

'Grace, would you go through to the kitchen please and collect the toast? I believe Mrs Warsow is hiding from us this morning. Wise woman.'

'Yes, Mrs Goodrun,' Grace said, in a small voice, before slipping back through the door.

'Laura, you will want to see this.' Ena passed me the newspaper.

'Up in a Balloon, Boys'
M. Gaudron's Ascent at the Exhibition To-Night
The Intrepid Aeronaut Will Rise to a Great Height,
Take a Leap and Trust to his Parachute

Underneath, there were two illustrations. The first showed Auguste ascending over a crowd, gripping the balloon's rope with one hand, doffing his hat with the other as he waved to the cheering people below. The other illustration showed the descent and this time, a balloonist in a short A-line dress held a trapeze and smiled.

'Is this supposed to be me?' I asked.

'Just read what it says. What my liar husband paid to have printed.'

M. Gaudron has been engaged for three more ascents next week. He is to go up Monday, Wednesday, and Friday and for the alternate days the Concessionaires have secured Miss Alma Beaumont, an aeronaut of great daring and increasing reputation. Thus, there will be one of these popular balloon ascents every night.

'I thought the name was just for show,' I said. Auguste nodded his head, not meeting my eye.

'The concessionaires have been putting pressure on me and they want a lady balloonist, a parachutist. Ticket sales. They were the ones who conscripted the newspaper man and arranged for this article. They decided what to print. And paid for it. That is not from my purse. Our purse.'

'But you can't offer what you don't have. You don't have Alma, no matter what they pay to print in the paper. I'm not doing this. And Laura's also already said no.'

'Has she?' Auguste asked. 'Perhaps she might change her mind? You may have surprised her with that quick pledge of yours.'

'Auguste, you are impossible,' Ena shouted, striking the table with her palm, and the knives jumped on the tablecloth. 'Have you signed anything yet? A new contract? Is that what's meant by *secured?* You can't do that.'

'I am simply trying to keep the employers happy. And the bills paid.'

'And I am trying to keep respectable. And safe. You said you would never pressure any girl into flying against her will. You will not do this to Laura. I do have a say in this business.'

'But you agreed to call her Alma. Here in this house when Mrs Warsow pointed out the . . . social difficulty. I believe "Alma" was your suggestion.'

'Auguste, we are simply not having this conversation. You are going to the concessionaires and refusing the contract. You are not flying again. We are going home today.'

'There are ways to manage this. And it has been advertised.'

'And it's lies. Please leave the room. We are eating our breakfast.'

He left, shaken. A blank expression on his face, and it was a long time before we saw him again.

The toast Grace brought through was burnt at the edges, the coffee not hot enough now, the sunshine too bright, too bright.

She came back into the room and sat down with a solemn look on her face.

'Thank you,' Ena said, softly. 'I'm sure you heard every word of that, Grace. I must apologize for the volume.' She picked up her coffee cup, put it down again, picked up a spoon and set that aside, too. 'Is Marina in the kitchen? Laura, can you see to her and make sure she's dressed for the day? I have her things laid out ready upstairs. Then I think you two young ladies should find somewhere else to be today. The tickets can wait for tomorrow. Monsieur Gaudron and I will need some time to talk.'

Marina was sitting up at the table, playing with her animals, eating peas from a bowl, Mr Warsow beside her, shelling them. He put the pods in a dish, the peas in a saucepan and every so often he reached over with a handful to add to her small bowl. He looked up and smiled when I came in through the door, then looked back down to his work.

'I think she likes them, she does,' Mrs Warsow said, standing by the back door. 'She's being lovely. Nicest little one around here in a while and no trouble at all.' She kept her voice quiet, her eyes on Marina. I was glad enough she didn't have a question for me.

She took a glass from the shelf and poured me a glass of water without checking, then said she'd bring Marina up the stairs in a minute for me. I was to go on up ahead.

'Take a moment. She's not quite ready to be shifted yet.'

I climbed the stairs to the bedroom and sat down on the bed. Mrs Warsow must have made it when she took Marina downstairs. Ena probably didn't, though the clothes were there, laid out like she said. The quilt was white, stitched all over with tiny stitches like tiny seeds, and I lay down on my back with my feet hanging off the edge, my hands flat on that whiteness. They still felt like seeds even if you couldn't see them, and the room felt hot.

Alma and Julia had told me it was best to keep careful about children. Girls like us could get saddled with minding people's kids and what good would that do? They'd warned me only to do it if there was pay and the pay was fair, which it was with Marina.

I liked helping with her. She was solid and soft, always smelled of soap. A strong little thing, not scrappy like the kids in Paris, indifferent to how I hugged her, nuzzled my face into her neck, but sweet sometimes, too, and giggly, and she didn't kick.

Mrs Warsow brought her up and did the dressing herself. I sat there on the bed, watching. She knew what she was doing, and she gave me a smile like she understood something, and then I went down to the street to find Grace.

'We could go find the boys,' Grace suggested. 'See if Johnny's up for some fun, and pick up Douglas, too. You like Douglas, don't you? Only we can't because he's visiting his family today. Don't look at me like that. Johnny told me.'

The street wasn't empty. There were people walking together, probably on their way to chapel. They looked well brushed and solemn. Grace bounced beside me, talking on, and the sky was sharp and blue. That felt like a change of sorts from the muggy weather, and I hoped it wouldn't be so hot today. A warm wind shifted along the street with us, pushed our skirts, pulled at our hair, and Grace spun around, teasing me. 'You do like him,' she said, reading into my silence. 'Well, that's nice. I think he likes you, too. Well, he likes Alma, at least. Oh, goodness, he's going to see that newspaper notice and think it is you, isn't he? Blimey.'

'You should stop.'

'Fine, then. We'll talk about something else.' She fluttered her hands about like she was trying to catch on to something and I tried to push thoughts of Douglas away. Douglas and Auguste and Ena. I quickened my pace.

We walked past closed shops and nothing corners, everything sleeping or shut. I thought of Paris and slow bells, then home and cowboys Sunday-sleeping under trees. Grace took off her hat and swung it by the ribbon, behaving like a hooligan or a child.

'There's no one out, really,' she said, when I looked at her. 'No one will see.'

Then a little later she said, 'What I don't understand is that Auguste told me days ago they were staying. He said he and Ena had decided. So, what's this show about now? She doesn't seem very decided about it.'

'You heard what she said. We're not staying around.'

'You think she'd leave without him? Just you, her and Marina?'

'No. I don't think so. I think she'll get her way.'

'Whatever that is. Well, you'll leave that Douglas crying, then. Probably for the best. If you're not looking to settle down.' She grinned at me, then added, 'Only there's one more thing I should tell you. He wants to see you Monday. He told that to Johnny the same time as the bit about seeing family today. That was the other part of the message. You shouldn't have cut me off before I'd finished.'

We spent the day walking about, not going anywhere. All the streets up to Queen Street then past the bigger shops there and down towards the Castle, but we turned at the church to look up at its tower. It was older than anything else around, solid, square and in the wrong place because it felt wrong surrounded by new streets and shops. Its stones needed the contrast of weather, grass, open sky, not the smoke of this growing city. It needed land where it could cast a shadow. The church doors were shut, but it was probably full, with people crowded in and quiet in the pews. I was glad to be outside, away from all those strangers.

We followed a path that cut through the churchyard, fresh painted black railings separating the paving from the graves. Grace slowed her pace and I slowed, too.

'How many dead people do you think are there?' she said, slowly.

I didn't know and kept silent. I wondered how many people were in the church.

'They're all dead in there. Ha! Caught you with that one.' Her loud laugh sounded on the walls around and I told her to fix her hat.

Ahead, the market building loomed up like a train station and the gates there were closed, too, and locked. There was a smell of yesterday's fish and old vegetables, and further along, of hot oil and frying potatoes. We walked past the new public library where Athena's head looked down over us, and then followed the tram tracks past the brewery, under the train bridges and through streets and streets of terraced houses stretching to the water.

Grace saw windows with signs for *Rooms*, pointed them out, and said she hadn't tried here when she was looking first.

'Might have, though. It's closer to the train station. Could have saved myself a walk.' She looked back and forth, considering. 'Might not have worked. Might be a bit rough? I wanted people who'd recognize Mr Goodrun's name.'

She told me she'd said she was his sister to look respectable. That opened doors, she said, but later when he didn't show up, the landlady got suspicious and that kicked off the trouble. She said she should have come up with something better.

The way she told this story, I didn't think it was true. She glanced at me sideways, and her words felt rehearsed. This couldn't be the story she told Auguste and Ena the night she knocked on the door. So why tell me now? What other lie was she smoothing over? Only I didn't want to push, so I nodded and let her go on.

'I was glad to find him anyway – well, them actually, I guess – and they did help me out which was the main thing. As I knew they would.'

Another bit here that didn't fit, because why didn't she ask the Gaudrons for work, if she was in fact looking, and she already knew Auguste? Or had she and he'd said no? That would be money, of course. Ena wouldn't have agreed to spend more on wages when we were managing the work and there was no way Grace could replace one of the hired men for the launch. And if she had her eye on my job, well, she'd need to learn to sew first, wouldn't she? I imagine Auguste had promised her help down in Cornwall, and when Ena found out, she'd be right to be angry. Another thing on a growing list.

A lady balloonist in Cardiff. How was he going to get out of this one? Because, if there was a contract, he couldn't just walk away, could he? It was in the newspapers. There might be time to send word to Alma and convince her somehow. Was there money for that? If the fee was good, there might be, if Alma could be persuaded. Or Auguste might try putting the pressure on me, but I wouldn't dare. Wouldn't want to come between them because where would that leave me? Out on the streets, here with Grace, walking on and on, looking about for work and somewhere to stay.

'So, this job you've sorted,' I said. 'Is it settled then?'

'Oh, I should think so. Looks promising, at least.'

'And you got it just by asking? Or did you end up talking to an agency?'

'No, nothing like that. I had – someone helped out. A friend.'

'That's lucky.'

A friend. Another lie? Or someone at the Exhibition. But she'd say that, wouldn't she? Tell me it was Johnny or the Gypsies or whoever it was. She might mean her mother. She'd dodged mention last time I brought her up. Probably, she regretted mentioning her to me in the first place, but she might still be in town and if she was, she'd probably pull whatever strings she could for Grace to set her up with some kind of role in one of the Exhibition shows. Only, if she had, it would be something wonderful and Grace would be bragging.

We could see the water now, the ships in the bay. Huge steamers and sailing ships, masts like a forest. We walked to the edge. There were people busy everywhere, not a Sunday at all here. Everyone was working. Again, I saw brown faces, black faces, white, worn, and everything so much more like the wide world than Holloway Road. It felt like New York, all those faces, all the business everywhere. I'd like to see New York again. Find a way to get on one of these steamers and set off for something new. Start all over, all over again.

The tide was in and the ships all riding high against their moorings. Further along, the red-brick Pierhead building rose up like a cathedral, and there was a band playing with trumpets and drums, and Salvationist banners flying. I could smell coffee and something baking, cheap fat, something sweet. As we came closer, we saw a well-dressed woman standing on a raised stage. She looked taller than Ena, more serious, too, and with a rougher complexion. Grace and I stopped to hear what she was saying, balancing our weight back and forth on tired feet after all that walking.

She told a story of a poor child she'd met on the streets of Tiger Bay. His mother had gone to the workhouse last winter and died there, and the boy had told the woman an officer was sent round to catch him, but he was too quick and ran off and hid. He'd said his mother always told him to keep out of the workhouse if only he could, and now he was trying to listen to her, running away like that.

'But who was going to look after him now?' The woman paused, sad-eyed, letting her question hang in the air, then looked up to heaven as if it might provide the answer. But she must not have heard anything and neither did we, though it was impressive how tragically she shook her head. Then she spoke of the need for families to look out for each other, even in the roughest streets, and when there was no help at hand, to turn – humbly – to the Salvationists for holy help. There was always something on hand to give to upright families, she said. Always help for those in need.

Grace got bored and turned a circuit of the square, seeing what else she could see. When she came back, she had a lunch to share and told me about the ladies who gave it to her.

'Completely free, would you believe it? They said it was for anyone who felt hungry, then they didn't even ask if I was, just handed it right over. I was worried there might not be enough so I told them about you and how I'd take it to you, if that was okay. They were fine with that, really friendly actually, but they wanted to know if we were kept girls.'

She laughed at that as if it were ridiculous and I asked her what she said.

'That we keep ourselves, thank you very much.'

It sounded so easy, like that, as if we could just keep going and going.

The afternoon was hot again and humid when we walked back through town, and by the time we got to Edward Street, I wanted to wash. I didn't think Mrs Watkins would be thankful if I asked her for water, and it was almost evening, so we knocked on number 19 for Mrs Warsow.

'Oh, I am glad to see you, girls,' she said, with surprise and relief in her voice. 'Come in, come in.'

She took us through to the kitchen, where the table was ready with two settings. Mr Warsow stood by the back door, but as soon as he saw us, he nodded and slipped outside.

'We don't want to disturb your tea,' I said.

Mrs Warsow smiled. 'Those places aren't ours, lovely. We like to eat later, particularly when it's warm like this. But I was hoping you two would be coming over for something to eat. I've been waiting and wondering, you see.'

She didn't ask where we'd spent our day or if anything was resolved, only piled plates with cold ham and thick sliced bread with salted butter and poured tall glasses of water.

'The Goodruns will eat later,' she said. 'They didn't want you to wait. You eat all you like and pudding, too, and when you're ready, you can get over the street to get your feet up.'

She touched Grace's arm gently, and I wondered where Marina was. I couldn't hear anything, so it was likely she was with her parents. I hoped they were all together.

* * *

She would wear a blouse striped blue and white with a square, nautical collar, puffed sleeves and gold braid on the cuffs. Dark blue knickerbockers. Dark stockings. Black patent leather ankle boots, shiny as French jet. A wide hat with pale distracting veiling to catch the wind and the attention of the press.

He was holding that hat when she came into the room, responding to his invitation, and the rest of the costume was still hidden, folded carefully away in a plush new carpet bag. As he described it to her, he removed each piece slowly, held it up for her to see and attentively watched her reaction. He mentioned the lining – silk – the buttons – mother-of-pearl – and that everything had been made to measure so as to fit her perfectly.

'The seamstress was up all night,' he said, and she felt encouraged to smile as if that were a compliment. Perhaps it was. All of it.

So, she took the costume and asked him for privacy. He smiled, too, nodded and turned away politely, and she quickly undressed and stepped into the costume. The fabric felt thin to her fingers, inconsequential despite its sheen, and it smelled of cheap starch. There were clips and hooks in strange places and the blouse was too large for her.

'Here, let me help,' he said. 'If we tuck it in a little smoother here at your waist, a little tighter, it will be better.'

His hands at her waist now, the band tightening.

'Yes, that's better now,' he was saying. He sounded confident, convincing, and she wasn't sure, but she would be. She would need to be. She'd already agreed.

13/

Asleep, Grace was a liar. There was no way she'd been telling the truth about her age. I watched her breathing, stretched out flat on her stomach, her face flushed and relaxed against the pillow. I spoke her name, but she didn't stir. Must have been tired out from all our walking the day before. And now it was Monday morning and who knew where we'd all be sleeping that night?

I left Grace in the room and made sure I was quiet on the stairs, hoping Mrs Watkins didn't hear me. Looking in the window at number 19 across the road, I could see there was no one at the table yet, so I chose to stay outside. I didn't want to be the first one there and run the risk of either Auguste or Ena catching me on my own. I couldn't afford to come between them.

The morning was already warm, an unsettled wind sweeping up the street, and I watched as people came out from the houses to start their day. I adjusted my hat, wondering what to do next. Standing around felt awkward with nothing to do, nowhere to go, until I remembered what Grace had said. Douglas wanted to find me on Monday morning, didn't he? Well, maybe I could go looking for him.

I walked away from Edward Street towards the Castle gardens, the same way I'd walked all week, except for yesterday. It had been good to see some more of Cardiff then. I'd expected Wales to be all sheep and green grass, and this town wasn't like that at all. It was full of new buildings and new straight lines, windows and details and decoration. Colourful tiles beside all the doors and shining shops and well-dressed crowds. And money, in places; in others, none at all. Backstreets and dirty children and more crowds there, too, so many voices in so many languages, so many eyes watching.

Cardiff seemed a town people came to for work, a hub of industry and a magnet, but no promises, so not like New York. No pursuit of happiness. No rising views. It would be nice to have a hill to climb, somewhere I could get above things and look down, and a climb would be good, too. A proper leg-stretch to get some air in my lungs.

At the corner, a cart was stopped, and a boy stood by the horse with his back to me. Douglas. Maybe. I flushed and slowed my pace, not ready to see him yet. And I wasn't sure, actually, the way he stood there, one hand on the horse. What if I called and it wasn't him? I wanted to turn round and go another way. I didn't need to do this.

'Hello!' A voice behind me, and the boy turned, but it wasn't

Douglas at all. A darker boy in rougher clothing, and in his cart, crates of chickens, white feathers in the air. I saw that now and lengthened my stride.

'Hello!' That shout again, then, 'Laura!'

I turned to face Douglas coming up the street behind me.

'It is you,' he said, a little out of breath. 'I wasn't certain. Laura, yes?'

'Yes, of course.'

'Of course, of course,' he said, closer now and grinning. 'Only Grace said there was something about your name. I wasn't sure what she meant.'

I told him Laura would be fine.

'Ah, yes,' he said. Then, hurriedly, 'A simpler way forward.'

'Grace complicates things,' I said.

'She did tell you I'd be looking for you, though? That today was a good day to see you for me, if you were staying after all. She told you that?'

'Yes. Actually, I was coming down to the gardens to find you.'

'Were you? That's convenient. I mean, nice. That's nice. I'm sorry. I don't mean to be – this is getting awkward.'

'No,' I said. 'It's not. It's nice.'

He carried his body lightly today. A lean face. A clean shirt. He laughed and asked me if we could go walking together. 'I thought we might go to the Sophia Gardens over by the river? It's a nice place to walk. Unless you want to sit down somewhere.'

'No, not yet,' I said, as if I thought there would be a time when I'd be ready for that sort of thing. Sitting down together. I could hardly breathe.

Stone pillars guarded a fancy gate, and everywhere, there were flowers in full bloom, the air heavy with the hum of bees. Under our feet, the paths were made of tidy gravel, raked and clean, and ahead, there was a fountain, so we walked towards it. I was thinking about Paris right then, because of the paths and the gravel, and I thought about telling Douglas, except it might sound like I was showing off and I didn't want to do that. And I didn't want to talk about Ma, either, so I kept silent, and walked along stiffly beside him.

The fountain was substantial, the pool a wide stone circle with a tall cast-iron tower in the centre. Jets of water emerged from lion masks, and above them, a fluted bowl was topped with entwining figures dancing and dolphins leaping. It was beautiful, all that falling water catching the light, and ripples coining out, every surface catching the light, throwing diamonds everywhere.

'I bet where you're from,' Douglas said, 'a fountain like this wouldn't work. It would freeze in winter, wouldn't it?'

'I guess so. I don't think we had any fountains. I never saw them.'

'Because of the cold, I'd say. We don't get that kind of cold here mostly.'

He took off his hat, and I could see the red line on his forehead where it sat. I wanted to touch it, to smooth it away, but he saw me looking and raised his own hand then rubbed like there'd been a smudge of dirt.

'That better?'

I smiled. 'You're fine. There's nothing.'

'Thanks,' he said, putting his hat back on. 'Garden dirt gets everywhere.'

We walked round the park three times, talking about nothing, just walking close, sleeves touching, friendly, then he mentioned the fountain in the Exhibition Grounds, and I said I hadn't seen it. He told me it was at the far end of the lake, that he'd seen it when he was delivering leeks to the kitchen.

'It would be nice to see. To compare.'

He shrugged and said he had no excuse to get in the grounds today and no money to spend on an entry ticket.

'I suppose we might get in through the garden, but Mr Pettigrew has asked us not to.'

'I can get us in,' I said.

He looked at me questioning, but I nodded and linked my arm in his. And why not? Might as well see what could happen.

We crossed the river again together and walked back past the Castle, up Park Place and to the Exhibition entrance. The man at the gate looked wilted with heat, his face flushed and red.

'So, I'm working for Mr Goodrun,' I said, wearily. 'This man, too, only he's only been signed on this morning and Mr Goodrun hadn't the courtesy to introduce us, only I'm to bring him in with me. I thought I'd been hired as a seamstress, but it seems I'm a delivery courier, too, like. You'll find my name on the list but you'll need to make one up for this man. I think he's French like Mr Goodrun hisself.'

As I spoke, the man smiled sympathetically, and then he told me he'd heard the flight team was expanding, and I laughed, roughly.

'You might say so. And so, it seems. I can't fathom the Frenchman and what he's trying to get away with here. All about money, but I won't say more.' I sighed, again, and he ushered the two of us through the gates and into the Exhibition Grounds.

Once we were out of earshot, Douglas turned to me, laughing, too. 'Look at you, cool as glass.'

He followed me down the path towards the Avenue. And what did we talk about then? Bute's trees, now, and fruit trees, and electric lights. He told me how at night the Avenue's lights shone over the garden wall, and the apple trees in their bird netting looked like pale ghosts. I told him about the moonlight towers we had at home in America, tall pencil-thin towers topped with arc lights bright enough to illuminate wide city blocks. At midnight, you could read your wristwatch a quarter mile away. He said that sounded strange and I agreed. It was stranger than moonlight because it wasn't real.

We stopped beside the lake and he slipped his arms around me as if there was no question at all about what he was doing, and it wasn't a problem with people around and watching and we had all the time we wanted. He kissed my mouth again, warm and easy. The first kiss had been a surprise, but this was different. It started and kept going, like a conversation, beginning, continuing things said, starting what might come afterwards and I had things to say, too.

Later, he asked me if I really was staying. I wished he hadn't. Without that train-ticket certainty of London ahead, a layer tore away, and I felt raw. A freedom exposed I wasn't ready to look at. I told him I was here today and didn't know about tomorrow.

'You won't be part of the new act, then.'

'I'm not sure there will be a new act, actually. That's a point of contention.'

'But in the newspaper . . .'

I interrupted. 'I know what it said. Monsieur Gaudron put that in. But that's not me. I promised Ena I'm not flying like that. Mrs Gaudron.'

He didn't ask anything else, just stood with me, close.

I was aware now, more than anything, that I needed to talk to Ena. When had I seen her last? Not since yesterday morning when she told me to take Grace away from the house. I didn't know what she was thinking now. Or when we were leaving. What were we staying in Cardiff for?

At the end of the lake, a crowd was gathering near the bandstand. A concert, maybe, or some spectacle getting the crowd excited. A stout well-dressed man stood on the stage, looking towards the Exhibition buildings, and I heard the sound of a trumpet, so here comes the band. But it wasn't a band arriving, just one trumpet player marching, dressed all in white, high-stepping down the path, and the crowd drew back to make space for him. The man on the stage looked past him, smiled, held his arms wide in welcome, and it was then I saw Auguste strutting behind.

He lifted his hat and waved, smiled and laughed, clapped his hands and the crowd drew close, getting in the way, only not before I saw her in his wake, her flamboyant hat hiding her face.

Douglas must have seen Auguste, too, because he gave me a look and then, without speaking, we started walking and joined the crowd. As we came close, the stout man held up his hand for silence and the crowd stilled.

'What a delight to gather an assemblage together like this for an announcement! I would like to extend my profound thanks to all who have taken time from their morning arrangements to be present with us. Ladies, gentlemen, and pressmen, too, please incline your ears and listen to these words from our own famed aeronaut and innovator, Monsieur Auguste Eugene Gaudron!'

Applause, more trumpets and shouts from the crowd. Pressmen jostled to take central places as Auguste stepped forward, and I couldn't see Ena, but she'd be front and centre, too, her eyes fixed on his face.

I thought the crowd had it wrong, expecting some new marvel when all they were getting was an apology. I thought Ena had convinced him, crafted some careful wording, rehearsed him within an inch of his life and brought him to heel. It was almost funny, seeing him standing up there, paused before what he now had to say. I stood there, waiting with everyone else, watching his face. Douglas held my hand, and I kept my eyes on the stage, looking at Auguste.

When he started to speak, he misjudged his volume, and I couldn't hear him at all. He smiled and looked relaxed, then someone towards the back shouted for him to speak up. He waved and started again, but I still couldn't hear well. Words came in scraps, torn by the wind.

'*. . . ballooning demonstrations! Quelle surprise! . . . as I have been asked and you have asked . . . Wonderful! Wonderful! I*'. . . His accent thickened and his voice boomed, but it didn't seem he was yet at the apology stage.

Then more clapping and the front of the crowd shifted, someone coming through.

'La belle Mademoiselle Albertina!'

Auguste's voice rang out, and Grace stepped forward onto the stage. She waved with both hands, grinning, crazy. Grace on stage, and Ena wasn't there at all because that had been Grace's wide hat, and Grace wearing a weird nautical costume, stripes and puffed sleeves and all that waving like she wanted to be there.

'Mademoiselle Albertina, the celebrated parachutist, famed acrobat, aeronaut, aerialiste! Si belle et merveilleuse, n'est-ce pas?'

14/

That costume fit her well. Blue was a good colour for her, and the stripes drew the eye, filling her out. The ankle boots made her look tall and the sun made the patent leather shine like mirrors. Not bad for performing clothes, though the skirts looked uncomfortably short. I hated that, hated seeing my legs walking along, all angles and eye-catching.

She'd changed back into ordinary clothes by the time she found us. Douglas and I had left the bandstand without saying anything. Of course, he had questions, though I had no answers. I didn't know why Grace was doing this or if she had any experience or when Auguste had made this plan. I couldn't tell him what I thought because I didn't know. Now, we were standing by the baked potato stand, waiting, and here she was, running up and grabbing at my sleeve, laughing.

'Laura!' Grace bellowed. 'You saw me! I saw you there, you

two, and you saw me! Isn't it wonderful? I told you I found work. See? You didn't need to worry about me after all!'

'I didn't realize this was what you meant.'

'Well, I couldn't tell you about it because I promised. Auguste said not to breathe a word. Anyway, there was a complication about the contract and then a fuss about the name I'd use. Do you like it? Very elegant, I thought. Al-ber-teen-a!'

'Quite patriotic,' Douglas said, slowly.

'Yes, I suppose. But French, too, so mysterious. Only we found it in the newspaper, in the shipping news. It's a steamer out of Newcastle. Without the *Mademoiselle*, of course. And together, it just feels right. I plan to use it for a long time.'

I looked at her and maybe I looked worried because she pouted.

'Well, I like it anyway. And the crowd clapped, so I think they like it, too,' she said, turning to smile at Douglas. 'Nice to see the two of you together.'

'I can't stay,' he said. 'I'm afraid I need to go right after lunch. I have some weeding to do this afternoon.'

I asked if I'd see him later, and he nodded, smiling a little. He bought three potatoes, and we ate them on a bench by the canal. The skin was crisp and sprinkled with salt, the water rippled by the wind, and I sat in the middle: Douglas, then me, then Grace. He felt solid and reassuring, and she was jittery. The potato was too hot, and I burnt my tongue.

Douglas asked about her last balloon flight and she said something about Redruth and Miss Alma helping get her ready. She stopped and started, her sentences breaking up between bites of potato. She told us she was so glad it had worked out, that after everything she'd ended up with such a fantastic position.

'And did you hear Auguste is flying tonight, too? It's flights all week, all sorted. He's to fly again tonight, Wednesday then Saturday, and it'll be me tomorrow, Thursday and Friday, and he'll be using the old balloon, leaving the new one for me. He says the fabric's brighter and prettier.'

Playing on her vanity, but who could blame him? You do what works.

Then she told me Auguste had said we weren't needed tonight, that he and Ena would manage on their own with the hired men, and we had the night off.

So, another shrug from Auguste. And from Ena, silence. He could use her name all he liked. I didn't believe she'd agreed to any of this. Grace, beside me, was taut.

'Probably he wants you to be relaxed and ready for tomorrow,' Douglas said.

'I don't know,' Grace said. 'Maybe. I guess that might be it.'

Douglas left us sitting there on the bench, and I watched Grace lick the salt from her fingers. Then she started a story about a pressman who'd tracked her and Auguste down before the announcement.

'Of course, they mentioned Mademoiselle Albertina in the newspaper this morning, but somehow, he knew we were going to say something, too. Auguste only told me this morning and it was all supposed to be a great surprise. Anyway, you would have laughed to see how tall this pressman was, all arm and leg, but Auguste didn't slow his pace at all when he tried to stop us to talk, so the pressman started walking backwards to stay close as we kept going and Auguste refused to let him speak with me.'

She must have liked that, that kind of protection, attention, but it would all be part of Auguste's act. He liked to build a mystery to grow a crowd. The interviews would wait until after her first flight so any story they printed could have her victory in it, too. Better publicity, that way.

'Anyway,' she said, 'really he was being clever because he told the pressman that if he wanted to hear more, he'd need to be at the bandstand in forty minutes. That made him jump, but when he was gone, I told Auguste it couldn't possibly take me forty minutes to get to the bandstand. We were halfway there already, and I could have circled the Exhibition Grounds half a dozen times by then. And what did he say? That the forty minutes wasn't for me, but for the pressman because it might take *him* that long to spread the word around and get back and, in that time, maybe he'd even manage to find an illustrator. So, wasn't that clever? And what a crowd we had! It's so exciting.'

She kept talking on, prattling excitedly, and I only half-listened because I wasn't going to let this happen. This was a ridiculous idea. Grace didn't actually know the first thing about flying. She said she did, but she said lots of things, and why Auguste believed her, well, who knew? I'd like to tell her there were other ways to prove your salt, because that's all she was trying to do, wasn't it? Prove that she could. Make the lies turn true.

She wouldn't take it well, me telling her she wouldn't be flying.

And what would happen then? How could I make it happen? Only by doing it myself.

Of course, it's what Auguste was hoping would happen all along, one way or another. That I'd like the idea of being Alma or be tempted by the newspaper attention or even now by the new glitzy costume and the crowd. Why should this upstart newcomer get that glory? This ploy would have worked on the real Alma, this jealous switch, and who knows, maybe on Julia, too? But not me.

And why not? It was a solution, after all. Someone needed to go up and if Grace did, there was no way she'd be safe. I knew what I was doing with a balloon and could manage just fine. And a crowd could be handled, all those faces ignored, if I tried. I had to. It might as well be me.

Only what would Ena say? She'd said so much already and done so much to keep me safe. I'd lose the argument for her by switching with Grace.

Then Douglas. How could I explain this to him? There'd be too many twists in the story, and I'd look too complicated, shifty even. He wouldn't understand. There'd need to be another way.

Grace crumpled the empty paper from her potato. She'd stopped talking and was looking out across the field, where some men were tending the grass.

'Probably an afternoon show would be the wrong thing to do today,' she said. 'Too many people crammed up together. Probably be better to just go for a walk.'

We circled the Exhibition Canal and watched people standing

on bridges, looking down at the water. The fountain in the lake wasn't as nice as the one in the park, but people threw coins in anyway or maybe it was just pebbles. I couldn't tell from where I stood, and I couldn't see the ripples either. With a fountain, the water was always moving, and throwing things doesn't matter.

'We should go back to the house,' I said. 'Mrs Warsow will be waiting. She's making gypsy tart for pudding later.'

Grace nodded, but then had another idea. 'We might stay, though. Might be a good idea for me to watch another flight getting ready. Before it's my turn tomorrow.'

'You don't have to do this, you know. You can change your mind.'

'No? But why not? This is a great opportunity. This is going to be great.'

Then, she talked some more about Cornwall and working with Alma and Auguste there and what fun to be able to do it all again here in Cardiff. I didn't say much. I didn't have the right words yet, the right plan to put a stop to this. I told myself she might as well be talking right then, that it might be good for her to hear her own words out loud, her own way of describing all this. So, we stayed at the Exhibition Ground and I bought her another potato and let her talk on as we waited for the evening flight.

After seven o'clock, we joined the crowd and someone was taking home money that night, because you couldn't see for shoulders. Grace grabbed my hand, ducked down and squeezed through like a kid, pushing to the front to find us a good spot. I didn't want to get too close and craned my neck but couldn't see Ena which probably meant she couldn't see us. Grace kept looking about, too, every direction, and looking into faces like she was searching for someone.

'Grace!' A boy's voice volleyed up and caught us, his hat held waving in the air. 'Over here!'

She turned towards him and hollered. 'I see you there, John Owen! You come over here and watch with us.'

I put my hand on her arm, hoping she wouldn't shout out loud like that again, and John Owen pushed past the people to stand beside us, grinning. Up close like this, I could see how tall he was, a good head and a half taller than Grace, and she beamed up at him like a little sister.

'What are you doing in the throng? Shouldn't you be out there holding ropes or something front and centre? Or do you get a night off for good behaviour?'

'Something like that,' I said, and Grace laughed, standing on tiptoes, trying to see. The balloon was almost full now, ready to rise, and the band struck up a new tune.

'I can't see anything from here,' she said. 'Let's shift.'

'But we're here at the front. There won't be anywhere better,' I said.

She gripped my hand again and ran, pulling me through the crowd, faster the further she pushed. I held tight and hoped John Owen was following. We'd never find him again in all these people if he lost us now. I tried to look back for him, but Grace jerked my arm, her nails in my skin.

At the edge of the crowd, she let go of my hand, her face pale. Behind us, a loud cheer and the balloon must be lifting. We didn't turn to watch, only sat down together on a bench, and her eyes were wide. And anyone would think we were on the best of terms, sitting side by side like that.

'You really don't have to,' I said, quietly. 'You can still say no.'

'It's not – I'm – no.' Mis-strung words collapsing. 'No. Not – don't be silly. I can't. Won't. I'm going to – fly.'

So, what next? What could I do? Thumb on her neck? Reach out and twist her ear? Would that work with Grace?

Another cheer and shouts across the field and clapping and a rush like an engine as the crowd erupted, delighted, alight.

'Have you told John Owen?' I asked.

She nodded. 'Told him yesterday.'

'Yesterday?'

But he was there beside us before she could answer and now, she was grinning again.

'What a crowd!' she said, reaching out for both his hands. 'Do you think it will be like that tomorrow? Maybe not because there's so many today – but once I've flown, word'll spread, and they'll all come out for me. You think?'

He took her hands and, smiling, pulled her up to her feet, but she grinned and twitched her hands away to dance past him towards the refreshment stalls and we followed after, John Owen and I, like children and the piper, like ducklings in a row.

The lines for lemonade were thick with people, everyone thirsty on a hot night. John Owen suggested the performers' caravans, that there'd be something to be had there and a quieter spot.

'Because there's something I should be saying. Should have said it yesterday, but it's not too late now.'

'Worrywart,' Grace said. 'You can't talk me out of it. I have a contract.'

'Do you now?' he asked, nodding. Then he turned to me and asked if I'd been round the caravans before, and I hadn't, so he talked on about the different kinds of people, the actors and the boaters from *Santiago*, the animal minders and the stalls' folk. 'A different city back there. Makers and minders. Fair folk, too. All travellers.'

I told him about the westward wagons at home and the kind of travellers we had. I thought they'd be different from these caravan people because their travel was temporary. Only a stage, a way of getting to a new place, because wagon families were settlers, planning to farm. They'd dig themselves in and stay planted. Take their wagons apart, use the boards to roof sod houses, the hoops to grow beans and they'd teach their horses to pull ploughs in summer and sleighs in winter.

'Sounds boring to me,' John Owen said, and Grace laughed, but her voice sounded strained and shrill. 'You okay, Squirt?'

'Bit chilly. Weather must be shifting with the sun going down.'

'We'll go to my digs and get you a blanket. Wrap you up warm.'

'Th-thanks.'

She was trembling now, and John Owen caught my eye, twisting his mouth to a brave smile which I didn't understand.

When we got to the caravan, he knocked on the side but there was no answer, so he climbed the steps and opened the door. 'It's all ours. No one else about. Didn't think there would be, but always good to check around here.'

Inside, the space was close and clean, though it smelled of salt, sweat and rough cloth. He took a folded blanket from a narrow bunk, wrapped it around Grace and had her sit down on the coarse ticking.

'You sit tight and calm, okay? I'll find something else to help now.'

There was another bunk on the other wall, and I smoothed the blanket and sat down, watching as John Owen pulled a box from a shelf, took out a bottle and two glasses, and set them on a stool. Then he splashed some whisky in one and handed it over to Grace.

'Get this in you,' he said, but Grace looked fierce and refused.

'You're trying something, the two of you. I can see that.'

'Nothing of the kind. Just being hospitable. It's what I've got. Laura, would you like some?' John Owen smiled, saying my name, and there was something else Grace had let slip, all these lies and secrets coming out.

'Thank you.' I held out my hand and took the glass. John Owen turned back to Grace. 'Water better?'

'I'd rather have milk. If you have any. Best thing in the evening. And before and especially after a flight.' She was trying to look steady, but was saying too much, too fast. 'I always drink milk after a flight. Make a point of it. Calms me right down, it does. After all the exertion.'

'Well, you look like you need some calming down tonight. But I don't have any milk. I could go find some, if you like.'

'No, don't bother. Whisky'll be fine,' she said. 'Just a little, though.'

'You can share mine, if you like,' I said.

John Owen gave me a crooked smile.

A sound outside, someone up the steps, now knocking on the door.

'John, you in there?' Douglas's voice called out. 'Open up.'

I stood up and John Owen opened the door and Douglas could see me behind him. I could see him, too, his face flushed, confused.

'Ah, good, Douglas, you're needed tonight,' John Owen said.

'Laura?' he asked, still looking right at me.

'Ah, so you know, too,' John Owen said. 'She hasn't quite finished my whisky, but I'm hoping she might help me talk clear with Grace, like I told you about. And you might help, too.' He stepped back, making space for Douglas to come inside, and I sat down again, not knowing how to look at him, knowing what he'd thought.

'Laura,' he said. 'I didn't expect—'

'We ended up staying for the flight after all. And Grace wasn't feeling well, so we came here to sit a while.'

'I'm actually fine,' Grace said. 'Had a quiver, that's all. No problem at all now.'

'Well, we might as well all stay a while. Give the crowds time to clear,' John Owen said.

I agreed that sounded best and tried to look at Grace.

John Owen caught my eye. 'You don't think tomorrow's a good idea, either, Laura?'

'Mademoiselle Albertina? No. I think Grace has got caught up in something.'

'I have not,' she said, in a small voice, but defiant. 'I needed work. You know that.'

'And I know the Gaudrons are fighting and you're letting yourself be used.'

'And you're not? Miss spinster-chained-to-a-sewing-machine?'

'I'm staying on the ground.'

'I could do something about the balloon,' John Owen said. 'Steal it or . . . or burst it or something.'

He laughed, trying to change the tone, and passed Douglas the second glass.

I tried a sip of the whisky to look relaxed, but it was damned fire; a torn cough swallowed, my nose rusted through. When I opened my eyes, Grace was looking at me, smiling, perked up like she was getting ready to laugh.

'You're both just sillies,' she said. 'There's no need to worry. I know what I'm doing. I've tons of experience and Auguste knows that. And crowds love it when a girl jumps.'

'But you're nervy, girl. We aren't blind,' he said. 'So, we're worried. And your family must be worried, too. Your mam and dad?'

Then she really did laugh or made a rough, choked-out sound, anyway, and said she didn't have any.

'And even if I did, it wouldn't matter.' She looked at me fiercely, brightly, then held out her hand for the whisky glass. I gave it to her, and she took a ready sip, showing nothing.

'Have you seen your mother again?' I asked.

'Me? No, I think I made a mistake about that. Probably wasn't her at all. Somebody else.'

'Easy to do, all the crowds we're having,' Douglas said. 'I was mistaken for someone's fisherman brother yesterday. Can you imagine me, off at sea?'

Grace laughed again, shrill and too much, and Douglas watched her face. He sat beside me, his elbows on his knees, looked down into his glass, then to John Owen. The whole thing made me tired. What good would all our talk come to? All these worries and her so stubborn? I had some more whisky and so did Douglas, looking at me now, finding my eye. This was better, and then something got the better of me, and I reached out and put my hand on his knee. The hollow round of my palm fit his kneecap perfectly. He smiled, too. Owen was asking Grace if it was love, if she'd been jilted, and she laughed again and said no.

'Stage fright. Happens all the time, right Laura? Or maybe, maybe I do have something on my mind but I'm going up anyway. I just don't care, okay? Now, let's drink up the whisky and talk about other things. Who are you in love with, Johnny John Owen?'

What we needed was a failure. A burst balloon like John Owen suggested, and that would be easy enough to craft. No disaster, only a small malfunction. A few snipped stitches, to weaken the seam I'd repaired. A slow leak to disrupt the inflation. Something impossible to spot until the swelling balloon failed to rise properly and then, too late. The flight aborted, a perfect failure and Grace wouldn't fly.

John Owen was laughing, taking a drink from the bottle.

'I'm simply looking out for you, kid. I want to be helpful.'

'You know what you can do? You can come collect me when I'm down again. Get a cart and pick me up, okay? I'd rather not hike back from the Moors.'

'But Auguste will be sorting that, won't he?' I said. Douglas put his arm around me, and I leaned into him, thinking things through.

'Oh, probably,' Grace said. 'But it would be nicer if it was Johnny. And you could bring me the milk, couldn't you? That would be grand.'

And where would I be then? In that cart beside him? Waiting at the shed? Or kept at the house with Marina? I couldn't see that far, didn't want to, so I'd plan for the morning, instead. I'd come early to the shed, first thing, and my workbox already there, my scissors. When the Gaudrons arrived later, I'd be diligently working, and if I said I'd checked the balloon thoroughly, was it likely he'd bother to check again? He'd be trusting. One seam. Enough. And what good would that do? It would keep Grace on the ground, at least for Tuesday. One more day, or two, because Auguste would take the flight on Wednesday, and Mademoiselle Albertina wasn't scheduled to appear again until Thursday. By Thursday next, certainly, everything would be changed and fine and safe for good.

Douglas walked us home to Pearson Street, Grace still laughing, me and Douglas walking behind. She was looking up at the sky, the stars pricking through light cloud, and it was clear what she was thinking. I slowed my pace to speak with Douglas, but this wasn't going to work, as Grace kept spinning round, singing out at us, teasing. I had so much to say but no way to explain now. I'd need to keep it simpler.

'Tomorrow morning?' I asked, softly, under my breath. 'Can you get the shed key early? Meet me there?'

He smiled, nodded, gripped my hand. He'd understand what I meant.

15/

How long is a night? As long as darkness lasts? Or silence? Silences grow in the dark and in the spaces between our words and the things left unsaid. Unheard chasms. You can fall a long way at night, waiting for the dawn to come. Night is tidal, shifting, flooding, and in darkness, shadows swell like silence, spread, stain, and blind all who would see, saltwater sting or sand's dryness.

At last, it was almost dawn, and beside me Grace slept, her mouth open, her hands relaxed. I shifted my weight slowly, slid from the bed and into clothes, then left the room, closing the door quietly to leave her be.

Outside, the sky was grey and pale in the east, the air cool but not clean and the street felt gritty. Somewhere, burnt bread and wood smoke, and the milkman's horse wore a dusty coat. I walked quickly, thinking of scissors. I needed to know they were safe. I should have locked them away like the sewing machine, and decided that when I got back to London, I'd ask one of the factory men to make me a compartment inside the machine's case where I could keep things like scissors, hidden and secure. My good measuring tape. Needles and pins.

I felt sick and thought that meant I was scared. It was no use to think of this. It didn't matter.

Halfway to the shed, I decided I wasn't going to tell Douglas what I planned to do. It wouldn't be fair, forcing him to keep a secret like that. It wasn't lying, though, at least I didn't think it was. I'd tell him I was worried – he knew that anyway – and that I needed to inspect the balloon. And if he asked? Well, then he was clever, and we could talk about it and it wouldn't be me telling him.

He was waiting already, leaning on the door, and when he saw me, goodness and I couldn't speak. The wind brushed through the weeds and tall grasses, and he was smiling, standing there, waiting, smiling, and I walked right up to him and stopped.

I thought he might take my hand – what, and shake it? – only he put his arms right round me like he'd done by the lake, and he pulled me close and put his face in my hair. My cheek against his chest. He was solid and smelled of tobacco, his arms strong around me and everything felt familiar, everything strange.

'I'm glad you thought about this morning,' he said. 'Might be the easiest time to meet. Most days at least. Some days, there's work.'

'Yes,' I said. 'Me, too. Actually, yes, I do need to do something this morning. With the balloon, the one Grace is using today. You did bring the key?'

'You're still worried,' he said.

'I want to check the seams. It needs to be safe.'

He held my look for a moment, then opened the lock, and we stepped inside together. No questions asked.

'I'll be right here by the door if you need me,' he said. 'Don't be long.'

It was much blacker in the shed than I expected, and I moved carefully. Last night's balloon would be left on the floor, a jumble to sort out in the morning, only when my eyes started to adjust to the dim space, I could see it wasn't there. More trouble in the night? I hoped the balloon hadn't ended up in the bicycle shed again. Then I saw the shadows at the far end, the two balloons hanging from the rafters together.

It must have been tricky work hauling up the old balloon last night in the dark. It was hard enough in daylight and the second balloon was always harder than the first because the ropes could catch and both balloons start swinging. There must have been lanterns looped on nails round the walls as Auguste and the hired men worked together, pulling hard, and Ena directing the whole affair, fixing her eyes on the lines to stop them from twisting, calling out warning and encouragement, and keeping everything ordered.

I found my workbox on the table and felt inside for the small scissors which I wrapped in a scrap of cloth and tucked in my pocket. This shouldn't take long. A moment or two and then? Douglas was waiting. Only which balloon was which? In this light, they were indistinguishable.

'Can I help at all?' Douglas asked, and his voice startled me, got my heart pumping faster again, and the two balloons hung heavy in front of me like huge, dark fish, like whales. Which was old? Which new? Why was it so hard to tell? If only I could focus.

'I need the ladder,' I said. 'I don't know where it is. I need to climb up to see properly.'

'It's too dark yet,' he said. 'You won't see what you're doing.'

'It's the top I need to check. Can you find me the ladder?'

'Aye, all right.'

I could snip both balloons. Then either would give Grace an escape. Only twice the snipped stitches meant twice the chance of being caught and wasn't that dangerous, too? I reached out my hands to touch the cloth as if it might be warm or wet or breathing, as if it could speak and tell me which balloon was meant for Grace.

Douglas was moving behind me. I heard the ladder scrape against the floor, then a quiet thunk as he set its top on the rafter, adjusted the angle and settled its feet in place. 'I'll hold it here. Keep it steady for you.'

I set my foot on the first rung, and he stood close. I braced myself to step up, not falter, not quiver, and that was a strange word when you thought about it. Quiver. To feel you were carrying arrows that wanted to fly, to try to contain them all. As I stepped up, he stepped closer, fixing the weight, and something shifted above and my foot slid backwards, off the rung.

'Wait till it's lighter,' he said, softly, persuading. 'It will be easier then. There's still plenty of time.'

'Yes?'

'Oh, I think so. Patient things, balloons.' He sounded like he was smiling, waiting, and this was what I wanted, too. Time together. Because his waiting meant there was time, didn't it? There really wasn't enough light to see about a seam properly and it might be dangerous to plough on uncertain, feeling my way with my fingers. There was time enough ahead.

I let go of the ladder's railings and turned round to face him, reaching my arms around him, pulling him close. My mouth found the hollow at his throat, that tender exposed place, soft but rough too from a razor.

'You're shivering,' he said. 'Must be the dark making you cold.'

Only later – too soon – sounds on the gravel outside. Shoes and the ticking of a stick. Auguste was out early, walking. When I realized, I wanted to hide, because the shed door was unlocked, and he'd just walk right in, but Douglas said he'd step outside first. He pulled away and I did feel cold then, light without his body against me. Then I heard the hellos and the two men talked about the weather. Another hot, uncertain day, and Auguste agreed, said he hadn't slept well, which was why he was out walking and when he came past the barn, he saw it open.

'And I worried it was my fault,' Auguste said, slowly. 'That I might have left it open when I left last night. And with my balloons and equipment inside and Mr Pettigrew's property, well, you know it would never do to leave this shed open for any hooligan to get in. But you have the key, do you?'

'Yes, sir. Mr Pettigrew says the strawberries are best picked with the dew on them. I needed extra baskets. A good crop this year.'

'Of course. All the heat, to be sure.'

'Sweetens the berries though it does make it difficult to sleep. And you aren't the only one who couldn't sleep. Your seamstress came by a few minutes ago and wanted to know if she might get in, too. Something about a sewing machine.'

I stepped out of the shed and smiled at Auguste.

'Bonjour, Auguste,' I said. 'Isn't it a beautiful morning. I was glad to see the balloons both hung up already. Did last night's flight go well, then?'

'Ah, yes. Laura.' He smiled back at me as if my voice didn't sound strange at all. 'All went quite perfectly. And today will be completely splendid. I know it will. Everything is going like clockwork. You will help me inspect today's balloon when the light grows stronger, yes?'

A clench inside. No time now, all time spent.

'Yes, of course. I will help you.'

'But first, breakfast? There are plenty of hours before the flight.'

We went together and bought buns and coffee and still no Ena. Maybe she'd gone back to London on her own. Maybe Auguste had sent her away. Or she was hiding, deliberately keeping away from the Exhibition. Or from me. I didn't know what to ask.

Auguste filled the day with smiles and small jobs. He never mentioned Laura-Alma nor said anything about Mademoiselle Albertina, and we both worked hard, inspecting everything. My scissors stayed in my pocket, waiting for him to step outside, turn away for a moment, but he never did, and I couldn't risk it. If only I could will it to happen, for that seam to unpick itself. Think so hard, wish so hard, the stitches would unravel and start to fray. Did I believe I could still make things happen like that?

All morning, I returned to that question, no matter what my hands were doing. Every breath for the thinning of threads. By noon, the skies had clouded over, and rain seemed likely. So, a different kind of reprieve. That was almost a miracle. They'd never fly her in a storm.

In the afternoon, Auguste sent me again to the basket shop with another errand, and then I was to return to the house to collect Ena. Relief, though I hoped he didn't see my expression. If I was to get Ena, there was still a chance to solve all this. Ena would help. She'd never let Grace fly, not sight unseen like this, not without a practice flight, not with crowds like these. Only when I got to Edward Street, it seemed Ena had gone on already. Mrs Warsow said she'd left me a message: I wasn't needed at the flight that night. All would be managed, and I was to enjoy an evening to myself. Shrugged away again, more damned time off, and no closer to setting anything right.

I went anyway, shouldered and elbowed my way in like Grace taught me. Got right to the front and didn't care if they saw me because I needed to see everything. There was Ena, standing grinning on the crate, directing the hired men: the ropes straining, the balloon filling too well, all stitches strong, the band playing jubilantly, and everything just as expected, the way a bad dream repeats, getting worse. A wind had sprung up from the west and scattered the clouds, so the sky was dazzling blue. A clear atmosphere, the newspapers would call it. I could see that printed already.

Then, a path cleared through the crowd, that damn trumpet

boy again and Auguste marching forth leading Mademoiselle Albertina. That sailor costume, those small shoes. Over her brand-new clothes, she wore a lifebelt, a fat cork thing with straps over the shoulders and one behind the back. Auguste paused and reached for her hand, gallantly raising it to his lips and the crowd cheered as he ushered her towards the balloon, but I saw him look to Ena as the crowds erupted with shouts and applause. His bright eyes. Her set, smiling jaw.

Grace waved with both hands and skipped, jumped up and waved again. She threw her arms around Auguste and kissed him on the cheek, and he threw his hat into the air with delight. A show! A marvellous show! The crowd loved it. Then Grace took off her hat and solemnly handed it to him, approached the balloon, and took her place on the webbing seat. Did she clip on the harness? The crowd pushed around me, and it was hard to see, and John Owen rushed up then right to the front so Grace would see him, calling out something I couldn't hear.

She grinned and kicked her boots. 'Don't forget the milk!' she shouted at him.

Then I heard him call again and saw him wave his hand.

'Goodbye!' she cried back. 'Goodbye and tra-la-la!'

And up she lifted, high and fast, puckering the skin of the sky and all the bright blue emptiness drew towards her, all eyes below caught, locked, kept. A black smudge, lifting, lifting away.

FALL

Cardiff: July 21st, 1896

1/

THE BALLOON CARRIED GRACE TOO FAST AND TOO HIGH. The wind was strong, the evening light lovely, and it must have been gorgeous up there in that cleared sky. I could imagine long city shadows raking out to the East Moor, the sea itself stretched, flooding with sunset to the west. I was almost jealous, watching her rise, only it was all too fast. Five thousand feet already, then six, seven. I saw Ena raise her field glasses and Auguste stood beside her with his face pointed to the sky. Even down here, the wind was too strong.

Grace was east of the town centre already, passing the Infirmary, but she didn't let go. The crowd cheered on and on, not understanding as she flew up higher and higher – eight, nine – and now, it was hard to see her against the sky. The wind kept up. Even with a basket, a windy flight like that would be frightening, and Grace sat on the webbing, with the ropes in her hands.

'Laura!' John Owen shouted, his face split in a grin. 'You coming? I'm off to get her.'

'You want me to tell the Gaudrons?'

'No, it'll be a race. See if we can get to her first. I've got a cart ready and waiting, and it's got a quick horse, least that's what the Gypsy who lent it to me says.'

He held out his hand to me and I took it then we pulled each other through the shifting crowd and out towards the road. The horse stood, a grey, tired thing, but ready with a cart that looked light. John Owen helped me up to the seat and pulled out a basket from under a rough horse blanket.

'Can you hold this? I'd rather the milk doesn't spill.'

'She has you wrapped round her little finger.'

'Friends help out. She's a good kid.'

We headed south through the streets and there was still light in the sky, even sun catching on high-up windows as we passed, throwing out spotlights. What a show this was. That windy flight, now a race to the East Moor and, at the centre, Grace. I'd be happy to see her safe on dry land.

I'd imagined the East Moor as a wide-open place, a kind of prairie at the edge of the city – cornflower, wild grass and birds flying up – but it wasn't like that at all. I could see why Auguste said it was a tricky town to fly out of. He'd mentioned the steel-works, but that was just the start. Engine works, gas works, chemical works, distilleries, brewers and the smell of beer, wagon works and foundries and railways everywhere. The cart wheels juddered over them and I thought the whole cart would rattle to pieces.

'Hang on tight,' John Owen said. 'We can't be far, I think. East Tyndall Street, then the Lewis Road down to the Copper Works. Douglas said we'd get to the shore near there.'

There were people crowding up ahead now, all looking up or facing out to sea.

'Can you see her?' John Owen asked. 'Is she up there somewhere?'

But I only saw an empty sky and chimneys, all these buildings blocking the view. Down at the shore, so many more people, all looking, and still I couldn't see. John Owen found a place for the horse and cart, and I followed him through the crowd as best I could with that basket.

'What else do you have in here?' I asked. 'Milk can't be this heavy unless you brought the cow.'

'Very funny. Just thought she'll be hungry, too. She might not have managed to eat anything today so could need ballasting now. She was pretty nervy, wasn't she? And I haven't had anything since midday and what about you? That's why I put together a picnic. Just don't open it up till we get her, okay?'

'Too many people about anyway.'

And there were a lot of people. People and people and people. John Owen thought maybe a thousand, maybe more. Most of them stood on the flat mud of the tidal field, but some were up on the embankment and I thought that would be the best place to look from because we might get a better view.

'No sign yet?' John Owen asked the man beside us.

'Sure. Went past a bit ago. We had a fine view up here of the balloon and the woman, too.'

'Did she land, then?' I asked, and he laughed oddly and said not land, but sea.

'The parachute came down and went under, it did,' he said. 'Right under the waves. So, sea, as I said.' He seemed amused at his own joke and John Owen started to walk away down towards the shore, but the man caught my arm and talked on into my face, louder now and rough, so John Owen came back and listened, too.

'She went in, of course. As she were coming down, she worked her feet about as if she was trying to avoid the water, but she could not resist the wind, and it carried her away from land.'

'So, she landed on the water, then?' I didn't want to imagine what that was like, out at sea.

'Aye. Took time, but at length her feet touched the surface.'

'How far from the embankment?' John Owen asked.

'Oh, I should say she would be as far from it as Westgate-Street to the Custom House Bridge.'

'And she's ashore now?'

'No, I can't say I've seen her dry. The parachute stayed up five minutes or so, then the wind seemed to get under it and turn it over. Filled with water and sank.'

'And the girl?'

'Moved her body and arms about a lot. Seemed to be trying to extricate herself.'

'Swimming, then?'

'No, not that I saw.'

'What, then, did you think she was trying to do?'

'I believe she found her feet stuck in the mud, and she was

fast. Ten minutes or so at least. Then I couldn't see her any more. Must have gone under.'

'Didn't anybody attempt to rescue her?' I wanted to scream at him, scream at them all, but he kept on talking in his slow, intent way, still holding my arm, his thumb pressed painfully against the inside of my elbow.

'No,' he said now. 'There were no boats, but there were two fishermen with their nets.'

'Did they not try to help her to shore? She'll be with them now, won't she?'

'No.'

'Do you think they saw her?'

'Well, the crowd here on the bank cried out to them, but they did not seem to take any notice. They went on attending to their nets.'

I wrenched my arm from his grip and rushed down the embankment towards the flats, someone quick behind me. A woman, catching up with me, her face aflame.

'Don't listen to him. He saw no such thing. The balloon was still high up over the works when I saw it and I didn't see her fall at all.' She looked me right in the eyes as she spoke, a different kind of bruising. 'You know her? You her friend then?'

'Yes, sort of,' but I couldn't say anything else and then she kept talking.

'I think she went right over the water, she did. All the way across. A haze comes up here when the sun goes down and that's why we stopped seeing her. She'll have flown right over to Somerset. Weston-super-Mare, the like.'

She let me go, stepped back and was gone, into the crowd again. All these people milling about, and she was right because the sun was going down now. John Owen and I walked down along the flats, still trying to look, and the ground was muddy and awful, but we didn't find Grace and everyone we spoke with had a different story. Half of it didn't make sense because they didn't know about balloons and how the parachute came off and when. Some weren't even sure it was Grace at all and would swear on a Bible they'd seen the Frenchman – know him anywhere with that continental moustache – and the girl might have been a mermaid for all they knew.

There was no sign of the balloon anywhere on the mud, so we walked back along the shore, then around the Timber Yards at the end of Roath Dock, checking there, too, in case we might find the balloon. Looked in-between the ships and along the jetty, by the coal staithes and the dolphins with their posts and mooring points and John Owen kept talking, telling me all the names of these stages and structures around the dock because he knew these things and liked pointing them out as we looked. I didn't mind. Mostly, I nodded my head and just kept on looking.

The light was dark now, the sun down, and the air felt wetter like a fog was coming in. That haze drawn close. Then it wasn't long until it was too dark to look, and all the shadows looked like Grace, all the waves her voice.

Eventually, we went back to the cart. Told ourselves she probably came down somewhere altogether different and, anyway, Auguste and Ena would have found her or their hired men, and look at that, we'd just lost the race. Grace would laugh when she heard about all these silly people out here in the mud.

On the way back to the Exhibition Grounds, we ate thick-cut cheese sandwiches, but we left the milk in the bottle, waiting for Grace.

She wasn't there when we got back, and neither were the Gaudrons. It was almost ten o'clock, the clock hands still pointing up, but where was everyone? Everyone? No. The bicycle track was crowded, people waiting to welcome Grace back. They weren't interested in John Owen and me, and it took an age to get through to the launching platform where electric lights were lit and men stood around, leaning on the railings, waiting. These were the Exhibition officials, suited men with good hats, and John Owen asked where Monsieur Gaudron had gone.

'You work for him, then? You one of the hired men? He's gone off to the sea. The Rhymney River. Somewhere in the east there. He received a telegram saying the French girl had fallen in, and there was a boat after her. Monsieur Gaudron, and his wife, too, set out at once to collect her.'

'Is she all right then? Any word how Grace is?' I asked, and the official looked at me with surprise, and John Owen said what I meant was Mademoiselle Albertina.

'Can't say. A telegram's a short thing. Said she waved though, so she must be all right.'

A noise and a cheer, and a horse-drawn cab split through the crowd, stopping at the edge of the bicycle track. Auguste emerged first and the crowd erupted, louder than before. He turned and looked at them, then tried to wave, a sort of half-flap, before he turned, helped Ena from the cab and closed the door behind her. They walked quickly, crossing to the platform where we stood, and Auguste held out his hand to the official then spoke in a loud voice.

'Ah, Mr Cundall, Mr Webster, I am afraid I must disappoint you and all these people. The lady has not yet been collected.' A groan from the crowd and a few shouts as the news was passed around, but Auguste held up his hand and spoke again, smiling.

'I have been informed that Mademoiselle landed in the water near the East Mud and, before I could arrive to assist her myself, she was collected by a sailing boat from Newport which now has headed back to port. So, though she is not here, she is safe.'

Another cheer, but more subdued, and Auguste turned to speak quietly with the officials.

Ena saw us and came over, her face as concerned as Auguste's was calm.

'Is she all right?' I asked. She hugged me close, tight and fast, and I felt the scissors' weight in my pocket, still wrapped up safely in their cotton scrap. Innocent enough, weren't they? They had no story to tell.

Ena pulled back to look in my face and I shivered like a dog before a thunderstorm.

'I don't honestly know, Laura,' she said. 'She isn't here yet. I don't know anything.'

She looked at me like she'd say more if she could. Like she couldn't. I didn't know what to think.

21

WE WAITED ANOTHER HOUR, HOPING FOR MORE NEWS, but nothing happened. The sounds of men drinking. After a long while, Mr Cundall decided to close the Exhibition. There was no point in keeping the city awake like this, waiting. There was sure to be news in the morning.

'Most likely,' Auguste said, as he joined us again, 'most likely, she'll have a badly sprained ankle which renders her incapable of movement. Our poor Grace. I hope she sleeps well tonight, though it can be difficult with pain like that. If only she were closer, we could take her brandy.'

He found a cab and we travelled back to Edward Street. Ena asked if I wanted to stay with them in the rented house.

'No, I'll be fine,' I said. 'Mrs Watkins will be worried if neither of us come back. I'll want to tell her what we know.'

'It's very little, I'm afraid,' Ena said, squeezing my hand. 'Come back over as early as you like. I don't imagine I'll be sleeping much tonight.'

Auguste walked me across the street, thanking me for coming out tonight and helping, and I think he'd forgotten that I hadn't. He talked on, distracted, about the changing weather and the wind, the instructions he'd given Grace before she flew, and I said nothing. He rapped on Mrs Watkins' door with his stick, drawing himself up tall and putting on a smile. There was a light on inside and we heard Mrs Watkins' shuffling steps in the hallway. When she opened the door, Auguste introduced himself as if she might have forgotten who he was and briefly, smilingly, gave her an account of the evening.

'So, we're not expecting Miss Grace back this evening after all, but she will be here again tomorrow to be sure.'

'I hadn't even known she was a balloon girl,' Mrs Watkins said. 'This one, too? Do you do that sort of thing, Miss Alma?'

Of course, I nodded, but what could I say?

Auguste explained how tired I must be, and I really should be getting right to bed, shouldn't I? So, I did. Up all the stairs to the little dark room and the thin blanket and the two pillows and my trunk under the bed. The only thing Grace had left in the room was her brown paper packet, small and tied with string.

I put on my nightdress and lay down. My arm felt tender, the bruise on my inner elbow nursing my pulse, and the room itself was a dark bruise, dark as mud, as the hidden night sea. No sleep came. I felt restless. Angry. Got worried. Wept. Got lost in thoughts and listened for church bells. The Exhibition clock with all its excellent time was too far away. Edward Street was quiet. No trains ran that night.

In the morning, I crossed the street and found Ena sitting at the table, looking pale and fidgety. When she spoke, her voice was strained and anxious.

'Auguste has gone already, off to the Exhibition grounds,' she said. 'I can't imagine she's got back there already. Do you think she'd go straight there? Or come here and find us?'

I didn't know. I didn't know what I'd do either. Not sure I'd even come back after a flight like that. With all that wind? And a first flight, too, because I was sure Grace hadn't flown before. Poor excitable kid. It should have been different for her. Auguste should have been there to help her with the landing, gathering up the parachute and everything. It was always a tangle and she would be exhausted from holding on. It wasn't really like you imagined beforehand, especially not with a webbing seat and not even the side of the basket to hold on to. And the ground rushed up so fast and even when it caught you and you stopped moving, it felt like it hadn't, like you were still falling and falling, and more so that first time. You needed someone there to hold you and tell you that you'd made it down.

I hoped some nice family had found her and taken her home. Wrapped her up warm if she had the shakes and made her something good to eat. Poured her a cup of milk like she wanted. If I was her, I'd have stayed with them all morning, maybe stayed for ever, except that was me and not her at all. I wanted quiet.

Stillness. She wanted fuss and celebration. She'd never want to hide away because then she'd miss the crowds with their cheering and their noise.

'I don't want any breakfast at all, do you?' Ena asked, standing up before I answered. 'We'll go join him now, I think. I can't stand the thought that he might know something before we do.'

At the Exhibition Office, police had their notebooks out, weight backfooted, chins tucked in as they copied down every story they heard. Word must have got out they'd be there that morning because half of Cardiff seemed to show up, everyone wanting to tell what they'd seen.

There'd been a man waiting for us at the entrance, directed to lead us right through to the Office, and when we got to the door, Auguste came out and pulled us aside, his face grave and excited.

'The newspapers want a statement,' he said.

'But we expected that,' she answered, hushed. 'What about the police?'

'Collecting witness statements. That will take all day, I should think.'

Several pressmen stood listening to the witnesses, a young policeman trying to block their way.

Auguste pulled Ena a step away and said something in her ear. One of the pressmen called out in a gruff voice.

'You going to be talking soon, now? Don't need to talk to all these fellows; you might just speak with *The Barry Dock News.*'

'Think that's likely, mate? You don't speak French.'

'Same as Welsh, innit? Muddle an' a squint eye.'

They all laughed like it was funny, then Auguste clapped his hands.

'No statement yet,' he called out in a strong voice, and the pressmen carped, but quieted to let him say more. 'Primarily, I would like to speak with the Exhibition authorities and hear what the police say. Then, when that is complete, I will be ready to speak with you. Or some of you.'

Another laugh, and this time, Ena laughed, too, but with no light. She kept close to Auguste as he drew away to speak with Mr Cundall and the police officers who stood with him, and I was left standing on my own. A tall pressman came up beside me, somehow got past the young officer. I wondered if he was the same one who'd impressed Grace on Monday.

'You look like you'd like someone to talk to,' he said, slowly.

'I've nothing to say. I only help with the sewing.'

'Is that right? Then, can you talk about what the French woman was wearing, then? Any small detail might make a story, you know.'

What could I say? Only told him the clothes were new, then kept my mouth shut. What did I know about talking to pressmen? He should have got the hint, but he didn't and seemed to decide I might say more if I heard more, so he told me the news from Penarth. He'd been up that way that morning, trying to get a story from someone who'd had a good view.

'Folk up at the Kymin – that's the grand house that overlooks the pier – they told me they had a good view down the water and watched the girl through field glasses. Some said they saw her descend with great velocity, and others said slowly, slowly, but then they all said they saw the parachute open and head off towards the Dowlais Works by the Cardiff Docks and there the story came with conflicts again. Some told me they saw her touch down and some that it fell in the water, and one told me how the parachute stayed off the water and a haze came in. They didn't see any boats from Penarth, but I've heard others did. Schooners and steamers and small boats and somehow I need to make a story out of all these parts. Only story I can see is conflicts.'

I didn't want him to ask me, so I asked him what he'd seen himself, and he told me he hadn't been anywhere close at all. He'd been working at the newspaper offices on another story.

'When I looked out the window, she was too far away to see properly, hanging in the dangling rope like a mere speck, like a dot at the base of a note of exclamation. A good word picture that, actually. Might use it.' And he took a pencil from behind his ear and jotted the words down in his notebook, nodding as he wrote.

'I'm going down Roath way next,' he said, still looking at his page. 'They might be better placed than this scrabble here to know something that really happened. I was there at the park for Gaudron's flight on the first Monday and wrote about it, then, too – his balloonic ascent and parachutic descent. Thought that phrase turned out nicely. He came over and thousands of men, women and children showed up of a sudden like magic, panting and blowing and flushed with heat and eagerness to get a near view. Should have been plenty last night, too. Have you heard anything about tonight's flight?'

A quick, sharp question and I might have answered without thinking if I did know anything, so it was lucky I didn't. But he was right to wonder. The Exhibition authorities were going to be in a sticky place. Were they going to let Auguste go up? On the one hand, the town was full of ticket-buyers who might be fiercely disappointed. But on the other, how would it look if Grace wasn't back yet? Flight preparations needed to start in the afternoon. How callous would it be to send up another balloon if they didn't yet know what happened to the first? They couldn't exactly claim he was going looking for her, could they?

The pressman was looking at me, and I shrugged.

'Dunno,' I said, hoping I looked dumb.

He shrugged, too, and said he'd be back later if I thought of anything or learned anything new. I watched him walk away, a tall man through the crowd.

'It's so hard to know what to think,' Ena said. I hadn't seen her walk towards me, but here she was. 'So many stories don't fit together.'

'Do they know anything yet? Is someone out looking?'

'We know too many things. Everyone thinks they know exactly, but none of the stories are helping. And they're keeping Auguste in the office, asking him everything under the sun as if asking him questions is going to find her. I can't fathom these people.'

How we got through those hours, I don't know. Waiting and people pushing up, coming and going, and the clock kept chiming and Ena kept talking about the weather, the colour of the sky, the temperature in the morning, the afternoon, then already the evening, and still no Grace. We went back to Edward Street without her again, and Mrs Warsow put plates in front of us, chops and dry potatoes and peas.

After a while, Mr Warsow came in and set the evening edition of the paper on the table and left quietly again. Auguste picked it up and read the story out loud.

LADY PARACHUTIST'S FATE
The Ascent from Cardiff Exhibition
FALL INTO THE CHANNEL
Then Disappears from View
IS SHE PICKED UP?
NO TIDINGS AFTER MANY HOURS
Intense Excitement in Cardiff and South Wales.

Speculation is growing that Mdlle Albertina, the famed lady aerialist who made her first ascent from the Cardiff Exhibition on Tuesday evening, has become a victim of her own hazardous enterprise. Since her much anticipated balloon flight with parachutic descent, she has not been seen nor sent word, and many concerning and conflicting stories are now circulating widely.

Her flight began with a balloonic ascent at the appointed hour of 7:30 in the presence of a large crowd. The weather, which threatened rain, had improved beautifully with a smart breeze blowing from the West North-West, promising to afford a splendid view to the spectators. Mdlle Albertina was in fine spirits, wearing a nautical hat, striped blouse, and jaunty knickerbockers which Monsieur Gaudron attested she designed and stitched herself, and she cheerfully thanked the crowd for their attendance. Upon launch, the balloon – the aeronautical company's newest and most modern model – was carried swiftly towards the east. It has been verified that M. Gaudron instructed the lady to leave the ropes of the balloon east of the town centre towards the location of the Infirmary, to land safely on the East Moors. Many spectators have attested that she did not follow this counsel and did not essay descent until above the Channel. As she left the balloon, her parachute expanded, reports to the contrary notwithstanding. M. Gaudron has assured the press that, though fastened to the parachute for safety's sake during the descent, the aerialist was utterly and simply able to release herself whenever she desired. Mdlle Albertina's skill as a swimmer was well known and M. Gaudron believes she would not be unnerved or even frightened merely by a fall into the water.

Spectators both in the Roath and Penarth districts witnessed the lady's slow descent. The coastguardsman at Penarth, watching through his glass, attested that he saw her drop to the ocean's surface with no difficulty or struggle, and she walked the water for many minutes, but sadly, he lost sight of her after a time. Later, he witnessed the approach of a schooner near the place where she was last seen, though, at present, there has been no confirmation concerning either boat or rescue.

As the young lady's tutor, Monsieur Gaudron is naturally consumed with great anxiety and is pursuing every possible course of action to find Mdlle Albertina. He informed this paper that he has known the lady for approximately four months, having advertised for a female aerialist in the London and Paris newspapers. Mdlle Albertina first performed with M. Gaudron from a captive – that is, tethered – balloon at Dublin, and since then, descended throughout the West Country at many fairs and exhibitions. Last night's solo ascent was her sixth.

3/

Marina was glad to have me back in bed that night. She wrapped her arms around my neck and would not let me go. All night, she locked me in, her breath hot in my hair, her knees pushed into my belly like knots, like fierce clutching life that made me glad.

In the morning, I woke in a panic because suddenly she wasn't there. Then I heard her singing just outside the door and Mrs Warsow came in with water and a clean towel, the small girl following after.

'Ah, you are awake then,' she said. 'You'll be wanting me to look after Miss Marina again or will you be taking over now? I only thought she might do with a wash first thing. Had a bit of a turning night, I think, judging from that matted tangle of hair. I'm happy to see to her, if you like.'

I sat up in bed and nodded, said that was fine.

'No need to spring up, then, lovely. You stay put and I'll see to the child.'

She filled the basin with water, then pulled Marina's nightdress over her head and removed her underthings. Her dark hair curled, her skin glowed pink and dimpled. She stood on tiptoe on the rag rug, fists clenched, waiting as Mrs Warsow dipped the cloth in the water, squeezed it out, lathered it with soap and reached for the child. I watched the water dripping, bare arms held up, folded down, soft belly scrubbed round in a circle, then the narrowness at the back of the girl's neck. I watched, wishing I was small again and she'd wash me. Ma's red-rubbed hands and a rough cloth. Cold water in summer. The smell of lavender soap.

'Might suggest,' Mrs Warsow said to me as she worked, 'that you go across the street this morning. You'll want clean things for yourself from that trunk of yours, but also Miss Grace took a package over, didn't she? Probably worth collecting before someone else tries to. Landladies get all sorts of odd offers once a name's in the paper. Always best to be careful.'

She'd give me a basket, if I liked, so I could carry things easily. I'd find it down in the hallway, waiting for me, whenever I was ready. Perhaps there would be time to go over before breakfast, too, all quick and tidy.

Mrs Watkins didn't mind. She let me in and offered a cup of tea in the kitchen, but I said no. She told me Monsieur Gaudron had paid up for the week already. I went upstairs to the room and unlocked my trunk, took out a fresh dress and a clean night-dress, and put them in the basket. Grace's packet sat on the shelf, still tied up. I put it in the basket, too, then put a fresh blouse on top. If the pressmen came by, snooping, I'd rather Mrs Watkins had only boring things to say.

Marina was eating at the table with her parents when I came through the front door. I could hear the three of them talking softly, a regular kind of morning, no rush, no bother. I took the basket upstairs and put it down on the bed. Mrs Warsow had made it already, its counterpane pulled flat, an empty coat hanger lying there.

I emptied the basket and picked up my dress to hang. And there she was, Grace in the room in my clean dress. Grace right there, but she wasn't. Just my empty dress held up to keep smooth. A fabric ghost I shut away in the wardrobe.

I sat down on the bed and picked up her packet. The string was knotted too tight to untie, but who was going to stop me? I snipped it open with my scissors, and found nothing special inside, just a shabby dress. I smoothed it and my hand brushed paper. A letter in a pocket. Two letters when I pulled them out, each postmarked 'Bristol' and addressed to *Grace Parry, Hancock's Circus, Devonport.* A woman's handwriting.

It was easy enough to open them up having already cut the string and reached into that pocket. The trespass had already happened, so what were letters?

Each was headed *Crinks Tea Gardens, Conham, Bristol.* Each short. Loving, full of questions and care.

Coming downstairs with the letters in my hand, I could hear Ena's raised voice.

'. . . but a *sixth* flight? I can't believe that for this girl. And a swimmer? That's as bad as the lie about her sewing her own costume.'

Auguste's answer was quiet, and Ena interrupted him with a wordless frustrated cry. Then a pause. Something dropped – a spoon maybe – and Marina's small words started again. I could turn round. Go back up the stairs or just put the letters in my own pocket, lighter than scissors. I could wait for a better time. And when would that be? What kind of better would waiting bring?

I stepped more heavily on the stairs and then in the room, put the letters on the table next to Ena's cup.

'They're Grace's,' I told her. 'I think her mother needs to know.'

'Her mother?' Auguste asked, his voice quick. 'We have no knowledge to share, do we? We do not yet *know* which hospital she is in or even which home. We know nothing. When we have found her and spoken with her, perhaps, but then perhaps she will not want to speak with her mother.'

'Auguste,' Ena said, and she looked at him as if she had nothing else to say, only his name which hung in the air between them. She looked down at the table, picked up the first letter and took it from the envelope. She looked at it, then at me, and turned the letter over and read out the ending.

'*Keep well,* she says. *Cheerful. Happy. Safe . . .*' Her voice shuddered, but she gathered herself and kept reading. '. . . *and healthy. Be kind. Enjoy your adventure every day. Yours with motherly love, Mary Crinks.*'

Ena let the letter fall, biting her lip.

Auguste looked over her shoulder at the paper in her hands. 'The handwriting is plain, no? But the feeling sincere. It would be interesting to know when the girl last wrote to her mother.'

'These are from April when she was with the Hancocks. Maybe we should be in touch with them, too. She might not have left a forwarding address.'

'We still know nothing.'

'We know more than they do. Or they might know something, too. There's a thought. Maybe she's sent word there.'

'They will be touring somewhere. Hard to find out where in a hurry. Somewhere in the Midlands or even the North.'

'Then I'll go through to Bristol. We have a responsibility to be in touch with her mother. Imagine if it were Marina.'

The small girl looked up when she heard her name and her mother smiled at her, then turned towards me.

'And what about you, Laura?' she said, business-like again. 'Would you like to come to Bristol with me?'

'No,' Auguste said, quickly. 'She shouldn't. She should stay here. If any news comes, I want someone in the family to receive it. Ena, I will come with you.'

The family. Was that how it was then? Or just the return of an old convenient lie?

I thought they'd rush off to the train station right then, but they finished their breakfast, and asked for another pot of coffee. Marina kicked her chair legs and Ena asked me to take her out to the garden for some air, so there I was, back to playing nursemaid. Maybe they'd leave her with me when they went to find Grace's mother. If it was her mother. The name didn't say, but Parry might have been her father's name. She'd told me she didn't know him. Actually, she'd told me she didn't know either of them, that she'd been raised by her grandmother, so maybe that was Mary Crinks. *With motherly love*, whatever that meant.

Outside, the garden smelled green and wet. Marina crouched down, her short skirts brushing the paving stones, as she finger-tipped for pebbles. There'd been rain in the night after all and her clean white clothes would mark with garden damp. Something else for Mrs Warsow to fuss and scrub, but she'd like that. All around us, the leaves were wet and green – think strawberries, think Douglas.

I needed to see him, but how was that going to work? If I went to the shed after the Gaudrons left, if I looked for him in the gardens. He'd be working, but we could make plans.

Ena stayed at the table all morning with a pile of newspapers and her clippings book. No rush to the train, after all, only the quiet turn of pages, the snick of scissors. Mrs Warsow claimed Marina from me, scooping her up and taking her through to the kitchen, so I sat down at the table, too. I didn't know how to leave the house.

Ena read nothing out loud and made no comments. Sometimes, she wrote something down on a bit of notepaper. She didn't ask me to do anything, didn't seem concerned or comforted by my presence. White paper all over the table and a little breeze in through the window, but this was nothing like Paris and she was wearing grey.

It was almost noon when Mrs Warsow came into the room and touched my shoulder, tilted her head so I might follow her into the hallway.

'He's brought back your trunk from over the street. Mr Warsow, I mean. So, you can have your things here and clean and don't need to go back and forth. I've been over myself and done a once-over on the room and it's empty now. I found Miss Grace's hairbrush and her eau de cologne. All that's upstairs, if you like, tucked into that basket. Thought you might like to know.'

Mrs Watkins would be renting out the room again. Mrs Warsow didn't say it, I could tell that's what would happen next.

When I sat down at the table again, Ena asked me about the weather.

'A bright day, isn't it? Clear sky?' She said she hadn't slept well with the rain and asked if Marina had been restless, too. I told her she hadn't and seemed to sleep well. She told me I looked pale.

'I'd like to go out later,' I said. 'If you don't mind. A walk would do me good.'

'Would you like company?' She looked up at me, her eyes grey, too.

'No. I'll be fine on my own. I won't go just yet. Sometime later. I'll let you know.'

Auguste came back to the house for lunch with more newspapers under his arm, and found letters waiting for him to open. He read through them quickly, and Ena asked what they were.

'Les folles,' he said. 'Crazies, all, these English girls. Ten letters I've had this morning from girls asking if I've advertised yet and am I hiring? All wanting to be my next pupil, my next Albertina.'

'They want to replace her? You haven't – you haven't spread word that you're looking to?'

'No, no, of course not. You can't think – but no. And, yet, they ask. What offers. Madness. And one girl – there is one girl who has travelled from I-don't-know-where, but a distance I'm sure, and she stands by the entrance of the Exhibition and *waits* for Mademoiselle Albertina to return. Says she is determined to be the first to welcome her back. With tears in her eyes, she *waits.'*

Ena folded her hands and looked at him. He held her gaze and I looked away. She spoke in a quiet, steady voice.

'There will always be another girl, won't there? As long as there are crowds and balloons, there will be girls risking everything. And men who ask them to, one way or another.'

He put the letters down on the table and tidied them into a neat stack. He tidied the newspapers, too, and looked at his wristwatch. Then he said Bristol could wait until the next day. It would be better that way, he said, and though there was no news yet at the Exhibition Grounds, they must have news by tomorrow and would know where Grace was resting. He said word had been sent to the hospital in Newport and the Somerset ports. Ena's lips tightened to a thin line, a taut rope, but she didn't argue with him. In the afternoon, she'd work at the table again, filling her book with clippings, her paper with careful notes.

And I went out.

Everything outside seemed normal. People just as usual and I couldn't see how, not with the headlines in the papers, but there were no newsboys on the corners. Must be too early for the next edition and the last one sold out.

The streets were dry now and the air fresher than it had been for ages. Too bad Ena was staying inside; this air would be good for her. And open space, though the streets weren't that. Trams and carts crushing past, horses and workmen and dogs. Two cabs passed at speed and a group of women walking crowded the pavement, so I stepped back against a shopfront and looked in a window, postered with advertisements for spectacles at the Exhibition.

The Trypograph:
The Best and Cheapest Copying Apparatus.
Duplicates Many Things.
Suitable for handwriting or typewriting.
Zuccato's patent for drawing, music, etc.
Zuccato & Wolff – 15, Charthouse Street,
Holborn Viaduct, London
See it in operation!
Stand #26, Machinery Section, The Cardiff Exhibition

Duplicates Many Things, does it? Well, that would be a different way of solving problems, if only it would work. I could duplicate myself and send one version back to Edward Street, a dutiful copy to tend and attend while the real me, did what? Where? A thought.

Or maybe I'd duplicate Grace. One Grace could be wherever she was, safe or hidden or lost, and the other, the sought-for Grace, could be returned safe and sound. Would that solve everything or anything? We wouldn't have to worry about what was wanted or aimed for. Just be split and have it all. If only it worked that way.

The sun hit the shed door full force and tucked in the lock, a roll of paper. A note.

L: I can't today. Will try tomorrow. More crane fly. Fingers crossed. D.

I walked through the Exhibition Grounds, back by the lake and the fountain, and the clock struck the hour. There would be boats out on the water this afternoon looking for Grace. That's what Ena's papers said. A tugboat and several smaller boats, too, working the mouth of the Rhymney River with grappling irons and large fishhooks. They typically used hooks like those for that sort of work, scratching through the thick mud, searching. They sent out boats together to cover the area when the tide was favourable. It was a good way of looking and often yielded results. The boatmen reported they were confident they'd have news by evening, but when Auguste brought the evening newspaper to the table for Ena, there was still nothing certain. Grace might still be anywhere.

Tomorrow, Ena and Auguste would go to Bristol. They made plans in the evening in hushed voices. Neither of them knew the city or what they expected to find. Mrs Warsow bathed Marina in the kitchen, the sound of her cheerful splashing difficult in the still house.

Another night without Grace, and the room became the thread-thin sky. Voiceless birds circled. Clouds caught on the curtains, on the window's hook and catch. The thin sheets, the torn parachute, every stitch a weakened seam. Night deepened, darkened, and now the room became the sea. The bottom of the sea, the fishes' home. Sailors might look down and see me stranded on this bed, like something in a bucket, eyes still open. Marina slept beside me, but I felt the weight of the water all around us both, and, on the bottom of the room, the rough boards lay uncarpeted.

I tried not to think of shining hooks and thought instead of the fountain and the pebbles we threw in. They'd be there now, washed clean and the water would keep on falling, no matter what happened. That's how a fountain works. It rose and fell without stopping, a constant running flow. I pictured it in the sunlight, the falling water like crystal or ice, and everything shining and bright with reflections. If I could learn to make the fountain stop, its bowl would settle and hold the face of the sky.

41

THE NEWSPAPER PRINTED A SECTIONAL DIAGRAM WHICH explained what happened. **A.** was the Exhibition where the balloon started from. **B.** the point over the Infirmary where she should have dropped, according to her instructions. **C.** the point at the Docks where she would probably have landed, instead of which she mounted to **D.** and dropped into the Channel at **E.** with a dotted line showing the course of the parachute.

It was explained that 'contrary to the opinion of many people who understand nothing at all about the subject', the weather that night was 'one of the best possible for ascent and descent'.

The illustration was clear, with the town, docks, mud and Channel all marked, as well as the direction of the wind. It looked like a large pyramid, a persuasively scientific diagram. Any who saw it would be convinced.

'Why do they print this nonsense?' Ena said. 'Filling pages with hypotheses and blather!'

She blamed Auguste, telling him the words reeked of his logic.

'They come and talk to me,' he said. 'They want to know. And I want to make them happy, so I talk. I can't control what they choose to print.'

'You'd do better to be circumspect. We'll lose the thread of what you've said.'

'We'll take that newspaper with us to Bristol, I think,' he said. 'Her mother would like to see that illustrated one, perhaps, and your clipping book can wait.'

She left it on the table when they went to catch the train. They took Marina with them and left me on my own. I opened the book to look through the fragments.

Only a few days, but so many stories and pieces of stories all piled up like pebbles. So much duplication, too, as stories echoed into each other, and the same lines rippled out. *Hundreds of binoculars and telescopes watched the lady . . . aroused so much attention . . . widespread interest . . . intense and growing excitement.* It seemed every working hour since the flight, people had gone into newspaper offices to share what they knew or what they saw or what they thought they knew. And this was news. These cobbled-together bits and pieces of witness.

A nervous-looking man told how he'd been out on the Moors, reading a newspaper, when the parachute came close overhead. He couldn't see if the parachutist was a man or a woman, but it came down quite close and he ran and grabbed hold. The wind was strong, and the parachute still held the air, so the man was carried, bumping along until he was obliged to let go, and what happened then, he could not tell. It was getting too dark to see.

Mr William John, a driver of a Bute Dock pilot engine, gave testimony of his Tuesday evening whilst bringing down wagons to the Taff Vale branch. He saw the lady clearly, clinging well to the parachute and, coming down, she almost touched the top of the mast of a large ship in the dock, and passed out towards the Channel. 'Thought I'd have a good chance of seeing her,' he said, so he put on steam and ran the engine out to the eastern signal box, and all the men climbed down to watch. They saw her pass over the mud, then out to the water a mile or two from shore, and Mr John reported how the top of the parachute touched the water and floated for some few minutes. 'Like an egg,' he said, 'then gradually flattened down, became smaller and smaller, and finally sank.' Then his men called to a fisherman named Partridge, living at Rhymney, who got a boat out and before it got near the place where the men supposed that the parachute had sunk, all trace was gone.

The papers reported she had known the Gaudrons for four months. That her real name was Grace Parry and she only worked as Mademoiselle Albertina. That she spent her winters acting in pantomime performances, her summers on the flying trapeze. That a lifebelt like hers would never let a person sink.

One source said she landed at Newport.

One source said she was seen by Monkstone, walking along the road.

One source said telegrams had been sent to Clevedon, Bristol and Newport, to Sharpness, Avonmouth and Portishead, asking if any boat had put in with the lady on board.

One source said word was yet to return.

Two sources reported that the girl, having been rescued by a schooner, had been taken to the Marine Hotel in Penarth where she passed a comfortable night.

One source said she'd been found in Penzance and soon would be leaving for France.

I read every word and learned nothing. You couldn't set all this together and build anything sturdy. Everything fell apart and the strongest story didn't win. But I read them all again, looking for the scrap of truth, looking to pass the time, turning every page, the smell of paste, the dry paper between my fingers.

Douglas's note said maybe Friday, but I didn't know when to go looking, and he never came for me. I might have gone out to the gardens myself or lingered at the shed, waiting, only I didn't want to hover about, looking hungry. Where was the strength in that? So, I'd stay at the house, and think about him. I tried to make him come that way. Thought and thought for a knock on the door, except it didn't work. I couldn't witch him there, not even when I tried. Maybe it didn't work any more.

I read the clippings book again and the cut-away bits of paper Ena left behind, all that newsprint windowed through with holes. Advertisements, news of trials and rewards. *Fifty Pounds promised by the Proprietors of the Evening Express to the person who will furnish first-hand to the Editor such information as shall lead to the apprehension and conviction of the murderer of David Thomas at Fairwater on Friday July 10th, 1896.*

Eyewitness. First-hand. But eyes blink or look away and what did hands know? Only what they want to do, try to do. Touch and strength and holding on. But hands break, too. Get slapped, grabbed at, torn like hair in the loom, lose grip, shake, tremble and what then? Just another story with a missing centre, cut away with scissors as easy as paper, easy as string.

No word from Douglas all day. Meals and time and a hot afternoon. No news from Grace either.

When Ena and Auguste came back in the evening, they were spent and pale.

'Nothing?' Auguste asked before I could speak. Mrs Warsow held the door, but he looked at my face, seeing the truth of it already. 'No. I thought not. But we do. Have news, but not useful.'

Ena carried Marina's sleeping weight on her shoulder. 'She's slept since Bristol,' she said, almost whispering. 'Fell asleep as soon as we got on the train.'

'Would you like me to take her upstairs?' I asked, but Ena shook her head gently and walked past me into the front room.

'Let's go sit down,' Auguste said. 'We are all fatigued but should talk before sleep. Best share our small news quickly.'

'Hardly news at all, I'm afraid,' Ena said, keeping her voice low. 'We found Mrs Mary Crinks and told her what we could, only it seems there were things she could tell us, too. Grace isn't Grace. Her real name is Louisa. Louisa Maud Evans. Grace Parry was a cousin's name that the girl assumed. At home, she goes by Louie.'

'And Mary Crinks is her mother?' I asked. 'Or grandmother?'

'Actually, neither. Her adopted mother. Her real mother was some sort of a performing girl, and Mary Crinks a neighbour who took the child in. Gave her the security her real mother couldn't. And it turns out Grace – Louie, I mean – isn't a performer at all. She'd only been hired by the Hancocks to watch the children. And she's a child herself. Fourteen.'

'But how do we know *that* is true?' Auguste asked. 'She said she was eighteen, twenty. Something like that.'

'We did know that was a lie, though. Just look at her.'

'Well, perhaps. But I never would have guessed so young. She is so confident.'

'A performer,' Ena said. 'And eager for it. That was something he asked about, almost harshly, I thought. Mr William Crinks. Asked if we'd . . . persuaded her, talked her into tomfoolery, but his wife reminded him Louie liked play-acting already, was always trying to get attention.'

We went to bed after that, but I didn't sleep for the stories I told myself about her. Her actress mother. Her grand machinations. And I kept thinking, too, of scissors and paper and seams and wishing I'd managed to stop her. I should have tried harder, tried something else. She should have sent word by now if she could. Word from Penarth or Penzance or half-way to Paris. She might have crossed the Channel, if she held her nerve. Washed up on a Brittany beach like a mermaid or an angel tumbled down. She'd definitely send word about that if she could. And if she couldn't? Another story starting and I was afraid of that one. I thought about the safety harness clips, the way the parachute worked, the way ropes swell in water. The night grew fat and heavy around me and I held on to what I could, which wasn't much. Thoughts of seams, snipped lengths of thought.

And then word came.

A knock on the door in the middle of the night and, for a moment, I thought I'd done it. The best trick of all. I'd wished and folded time and here I was, back in bed with Marina sleeping and everything happening as it had before. Auguste and Ena were coming in late, arguing in hushed tones, and I'd stay in bed. I was glad to hear both their voices and know they were home safe and Grace downstairs, too, in the hallway now with her pale face and those eyes, asking for a place to stay the night. The first time all over again.

Another knock.

A man's loud voice.

Feet in the hall and Mr Warsow's voice, then Ena's and a shout from Auguste, a cry. I heard the door close, and voices continuing. I stayed in bed, closed my eyes, tried to believe what I knew wasn't true, and Gaudron cried out again.

Grace was found.

51

SHE WAS FOUND BY A GIRL HER OWN AGE, MARY Waggett, who lived in Nash between the lighthouses. They were built to warn ships of the strong currents and mud, there where the Channel met the Severn and the Usk. It was a place where things washed in, and Mary was out, looking for driftwood to burn at home. She thought she'd found a drowned sailor, lying wave-washed on the flats as the tide went out. That blue, those stripes, and a cork vest. The kind of person who would be lost at sea. But the boots were so small, and then she saw small hands, pale and open. She went straight home to tell her mother.

Who can say if she ran or walked? The newspapers would tell the story as they chose, just like every other story. Still, we knew she went home and moved the story along. Her mother sent word to the police and they came out to find Mary who led them through the dark back to the shore to the place where the drowned girl had been.

I hid from this news until morning, when Ena came into the bedroom and sat on the bed with thumbprints under her eyes. She told me about the man who'd come in the night, knocked on the door, and woken Mr Warsow who woke the rest.

'Maybe you didn't hear him because of the rain,' she said. 'I didn't sleep at all, wound up by it. Or maybe, somehow, I knew news was coming and I was keeping awake for that. He made such a noise at the door.'

She reached out and stroked Marina's hair, the child still sleeping beside me.

'Poppet,' she said. 'Mummy's here.'

But Marina stayed sleeping, her breathing even and sweet.

Ena told me Auguste would go to Nash to identify the body. He'd already left the house for the Newport train.

'The police want to know for sure who it is, but there doesn't seem to be much space for doubt.'

'Is he going to tell them?'

'Of course. He can't rightly deny now.'

'I meant about Grace not being Grace.'

'Oh, I don't know. Probably. Yes, I hope so. We need to come clean about everything we know. There will be an inquest quite soon.'

Then Marina opened her eyes and was awake. Funny how kids can do that. Fall out of sleep as easy as that. She looked at her mother, smiled and sat up, then started bouncing. Ena shushed her and held out her arms, but the little girl laughed out loud and kept bouncing.

'You rascal. You're going to fall off the bed if you keep doing that.' And she caught the child and gathered her up, burying her nose in the soft tumbling hair. Under the bedsheets, I straightened my nightdress and pulled it down over my knees, then got up to start the day.

All morning, it kept raining, and the wind was loud. Mrs Warsow took Marina into the kitchen and Ena sat at the table again with her clippings book. Scissors and paste, pencil on notepaper, passing the time.

'It's for the inquest,' she told me. 'They'll want to know who's to blame. I'm trying to keep the story straight.'

Auguste had given interviews every day and said so many things that didn't hang together. Ena said she wanted to gather them up and see what she could do to limit the damage. Not that she didn't care about the girl, of course, but she needed to know what Auguste was claiming if this was going to go well.

'The girl,' I said.

'Yes. Grace. Louie. Louisa Maud. Do you think the Evans means she has Welsh roots?'

I wanted to go outside. Walk away right then. Get some air. I told Ena and she said it wasn't wise.

'There are pressmen outside. One knocked on the door a little while ago, and Mrs Warsow sent him packing, but there's another one – or maybe the same one – standing across the street. You'll see him out the corner of that window. He'll hound you if you emerge. I wouldn't if I were you.'

I tugged back the curtain and it was dirty weather out there all right, and there he was leaning on a lamp post across the street, looking at the house through the rain. I looked the other way, and coming up the street, I saw the tall pressman striding.

'Someone must have passed the address around,' Ena said. 'I wish they wouldn't bother us. They seem to be able to find all manner of people ready to talk without hassling us. They've even spoken with Alma. Actual Alma in London. And your friend John, too. Here.'

She passed me a newspaper page, an interview from John Owen. Poor Johnny. He'd told them about her tra-la-la and the milk and how she'd been trembly the night before the flight. He also confessed that he'd promised to burst the balloon if she was still nervy the day of the flight and that she'd laughed at him. All true, more or less, but it looked strange put down on paper, like the way a story works, one thing leading to another like stepping-stones in the dark. Everything looked inevitable. Was that because we knew the ending? Only what happened at the caravan Monday evening hadn't set anything in stone. I still might have managed with the scissors in the shed, and then none of the rest would have happened. Only a different ending, after all and what would the trembling mean then? Something altogether else, wouldn't it?

Ena sighed. 'Some of these stories are absolutely florid,' she said. 'All exaggeration and plenty of probably-s and a purple writer who calls himself Morien who dresses all the events up as poetry and embellishes everything to the skies. Preserve us from pressmen.'

A knock at the door and I jumped, or rather both of us did, only it wasn't the front door, and just Mr Warsow coming in.

'More newspapers for you, Mrs Goodrun.' He set down a bundle on the table. 'Latest editions. I walked a ways but brought back several. They're selling fast today. Everyone wants the story in their hands. Sad stuff.'

'Thank you. It was kind of you to venture out in that.'

'Needed to get one for the missus, too. Not every day she's recorded like this.'

'Did they get to her, too? Oh dear,' Ena said.

'And I've a letter for Miss Laura, too.' He held out an envelope to me. 'Laura-Alma, is it?'

'Thank you,' I said and took the envelope quickly. It had been used before, or at least the paper had. Creased already, then cut and folded to contain what? A note of some kind. I took it and thanked him, then turned away and opened it up.

An empty seed packet, that's what it was. Green beans. I saw the printing when I pulled the paper out. Clever hands to save the packet like that and reshape it into something useful, and I turned the notepaper over to see what it had been before, but that was blank on both sides, save for the writing.

Dear Laura,

Don't come looking for me and don't go to the shed. The police have it guarded and won't open it up till after the inquest. But come find me tomorrow? You could go out early as if to Chapel and walk west past the Castle. I'll meet you up the road. D.

Soup for lunch. Lamb with barley and carrots. Circles of fat on the surface. Good bread, too.

Auguste came back from Nash in the late afternoon. He came in through the kitchen door with his trouser knee torn, so he must have climbed the garden wall to get in. Ena didn't ask.

Mrs Warsow brought a tray through to the front room and set it at one end of the table.

'Not coffee. What you need's tea. You're jittery enough as it is.' She poured it out without being asked, added sugar, and passed round the cups. 'I'm back in the kitchen now if you need me. Any help at all.'

Auguste nodded, looking down, and Mrs Warsow closed the door behind her.

He told us the train carriage was empty and smelled of fresh paint. He'd like to have slept, but the smell was sharp, and Newport wasn't far away. He went to the police station and the pressman was there and offered to drive him to Nash, which was convenient. The weather was better then; the rain cleared away and the afternoon felt serene when they climbed into the cab. But the horse was slow on the wet road and Auguste said the wheels sounded much louder than they should, noisy and scraping.

'You were tired, my dear,' Ena said. 'We all are today.'

On the way to Nash, the pressman was kind or at least quiet. He asked a few questions, but did not press hard, and mainly he sat quietly and let Auguste do the same.

'We passed by powder houses down that way. The pressman pointed them out. Solid stone and windowless, buttressed, too, for strength. They keep gunpowder there,' he said, and I tried to picture that, but didn't know what gunpowder looked like. Dusty and black like snuff, maybe. The opposite of chalk.

'The pressman told me the girl's father works there,' Auguste continued. 'The girl that found her, that is. Mary. She lives just near the powder houses.'

He said Nash was a church and an inn, a few houses and trees. Not much of a place, and the land around was flat, cut through with ditches, and the trees were leafy and the church, a square stone tower with a tall sharp steeple, was the highest point around.

'The pressman told me they'd laid her in the belfry, and I thought that meant the tower. They would have had to carry her up so many stairs and I don't know why they did that. A safe place, perhaps. But no, I had misunderstood. The pressman explained she was in the space under the church tower where the bell ropes hung down. But first we went to the inn.'

The landlady met them, Mrs Sarah Jones. Auguste said he was to identify the body, and she brought out things to show him. The cork life belt, cut in two, heavy with water, which Auguste held in his hands, and he wanted to show them both how well it was made, the strength of the ribs and the solidity of the material, but what good would convincing them do? Mrs Jones had such a sad smile and handed him one boot and it too was heavy with seawater. Then a villager went to find the church key and there was a wait before the door was unlocked and then it was, and they had to go in. Mrs Jones held a candle out in front, making shadows of her skirts on the floor.

Auguste hesitated. 'I don't want to tell you any more,' he said. 'But I can't stop seeing what I saw.'

'Tell us,' Ena said. 'We should hear this.'

The girl lay on a bier against the wall. She looked swollen, a little at least, but calm, and the candlelight showed her face clearly enough and the sea-scoured clothing she wore. Mrs Jones said she'd tended to her the night before, loosened her bodice to lay her down properly, and tied her jaw with a handkerchief as was proper for the dead. Her mouth wasn't quite closed though, and her teeth were visible. Small and perfect, and Auguste said he hadn't noticed her teeth before then, so small and white.

'Was she hurt?' I asked. 'Could you see how she was hurt?'

He paused before answering and, for a moment, I expected he wouldn't, but I was wrong.

'Yes. Mrs Jones had told me to prepare myself for that. She had done her Christian best to honour the dead, setting the face with prayer and folding the arms, but she told me you cannot pray away mortal injuries. Les blessures. Mon Dieu.'

Then he told us about the large wound on her head, the way her scalp was torn, the red flesh exposed. The long blue mark on her neck. The torn skin on her arm, too, scraped off, and the flesh underneath was the colour of rust.

The pressman took notes on all this for the paper, writing quickly in the dark space, then turning to look right in Auguste's face.

'He asked a question, and I asked him to speak it again because how can you hear clearly in a place like that? But he wanted to know if I had any doubt as to the girl's identity. I had to tell him no. No, not the slightest doubt.'

He said the inquest would be held on Monday in Nash at the Waterloo Inn.

'Auspicious,' he said. 'Another French defeat.'

'They'll want to determine blame,' said Ena. 'We can help them with that. Show them how it was all an accident.'

'An accident.' He repeated her word, then told us how, looking at Grace lying there, he only had one thought.

'My own fate, lying there. Isn't that terrible? I should have prayed, no? A benediction, supplication for her soul, but I thought of nothing. Only myself. Is that an accident? Does that not prove I'm to blame?'

He wept then, and Ena waited, looking patient, drinking her tea. I didn't touch mine. Couldn't.

No one wanted any supper. The Warsows were both still in the kitchen when I took the tea tray through and set it on the table, the empty cup, the full ones. Mrs Warsow's eyes were red, and Mr Warsow was quiet, his hands folded and still. I told them I was thinking I'd go to chapel in the morning. I'd go out early for a walk beforehand, too. I didn't want them to worry about me.

Mrs Warsow said she'd be up early herself, and she'd make sure there was something for me to eat.

'Can't send you out empty, can I?'

She said she'd find me an umbrella to take with me in case it was still raining. Hard to tell in the evening what the weather would be like come day. Might be anything by then.

All night, rain fell, and I was glad for the sound of it, the ongoing sound. Marina lay curled in on herself and I didn't want to wake her. I tried to think about morning, about walking west and Douglas, but finger to a bruise, I came back to the inquest and the question of blame. Tongue to a broken tooth. An accident. A sharp edge. A fault, a crack, a weakness. Whose fault was it?

Auguste Gaudron was the logical villain. Foreign. Male. The one in charge. A stranger. Performer. Liar, too, and that was easily enough established. All those stories to the pressmen, contradictions and half-truths. And lies he believed. Were those his fault, too?

Because Grace lied to him, clear as day and wearing someone else's name. Was it all her fault then? Is that fair? She wasn't here to defend herself and blaming her would be neat enough, but honest? Are we to blame when our lies are believed?

Twenty, twenty-one, she'd said. How could he believe that? Had he even looked at her? *An acrobat, an aerialist, an aeronaut*, and *experienced*, a claim which sparked ugly rumours. The way she'd chased him to Cardiff. The way he flaunted her and she let him. That look in his eye. Her good looks.

The concessionaires, then. Mr Cundall and the rest. The Exhibition's money men who pressured Auguste for more flights and a lady parachutist, too, when Alma had already run off and wouldn't return, leaving Auguste alone, and the pressure was on. Who was going to fly? Who'd take the risk? Marriage, Alma told the newspaper, was a much less hazardous adventure. What was Auguste to do?

So, Auguste, again, because he succumbed to the pressure. A weak man. A Frenchman. A crook. And he lied to his wife, and though the world couldn't know that, I did. He lied and signed a contract before telling her the truth. Even advertised in the newspaper. Paid-for lies. And who paid for her costume? Her boots and that lifebelt? The lifebelt looked more than adequate and made to impress – who? Grace herself, or Ena? Convince her that all would be well? That might be it. Auguste could have spent his Sunday making it, cork cut, hoop shaped, the whole small-waisted thing rigged in the shed as the rest of us paced at the house and passed time. And the clips? The safety harness? Those stitches might be his, hidden away so they wouldn't show when she walked through the grounds, sashayed around the bicycle field. That felt like Auguste – innovation, but only for show – but I knew the idea had been mine. But not yet, not yet.

Ena then. How did she spend Sunday and what did she know? Or turn a blind eye from? Turning away was another kind of knowing, wasn't it? But she'd never admit to that. No, she'd say she'd always been scientific and practical, like her father, purpose-driven. And maybe she was right. She could do anything she set her mind to. Save me from Jacq. Change my whole life. Change the world, if she wanted to. That steely eye. That strength of jaw. How could this accident be her fault?

Because she knew him and could read him. Because she had her suspicions about him already and must have seen what he was planning. What did she think would happen? He needed a girl so how else could this end? With a girl and a balloon, Grace or me. Ena could only save one of us. She could choose and probably did.

So, me. We were always going to get there in the end. Was it my fault because Ena chose me? No, it was more than that and more fault mine than the rest, too. Was that honest? Of course it was. Because with the others, I could only guess. Piece together all the fallen pieces on the tabletop, the cut-out scraps of what they did and didn't do, what they knew and what they wanted – all guesswork. But for me, it was solid truth because I knew what I knew and what I did or tried to do. And even there, a lie. Did I try? Interrupted, I stopped. Later, I tried another way. And did I, for one minute, believe that would really work? I can't say.

Night in this room in this house and when I finally closed my eyes, I saw the prairie. Wide and pale, too real and bright, and I'm sitting on the rock, looking down at the trail and the wagons going past. There aren't many today. One and then another and a long gap. There's a wagon boy, too, a ways off from the trail and walking parallel to it, but up a slight rise, so I see him set against the sky. He's like a drawing, something a child would sketch, the horizon flat under his feet. I can see he's carrying a gun and looking about, but he doesn't see me. He's looking at the sky. Suddenly, a bird flying, straight up from the brush close to him and he watches it and raises the gun to his shoulder, all in one motion. He shoots. The bird spins, its wing torn, and it's brought down, the other wing still flapping as it falls. It falls. The ground kills it. The boy walks away.

6/

When I came down the stairs in the morning, I heard Mrs Warsow moving about the kitchen, and coming through the door, I saw Mr Warsow sitting at the table.

'Don't you worry,' she said with a quiet voice. 'We've both been to bed all right. Just up early again now. Old people don't need much sleep.'

Mr Warsow gave me a half smile and I sat down beside him.

'You be all right on your own this morning?' he asked. 'We were wondering if you might not like to come along to chapel with us.'

'She might want to be on her own. We shouldn't presume or pressure.' Mrs Warsow lifted a tea towel from a plate on the table. 'Welsh cakes again. I think you liked them?'

'Thanks,' I said. 'They're very good.'

Mr Warsow looked out the window, and it was dry after all that morning, the sky a swept blue, silent.

I did what I was told. Walked west past the Castle, all the animals on the wall watching. I thought Marina would like to see them again, maybe tomorrow. Ena and Auguste would be going to the inquest and I'd be left behind, probably. Most likely. We hadn't spoken about it yet. I counted the animals and kept walking. The river was as blue as the sky, swift under the bridge, and I walked on down the street, alone.

This was stupid.

Douglas hadn't mentioned a time or even a street. What if I had it all wrong and he meant some other street and was there now waiting for me? I couldn't know and he couldn't know, and we'd miss each other. And then? Everything wasted before we really had a chance.

'Laura.'

I looked over my shoulder and he was already there, coming up beside me.

'I don't think it's ever been so calm on a Sunday morning,' he said. 'No wind at all. There's always been some.'

'Lousy weather for a balloon,' I said. 'It wouldn't go anywhere.'

Douglas wore clean boots and dark trousers. He said he was going to see his grandmother in the west end of town and wanted to introduce me.

'And to Chapel, too? Is that your plan?' I asked.

'No. Not this morning, at least. My grandmother tells me she's old enough to miss a Sunday here and there, and she thought she might want help with her garden this morning. I only mentioned it in my note thinking it might be a good reason to suggest if anyone asked where you were going.'

'It worked, too. That's just what I told the Warsows. Offered to take me along with them, if I liked, but I said no.'

He laughed and walked quickly, and I quickened my pace to keep up. I hoped I wouldn't look too flushed when we arrived. We walked past the workhouse and the ordered new streets. This was a new neighbourhood and the streets smelled of wood and brick dust, the cows from the cattle market, and all the shops were Sunday morning closed. We turned from the main road and I saw a church spire needle up, sharp grey against the blue sky. Douglas was a needle, too, thin and quick, and I was the thread following after, past the red-brick houses, white window frames, all the bright tiles beside every door.

'It's a new town out here,' I said.

'A bit of a long walk, but we're almost there. Two friends shorten the road,' he said. 'Next street over.'

The houses were smaller here, flat-fronted, and front doors right on the street. The door to number 34 was open, but Douglas knocked anyway as he went in, then turned to draw it shut behind him. That was tricky – him through the door first, then me, and he came close to pull the door handle and where was I to go? Froze where I was as he leaned past and, for a moment, his body against mine. Moment. The door clicked shut. Quiet. Close. And his grandmother might be in the very next room. Couldn't breathe. Couldn't. And I don't know if he looked down at me, all close like that, because I was looking down, but he – but me – close,

close, close – and a breath, then he slipped past and away down the hallway.

'She'll be out back in the garden,' he said. 'The sunshine's there in the morning.'

I threaded my way behind him through another door down to the kitchen and he was right because there she was, sitting in the back, halfway outside, with the sun streaming in.

'And Douglas,' she said, like she'd come to the end of a thought. She looked up at him and smiled. 'Are you all right?'

'As ever, Gran.' He bent his face to hers and kissed her cheek. 'How are your legs?'

'Terrible,' she said cheerfully. 'But I can manage the kitchen and the garden, can't I? Hale and hearty.'

She was an old woman, thin like Douglas, and looked brittle as a stick. She'd pulled up her skirts and her legs stuck out into the light, bare and bony, with spidered veins, and her knees weak and wrinkled, old paper in the sun. She looked like she didn't care.

'This is Laura, Gran. She is working at the Exhibition.'

'Yes? Is it good work there? What are you doing? Selling tickets?' She turned her head at me and spoke quickly. I told her I was mainly sewing and that I work for the aeronauts, the balloon people.

'I know what aeronauts are,' she said. 'I read the newspapers.'

She turned back to the garden and I saw the child. A girl, about six years old. She sat on a stool under an apple tree with a fierce look on her face.

'Come out and see Douglas, will you?' the old lady shouted, but the girl shook her head and stayed where she was.

'Won't.'

'As you wish. You're being a grumpy girl.'

'I don't care. You made me grumpy.'

'I didn't,' the grandmother said. 'She's choosing to be grumpy. I only wanted her to sit in the sunshine. It's warm again today, isn't it? Your garden must be doing well, Douglas me lad. Did you bring me any berries today?'

'No, I'm afraid I couldn't, Gran. We're onto the last now and Mr Pettigrew sends them to the Castle kitchens to be made into jam.'

'Pity. It would have been nice to sit here in the sun and eat berries. Why don't you pull two more chairs out here? No, better. Help me right out into the light and then there will be space for us all. Maybe we can tempt your cousin out of the shadows if we sit around together and talk cheerfully. She'll want to join us then.'

'Won't!' the child called out.

'Don't worry, Flora,' Douglas said. 'You are fine where you are. I only came to see Granny anyway.' He helped the old lady stand up and she batted his hands away but let him take her chair once she was standing. She moved one foot at a time. It was hard work. I helped Douglas with the chairs and sat down when he sat down. The girl watched us, still looking fierce.

Beside her, there was an old garden trug on the ground, with a few green beans in the bottom. The wood was grey, and the boards pulled away from each other. Douglas told his grandmother he was going to find her a new one, but she told him she liked the old one just fine.

'I had her picking the first beans this morning,' the grandmother said. 'She seems to like them. Usually, she's a sensible girl. But I told her I was thinking of cutting down the apple tree to make space for more beans and that made her angry. She says not everyone likes the sun. Some people need shade. Do you think she'd be right?'

Douglas told his grandmother that I was American, and she said that was interesting. She'd left home, too, when she was young.

'Hard, of course, but it is good to really know how big the world is. Helps you understand people. There are so many of us.'

I asked her why she'd left, and she laughed, catching me off guard. 'Because of my husband, of course! The only reason. But you are too young to know about that. Why aren't you at home?'

'My mother. And father. He was French, so we moved to Paris.'

'Ah, yes. The same reason, then, but different. You should ask your mother about it.'

'She's no longer with me,' I said.

'Oh, you mean she's dead. A strange habit not calling dead dead. Are Americans poetic in that way? Or squeamish? Maybe your war did that. You haven't yet had many wars, have you? But you are too young to have known the war.'

'I'm not yet twenty.'

'No. And I'm not yet one hundred. You have a funny way of talking.'

The girl in the shadow stomped her feet and we stopped talking. She stood up and looked at Douglas.

'Did you really only come to see Granny?' she said.

'No. Not really. I thought I might see you, too, but you're not cheerful.'

'You don't need to only see cheerful people.'

'No, I suppose that's true.' He stood up and went over to join her in the shade.

'Her mother's dead, too,' the grandmother said. 'Something we all have in common, then, but she doesn't see it that way. She doesn't believe I ever had a mother.'

'Maybe I should tell her about mine.'

'If she comes over here. I wouldn't chase her, if I were you. She's in a difficult mood.'

Douglas was squatting down next to Flora now, talking, but we couldn't hear what they were saying. Three sparrows flew over the garden wall and settled near the kitchen door, pecking for crumbs.

'It's the Frenchman you're working for, isn't it?' she asked, watching the sparrows. 'The one with the lost girl that was found. She must have been a friend of yours.'

'Yes. Grace . . .' but what could I say?

The grandmother reached out and patted my hand. 'Grace is a lovely name. I see why she used it. And where is she now? Have you been able to see her?'

'No. She's at the church in Nash. Monsieur Gaudron went to see her yesterday. She's in the belfry there, under the bells, and he said they're refraining from ringing them and there's to be no church service today.'

'Fitting,' she said. 'Fourteen, wasn't she? I was married at fourteen. Far too young. You're sensible to be waiting.'

Douglas and Flora were walking back to the chairs now and when Douglas sat down, Flora sat on his knee.

'Flora says you've been coughing at night, Gran.'

'When are you going to die, Granny?'

'Soon. But don't worry about that. I'll be eating up all the beans first. And the ones you haven't picked yet. Even the ones that are still flowers.'

'Gran,' Douglas said, but there she was, reaching over and patting my knee again.

'I like this girl, Douglas. She's more sensible than me.'

There was a luncheon the grandmother must have prepared first thing in the morning. She told Douglas it was waiting on the kitchen table when we wanted it. A sausage pie, some small tomatoes and sliced cucumbers, then a plate of drop scones with butter and jam. Flora was feeling better by the time the pie was outside and asked if she could fetch the plates from the cupboard.

'Be careful to close the door when you have them. And don't slam it, just shut it nicely.'

The girl closed her eyes when she was walking, but she didn't trip and didn't drop the plates and no one said anything about her eyes. She set them down carefully on the small table beside Douglas and watched while he sliced the pie. I thought about offering to do that, but I was the guest and sat quietly. The pie was delicious, the pastry flaky and good.

'I didn't make it,' the grandmother said. 'The neighbour did. She does things like that. Bakes two, she says, and gives me one. She checks in most days. The tomatoes grew in her garden.'

'They are very good, too,' I said.

'Douglas's are better. But these are nice.'

Douglas laughed. 'I'll bring you some the next time I come, and you can give them to her over the wall.'

'I'd like that,' she said.

After lunch, she wanted a sleep in the sun, and the girl took a book into the shade and sat quietly.

'We'll tidy the plates away,' Douglas said.

'Later, you can bring out a pot of tea,' the grandmother said. 'If you like.'

'Sleep well, Gran.'

'I'm not sleeping. I'm enjoying the sun.'

'In a little while then,' he said, and I followed him inside.

He heated a kettle and filled the wash basin. He rolled up his sleeves and I found a towel. It doesn't take long to wipe plates clean and when we finished, and the plates away again in the cupboard, he dried his hands and sat down and the other chairs were outside in the sun and I could only stand there, uncertain. And then he reached out and I did, too. He took my hand and he pulled me in close. One finger on my neck, my collarbone, the string that held the key. I put my finger on his lips till there was stillness and I sat on his knee and my hand in his hair and my mouth on his mouth and soft and strange and hard and good. This was better than before. I could open my eyes and see him, his eyelashes, his close-up skin as he kissed me. I could see the sunshine on his face.

Everyone talks of weather every day, and I always thought it was a casual, empty bent. Something to talk about to fill the time. But it isn't. It is the centre. I know that now. I need to know how the sun shines, how sky is swept blue today and the wind from the west, and the clouds overhead like wisps of white hair, and the shadows under trees still damp from last night's rain, and the air warm, and the sun bright and hot. I need to know these things because they are a part of me. I am part of the weather, part of the day, and part of the place where I stand. It must be the same for everyone.

71

BY THE DAY OF THE INQUEST, THE PAPERS HAD MADE a switch. No mention of Mademoiselle Albertina or the lady balloonist. Now the headlines read *Lost Child-Parachutist.*

John Owen had come to see me on Sunday evening at the house on Edward Street and asked if I'd walk out with him. He wanted to talk, he said, and he held a serious look in his beautiful eyes, a set look about his mouth. I excused myself from the family and said I wouldn't be long. We'd only walk up the street and back.

He told me he wanted to go to the inquest, and he wanted me to go with him.

'I don't have money to get out to Nash,' I said. An easy excuse, but it didn't work.

'I have money,' he said. 'The newspaper man gave it to me. Thirty silver pieces.'

'Oh, don't say that. They're trying to talk to everyone. You've done no harm.'

'Have they talked to you?'

'No. But they might if I went to the inquest. What good comes of going?'

'It's something we can do for her. Hear what's said when it matters.'

'They won't let us talk,' I said and, more than that, I didn't want to. I couldn't trust myself. Because what would I say if I did spill the beans? That she'd died because I didn't manage to stop her? That I didn't think hard enough, wish enough, *will* enough to keep her safe? That prayers and spells only work sometimes, and I couldn't bring myself to take her place? That it was my fault after all? What kind of reward would the papers give for that confession? It wasn't worth paper now.

John Owen stood under the street light, looking at me.

'I don't want to talk,' he said. 'I just want to hear. Make sure there's a friend close by, listening, for her. Will you do that with me? I'll pay your ticket. We can go together.'

'John, you're lovely, you know that.'

'And me, not even trying.'

When I came back to the house, Ena and Auguste were standing in the hallway in travelling clothes.

'We're leaving tonight for Nash,' Ena said. 'I don't want to be on the morning train with the pressmen.'

'There's a cab coming along shortly,' Auguste said. 'A quick and clever decision on my wife's part this evening, but we didn't want to leave without speaking with you. Because we haven't even asked if you wanted to come to the inquest.'

'I – I'm not sure. No, I'm not ready.'

Ena smiled, flatly. 'That's what I thought you'd say, Laura. And likely, there's no real sense in you going. The whole thing's simply a formality, really. Easy enough to see this is just one of those small tragedies that happen. Cut and dried. We should be home early tomorrow afternoon and can make our further plans for London then. Mrs Warsow is looking after Marina just now. We've already said our goodbyes to her.'

The house felt emptier that night and Marina kept waking. She wanted me to talk to her and wanted me to sing. In the dark, I felt bell ropes hanging down over our head, shadows everywhere and the taste of salt water on my lips.

In the morning, I left her sleeping in bed and met John Owen early in the street. There were pressmen on the train, but they didn't bother us. They talked together, telling too many jokes, not looking at the weather. We didn't talk much. He'd brought his basket with him again and told me it was a picnic for our lunch, and I tried to tease him about bringing a bottle of milk and he looked like he might cry.

'I'm sorry,' I said, and he held up his hand and wouldn't let me continue which was just as well because what else could I say?

I'd imagined we'd be walking from Newport, but John Owen

said if we stayed on to Llanwern station, it was only four miles to Nash.

'That's still a ways to walk if we want to be there on time.'

'But we won't be walking. I plan to secure a cab.'

'We'll be lucky with all these pressmen,' I said.

'I can be quick. First off the train,' he said. 'And you might distract them. Strike up a conversation as we pull into the station and buy me a bit of time. Maybe flash your French at them?'

'I'd rather not. Wouldn't that start the questions? Auguste hardly needs another sister lurking about.'

'Well, not French then. You'll think of something. But take your time. I'll hold the cab when I get one.'

The pressmen must have known about the other station as they stayed in their seats at Newport. Coming up to Llanwern, John Owen readied himself and got the door open before the train even stopped. The pressmen were still laughing, putting on jackets. I thought I didn't want them in the same room as Grace, all that laughing, but of course, that's what she liked, that kind of fun. And I had to stop thinking of her as Grace because she wasn't any more, was she, and never really had been. Just another act. Louie.

John Owen vanished out the door before I even noticed, and I did as he said and took my time. Fussed with the handle to the carriage as the pressmen stood behind me, kept fussing as they waited and I pretended to be flustered. Then a long moment before I stepped back and let one of the men sort it for me, and he stood back and let me climb down which I did slowly, too. Then, when I came out the front of the station, there was John

Owen with a cab booked and ready. He helped me in and gave me a wink.

More cabs in front and behind and carts and people on the road, all heading south to Nash. We passed houses and farms, faces at the gates, and hedgerows summer-tall and dark. Then the powder houses Auguste had mentioned, and I thought how he and Ena must have passed them last night in the dark. He'd have explained them again to her, their purpose and their strong design. He liked to explain things and mostly, she was patient. When we came close to Nash, the church tower drew my eye, and I saw it as another powder house, with Grace laid out inside. All these dangerous things hidden away by thick strong walls where the light can't get in.

The Waterloo Inn was over the road from the church, and people stood about in front, bunched up in groups, waiting. We didn't; we walked right in.

'No point in being here early and not landing a seat,' John Owen whispered at me, pulling me along. 'Chin up, shoulders back and look like we're supposed to be here. No one's going to say boo.'

The tables had been cleared away and benches and stools lined up to face a raised chair at one end of the room. There was a small table there, too, where three pale men sat, hunched over paper and pens. The ink pot between them looked overlarge and out of place, like an odd glass of dark beer in this changed inn. The raised chair was empty, but easy enough to see that's where the coroner would sit. I wondered if he'd come in with others or on his own. A lonely sort of work, deciding like this.

John Owen nudged me and pointed out other seats, set apart and squint.

'That's for the jury,' he said. 'Thirteen. Unlucky number.'

So, he wouldn't be deciding on his own then. A whole crew would do that work. I pictured them as sailors hauling ropes, sleeves rolled up, tattoos, arm hair.

The room filled up around us, the seats at the front stayed empty. Then a loud bang on the door, a loud voice and everyone stood up, too close together, and the sound of feet marching in. John Owen reached out for my arm, held on tight, kept his face frozen and grim.

The jury marched in, well dressed and solemn, and stood by their seats as the coroner came in. Mr Robert-Jones, a tall tower of a man, and big, too, like a working man who'd lift heavy things, not a suited man at all, but there he was, buttoned up and steady. He barked out words and the room sat down, but the jury stayed on their feet. He asked them something, words, more words, and they nodded and answered back.

'They need to be sworn in. Needs to be official,' John Owen said, and the pale men wrote the words down, ink on paper, black on white.

But now they were leaving again, these marching sworn-in men, all leaving the room like they'd finished, and nothing had happened yet, and their seats stayed empty and they were gone.

'Shouldn't take long,' John Owen said. 'I'm half wanting to go with them and more than half glad I don't need to. Hard to know they're all strangers, looking at her.'

'Where are they going?' I asked.

'Out to see the body. They need to before they hear the evidence. Not enough to read the details in the newspaper. But it shouldn't take long,' he said, again. 'They'll be back soon.'

I looked around, trying to get my ears right again, trying to feel the floor. There were open windows and birds outside. There were quiet voices talking, newspaper pages turning. People being calmed. There were empty chairs in the front row, too, I noticed now. I looked for Auguste and Ena but couldn't find them, so maybe the chairs were for them. The coroner sat looking at us all with heavy eyes. A woman walked up and gave him a glass of water to drink. I watched him thank her, then she turned and walked away, holding her face very steady in front of all the people.

The sound of feet again and the jury back in. Most looked down at the floor as they walked, and all voices were still. A storm coming, and they felt it, readied themselves for the pitching deck. They took their seats solemn-faced, ready.

'The jury has now viewed the body of the deceased as is proper. And have you, gentlemen of the jury, elected a foreman?'

One man stood. 'Yes. The jury has elected me, Mr Walter Collett, ex-county-councillor.'

'Thank you, Mr Collett. The County Constabulary will be represented by Inspector Carter, yes? And are the witnesses all present?'

More feet and heads turned, so I turned, too. Auguste was walking the aisle with Mr Webster beside him. I didn't know the others who came in with them. Exhibition officials, the money men Ena spoke of. Auguste's suit looked hard brushed, and he wore a new bowler hat. And Ena wasn't with him. Where was she? How could she not be there? I didn't want to turn and be seen, looking.

Then voices at the front and the first witness was called: Mary Waggett. She told the same story we'd all read in the newspaper, though added mention of telling a hay cutter who was working near the shore before she told her mother.

'I told him I'd seen the body of a sailor,' she said. 'He told me to go on to Nash to see if anyone would go and find the body again.'

The coroner didn't ask any questions, and the pale men wrote everything down. Then the girl remembered what she told her mother and how the police had come and she told them about finding Grace's body only she kept saying *it.*

'. . . it was then on the dry stones, and it was in the place when the police accompanied me to the spot.'

The small word grated, and my fists tightened on my lap. I hated *it. It* was a scratch, a tear, a biting flea. *It wasn't Grace.*

The coroner received her testimony and said she had spoken clearly for one of tender years, and she returned to her seat.

'Are the relatives of the deceased now present?' he asked. A police constable explained they'd yet to arrive. They were coming from Bristol and would have to walk from the station.

I pictured them on the road right then, walking past the hedgerows and the powder houses, all the cabs gone on before, and I felt guilty. I wondered when their train came in, and if we'd passed them and who they were.

Then I saw Ena, two rows in front of me. She must have been sitting there all along, but I hadn't seen her. The back of her head, her neck. She wore a blue high collar, a gorgeous colour but too hot for a warm day, and sat up straight. She couldn't see me without turning right round, but she might have noticed me on the way in. Felt like I'd been sitting there a long time now.

When a single woman walked up the aisle past her, she tilted her head to watch. The woman was all curved down, her shoulders held like she was old, but I saw she wasn't, only heavy in her cheap dress like this room was the last place she wanted to be. Ena sat very straight as the woman lowered herself into one of the empty seats at the front. Then an older couple joined her: a woman in an out-of-date hat, a man in a dark coat, too heavy for the day. The family we'd been waiting for – the Crinks and Grace's mother – and Auguste half stood at the end of the row, bowing his head towards them all. Ena sat up straighter.

A police officer came forward, carrying a lifebelt. The fabric was water-stained, and the straps looked sliced through. The officer held it up for all to see, then showed it to the jury. When they had finished with the belt, it was placed on the clerk's table and Police Constable Boucher was called on. He told the story of going to the shore to see the body, and of examining the lifebelt the deceased wore.

All these pieces of the story overlapping felt like the newspaper clippings all over again except the lifebelt was there on the table, something real and true, and Grace lay in the belfry, another kind of real.

One of the jurymen called something out, and the coroner said he'd now call for evidence.

'I was going to ask whether the lifebelt is a proper lifebelt,' the foreman said. 'It's the only one I have ever seen like it.'

The coroner replied it was an ordinary belt for saving life.

The police officer added that he believed it was a Board of Trade regulation lifebelt.

'What about the hooks?' the foreman asked.

'The hooks have nothing to do with the lifebelt,' the coroner said. 'They were for fastening the parachute.'

'They seem to work very loosely.'

'That would be all the easier for the girl to disconnect herself from the parachute when she reached the water.'

They talked on about the belt and the clothing she'd been found in. The police constable said he'd shown items of the clothing to her friends and they had been swift to identify them. There was no doubt about identity. So, piece by piece, the story came together, the jury listening. I was wrong to think of them as sailors on a ship. Sailors, maybe, but factory-bound now, making the story, piece by piece. Needle through the canvas, varnish on with a stiff brush, wood steamed and bent and shaped.

Auguste was called to the stand.

'Mr Auguste Eugene Gaudron, of Seven Victor, London. Occupation: Aeronaut. Eighteen years' experience.'

He said he'd known Grace for two months and spun a story about Cornwall and the Hancocks, then about advertising in the newspaper and Grace answering. He called her *the deceased* when he spoke which sounded strange in his accent and he kept talking, about salary, about past employees. The coroner interrupted him.

'You say that you have had eighteen years' experience?'

'Yes.'

'What age are you now?'

'Twenty-seven.'

'Then you began when you were nine years of age?'

'No, when I was twelve.'

'Then you have only had fifteen years' experience.'

'I began when I was twelve. Yes, it is fifteen years then.'

The coroner pressed him on Grace's experience, her real name, and what instructions he'd given her about flying from Cardiff. Words and words and nothing could change. Auguste looked weak and unreliable. Ena sat too straight. In the front row, the single woman was slumped and crying. The room was hot. The smell of sweat. Dust. Dirt. Someone coughed up in a handkerchief behind me. My boots felt too tight.

More questions for Auguste about the map he'd drawn for Grace and I wanted to believe it, wanted to know he'd taken the time to prepare her like that. But who knew what he'd even said to her and if she'd been in any state to hear. She'd been so sick with excitement about the whole thing. And with something on her mind. She'd said that in the caravan, hadn't she? And I hadn't pressed – John Owen and Douglas and I – none of us had, so that was a guilt as bad as scissors, now. We might have. Or I might have earlier when I heard her say *she waved at me – like she wanted my attention.* If I hadn't been quiet that night in the dark room, only wanting to sleep, she might have said more and maybe we'd understand.

Only it was too late for that and now her crying mother sat in the front row. If I called out, she'd hear me. Or stood up and leaned forward, I could even touch her. She was that close. Her neck rubbed raw from a bad neckline, her dress printed calico. Yellow.

The coroner was talking experience now. He wanted to know how practised the girl had been before the jump and Auguste told a tale about what he believed and what he'd been told. None of it sounded at all credible.

'Did you not ensure she had jumping experience before you authorized a performance of this nature? This was not your first student, I believe?'

'No, I have had many, many students before, but there is no practising in parachutes. You simply need to do it. Tell and talk all you like with maps and little arrows and advice, but there must be a first time, mustn't there?'

'And this was the deceased's first time?'

'Yes. I tell you the truth now. I believe it was.'

8 /

Mr Crinks was called as a witness, and when he sat with his hat in his hands and told the coroner he was the girl's adopted father and her full name was Louisa Maud Evans, his voice was heavy and certain.

'She was fourteen the sixth of last December. With us since she was sixteen months as her mother was a travelling player who worked the shows and now Louie's a girl that grew big, but she had an infantile face.'

He paused and looked about the room. The coroner let him take his time.

'I last saw her alive at Taunton just before Easter when I went to do some work for the Hancocks.'

Another pause before he told the court about her father. Andrew Evans was a seaman in Her Majesty's service and he'd not been heard of for eleven or twelve years. Crinks mentioned her mother, too, saying she'd given the girl permission to go with the Hancocks in the spring, though he himself had been against it. 'She'd be a companion, make a cup of tea and things of that sort. There was no talk of any performing at all. Mrs Hancock is a friend of mine.'

He'd had a letter from Mrs Hancock dated July 14, saying that the girl went away from them on Saturday night without any provocation, and they did not know where she went.

'Only that she'd become very thick with the balloon man,' he said, and the coroner interrupted him.

'That has nothing to do with the cause of death.'

Mr Crinks held his hat and said no more. The coroner thanked him and called for the next witness.

In the front row, her mother stood up and gave a weak curtsy, a damp handkerchief tucked in her hand.

John Owen leaned in and whispered at me. 'Mrs Evans, is it? Well, look at that. Is she what you expected?'

She was trying to keep her tears under control, her shoulders held awkward like broken things. The coroner confirmed her name and asked how close she was to her daughter. She stared at him and he repeated the question.

'How often did you see her, having given her up for adoption as an infant? Did you know each other well?'

A choked gasp before she tried to answer.

'I . . . I had her in my sight all the time. From infancy . . . all the time till she went away with the Hancocks. A week or so before Easter, it was. All the blessed time . . .'

She broke down then, sobbing fiercely and the coroner watched, unable to ask another question. But Mr Crinks stood up again and held a piece of paper above his head so everyone might see. One of the pale men took it from him and gave it to the coroner.

'Marriage lines, is it? January 1881 – Mary Ann Fussell, eighteen, and Andrew Aiken Evans, twenty-one. I see.'

Mrs Evans straightened. 'And the girl was born . . .' she called out with a strong, strained voice now. 'She was born ten months and a fortnight after our marriage.' She worked to keep her face straight, but having nothing else to say, she crumpled again into tears and hid her face in the handkerchief.

The coroner handed the paper back and nodded to a police officer who stepped forward, helping Mrs Evans from the room.

A doctor's turn next and he described what he'd seen. Every bit of damage. He didn't say *it* but I still struggled to listen. The conditions were consistent with drowning, he said, and counted off every bruise and abrasion of skin, every illness she'd previously endured, every weakness she knew, and we all sat there in our bodies, listening as he spoke, air in our lungs, listening to the effect of sand and water and time. He told us he believed the girl fell into the water alive and was drowned, but he had expected to find mud or sand in her stomach and had not, which suggested she did not fall into the water conscious. A sigh in the room, and a straightening. He continued. One more thing he thought it right to mention because he understood there had been some suggestions made with reference to the girl's virtue. To this, he would say only this much: that she was as pure a girl as ever lived and aught that might have been imputed to her was absolutely false. Murmured applause throughout the room, and another sort of sigh.

A break before the final verdict and we left. The jury withdrew, the witnesses were led out by the police, and everyone suddenly on their feet, clearing the room. John Owen gone, too quick for me, and me, too slow. The aisle filled and everyone was moving. I had to wait, tried not to hear voices all around me. Then Ena was there, looking at my face. That high blue collar held her head up, and she looked right at me, her smile like a hand raised, blocking the view.

'Laura. You're here.' She stopped in front of me and the crowd of people moved around her. 'Are you well?'

'Yes,' I said. 'You?'

'Yes. Just need some air now. Like everyone else. The room feels close, doesn't it? With all these people.'

'There's so much interest in the proceedings,' I said. 'Or sympathy with the deceased.'

'You sound like a newspaper.'

'Yes. Well.'

'I didn't expect to see you here. You didn't tell us you were coming.'

'I hadn't decided. Then John Owen asked, and I thought I might.'

'John Owen.'

'Grace's friend. From *Santiago*.'

'Ah, yes. Not your young man, then.'

'No, just a friend. We're going back to Cardiff now.'

'Yes? I will . . . I will see you there then. Back at the house?'

'Yes. We can talk then.'

She looked sad, looking at me. I felt like I'd changed things or maybe she had. A different day.

Outside, John Owen found me and said he'd heard enough. He couldn't listen any more. We'd walk back to Llanwern and wait for the train. We weren't the only ones with the idea, but we walked alone, quick-paced away from the others. We didn't talk, or rather, he didn't. When I tried, he said later. He wanted to be quiet just then.

The hedgerows were loud with birds and Queen Anne's lace grew thick at the edge of the road, all those flat white clusters, delicate as netting. A few had gone to seed already, their edges curled up, cages, crinolines, balloons. I picked a handful, the rough stalks stubborn when I grasped them, but I wanted something to carry in my hands.

On the train, the stalks stained my hands green and the flowers' heads began to droop. They looked tired and we did, too. John Owen leaned on my shoulder, and I didn't mind. He brought his mouth close to my ear and started to talk, said he wanted to tell me about Grace's mother. She might have looked distraught and virtuous at the inquest, but she really was a piece of work. I whispered back, how did he know that? And he said he'd put it together. Things Grace had told him, and the pressmen had also dug out details, dropped hints when they spoke with him. They hadn't quite strung the pieces together, though John Owen did.

Mary Ann Evans wasn't a travelling player at all as Mr Crink said at the inquest. She didn't need to foster out her girl to make ends meet but chose to because her husband was long off at sea and she'd got pregnant. And the new man wanted her, which must have been good news to her, but it was hard to set up respectably with a stompy toddler in tow when she wasn't a widow. She must have been desperate. So, the neighbours – the Crinks – helped out. Maybe the new father was their son or a nephew or maybe that was gossip, but anyway they helped Mary Ann out and adopted the girl.

John Owen said Grace knew all this and said she saw her mother sometimes, and her little half-brother, too. Albert. A popular name in these days. She'd told John Owen, she'd missed him in Cardiff, but she didn't miss her mam and hated her and never wanted to see her again. And now she wouldn't. No use crying, that's just how it was.

After that, he looked out the window, all the grasses a blur, the flowers and the weeds and the swallowing sky.

By the time we got to Cardiff, the papers were full of the inquest. John Owen bought the *Evening Express* at the station so we could read together. There were details about the witnesses' statements and transcripts of the examinations, and through it all, Auguste's voice was strong. Had she obeyed her tutor's directions, she would have lived. Before going up, he had strictly instructed her to leave the balloon when she was over the Infirmary. Had she done so, in all probability, her life would have been saved. Final verdict: Death by accidental drowning.

'The jury were unanimously of the opinion that Auguste

displayed great carelessness and want of judgement in allowing so young and inexperienced a person to make a descent during such weather as prevailed on Tuesday last, and that they wished to censure him and caution him against allowing such a thing to occur again.'

The flowers in my hand were wilted, and I stood with John Owen in the street with my arms hanging down. Neither of us had any energy for more. Cardiff was noisy around us, the news of Grace everywhere. Louisa. A child. And men bought the news, horses pulled the trams, crows left their rooftops and flew away, but I felt sorry for the flowers. Their effort was wasted, all that holding on through the winter, then the spring push of their strong shoots, their pale flowers, just fit for the dust cart now. I let them fall.

The wind was still at last, and the sky clear, our friend far away. And all that I'd imagined? The stories within her stories, my reading between the lines? All wilted, too, left behind as we leave the dead behind. We turn away from the church tower, look away from the loss. We leave them because we can't stay beside them, but they stay with us, travelling on.

WINTER

EPILOGUE

The bones of the hills are traced with snow and all this morning was a struggle. Dark, my feet cramped with cold and the house empty, aching around me. The afternoon brought snow, then everything grew silent and suddenly beautiful. Fat, heavy flakes like petals falling, and I was caught up, remembering your funeral. An out-of-time sort of feeling because that day in July had felt like spring with petals blowing about from all the flowers and a freshness in the air that comes after rain, but it wasn't spring, and it isn't spring now. It's December years after, and I find I'm talking to you.

Isn't that strange? So many years gone and all the way over here, but I'm reaching out to you, Grace. You'd tease me mercilessly if you could. Sentimental silliness. But no. It's like talking in the dark, tucked up in bed beside each other, trying not to feel strange.

I've always called you Grace, and I'll keep that up, if you don't mind. You never gave me another name to use and it feels wrong to change now.

There's been no wind today and the hills that looked stark in the morning are softer now. The iron-bristled trees are smoothed, their branches padded with new snow and all edges blurred and yielding. Between me and the hills, snow fills the sky, every flake fatter than the last and lovely. I try to focus on just one, watch and follow as it spins down in its private spiral dance, but I blink and it's gone, another in its place. A hundred thousand falling petals.

The flowers at your funeral were paid for by the concessionaires. Heaps and hills of white blossom covering your casket, piled in the carriage, and then more in baskets, too, at the cemetery for the mourners to collect and scatter. It felt like a wedding until the music started. The Old World Band from the Exhibition stood at the cemetery gates, waiting for the horses with their tall black plumes to bring you all the way from Newport that morning, and the roads were lined with people, men with hats off, women looking down as you passed by, as if down was safe. The children looked up at the horses, long as they dared, with closed-eyed mothers gripping their hands as the band struck up the first deep notes and the funeral began.

There were no questions left, with you found and the inquest over, all the ends tied up. Tied up, tied down. Which was it? The aerialist's difficulty which we all understand: the suspension of disbelief, gravity's battle and the familiar trick of knowing when to hold on, when to let go. You accused me of being tied down, didn't you? Not able to get away. But I did, when the time came, and whichever way we look at it, Grace, we're all tied anyway. Not one of us isn't tied. Even when we undo all the clips like you did and like my Ma, too. Try to get away, but it doesn't work. We're still tied together, linked and looped and circled through. Didn't the Gypsies teach you that when they gave you those earrings? Those tiny gold circles were rings to remind you of the ringed connections all around. Like that wide ring of people who came to your funeral. Everyone came. The Gypsies were there, standing in the rain as the Old World Band played and everyone listened. Mrs Warsow and Mrs Watkins, too, and Douglas and me, standing close and brave, and John Owen and a big group of men from *Santiago*. The concessionaires and the town aldermen, too, and all the crowds and the pressmen come to watch, then tell your story. You'd have liked that, all that attention, and probably because this is all so sad and so many people heard it then and felt it, they'll keep telling it, just keep on telling it and I don't know if that's good or bad, but it's beautiful, anyway, to know how you'll be remembered. I'll remember you.

I say everyone came, but that's not true. Auguste, Ena and Marina weren't there. They left Cardiff after the inquest because of a prior engagement. That's what was printed in the newspaper. But they contributed to the funeral fund, of course, and arranged for Mr Webster to buy a wreath on their behalf. They did what they could, but when they left for London, I stayed behind.

A lot of money was collected at that time. All those people who'd bought newspapers, eating up your story, wanted to put their money towards something good, and it was decided that the people of Cardiff would give you a marble gravestone, beautifully carved and engraved, with your story set out clear. I put some money in, too – everyone did – and it's a lovely stone. It's strange to think about people seeing it down the years, reading the words and knowing your story.

I think I was lonely this morning only because your birthday's coming up this month, and yes, that's sentimental, but the date sticks in my mind. Sixth December. I looked out at the cold garden, the sparrows pecking at the breakfast crumbs on the windowsill, the bent apple tree that looked so cold out there in the grey, and I thought about your mother. Is she still living? Is she thinking of you today? And is it cold in Bristol and is she living alone? We saw her at the train station, me and John Owen, after the inquest. She was waiting on the other platform, headed back to Bristol, and someone must have given her a lift because she was already standing there waiting when we arrived. She had stopped crying, and I couldn't see her face. She stood looking down the track, away into the distance, and I felt sorry for her. Then Mr Crinks came up and stood with her, before taking her arm and leading her away. She must have been confused because she wasn't going back to Bristol at all, but on to Cardiff, same as us. She'd be there for the funeral on Wednesday, so I supposed she and the Crinks were staying somewhere in town. Someone must have been kind and put them up. On the train, when John Owen told me the story about her and about giving you away as a baby, I kept seeing her there, looking out for the train. I see her like that still, looking and looking and everything's far too late.

After that time, Douglas and I moved away. We got married first at his Granny's chapel, and I wore the brooch Ena gave me for Ma, but I wore it for you that day. Remembering. It was a beautiful day, quiet, which I liked. No crowds for us, but that was better. Mr Andrew Pettigrew came and his wife despite her back, and the two of them held hands through the whole thing which was rather sweet. Their grown daughter Mary came, too, looking after them, I think, but it was nice to have them there and they gave me lilies from the garden to carry as a bouquet. Wasn't that kind? Flora carried white daisies to match and looked lovely in a blue dress. And after the ceremony, Douglas's Granny kissed me and asked me to take care of him and let him weed the berry patch because he'd always liked that kind of thing.

She'd like to see the garden we have now, I imagine. Where we've ended up, there's more space for growing things than we know what to do with because we went home. Well, home for me. Back to the States and out to Montana where everything was new for Douglas and Flora and there's plenty of fresh air and good land. When Douglas first suggested it, I thought he wanted to farm, but he didn't. He told me he'd trained as a gardener and should keep at it. No wheat or corn or cows for him. We live just outside town and grow all sorts of things: potatoes and tomatoes, peas and beans and pumpkins, but more than that, flowers. We sell them to the hotel by the railway station and in town, too. We have boys now and they are big enough to push a cart and take it round the houses and bring home money smartly enough. All summer, they worked so hard, but it's winter now and they're both in school, learning all they can, even though it's Flora teaching them and they need to remember to call her Miss Harris and sometimes they don't. But they're good boys. You'd like them. We called them Johnny, after John Owen who was a good friend to us, and Louis after you.

I'm watching the sun over the hills now, hazy through the cloud. It's getting low and the day's slipping away. I think I'll make Welsh cakes this evening once everyone is home again and the house is feeling cosy. There's a pot of stew at the back of the stove and I'll peel a few potatoes and put them in soon. We need rib-sticking food in this cold, heavy rugs out on the floor and thick quilts on all the beds. Flora has been working on one of her own in her spare time, though there's little of that for a teacher. She's making it complicated for herself, too, a design all curves and circles and interlocking rings. A lovely thing, but she'll do her eyes in with it. Once she's got it all planned and organized, I'll be helping her with the sewing machine, and I shouldn't be surprised if she's working up to an announcement in the new year. She's keeping rather private about it now, but there's a young widower whose small boy is in her school and he's very keen on buying our pumpkins. Poor child must be living on the stuff, turning half orange.

Maybe it's strange talking to you like this, telling you all these faraway things about people you'll never know. I should be telling you about the Gaudrons instead, Auguste and his own balloon accidents, and Ena quoted in the newspaper, condemning the whole thing and asking the government to put a stop to these sensations, which aren't proper balloon ascents at all. Can't you just hear her saying that? Her voice, right there.

Auguste's been dead now several years and I don't know whether to blame another accident or maybe an illness, only one way or another, he's ended up buried in Highgate Cemetery with Ena's father. Forty-five was too young by far. And we thought him old back then, didn't we? But there was Ena, a widow too young, too, and Marina, a young woman herself, both left adrift. I imagined the family would look after them and, of course, there was the factory, but next I heard was in a letter with an American stamp. She wrote they'd relocated, come west to pioneer their way on the Great Plains, and Ena planned to farm. She told me she'd been reading all about modern machinery and would learn to drive a plough and can't you just see her at it? That was three years ago and now they've done it. Bought land and found husbands, too. Brothers, of all things – imagine that. She told me there was still time for a life and she was determined to have it. I can only wish her well.

Outside, the snow is building up now, the garden getting its tucked-in look underneath the blanket. The road will be wet when Douglas comes home, and I'll need to dry his boots by the fire. It's always wet or muddy or cracked with heat, this road, and the dust comes in through the windows when the carts go past, but I don't mind. We cope just fine. Most years, we reap what we sow.

I remember you telling me about the road you travelled that spring. You'd never been on a road before, not travelling like that. Every day, you walked to the cloth factory, and down the Bristol streets, but this road across the country was different. Stretching on and you were going somewhere at last with all those people and a reason to be there. The Hancocks travelled south that Eastertide, taking the whole show with them, down through the West Country. All the carts and painted caravans and the animals in their cages, the stalls folded up cleverly into wagons and tents and flags and everything, everything. The Hancock children made a fuss of you, asking questions, wanting to hold your hands, and the road stretched on and on and it was spring. Out from Bristol and down to Taunton and into Devon and the rolling hills.

Then you came to a place where a green valley opened ahead and the sky held birds, black birds hovering all together in the wind. They were almost still, high above the earth, holding their wings just so and staying in one place like things suspended. Strange birds, you told me. You didn't know what they were. Not crows or jackdaws but something else, something new. And you told me how you watched them as you walked down that road and then there was some business with the children, some distraction, but I can't remember your story about that and, in a little while, when you looked up again to the black birds, they were gone. You kept walking and the carts and wagons all kept moving, and then you thought to turn round. And there they were, behind you, changed. The sunlight caught them and you saw their feathers were white, their shapes familiar. Just gulls. Like every other common gull, white against the sky.

THE END

In Memory of
LOUISA MAUD EVANS
Aged 14 ½ years
Who met her death on July 21st, 1896
On the day she ascended in a balloon
From Cardiff, and descended by parachute
Into the Bristol Channel. Her body was
found washed ashore near Nash (Mon) on
the 24th July and was buried
here on the 29th
To commemorate the sad ending of
A brave young life
This monument is erected by Public Subscription
'Requiescat in Pace'
Brave woman, yet in years a child
Dark death closed here thy heavenward flight
God grant thee, pure and undefiled
To reach at last, the light of light. CTW

A NOTE ABOUT HISTORICAL REFERENCES AND MANY THANKS

This story is based on the true story of Louisa Maud Evans. Many of the people depicted are drawn from the historical record. Others have been invented by the author to fill the gaps history leaves behind. The story of Laura and Douglas is entirely fiction.

I would like to gratefully acknowledge the usefulness of

John Camden Hotten, *The Slang Dictionary,* 1873
Charles Spencer, *The Modern Gymnast,* 1866
Nick Peacey, *The Inflations and Deflations of the Spencer Family: balloons, bikes and electric camels,* Goggled Dog Publications, 2013
Ruth Goodman, *How to Be a Victorian*, Penguin Books, 2013
Rosemary Chaloner, *The Balloon Girl: The First and Fatal Flight of Mademoiselle Albertina*, Jelly Bean Books, 2016

Diolch yn fawr to the Glamorgan Archives for primary information about the 1896 Cardiff Exhibition and to the National Library of Wales for their extensive digitized collection of nineteenth-century Welsh newspapers which proved invaluable during my lockdown research. Also to Gladstone's Library for space to read, write, and reflect.

I would also like to thank my agent, Cathryn Summerhayes, for her encouragement and support; my editor, Ann Bissell, for her persistent sharp eye; and my publicist Amy Winchester and all the team at the Borough Press for all their dedicated work in sharing Louisa's story with the world.

Special thanks to Mahsuda Snaith, Samantha Dennis, Tọlá Okogwu, Lauren Brown, Katherine Stansfield, David Towsey, Carole Burns, and Sarah Agnew for companionship, reading, and good advice. Thanks to Russell Howells for the tour of Highgate Cemetery and his above-and-beyond research and gravestone photography, Bethan McKernan for the line about Yemeni Arabic, Mark Takel for late-night chats at St Canna's about our shared interest in this story, Darlene McLeod for help with sewing terminology, Janet Gellately, Emily Sturgeon and Will Hay for encouragement and checking historical details about sailing ropes and sewing machines, John Hay for getting the song stuck in my head, Hilary Hay for loving enthusiasm, and Michael Munnik for everything.